*Laughing Boy*

a&b

*Laughing Boy*
STUART PAWSON

Allison & Busby Limited
13 Charlotte Mews
London W1T 4EJ
*www.allisonandbusby.com*

A CIP catalogue record for this book is available from
the British Library.

First published in the Great Britain in hardcover by
Allison & Busby in 2002.
Published in paperback by Allison & Busby, 2003.
Reprinted in 2005, 2006 and 2008.

10 9 8 7 6 5 4

ISBN 978-0-7490-0647-1

Printed and bound in the UK by
CPI Bookmarque, Croydon, CR0 4TD

To Doreen

# Acknowledgements

I am indebted to the following for their help:

Dennis Marshall, John Crawford, Clive Kingswood, Dave Mason, Matthew Perkins, Ron Ellis and John Mills. Special thanks to Greg and Shelley Davis of Blue Coyote and extra special thanks to the genuine Tim Roper and Fool's Progress, whose 'music, when soft voices die, vibrates in the memory'.

Time's vibration falters
Caught mid-breath
Between the parchment past
And wide-eyed tomorrow
Silence dangles
Fecund, ripe as plums
So pluck the best
And leave the rest for fallow
Until with leaden head
And lidded brows
Engulfed and mellow
You find the time
To be
Embalmed by the warm
But watch out for that needle, Son
This is the eye of the storm
This is the eye of the storm

Complacency seduces
Enfeebles from within
Enervates the core
To draw the marrow from all desires
Voiceless ashes turn
Where once burned bonfires
As unquestioning as a faithless friend
Whose answers like smoke rings
On falsehoods are borne
So watch out for that needle, Son
You're in the eye of the storm
This is the eye of the storm

Tim Roper (1944–1969)

*California 1969*

The tiny figure jerked across the stage like a clockwork matchstick man, dwarfed by the paraphernalia of the rock concert that surrounded him. Banks of dry ice gas piled upon each other, violet and pink, and the flickering strobe lights made the set look like a vision of hell from an early movie.

*"It's been a good day in the war,"* he yelled into the microphone, and the capacity crowd standing before him screamed their approval and swayed from side to side, arms aloft, holding burning cigarette lighters and candles, girlfriends on their shoulders, bandannas around heads, long hair swirling to the beat.

The singer was stripped to the waist, his whiteness heightened by greasepaint and sweat that sent the spotlight beams glancing off into the night sky. All he could see was an ocean of faces, each one illuminated with religious fervour, adoration even, as the group hammered out the bass line. This was what they wanted to hear. This was power – the power of music. Hey man! This was love!

> *It's been a good day in the war,*
> *And ain't that just the TRUTH!*

He howled the last syllable and the sound system amplified his voice a thousand times.

> *Pratt and Whitney are up ten,*
> *And Boeing are through the ROOF!*

The guitarists that flanked him, Carlo on rhythm, Oscar on bass, glanced across at each other and grinned, but there was a hint of fear in their smiles. This time he had the audience, he really had them, and if he didn't bring them down there could be trouble. Two youths had been stabbed to death after an earlier concert, and it was written into the contract that they would end the show with a slow number to lower the tension, cool the emotions, before five thousand disciples of anarchy were loosed out into the night, on to the streets of downtown San Diego. Behind them, Zeke on the drums and Eddie on keyboards had no such inhibitions. Eddie was the oldest member and the musician of the group. Brought up among jazz bands, he'd seen the writing on the wall and made the transition to rock. He gave the group, who called themselves The LHO, respectability, injecting long solos and complicated twiddly bits into the ceaseless beat and mundane tunes.

Zeke was on the most fantastic trip of his life. Earlier in the day his wife had gone into labour and at that very moment was giving birth to their firstborn in St. Catherine's Sisters of Mercy hospital. He laid stick against skin with a verve that threatened to burst his drums asunder. His musical theory was simple: If you hadn't hit it for a while, do it now, and do it hard. Eddie glanced across at him and winked. "This is the life; this is what it's all about," was the message that flashed between them. Zeke grinned back and hammered the cowbell.

> Body bags are doing well,
> And so is Uncle SAM.
> He can pay his debts now,
> Thanks to ol' VietNAM

Tim Roper, the lead singer and creator of The LHO, windmilled his right arm, bringing his musicians back into time with each other and winding down the tempo. Zeke slowed the beat and Eddie went into the band's standard finish, ending with a drum roll, a few wailing chords and a final crash of everything that made a noise.

The audience, almost all living under the threat of draft into the army, went wild.

City ordinances demanded that the concert end at eleven p.m., and it was nearly five to. A roady in the wings tapped his watch and held up five fingers. Tim nodded an acknowledgement. Breach of the rule would mean failure to obtain licences for further concerts.

"Let's do the breakfast song," Tim shouted at Eddie, intoxicated to a height that drugs alone could never reach. He was reckless, wanting to live dangerously. *Fuck* the city ordinances, he was thinking, and if a couple of dope-heads were stabbed it wouldn't hurt record sales. They'd given one encore, but the crowd was shouting for more; waving arms and stamping feet until they gradually fell into time with each other.

"We can't, man," Oscar yelled back. "We finish on 'Storm'. We agreed."

Eddie heard the exchange but didn't argue. He just played the riff from 'Eye of the Storm' without waiting for a cue and the foot stomping changed to a cheer of approval. Tim had been overruled. He didn't like it but there wasn't much he could do. Carlo picked up the melody and Zeke fell into the rhythm as easily as falling into a warm bed. In ten minutes he'd be out of here, on his way to St. Catherine's. Eddie pulled a face at the girl in the front row with devotion in her eyes and what could have been a small family of illegal immigrants inside her T-shirt. If the roadies did their job well he could be having sex with her before the night was much older. Tim yanked his guitar back into position with a scowl and spread his fingers into the appropriate chord.

"*This is the eye of the storm*," Tim sang. It was his most popular song, their only small hit, and a slow number in contrast to the thrashed metal that they were moderately famous for. "*Watch out for that needle, Son, 'cos this is the eye of the storm.*"

Blue Coyote sound studio where the band hung out was in Sherman Oaks, a district of Los Angeles adjacent to

Hollywood and all the film studios. It was in a basement below a converted garage and run by Eddie's younger brother, Pete. Pete was one of the finest saxophonists on the West Coast, and heading for a great future, until he discovered the hard way that Harley-Davidsons with bald tyres didn't go round corners too well and didn't go through brick walls at all. He came out of hospital in a wheelchair, with a permanent tremor in his left hand that meant his playing days were a memory. Eddie organised a series of gigs, added his life savings and set Pete up in Blue Coyote.

Three days after the San Diego concert the members of The LHO congregated at the studio. It was the first time they'd met since the post-concert party, and there was much to talk about. Outside, the streets flinched in the glare of the morning sun, but down in the cellar all was cool and dim. Carlo was drinking coffee, Oscar and Tim sipped the vodka laced with jalapeño chillies that had become the band's favoured tipple. Guitars leaned against music stands, amplifiers lined the walls, blinking in time to the sound of Tim's voice coming from the slowly-turning reel-to-reel recorder that had captured the last performance of 'Eye of the Storm.'

"You sound good," Pete told Tim. "Real good. Lots o' soul in it." He was insincere. He regarded the band as talentless amateurs and he couldn't stand Tim, but if it kept him in joints who cared about a few white lies and a little hypocrisy? Pete had a reputation for his prodigious consumption of marijuana, but he took it for the pain, not the highs. Pete knew a lot about pain, in all its forms. He spun his wheelchair in the area of clear floor next to his control desk and adjusted the bass balance.

Eddie was next to arrive. He poked his head tentatively round the door until the others yelled at him. "Hey, man," he said, "the friggin' red light's on. Been waiting outside nearly two hours."

"Two minutes, more like," Carlo responded.

"Whadya know!" Tim exclaimed. "That was me." He'd

been playing about with various switches and had activated the Recording in Progress sign on the door. He found the switch and restored it to its proper position. He was wearing a skin-tight T-shirt with velvet flares and his hair was tied back in a ponytail. "So," he went on, "tell us all about Miss San Diego 1969."

Eddie removed his dark glasses and shook his head. "You wouldn't believe me, Old Son. You just wouldn't believe me."

They almost always held some sort of party after a concert. Nothing very grand or organised: drinks and draw in the hotel, fried chicken or Mexican food, and some music. While the band were playing the roadies handed out invitations to the likeliest- and sexiest-looking girls in the first few rows, carefully avoiding the weirdos who followed every group. This time they'd done well, and Eddie had quickly found himself chatting to the girl he'd made eyes at during the performance. He gave a brief smile, aware of Pete, sitting in the corner, in the shadows, in a wheelchair. "She was... OK, a nice kid," was all he added, downbeat.

The door opened again and the grinning head of Zeke appeared. He looked around then bounced into the room, carrying a bundle in his arms.

"Hey! Zeko!" they called. "Whadya got there?" He was followed into the studio by his wife, fragile looking in an ethnic jacket and tie-dyed wrap. "Carol-Anne!" they greeted. "Come in; sit down; make a space for her."

They took turns to embrace Carol-Anne and shake hands with Zeke. He unfastened the baby's shawl and formally introduced him to each band member. "Theo," he'd say, "I'd like you to meet Tim. Tim's lead singer with The LHO and the best goddamn singer-songwriter in Sherman Oaks."

"Theo, eh," someone remarked. "After Theodore Roosevelt, I suppose?"

"No," Carol-Anne replied. "After Theodore van Gogh. He looked after his brother, and we hope this little feller will grow up the same."

"Which reminds me," Zeke interrupted, turning to Pete. "*This little feller*, this little chickadee, is going to need a godfather. We, er, we were talking on the way over, like, and, er, well, Pete, we'd be mighty pleased if you'd agree to take on that responsibility."

Pete sat silently for a few seconds, looking confused, then said: "Sure," and reached out for the baby. Carol Anne walked across to him and put her arms around his neck as he nursed young Theo.

Tim sprang into life like a jack-in-the-box whose time has arrived. "Hey!" he exclaimed. "I've written a song."

"A song?" they echoed with mock enthusiasm. "Wow, Tim's written a song." Jeez, here we go again, thought Pete.

"Yeh. When you rang me, Zeke, to tell me about young Theo, I just thought, you know, like wow! I flipped, man, I just flipped. A new life, procreation an' all that. What you've done is, like, well, it's incredible."

"No it's not," Eddie interrupted, "it's natural. The difficult bit is not to have kids," and the others laughed.

Tim blushed. He was the driving force behind the group, but was the smallest and youngest of them. "Well, man, I just thought I'd make our newest member a little present. It's nothing, really, just a little nonsense thing, y'know. I have it here, somewhere." He retrieved his leather jacket from the back of a chair and delved into the inside pocket. "I, er, ran off a few copies. It's hardly finished, might need a few touches."

"We gonna lay this down?" Pete asked, handing Theo back to his mother and switching on the eight-track deck.

"Why not." In a few seconds the room was filled with the noises of guitars being checked for tuning. Tim ran his thumbnail across the strings of his Fender, made a slight adjustment and looked at Pete, who was blessed with perfect pitch. Pete nodded. Zeke manoeuvred himself behind the drum kit and rattled off a few trial rolls.

"We won't need the cowbell for this, Zeke," Tim told him with a smile.

"I like the cowbell," he protested.

"It's just *tum ta-ta tum ta-ta tum*," Tim said, tapping out with an imaginary stick, and Zeke responded with the real thing.

"Nothing intricate, just C and F, going to G and G-seven," he told the rest of them. They clipped the sheets on to music stands and shuffled into their seats. Only Eddie, the keyboard man, didn't take up his instrument. He lifted Theo from Carol-Anne's arms and walked round the studio with him, pointing to pieces of apparatus, saying: "And that's a Radio Shack 500 watt amp; and that's a Yamaha state-of-the art keyboard; and that's..."

"*One two, buckle my shoe, Uncle Joe is stuck in the glue,*" Tim sang quite slowly, strumming the appropriate chord just once at each change. "*Two three, he'll never get free, as long as he sits there in that tree.*"

The others joined in as they picked up the melody, nodding their heads and foot-tapping to inject some rhythm.

"Hey man, this is cool!" Oscar shouted.

"I like it," Carlo agreed.

"*Call the fireman, call the vet, call the doctor but don't call me.*"

Carlo suggested a couple of key alterations to add some variety and they ran through it again at the proper speed. Third time they put it to tape. Pete wrote the details on the label, then asked for another run-through, saying that he'd like Oscar's bass guitar bringing more to the fore. "Then maybe Eddie can add some flourishes and fancy bits later."

They all agreed and played it once more.

"Hey, Tim," Zeke said when they finished, "that's cool, real cool. I'm touched, man, touched. It's the best present young Theo could ask for."

"It's real sweet of you," Carol-Anne agreed.

"No problem, man," Tim replied. "As long as it stays

within these four walls. If it gets out that I wrote it…well, man, my reputation is shot to pieces. Can you imagine? Gee, I'd be dead meat."

Pete wrote the labels and fitted the reel into its can. This was the most commercial thing that The LHO had ever done, and one thing he was certain of was that it wasn't going to stay within those four walls. He spun his wheelchair round to face Tim and said: "Yeah, man, real cool. Anybody need some draw?"

Three days later KWOV, Sherman Oaks' very own radio station situated on the corner of the same block as Blue Coyote, broadcast 'Theo's Tune' to its peak-time audience. They received three enquiries from listeners wondering if it was available as a single.

"Three," Pete repeated when he heard the news. "That's not many." He was sitting in the outer office of the station, sharing a joint with the station's owner and chief DJ. With their long hair and Pete's headband they could have been pirates, discussing a raid, and in many ways they were.

"Hell, man," the DJ replied, coughing as he drew on the joint, "I don't wish to minimise the influence of li'l ol' KWOV on the good residents of downtown LA, but if you took three as a fraction of our total audience, then multiplied it by the population of the entire US, it'd prob'ly work out at about a hunnerd million people. That's a hit by anybody's standards."

"You reckon?"

"I reckon. Hell, man, we only had *two* calls about the moon landings."

Pete had a demo disc made and it was played by several other local stations. One by one the band members heard themselves on radio, belting out 'Theo's Tune', and were pleased and bemused. They were in the business to be heard and to make money. Artistic integrity didn't pay the bills.

Tim didn't agree. He called Pete as soon as he found out what was happening and said some things he later regretted. Pete, fortunately, had just taken delivery of a stash of Aztec Honey and was feeling particularly mellow. "Hey man," he responded. "I made you famous. I made you goddamn famous."

They held a meeting and Tim berated them all for not respecting his *intellectual property*, as works of art are known in the business. He told them that The LHO had built up a reputation for its anti-establishment, anti-government, anti-capitalism, anti-war, anti-*everything*, stance, and that could be destroyed by a silly sentimental song like 'Theo's Tune'. They had a growing audience of young disaffected Americans, black as well as white, and they could easily lose them.

Eddie put the opposite view forward. Much as he enjoyed making good music, he was in it for the money. There were places he wouldn't go, depths he wouldn't reach, but 'Theo's Tune' wasn't quite there. He was happy to be associated with it. "An' listen, man," he concluded, "if we don't do it somebody else will, and we can always use the bread."

Tim was adamant, but eventually a compromise was reached. They'd release 'Theo's Tune' as a single under the name of Blue Coyote, with a Bobby Vee number on the B-side. Everybody was pleased.

The record was a slow burner, as they often are in America. There is very little national exposure but local stations play certain discs *ad nauseam* and listeners on the fringes of the reception areas then ask their own stations to play them. So popularity spreads across the country like an infectious disease, or a plague of crop-devouring insects. But once the momentum starts, there's no stopping it, and soon Blue Coyote's only record had sold more copies than The LHO had in its entire career. There were rumours about Blue Coyote, and one or two more perceptive rock journalists noted that Zeke's new baby was called Theo and drew the obvious conclusions. But when they printed their theories the boys just grinned and said: "Not us, man. No way."

The summer season ended with sell-out gigs at the Greek and Balboa Park, and The LHO settled into a tour of the various indoor venues around LA, with names like It's Boss, Le Parisien and Gazzari's. They'd hammer out their own special brand of folk-rock and garage-band, Tim yelling his anti-war lyrics to an audience who lived in fear of finding a US Government letter in their mail. A letter that might say they were required to report for training, or, God forbid, that a brother wouldn't be coming home.

Towards the end of every concert some joker in the audience would shout a request for 'Theo's Tune'. "Not us, man," Tim would respond, and go straight into his new hit song – 'Breakfast at Da-Nang,' or 'Eye of the Storm' if it was curtain time. Nobody argued, although Eddie firmly believed in giving the people what they wanted. Meanwhile, 'Theo's Tune' kept clocking-up the air-time. They heard it in hotel foyers and on garage forecourts; bus drivers sitting in gridlocks tapped their steering wheels to it and hopefuls on second-rate TV talent shows hitched a ride on its popularity.

The day before Thanksgiving they played the Graffiti Club on the edge of Compton, a largely black and Hispanic quarter of Los Angeles. Tim, for some reason, wanted to start with 'Eye of the Storm'. The others pointed out that they usually finished with it, to bring the audience back to ground level, but Tim just said: "OK, so we reprise it. What's the problem?"

There wasn't one, and it went well. The audience identified with the lyrics – those they could hear – and bounced along to Zeke's driving rhythms. The aptly named Graffiti was a large converted cinema with the seats torn out, and every ticket was sold. Eddie let rip on the keyboards and Oscar laid down a bass line as solid as stepping-stones across a river. Tim turned as Eddie played the opening bars of

'Breakfast at Da-Nang', and grinned at him, nodding to the beat. Eddie added a flourish and Tim launched himself into the song:

> *It's breakfast time on the Mekong Delta*
> *The PFC in the mess hall's making a brew.*
> *How d'ya like your napalm? Over easy?*
> *That's the way he'll do it, just for you.*

The audience loved it, some swaying to the music, others jiving with or without partners. Eddie cast an expert eye over the girls and wondered whether the roadies would invite any black chicks to the party. It might not be wise.

> *We're cooking toast, here at Da-Nang.*
> *Do you have a preference? Brown or white?*
> *Or how about a crazy shade of yellow?*
> *So as not to give your mother such a fright.*

The irony of the song was lost on the audience. The mood now was "Let's bash the Commie bastards." Napalm was what they deserved. Eddie saw a black girl with eyes like moonrise in the desert and fell instantly in love with her. He smiled and she smiled back at him, reflected light from the spots glinting off her tooth brace. He fell out of love just as quickly as Tim went into the last verse:

> *Man, you sure look groovy in those pee-jays,*
> *I guess you didn't have the time to change.*
> *Is black the only colour that they come in?*
> *And have you any others in my range?*

The applause came like the surf down at Redondo Beach, crashing and tumbling as each new wave filled the trough left by its predecessor. Tim lifted the strap of his guitar over his head, took a step forward and bowed. It was his sign that the concert was over. Oscar looked at Carlo and they both looked across at Eddie. Eddie shrugged his shoulders and shook his head. The applause from the audience settled into a rhythm, the calls for more growing until it was a battle of wills between the audience and the band. Tim turned and took his place in the line again, absorbing the adulation but determined not to play any more.

"I thought we were doing 'Storm'," Carlo shouted at him.

"We did it."

"A reprise."

"We did it once."

"We can't leave them like this."

"Wanna bet?"

The applause had settled into a chant. Then somebody near the front shouted: "Do 'Theo's Tune'!"

"Yeah! 'Theo's Tune'!" came like an echo from the back of the hall. Soon everybody took up the call: "Theo! Theo! Theo!"

"Let's do it," Zeke shouted from behind the drums.

"No!" Tim screamed back. "That's it! We're through."

"Theo! Theo! Theo!" they chanted.

The club owner, his face etched with panic, strode onto the stage trailing a microphone lead. He attempted to speak into it but didn't make a sound and only encouraged the crowd to double their efforts. He was wearing a business suit that immediately marked him as part of the enemy, one of the fat cats living off his warmonger shares. He tapped the mike then abandoned it. "You can't leave 'em like this," he appealed to Tim. "They'll tear the fuckin' place down. Play something slow, for Chrissake."

"We don't do slow," Tim replied, stepping away from him to take what he intended to be his final bow.

"Theo! Theo! Theo!" they chanted.

Eddie took over. He slid the controls on his keyboard over to maximum, turned to do the same with the volume on the amplifier, and played the opening riff of 'Theo's Tune'. It cut through the hall like a jet plane and the chants turned to cheers of approval.

*Dum dum, di-dum dum dum*, he played again, and the crowd fell almost silent.

*Dum dum, di-dum dum dum*.

The others looked across at him, Zeke grinning, Oscar and Carlo confused and Tim's face hollow with disappointment.

*Dum dum, di-dum dum dum*.

Zeke took it up, adding his *tum ta-ta, tum ta-ta, tum* behind Eddie's keyboard, and Oscar thought, What the hell! and laid on his bass line.

Tim stood for a moment, his back to the audience, guitar held by the neck in his right hand. When Carlo started to pick out the melody he hurled the three hundred-dollar Fender at Eddie, catching him a glancing blow on the shoulder. The instrument, mute without its power lead, hit a speaker and fell to the floor. Tim stormed off the stage.

"You take it," Eddie shouted at Carlo, who duetted with Tim on several numbers and had the better voice. Carlo stepped forward and the band fell into time for the first public performance of 'Theo's Tune'.

*One two, buckle my shoe*, Carlo sang, and the bemused audience stopped laughing at Tim's antics and sang along with The LHO's new front-man:

> *Uncle Joe is stuck in the glue.*
> *Two three, he'll never get free,*
> *As long as he sits there in that tree.*
> *Call the fireman, call the vet,*
> *Call the doctor but don't call me.*

Tim was in the waiting car and heading back towards Sherman Oaks before the song was finished. He picked up his own Corvette and drove aimlessly across the Valley, through Pasadena until he found himself on I-210, heading out of town. It was a cool, clear night, and the roads were busy with people doing the rounds that everybody needs to do the day before Thanksgiving. Through Arcadia a police car tailed him for a while and he realised that they'd have a bonanza if they pulled him over, what with the vodka he'd consumed before the concert and the king-size joint he had in his pocket. He slotted into the right-hand lane behind a 1960 Eldorado Biarritz with bigger fins on its tail than Apollo 11 and the cop car cruised by without a glance. Tim turned off at the next exit, heading north into the San Gabriels.

He parked in a viewing area overlooking the reservoir and lit the joint. Away to his right were the lights of town; behind, before and to his left was the empty blackness of the reservoir, the mountains and the desert; above him the Milky Way trailed across the sky like the train of a bride's dress.

City of angels, city of dreams. Less than an hour ago he'd held them in the palm of his hand. Every jerk of his head, every strangulated vowel, and they'd bayed their approval. And now he was up here, alone, destroyed by those he thought were friends. Judases, every one of them. People down there were doing deals, pulling fast ones, making money by the strength of their talents. Or, for some, by selling their souls and their bodies. He took a long pull on the joint and closed his eyes. They'd learn, he thought. They'd learn. It could all come crashing down. Los Angeles might be the dream factory, but it was surrounded by desert. And it was built on an earthquake zone.

As dawn broke he took the I-10 towards Palm Springs, drawn inland by thoughts of a reunion with a girl he'd had a brief affair with earlier in the year. Twenty miles from her home he realised that she wasn't the type to be eating alone, and in any case he didn't have the gall to arrive at her door and invite himself in for Thanksgiving lunch. He made a U-turn and drove all the way back to La Habra, the suburb of LA where his parents lived.

"Hi, Mom, hi Dad," he said as he breezed into the house. "Is my room still vacant?" Ten minutes later he knew it was a big mistake, but it was too late now.

He was the best Thanksgiving present they could have had, his mother kept telling him, between enquiries about his wellbeing and relating items of gossip. They were so proud of him, and he didn't come visiting anywhere near often enough. He took refuge in the bathroom, having a long shower and a shave with his father's spare razor. When he went downstairs an hour later lunch was ready.

Tim's father asked him what he'd like to drink with his meal, and was surprised when his son told him Jack Daniels. When pressed, Tim agreed that wine would be fine.

"Dad…" Tim began before they took their places at the table.

"Yes, Son."

"I was wondering. About my car. If people see it there they might realise I'm home, you know, and kinda come visiting. I was hoping for some peace and quiet. Would you mind if I swapped it with yours in the garage?"

"No problem, Son. You know where the keys are. Only trouble is, er, my gun's in the glove compartment. Bring it in, will you. Can't leave it there if the car's parked outside. I'd be in big trouble if that got stolen." Mr Roper owned two shoe shops, and habitually carried the day's takings in his car. The gun was a sensible precaution.

Tim's mother came in bearing a steaming bowl of pumpkin soup. "No time for that, now," she stated. "It's eating time."

Mr Roper said grace and Mrs Roper handed a basket of corn bread first to Tim, the prodigal son, and then to her husband. "I told Aunt Jessie you were home, Tim," she said. "I hope you don't mind, but we're so proud of you. She said she might drop by, later, and bring Shiralee with her. She's such a nice girl."

Tim winced at the prospect. Cousin Shiralee wasn't his proper cousin, unfortunately, so was considered a prospective bride for him. Nobody had noticed that he was skinny as an alley cat's shadow while she had averaged a weight increase of ten pounds per year throughout her twenty-three years. "That's OK, Mom," he lied.

"And she just loves that new song you did. 'Theo's Tune', is it? Why, it's so...educational. Mrs Gilfedder even has grade two singing it, and they all know it's by you." Tim reached for the wine bottle. "Why you said it wasn't you who wrote it I'll never know."

"It was, sort of...commercial reasons," Tim said.

"Well I don't understand all that commercial stuff. I know it's not like all the songs you wrote supporting our boys in Vietnam, but I reckon it's the best thing you've ever done. Why, Mr Summerbee at the fillin' station, he reckons you could be bigger than the Partridge Family, come Christmas. Now wouldn't that be something, George, if Tim's song was number one at Christmas?"

"Sure would," Mr Roper agreed, laying his spoon alongside his empty bowl.

They had corn-fed tom turkey with orange rice stuffing, cranberry and apple sauce, traditional mashed potatoes, mashed sweet potatoes, glazed brussel sprouts and roasted onions with green beans. Mrs Roper was a ferocious cook and helpings were copious in spite of there being an extra face at the table. When she put on a spread the table legs braced themselves.

"It's not as if I *like* all that rock 'n' roll stuff you do," Tim's mother was saying as he ploughed on through the mountain of food in front of him. "But I don't *like* all opera, either. Just some of it. But the good stuff kinda makes up for what you don't like, and it's the same with yours, Tim. *Refreshing*, that's what a song like 'Theo's Tune' is. Refreshing. Don't you agree, George?"

"Mmm."

"Any chance of some more wine, Dad?" Tim asked.

"I'll open another bottle."

"This is a wonderful dinner, Mom. I'm glad I came."

"So are we, Son. It's the best Thanksgiving we could've asked for. I can't wait to tell them at the Guild that you came by. Everybody's so proud of you."

They finished off with pecan pie and blueberry ice cream. When they'd left the table and were settled in easy chairs Mrs Roper said: "And now something I've been just itching to show you, Tim. Look at this." She perched on the arm of his chair, glowing like a log fire, and laid a big coloured book on his knee. "I found it at Books R Us. What do you think of that?"

It wasn't very thick and had stiff board covers with cartoon characters racing across the front. 'Theo's Tune' it proclaimed in bright letters. Tim slowly opened the cover and a tree came to life in front of him, rising hesitantly off the page like a new-born giraffe finding its feet. *One two, buckle your shoe*, it said. *Uncle Joe is stuck in the glue*. Uncle Joe was indeed stuck in the glue, up near the top of the tree.

"That's, er, neat, Mom," Tim managed to say, his voice a croak, as he turned the page to reveal a dancing nun. *Four five, saints alive! Sister Mary is learning to jive*.

"I got two more, for you to autograph," she declared. "One for Aunt Jessie and one for the girls at the Guild, to auction for funds. Aren't they the cutest things you ever did see?"

"Sure. I'll, er, do them later." He leaned forward and placed the book on a coffee table.

"Well I'll be!" he heard his father say. Tim turned and saw he was fiddling with the controls of the television set. "Well I'll be. Come and look at this."

"Come and look at this," his father insisted. "Ma, come and look at this."

"What is it, George?"

"Larry Johnson show. Listen. Just listen."

They listened, and watched. Four girls dressed in pilgrim costumes with lace bonnets but short skirts high-stepped across the screen, kicking their legs in a way that would have had them burned at the stake in 1621. Four men, appropriately but more modestly attired, tripped on from the right and merged with them, linking arms.

"What is it?" Mrs Roper asked.

"Ssh!" George replied. "Listen. Just listen."

Tim recognised the tune before his mother did:

> *Nine ten, I'll tell you when,* the dancers mimed.
> *You can bring your apricot hen.*
> *Come on an elephant, ride on a donkey.*
> *Come in a buggy with a wheel that's wonky.*

It was almost too much for Mrs Roper. "Oh my!" she gushed. "Oh my! That's wonderful, just wonderful! I don't believe it. Our Tim's song on the Larry Johnson show." Tim had picked up his wineglass but he had to put it down again because his hand was shaking. "And just look at him," she went on. "He's so modest. Anybody would think he was embarrassed by all the attention." She stepped forward and held her son in a bear hug that stopped him breathing for a few seconds. "Wait till I tell Jessie," she said as she released him. "Just wait till I tell Jessie. I wonder if she saw it?" She dashed off into the hallway, where the telephone was, to pass on her good tidings.

Tim and his father stood awkwardly for a few moments until Mr Roper Sr. said: "She gets kinda excited, Son. She's proud of you. We all are."

Tim picked up the glass again and drained it. He studied the empty vessel for a few moments, as if whether to have a refill was a big decision, then said: "About the cars, Dad. Do you mind if I swap them over now?"

"Why no, Son. The key's in the kitchen, where it always is."

"OK." He walked through into the kitchen, which still held the debris of the blow-out lunch they'd eaten, and placed his glass on the work surface. Just inside the top left-hand cupboard, where they'd been since his childhood, he found the keys to the garage's side entrance and his father's car. On the key fob was a Mickey Mouse he'd given his dad when they'd visited Disneyland the day it opened, down in Anaheim back in '55.

It was dim and cool in the garage, with motes of dust suspended in the beams of sunshine from the tiny windows. The car was the same old Buick that his father had owned for ten years, the maroon paintwork's glow reflecting the attention he gave it. Tim squeezed down the passenger side and unlocked the door.

He placed his hand between the door and the wall so as not to scratch the paint as he eased himself into the seat and sank into the deep leather. The door closed with the dull *clump* that took millions of dollars to perfect.

Through the windscreen he could see a pile of articles heaped against what had once been his father's workbench. Easily identifiable were Tim's first and last bikes, and two Halloween masks hanging on a hook. There was an ironing board, a convector heater that he'd had in his bedroom, and a pile of boxed board games that he remembered as being invariably disappointing. Sitting on top of them was the catching glove he'd been given as a twelfth-birthday present and, apart from briefly trying on, had never worn since. Not once.

Tim opened the Buick's glove compartment and raised the sheaf of documents that lay inside. The gun was underneath them. He lifted it out and inspected it.

The wooden grip felt comfortable, reassuring even, in his hand. It was a Taurus revolver, made in Brazil, bigger than a twenty-two but not quite a thirty-eight. There were four bullets in the gun, with an empty chamber under the hammer and another next to it. Tim smiled at his father's concern for safety. He could pull the trigger once and nothing would happen. Next time, he'd mean business.

Tim pushed the cylinder round one click, and then another, just to be certain. He turned the gun in his hand, threading his thumb inside the trigger guard, and placed the snub barrel in his mouth. It was as numb as the kiss of a faithless lover. As he applied pressure to the trigger he felt the cylinder rotate against his lip, bringing the next bullet under the hammer. And then he felt nothing.

Happy Thanksgiving, Mom. Happy Thanksgiving, Dad.

# Chapter One

There is no such thing as an ordinary person, so it follows that there is no such thing as an ordinary murder. I remember thinking that in the early days of the enquiry, after we'd raked through the ashes of Laura Heeley's life until our fingers hurt and our eyes burned. I may even have said it to the troops during one of my more eloquent pep talks.

Laura was thirty-eight when she died, and had lived in Heckley for all that time. Local secondary modern school; left at fifteen to be a machinist in one of the last mills in town; married a boy from the next street when she was twenty and had two children in the next three years. The kids were now fifteen and seventeen and had never been in trouble with the police, bless 'em. Laura played bingo twice a week, taking her elderly mother along for a game, and did her shopping at Asda on a Thursday afternoon. Through the day she worked part-time packing electronic components in one of the featureless warehouses in the new technology park at the edge of town and her favourite television programme was *Emmerdale*. Ordinary was a word that came charging out of the sunrise on a palomino pony as soon as you thought about her.

Until one evening in February, as she walked home from her mother's house after another moderately enjoyable but utterly fruitless game of bingo, her numbers came up for the first time in her life. One person in the entire United Kingdom was chosen to be stabbed to death that Tuesday evening, and that person was Laura Heeley. Somebody walked up behind her and plunged ten inches of razor-edged stiletto into her back. It penetrated C&A coat, BHS blouse, M&S bra, skin, muscle and finally her heart, with total indifference, leaving her to die at the side of an unlit lane.

That's where I come in. My name is Charlie Priest – that's Detective Inspector Priest – and I handle all the murders around here. For just over a month I've lived, breathed and slept Laura Heeley until I know things about her that would shake her husband out of the torpor that has gripped him for most of his adult life. I've drawn charts, read files, made cross-checks and stared at video screens until big blue tadpoles started swimming across my eyes. My staff have made over five thousand interviews and looked at the tyres on every car in West Yorkshire. I've consulted, co-operated and co-ordinated until I didn't know which was which and I've sat on a rock, high on the moors with the wind in my hair, and talked to the sky.

The sheep gave me some funny looks but no answers. They were right to be concerned: foot-and-mouth disease had erupted in Essex and Northumberland, and they had relatives there.

Laura Heeley, for whom the word *ordinary* was coined, just happened to be in the wrong place at the right time. She crossed paths with someone who, for reasons known only to himself, needed to kill a woman on that spring night. He'd had a row with one; caught pox off one; hated his mother, who was one; who can tell? Maybe he'd had a row with his mother after he'd caught pox off her. It's not unknown.

What was for sure was that I was summoned before an independent review team at HQ for a case meeting. Thirty days without a result and people in high places start asking questions. They want to hear about suspects, possible leads and lines of enquiry. It's not all bad news. If you're short of resources it's a good opportunity to make your case.

So I stood up and told them everything we'd done, which was a lot, and everything we'd achieved, which was diddly-squat. They had a few suggestions, nothing dramatic, and I accepted them gratefully. She'd been murdered by a random attacker who had no motive and no recognisable *modus operandi*. He hadn't killed again, so hopefully she was a one-off. The time had come to wind down the enquiry, re-deploy the troops, and I reluctantly agreed. I was treading water, and for the life of me didn't know what to do next in the Laura Heeley case.

If I'd known that she was number five in a series I might have had a few ideas.

Next morning we had a big meeting, crowded in the conference room. I told the troops about the review team's decision and thanked them for the hard work they'd put into the case. "Reports," I told them. "Get your reports finished and tagged, no matter how futile you believe them to be, before you resume normal duties. And meanwhile, let's have one last brainstorm. Anything you don't understand about the case, or any cockeyed theory you might have, now's the time to air it. Who'll start the ball rolling?" Individual officers have their own areas of enquiry, and can't be expected to know everything about the case. That's my job, to have an overview, but I have no illusions about my omnipotence and was at a stage where I would have accepted suggestions from the cleaning lady.

"Dave?" I invited, looking at big Sparky Sparkington sitting in the front row. He's a close friend and doesn't mind being put on the spot.

"Yeah," he began, shuffling in his seat. "We all know the statistics. According to them, it's a family matter. Are we really happy that the husband and son are in the clear?"

We'd covered this ground a thousand times, but it helped break the ice. I pointed at Jeff Caton, one of my DSs, and invited him to comment. We'd spoken to the family together, initially, handling them like one would handle any bereaved relatives. Then Jeff had called them in for a formal interview, "just for the record." It's a delicate situation, balancing sympathy for their loss with your suspicions that they may have done the deed themselves.

"I'm happy about them," Jeff told us. "The daughter's alibi is watertight – she was ten-pin bowling with friends and still had the receipts. The son and husband are not totally in the clear – they could have conspired together, but there's nothing for them in it."

"I'll go along with that," Maggie Madison interrupted. She'd worked with the family as police liaison officer. "Barry and young Billy are completely lost without Laura. They don't know how to boil an egg between them. Barry has never made a cheque out in his life and hasn't a clue about the washing machine or where the clean towels are kept. Laura ran the house and ran them. In short," she added with a smile, "they were a typical happy family."

"No skeletons?" I asked.

"Big row, two Christmases ago. He got drunk, had a fight with Billy. The daughter, Sarah, used it as an excuse to leave home and live with her boyfriend, but she's back now."

"Anything else?"

"Laura was friendly with an old man who lives nearby. Used to take him meals and talk to him, but there was nothing in it. He's a pensioner."

"Pensioners have their moments, Maggie," I remarked.

"Well, I hope they do. Did Barry know about this?"

"Yes, but he's not the jealous sort. He's not any sort. A couch, a television and a remote control and he's as happy as Larry."

"As you said, they were a typical happy family. Anybody have a question?"

"Insurance?" a voice asked.

"None," I replied.

"Are the kids his?" someone else asked.

I hunched my shoulders, pursed my lips and opened my eyes wide. "Dunno," I admitted. "They're supposed to be his, not adopted, that is. What do you have in mind?"

"Well, maybe somebody else put Laura in the family way, all those years ago, and he's born a grudge ever since, biding his time. It's just a thought."

"Yep," I said. "It's a possibility. Resentment smouldering away inside him. We have samples from them all but I don't think we asked the lab for a paternity test. We'll check it out. Thanks for that, anything else?"

We rabbited on for another hour, chewing over stuff that I'd grown sick of the taste of but was possibly new to some of the others. Unusual tyre prints had been found near where Laura died, and the owner of the vehicle that left them had been tracked down. They were cheap imports from the Eastern Bloc, and only two hundred and fifty had been brought into the country, so it wasn't a difficult task. He admitted being there, but twenty-four hours earlier, and had dumped a mattress and some other rubbish in a farm gateway. Forensics proved the mattress was his, witnesses confirmed it had been there when he said. We did him for littering and moved on, but the review team were not happy about this and I'd agreed that we'd have him in again. It was a waste of time but it made them feel useful. I delegated a few jobs and closed the meeting.

"Tea, Vicar?" Sparky asked, ten minutes later as he manoeuvred himself into my little office, two steaming mugs in his hands.

"Cheers," I said, pushing the papers on my desk to one side.

Noticing DS Jeff Caton sitting in my visitor's chair he said: "Oh, am I interrupting?"

"No," I told him. "Move that stuff and sit down."

"You want a tea, Jeff?"

"No thanks, Dave."

"So what do you reckon?"

"We reckon that there's a killer on the loose, that's what," I said.

"And we've failed to catch him," Jeff added.

"We will do," Dave assured us. "Wouldn't like to think I'd done a murder, these days."

"Optimism!" I retorted. "From you? What happened to the usual morose Sparky we all know and love?"

"I have confidence in you, Sunshine, that's all. Well, in

you and mitochondrial DNA."

"Oh God," I said. "He's been reading the *Sunday Times* again."

"Something will turn up, just you wait and see."

"Yeah, but what if it's another body?"

"Blimey, we are down, aren't we. Is there summat I don't know about?"

I shook my head. "No, not really. I'm just not happy about disbanding the team but I don't know what else we could've done."

"We need a morale booster," Jeff said. "Something entirely different to use up our energies and give us a high."

"Start the walking club again," Dave suggested.

"We can't. Everywhere's closed off because of foot-and-mouth."

"It'll soon be over."

"We're always starting the walking club. It fizzles out, mainly due to shift patterns."

"How about the London marathon? Or the Leeds marathon? We'd get entries in that."

"Too much commitment required," I said.

"And we'd look fools, training in our fancy costumes," Jeff added.

"You don't *have* to wear one, you wally."

"In which case you look a fool when all the fancy costumes beat you. Imagine buying all the best gear – the Adidas vest and shorts; Nike shoes; a headband – training for a year, running twenty-six miles and then getting beaten in a sprint finish against a Telly Tubby."

"Or Thomas the Tank Engine," I said.

"Good point. So what about Karate? Table tennis? Ballroom dancing? Five-a-side soccer?"

"Mmm, I don't think so."

"The Three Peaks?"

"We're always doing the Three friggin' Peaks. We've done the Three Peaks so many times my boots say: 'Oh no, not again,' when the car stops at the Hill Inn."

"Ask around, Dave," Jeff said. "See what the troops think. It'd be good if we could come up with something to keep the team together."

"Right," he replied, adding: "Now can I ask about the crime?"

"Which crime?" I asked.

"Mrs Heeley's murder."

"Sure. Fire away."

"That killing in Lancashire, near Nelson, the beginning of February. You brushed over it in the debriefing just now because there are no apparent similarities, but I think they could be connected."

"Robin Gillespie," I said. Robin was found dead on the edge of some waste ground just outside Nelson. He'd been hit once on the head with a hammer and his body brought to the spot. He was fourteen years old.

"That's right. Poor little Robin."

"You went there with me, Dave, and saw the files. What's troubling you?"

"It's a random killing, like ours, and Nelson is only thirty miles away."

"The MO was different."

"It's a progression. First one, a blow to the head – efficient but impersonal. Next one, a knife in the back – much more satisfying."

"Thanks Dave," I said. "That's really cheered me up. Just what I needed."

"Any time. Want me to have a word with our litter lout friend?"

"Yes please. I was just going to ask you. Meanwhile, I'll get the lab to check on the paternity of Mrs Heeley's children."

"And I'll go back to making the streets of Heckley safe for women and kids," Jeff said, rising to his feet.

When I was alone I picked up the telephone, but it wasn't

the lab's number I dialled. "It's me," I said when the front desk answered. "Spread the word. Sparky will be coming round sometime, asking about volunteers for extra curricula activities – walking, running the marathon, that sort of thing." After a couple of minutes' conspiratorial chatting I pressed the cradle and this time I really did dial the lab.

Sparky's belief that the two murders were linked worried me. Laura Heeley appeared to have led a relatively blameless, uneventful life. She was a bit of a gossip, we discovered, and was often the first to pass on information, suitably embroidered, about the downfall of any of her neighbours. Two brothers a few doors away had been put on probation for shoplifting and Mrs Heeley had been vocal and indiscreet in her condemnation of them to the extent that their father had called and had words with her, but stealing chocolate, even Ferrero Rocher, doesn't usually lead on to murder. In mediaeval times she might have been a candidate for the ducking stool when things were slow, but in modern, cosmopolitan Heckley she had largely lived her life unnoticed.

Robin Gillespie was a son that any father would have been grateful for. He played for the school football team and somewhat reluctantly in the school orchestra, on viola. He was killed while on his paper round, which he did to earn money for a proposed trip to Florida, and his body transported about a mile and a half to the waste ground. The local police found the spot where he died, in a dark stretch of road between two groups of houses, but no weapon. He had not been sexually assaulted and the pathologist found no evidence of previous homosexual experience.

Two murders, no motives, and little else to link them. But murder is relatively rare in this country, and random killing almost unknown, apart from among young tearaways. The more I considered it, the more convinced I became that Sparky might be right. I found my copy of the Almanac in the bottom drawer and thumbed through it until I reached the NCIS entry.

Chief Inspector Warburton shared a symposium with me at Bramshill a couple of years ago, talking about crime in market towns. It all went straight over my head. Rural, suburban or inner city, I just look for fingerprints and round up the usual suspects. The only difference, I told them, is the type of shit you get on your shoes: cowshit, horseshit or dogshit. I left a message for him to give me a ring.

It was Nigel Newley, a DS at HQ and my number one protégé who called me first. "Hi, Boss," he said. "It's Wednesday, are we going to the pub tonight?" He'll still be calling me boss when he's Assistant Chief Constable.

"Have you any money?" I asked.

"Um, a small amount."

"In that case, see you in the Spinners, usual time."

"Do we, er, have a lift home?"

"I'll arrange it."

"Smashing, I'll walk there, then. See you."

"Ta-ra."

DCI Warburton rang shortly after. We reminisced about Bramshill for a few seconds and then I told him about Laura Heeley.

"The husband did it," he announced.

"Ah!" I exclaimed. "Many a true word, and all that. He's not completely in the clear, but unlikely. It looks to be a completely random act." I then explained about Robin Gillespie, hardly thirty miles away. He was interested, and promised to have a look at the database for similar unsolved murders. Apart from that, I didn't know what else we could do.

Colinette Jones stood in the doorway of Mr Naseen's shop and watched the rain dapple the road and distort the reflections of the streetlamps. She shrank back slightly as a car went by, the spray from it chilling her legs, and pushed the umbrella out into the night before unfurling it. A hand fell on her shoulder and her boss said: "You'll get soaked,

Colinette. Let me ask Mrs Naseen to mind the shop and I'll run you home."

"No thanks, Ali," she replied, shrugging off his arm. "It's not far." Once before he'd offered, and she, on only her third day working for him, had gratefully accepted. He hadn't exactly tried anything when he drove straight past her street and stopped at a well-known lovers' lay-by, but he'd subjected her to a forty-minute description of the breakdown in intimate relations with Mrs Naseen since their fourth child had been born. It wasn't as if he was remotely fanciable, she thought. He was old, for a start, nearly fifty at a guess, and grossly overweight.

"It's no trouble, Colinette," he insisted. "I don't want you going down with a chill now that you are such a valuable member of my staff."

"It's nearly stopped. Goodnight."

"Goodnight." He watched her step on to the pavement and heard the click of her high heels as she vanished round the corner. In another four hours he'd close the shop and try another assault on the battlements that the redoubtable Mrs Naseen had erected between them.

Colinette gulped in the clean air, refreshing after the cloying odours of the shop. To the casual visitor they were exotic and romantic, stirring the tastebuds and evoking pictures only seen in TV travelogues. When you worked among them all day long they were nauseous. In eight minutes she would be home, just in time for a quick shower before *Coronation Street* with one of her mum's steak pies on her lap.

And on Friday, after he'd paid her, she'd be free of Mr Naseen with his curry breath and fat face that he liked to hold close to hers as they filled the freezer cabinets. Monday she would start at the health club, in a proper job that paid a wage and gave you a number you could quote when you applied for grants and student loans. Because in September...her heart gave an extra bump at the thought of it…in September it was back to college. Sports therapist.

And just as suddenly she was sad. College was only possible because her dad had died in an accident at work, and his employer had made an out-of-court settlement that the union solicitor had said was the best they could hope for. Fighting for more, he'd said, asking for justice, could have taken ten years.

The rain was coming heavier, and her feet were wet. She pulled the collar of her denim jacket up and lowered the front of the brolly until it was across the top of her vision, like the brim of a hat. A flurry of rain drummed against the stretched fabric and she tightened her grip on the handle. She'd reached the spot where, a year last Christmas, her life had changed, and she looked over the hedge into the recreation ground, as if she might see a remnant of her former self, or even the ring, glistening in the dark. Graham had been her boyfriend for seven years, since they met at high school. She was his lover at fourteen, engaged at fifteen – secretly at first – and still engaged six years later. Walking home from the cinema they'd had a row. Her parents were in so there was no chance of sex in her bedroom with its creaky bed, and Graham had wanted them to do it in the rec. Colinette objected and had hurled his ring, with it's diamond and rubies that would have cost a normal working lad a month's wages, out into the night. She smiled happily at the memory of what she considered the most decisive action she'd ever taken, and wondered if it was still there.

A car came past her, fairly slowly, and Colinette's footsteps faltered as it came to a halt thirty yards in front of her. As she approached it the driver's door opened and she quickened her step again as a young woman got out. She was smaller than Colinette, slightly overweight and perhaps a little older.

"Excuse me," the girl said, "but have you any idea where Burntcastle Avenue is? I've been driving round in circles for the last half hour."

"You've found it," Colinette told her. "On the left, in about two hundred yards."

"Oh, that's a relief. I've an appointment at number 238 for seven fifteen. Fitted kitchens. Will that be at this end?"

"No, at the far end. Um, two hundred and thirty-what did you say?"

"Eight. Two hundred and thirty-eight."

"An even number. I live at forty-four, so it will be on the right-hand side of the road."

"Oh, that's most helpful, thank you. Hop in and I'll drop you off."

"It's all right, thanks. I'm nearly there."

"Nonsense. Jump in. You look soaked already."

"Oh, OK then. I am a bit wet. Thank you." She slipped into the passenger seat of the hatchback and basked in the comforting warmth of the car's interior. The driver slammed her door and let the clutch in too quickly, spinning the front wheels. Colinette rocked backwards in her seat and then forwards, wondering if it was worth finding the seat belt for such a short journey. "Fitted kitchens, did you say?" she asked.

The car was still accelerating as it passed the end of Burntcastle Avenue. "It's a living," the driver mumbled, to herself as much as to Colinette.


"Cheese and onion?"

"Plain, please," I replied. Sparky juggled with the packets of crisps before tossing one at me. Nigel appeared behind him, three pints bundled together between his outstretched fingers, and gingerly lowered them on to the table.

"Cheers," I said, placing mine on a beer mat before I struggled with the crisp packet. We sipped our drinks in silence for a few moments, until I looked at Nigel and said: "It doesn't suit you."

He fingered his chin, which carried several days' growth of hair. "It's only been a week." Nigel came to me when he was on the fast track, and greener than a leprechaun's socks. He was a college boy, from the south, and an easy target for the locker-room cowboys, but I took to him for some reason. I don't know why, perhaps I saw a little of myself there, or what I would like to have been, and I steered him through the early days without damaging his reputation or self-esteem.

And now he'd grown a beard.

"You look like a rat peering out of a haystack," Dave told him.

"Thanks."

"What does Les Isles think of it?" I asked. Les is a superintendent at HQ, and Nigel's new boss.

"He said it's the first time he's seen one with teeth."

I turned to Dave. "What on earth can he mean by that, David?" I asked.

"No idea, Charles," he replied.

We stuffed crisps into our mouths and sipped the beer. The Spinners is an old pub in the middle of town, and the clientele had changed in the years we'd been using it. Not long ago it catered for market traders and the local business people who needed a drink at the end of a long day. Once there was a bar in a corner room called the Oddfellows, restricted to men only. A small clique of salesmen used to gather there every evening to discuss the day's business and delay returning to wherever it was they laid their heads at night, but they'd grown old together and retired or passed on. Now there was a pool table in the room. A burst of noise announced the arrival of a group of young men in sober suits and hysterical ties, probably from the Insurance Centre. They surged through the door, shaking the rain off their haircuts as they reached for wallets. Two young women followed, carefully folding umbrellas and leaning them against the wall.

"Spritzer for you, Natasha?" the first youth to reach the bar called out over everyone's heads, and one of the girls nodded her approval. If the men wore bright ties as a focal point, to draw attention away from their deficiencies, with the women it was short skirts. I watched her climb on to a barstool and cross her legs.

"I think I've gone off this pub," said Dave, whose back was to the bar.

"Oh, I don't know," I replied, groping for my glass.

"So," Nigel began, "you've disbanded the team and we'll be getting our men back."

"'Fraid so," I said.

"Nobody in the frame at all?"

"Nope."

"Why would anybody want to do something like that? A random killing. It seems so pointless."

"It's whatever turns you on, Nigel. There's some funny people out there, as you well know." Natasha closed her eyes and pursed her lips to take that first sip from her drink. I tore my gaze away and turned to Dave. "I've had a word with NCIS," I told him. "Asked them about other unsolved, apparently random killings."

"You think it might not be a one-off?" Nigel asked.

"Dave wonders if it might be linked to the paperboy who was murdered over near Nelson, two weeks before Laura Heeley was killed."

"Poor little Robin. It's worth pursuing, I suppose," he said, unconvinced.

"But meanwhile…" I announced, brightly, "he's busy trying to organise some activity to boost our flagging morale, aren't you, Sunshine? Any luck with it?"

He pulled a pained expression and shook his head.

"What?" I asked. "Has lethargy tightened its grip on the brave forces of law and order we used to know and love?"

He had a drink, opened his mouth to speak and closed it again.

"Go on," I urged.

"Well…" he began. "I asked around, but nobody seems interested."

"Somebody must be," I argued.

"Well, they're not."

"I don't believe you."

"Listen," he said. "I went down to the incident room at shift change and put it to them that we should organise something, preferably for charity, but nobody was keen."

"I'd have thought they'd be full of ideas," I stated.

"They're usually an enthusiastic lot," Nigel agreed.

"Well I asked."

"And nobody came up with anything?"

"No."

"Nobody at all?"

"Well, only one."

"What was it?"

"Big Geordie Farrell. He said he'd always had a hankering to learn Morris dancing."

"Morris dancing!" Nigel and I echoed in unison, and I added: "What did the others think of that?"

"They all agreed. Said it was a good excuse to work up a thirst and have a piss-up."

"That's true," I confirmed, raising my glass to hide the grin I was having difficulty containing.

Dave lowered his head and glared at me from under his eyebrows. "It was you, wasn't it?" he growled.

"Me?" I replied, struggling to adopt the expression of one of those baby seals just before the club bashes its brains in. "Me?"

"You set me up, you bastard!"

"How's that, David?"

"*Bastard*! I thought they were all a bit too eager. Well just for that you can get them in." He drained his glass and plonked it down in front of me. "And another thing," he continued. "We're doing the Three Peaks, whether you like it or not."

"Oh no, not the Three Peaks," I protested.

"Not the Yorkshire three, the three biggest in England,

Scotland and Wales."

"That's nine peaks," Nigel told him.

"You know what I mean, clever sod: Scafell Pike; Ben Nevis and Snowdon. The fire brigade are pretending to do them at Heckley gala, running up and down ladders. We'll do them for real, so start training."

I was laughing all the way to the bar. The youth who bought the drink for Natasha was standing next to her, shielding her from the attentions of the others, but she had twisted on her seat to listen to the words of wisdom that the oldest member of the group was regaling them with. I decided that he was the boss and that laddo didn't have a chance. As I pushed between them she caught my gaze and held it for a telltale few seconds longer than propriety dictated. She was a young lady on the make, checking out the talent. You notice it most of all when you're in the car. A woman is driving in the opposite direction. As she passes she glances across, slightly curious, to see what you look like. She probably doesn't realise it, and would almost certainly vehemently deny it, but she's interested and possibly available. The ones who are totally engrossed in and content with the life they are living go sailing blithely by. If you were wearing a purple gorilla suit with strobe lights they wouldn't notice you.

"Hello, 'Tasha," I said, before she could look away. "Long time no see." She blinked several times and laddo's mouth fell open. They could have been a double act from a kids' comic: The Owl and the Goldfish.

As I returned with the drinks Dave was explaining the logistics of the venture to Nigel. "The idea is to do it in less than twenty-four hours," he stated. "If you say three hours on Snowdon, four on Scafell and five on the Ben, that leaves twelve hours to drive about five hundred miles. QET."

"QED," Nigel told him.

"Pardon?"

"QED. *Quod erat demonstrandum.*"

"No," Dave insisted, "QET. Quite enough time."

I winced as I set the glasses safely down. "Don't encourage him, Nigel," I protested. "Some of us have to work with him. Ever since Sophie went to Cambridge he's been polishing the college doorknob on his way to work." Sophie is Dave's daughter, my Goddaughter, and we both take a keen interest in her studies. Last week it was Simon de Montfort and the foundations of Parliament. At about ten o'clock the other woman in Dave's life, his wife Shirley, would come to give us a lift home.

"What will you do," Nigel asked, "if the foot-and-mouth epidemic isn't over?"

Dave took a long, deliberate sip of beer and I could tell that his mind was working overtime. He replaced his glass on the table, licked froth of his lip and said: "I hope you don't mind me mentioning this, Nigel, but I know that you are a stickler for these things and that you've had a much better education then me – sorry, than I…"

"You got a C in woodwork, didn't you?" I interrupted.

"Religious instruction, actually. I got an F in woodwork."

"I thought you were good at woodwork."

"I am, but Mr Gravesend took us for the exam and he had a speech impediment. He told us to make an egg rack, but I thought he said roof rack. I used more wood than all the other kids put together. Anyway, as I was saying, as you are such a bloody pedant about these things, Nigel, can I point out that *people* have epidemics, animals have epizootics."

"Ooh!" I said. "Ooh! Talk yourself out of that one, Nigel."

He bit his lip, then said: "I think I'd better get the next ones in."

I was still smiling as I looked across at Natasha. After a few seconds she glanced my way and I raised my eyebrows in salute. One day I'm going to learn how to make them work individually. I practise every morning, as I shave, but it's harder than it looks. She returned my smile, just for a moment, until something behind me caught her attention.

"Uh-oh," I heard Nigel say, and Dave added: "Talk of the devil."

I looked round to see what the fuss was about. A man had entered the bar, a big man in uniform who dwarfed the doorway. He stood there for a few seconds, taking in the room, then wove between the tables towards us.

"Bet he hasn't come for his first dancing lesson," Nigel said.

"No, I don't think he has." I looked up at the figure as he loomed over me, and said: "What is it, George?"

PC Farrell, better known as Big Geordie, placed a hand the size of a leg of pork on the table and stooped until his face was level with mine. "Sorry to disturb you, Boss," he whispered, "but you're needed. It looks as if there's been another."

"Where?" I asked.

"Down a lane off the Oldfield Road, just out of town."

"Woman?"

"Young girl."

"Right."

We followed him out, oblivious of the three barely-touched drinks on the table and all the eyes, including Natasha's, that watched us to the door.

The hatchback reversed into the space outside the terrace house and doused its lights. The driver let his head loll back and reached across to take the hand of the woman sitting next to him. "Phew!" he exclaimed, and she squeezed his hand in silent agreement. Phew indeed. After a moment he felt into the car's ashtray and retrieved his door keys. They both got out and after unlocking the front door of the house he turned to use the remote control to lock the car. The hazard lights flashed to confirm it was done and they entered their home. When inside he carefully dropped the latch and turned the key. The curtains in the front room were already closed, and a gas fire gave off a comforting hiss as it kept the room temperature up in the tropical eighties. The only illumination was from the fire and a pair of wall fittings that cast semi-circles of light on to the high ceiling.

He led her into the room as if it were a new experience for both of them. She held back with feigned reluctance, like a schoolgirl who'd heard about men like this – not wanting to follow but at the same time driven by a curiosity that had to be satisfied. He tugged her arm and she shelved her doubts, allowing herself to be led.

When he was standing on the woollen rug in front of the fire he turned and undid the buttons of her coat. "Take this off, my darling," he said, "or you won't feel the benefit, afterwards." She shrugged it off and he tossed it over an easy chair.

"What about yours?" she said.

"I'll take that off, too." His jacket joined hers and he placed his hands on her shoulders, massaging them with a rotary movement. "You're good for me," he told her.

"We're good for each other."

"That's right. We're a team."

"Shall I put some music on?"

"It's in the player."

The girl turned away and pressed the play button on a Sony music centre that stood on a sideboard opposite the fireplace. After checking that the volume was right she moved back to him and he replaced his hands on her shoulders. She rolled her head, swaying to the music, and murmured: "Mmm, that's good, Timothy, that's really good."

"What!" he exploded, pushing her away. "What did you call me?" His arm swept in a wide arc and his cupped hand cuffed her at the side of the head, the noise it made more violent than the impact.

"I'm sorry," she sobbed, holding her hand in front of her face like the heroine of some 1930s paperback. "Don't hurt me! Please don't hurt me."

He grabbed her hair and pulled her head back. "What did you call me?" he demanded.

"I'm sorry."

"Say it."

"I'm sorry."

"What are you sorry for?"

"For calling you...calling you..."

"Calling me what?"

"For calling you Timothy."

"So what am I called?"

"Tim. I forgot. Please don't hurt me, Tim."

"I don't want to hurt you, you know that, don't you?" She nodded, her head still stretched backwards by him, her white throat exposed. "But you've been a naughty girl, haven't you?" She nodded again.

"And what happens to naughty girls?"

"I don't know."

"You do know, so tell me."

"They get punished."

"And do you think I should punish you?"

"I don't know."

"Do you deserve it?"

She nodded.

"And how do we punish naughty girls in this house?" he asked.

"With..."

"Go on."

"With...the strap."

"And where is the strap?"

"Down here." Her hand fell to his waist.

"You'd better fetch it then, hadn't you?"

She slowly lowered herself to her knees in front of him. Her fingers unfastened the big aluminium buckle of his belt and began to carefully unthread it from the loops of his Versace jeans.

Chapter Two

I pushed the possibilities out of my mind. Speculation is pointless when you are on your way to the scene. Go through the checklist, think about what you could have done better last time, try to put your mind into a higher gear. Some times, faced with a suspicious death, you need to act fast and decisively; others demand that you move with the deliberation of a chameleon stalking a fly. The trick is to know the difference. Everywhere we go we leave something behind, take something of that place with us. The molecule of spittle he breathed out or the single fibre that he picked up from a chair may be the only clues to link a killer with his crime, and it's my job to find them. Mine and the team of experts I have, a phone-call away.

The three of us piled into the back of the patrol car and Dave rang Shirley to tell her that we wouldn't need a lift, because "something has come up." The words are written in burnt dinners and disappointed children's faces across the life of every policeman's wife.

Big Geordie filled us in with the details. A motorcyclist on his way home from the wire works at Oldfield had stopped to shelter under a tree when the rain suddenly became much worse. He saw a girl's body lying at the side of the road and rang for an ambulance and the police. He'd felt for a pulse and said that she was still warm, but he'd thought she was dead. We dropped Dave off at the General Hospital, where the woman had been taken, and the rest of us continued to the crime scene.

There are not many trees in this part of the world. The sheep eat the ones that survive the winters and most of those that achieved a decent size have long gone to the chipboard factory. This one was a chestnut, in full leaf, at the side of the road where a kink in the wall to accommodate the tree had created an unofficial lay-by. Another patrol car was parked nearby, behind a little Honda motorbike.

By the light of the car's headlights the motorcyclist showed me the exact spot where her body had lain. The rain had turned the roadside into a quagmire, but the area under the tree was still quite firm, with lots of tyre marks. Big drops from the leaves pocked the surface as I looked at it, indicating that we hadn't any time to lose.

"Quick," I said. "Find something to cover the ground with, before it gets washed away." We spread their waterproof coats over the tyre prints, and radioed in for a tent.

I'd just sent the motorcyclist on his way when Dave phoned me. He confirmed that the girl was dead, and by the marks on her neck she'd been strangled. I clicked my phone off and turned to the four PCs. "It's official," I told them. "This is now a murder hunt."

"Timothy...Tim..." she whispered.

"Mmm."

"The music's stopped."

"Mmm."

"Are you asleep?"

"I was."

They were lying on the floor, under a duvet, with the gas fire turned down low. He tugged the duvet to cover their bare shoulders and extricated his arm from under her head. She turned on her side and wriggled backwards until they were fitted together like two garden chairs. He flexed his fingers to revive the circulation and reached around her, feeling for her tiny breasts.

"Shall I put it on again?"

"Yes, I think you'd better."

"Tonight..." she began.

"What about it?"

"Tonight...It was the best ever, don't you think?"

"Yeah. Definitely."

"I was...I was touching her."

"I know you were. Was it good?"

"It was fantastic. I've never experienced anything like it. I was holding her, you know, down there, and she just, like, faded away. And, and, it was like, electric. It was, like, power, coming to me. I could feel it, coming up my arm. Like, power."

"I told you what it could be like. Now do you believe me?"

"I've always believed you, Tim. You're so clever. And I love you."

"And I love you."

"When can we do it again?"

He propped himself up on his elbow. "I'm not sure," he said. "Doing two in Heckley was clever. They weren't expecting that. Now they'll realise that they are up against someone special, if they've made the connection, yet. I'll have to think about it."

"When we do," she began, "can we, do you think we could, you know, spend more time with…them?"

"With the target, you mean?"

"Yes."

"I've been wondering about that myself. It'd be good, no doubt about it. Lift us on to another level. We'd have to bring them back here."

"Would it be too dangerous?"

"No, not if we're careful. Leave it to me. I have an idea, but it will mean some heavy work. And I've a couple of targets picked out already. I think you'll like them."

She wriggled her bottom against his loins to show her approval, and felt him harden. "I thought you were putting the music on," he reminded her. She reached out and pressed the play button. After a few moments a simple rhythm filled the room, tapped out on a cowbell and soon joined by a bass guitar and keyboard. She turned to embrace him and he pulled the duvet over their heads as a thin, piping voice leaked from the speakers. "*This is the eye of the storm,*" it sang. "*Watch out for that needle, Son, 'cos this is the eye of the storm.*"

One of the important pieces of information we lacked was the identity of the victim. They went through her pockets at the hospital without finding anything, and we did a torch-light search of the edge of the field where she'd been found, in case her handbag had been hurled over the wall. Negative. Dave phoned me with a brief description and said she was aged about twenty. Same as his daughter, Sophie, I thought, and wished I'd sent somebody else to the hospital.

I went back to the station to check the missing persons' file, knowing it was a waste of time. My feet and shoulders were wet but the heating in the offices was off, so I found a portable fan heater that we're not supposed to have and plugged it in. Gilbert Wood, my superintendent, arrived, shaking his head and making sympathetic noises, and I rang a few other people to tell them to be at the station early in the morning.

"What do you reckon, then?" Gilbert asked. "Is it another?"

"It's another murder," I replied. "Whether it's another *murderer* is a different question." I've never understood the dread that people have that a series of deaths may be the work of the same person. Surely having one twisted hospital worker going round the wards turning off the oxygen is preferable to having a whole bunch of them who just do it once, for a kick? For the time being we'd treat this as a one-off, and do everything we could to find the perpetrator. If we were successful and could pin the other two deaths on him, so much the better. If we didn't catch him, we'd have to take a long and careful look at all the circumstances.

"Need any help from HQ?"

"Not at the moment, Gilbert. Let's wait until we know who she is. Somebody might leap into the frame."

Who she was, her last movements, who she was with. Often, with attractive young women, that was all we needed to know. Young blokes, and sometimes not-so-young ones, get ideas, build up fantasies. Magazines and daytime-TV soaps reinforce the idea that romance, perfect romance, is everybody's right. You see the girl of your dreams, she looks across and the feeling is reciprocated, as if love was some force of nature like gravity or magnetism, that obeyed rules laid down when the universe was formed. But it's not like that, and when we learn the truth it can be painful. Most of us just go home to play the Janis Ian records and sob into our cocoa. A few of us turn violent, and this looked like one of those.

The phone rang. "Priest," I said into it.

"It's the front desk, Charlie," I was told. "I've a woman on the outside line, saying she's worried about her daughter. She didn't come home from work tonight."

"Right," I sighed, composing myself for something that no amount of training or experience can prepare you for. "Right. What is she called?"

"Mrs Jones."

"OK. Put her through." I covered the mouthpiece and whispered: "This could be it," to the super. After a click and a silence I said: "Mrs Jones?"

"Yes," a quavery voice replied.

"I'm Detective Inspector Priest, Mrs Jones. You told the sergeant that your daughter hasn't come home from work."

"That's right."

"Could you give me your address, please." I wrote it down. "And what is your daughter called, Mrs Jones?"

"Colinette."

"And what time were you expecting her?"

"About ten past seven. She rang me at half past six to say she was finishing at seven, but she never came home."

"And how old is Colinette?"

"Twenty-two. It was her birthday on Sunday."

"And where did she work?"

At a nearby corner shop. It wasn't a proper job, just something to pass time until she went to college. No, she'd never done anything like this before. Her supper was ruined and she didn't have a boyfriend. I wrote the responses down, trying to ignore the knot that was tying itself in my groin. "She's dead!" I wanted to scream. "Your lovely daughter, the best daughter anybody ever had, is dead."

"Is there a Mr Jones?" I asked.

"No, Inspector. I lost my husband four years ago."

"I'm sorry."

"He was killed in an industrial accident. That's why…"

"Why what?"

"That's why Colinette wouldn't do anything like this unless…unless…"

"I'll have to come round and take a statement from you, Mrs Jones," I interrupted, cutting her off from speculation about her daughter's fate. The truth would be far more horrifying. "I'll be about…twenty minutes, half an hour. I'll…take a statement."

I replaced the phone and looked at Mr Wood. "Colinette Jones," I told him. "Aged twenty-two. What time is it?"

"Twenty-five to eleven."

"Maggie won't be in bed yet. I'll take her."

"Tell her I'll pick her up," he said. "I'll break the news to Mrs Jones, Charlie. *Noblesse oblige*, and all that balderdash. You get yourself home."

I dialled Maggie's number and didn't argue with him.

Colinette had phoned her mother at about six thirty, and left the shop a couple of minutes after seven. The three-nines call for an ambulance was timed at seven fifty-two and the body was found five miles from the corner shop. Around midnight Mrs Jones confirmed that it was her daughter.

We sent the team out, bright and early, knocking on doors, talking to neighbours. Mr Naseen at the corner shop confirmed that Colinette left on time and expressed his concern for her mother. Later that morning we spoke to a couple of Colinette's friends who were not too complimentary about her employer, so we brought him in.

"How long had Colinette worked for you, Mr Naseen?"
I asked, as we sat in interview room number one. Dave was
with me but the tape wasn't running.

"She didn't work for me."

"So what was she doing at your shop?"

"She just helped out, sometimes."

"That's not what her mother says."

"I don't know what she has told her mother, Inspector."

"Her mother says she has worked for you for over a
year."

"No, it is not true."

"She just helps out?"

"Yes, Inspector, as I said."

"You call eight hours a day and four on Saturdays just
helping out?"

"It is nothing like that Inspector. My wife assists me, and
Colinette sometimes calls in to help her with the children.
Perhaps my wife pays her for that. I don't know."

We'd come up against the Rice Curtain. It's an occupa-
tional hazard in this part of the world. I leaned forward over
the little table until I was as close to his face as I could get.
He'd had curry the night before, but I didn't mind – so had
I. "Mr Naseen," I began. "We are investigating a murder. The
fact that you employed Colinette Jones on a casual basis,
paying no National Insurance fees on her behalf, or deduct-
ing no Pay As You Earn, is irrelevant to this enquiry. *At the
moment.*" I loaded the last sentence with meaning, to show
that we'd keep it on the file if he didn't cooperate. "We've
also spoken to two girls who had the job before Colinette
did. Two girls who didn't stay with you for too long. Now,
Mr Naseen, can we start again? How long did Colinette
work for you?"

The expression on his face indicated that he'd got the
message. "As Mrs Jones told you," he replied, very softly,
"Colinette had assisted in my shop for about one year. You
must realise, Inspector, that the shop is in a very poor area.

My turnover does not allow me to employ full-time assistance and I have a wife and four very young children to support."

"Not to mention a Series Seven BMW," I added.

After that he began to cooperate. He confirmed that she'd left just after seven, in the rain, and told us what she'd been wearing.

"Was she carrying a handbag?" I asked.

"No, Inspector, an umbrella."

"But no handbag?"

"No. She very rarely carried one, unless she was going straight out with her friends."

"Did you fancy her?"

"What do you mean by that, Inspector?"

"I mean, Mr Naseen, did it ever enter your head that a more intimate relationship, even a sexual one, with Colinette would be very desirable?"

He sat back in his chair, one arm extended, resting on the table, almost as if he were enjoying himself. "She was a modern young woman, Inspector. Had lots of boyfriends like western girls of her age do. She was attractive and dressed in a very provocative way. Yes, I fancied her, as you put it. I fancied her to distraction, but I never did anything about it. I'm a middle-aged man, as you are, and feelings like these are part of the growing old process, I'm sure you'll agree."

"That's not what the other two girls say."

"What do they say?"

"They say you propositioned them constantly, until they had to leave."

"They were not very nice girls, Inspector. I caught them stealing. It is only natural that they would try to blacken my character."

"So where were you between seven and seven thirty last night?"

"In my shop."

"Can anyone support you in that?"

"I would imagine so, Inspector. I had a steady stream of customers and a couple of them paid their newspaper bills. I can furnish you with their names and the till receipts, which will bear the exact time that they paid. Will that be sufficient?"

I glanced across at Dave, who looked as if his strangulated hernia were playing up. "Yes Mr Naseen," I replied. "That should be quite sufficient."

"Bugger!" I exclaimed when we were back in my office.

"He's not exactly love's young dream, is he," Dave said.

"No, and I bet he runs close to the edge of the sexual harassment laws, but he's in the clear, if his story checks out."

"It will do."

"Mmm, I think you're right."

"Do you want a coffee?"

"No, we haven't time. I wonder how long Maggie will be?" I'd asked Maggie Maddison to attend the post-mortem because she'd be liaising with Mrs Jones throughout the enquiry, and there might be a flake of comfort for Colinette's mother in knowing that a female officer was present when they cut her open.

"A while yet," Dave replied. "They weren't starting until nine."

"OK. So you go round to Mr Naseen's and check his story. I'll report upstairs then see how the fingertip boys are doing."

The task force do the fingertip searches. Shoulder to shoulder, down on their knees, they miss nothing. It was nearly half a mile from the corner shop to 44 Burntcastle Avenue, where Colinette had lived. Ten minutes maximum, although she was wearing high heels. A long stretch of her route was on an unlit road past a recreation ground, and that's where we had started the search.

Usually it's a weapon we're looking for. If anyone finds

anything they raise a hand and the line comes to a halt. The sergeant in charge has a look and assesses the find. He might decide to photograph it *in situ* or just make a note of the place and bag it for later examination. When I arrived the sergeant was lying on his stomach, peering at something, and the rest of the line were sitting back on their heels. "What is it?" I asked as I crouched down beside him. The grass was wet and they were all wearing wellies and water-proof trousers.

"Hello, Boss," he said, pushing himself upright and extending his hand towards me. "A ring, possibly engage-ment."

I studied it without taking it from him. It was a thin gold band with a tiny diamond between two even smaller rubies, but it would have cost somebody all they had to offer, finan-cially and emotionally. "Mmm," I mumbled, not knowing what else to say.

"Been here a while, unfortunately," the sergeant told me. "Grass growing through it. Nothing to do with us, I'm afraid."

"Right," I said. If you keep quiet somebody always jumps in with an answer. "Anything else?"

"Not really. Usual rubbish, but no handbag. We've had a good look right along her route, but haven't found it."

"Um, no," I began. "We've been told by her employer that she wasn't carrying one, but I'll check with her mother. She was carrying an umbrella, though."

He shook his head. "Sorry, no umbrella."

"So what happened to it?" I wondered aloud. I pointed at the ring. "Put that in an exhibit bag, please, and I'll take it with me. It'll make an icebreaker. God knows, I'll need one."

"Rather you than me, Charlie," he replied, reaching inside his overalls for a bag.

I'd been told that 44 was on the right-hand side, the sec-ond one of a pair of semis. In reality it was the one with all the cars outside and a floral cross hanging on the door. As I approached I saw faces inside turn towards me, so I just waited on the step, without knocking. A middle-aged man came and invited me in after I'd introduced myself. Two women buttering scones in the kitchen squeezed to one side as I passed through. One of them told me she'd just made another brew and asked if I'd like a cup.

The front room was crowded and smoke-filled. Mrs Jones thanked me for coming and someone pulled an upright chair from under the dining table for me. I sat down and told everybody how sorry I was.

The consensus of opinion was that hanging was too good for the bastard who did it. I let them bounce their anger off me, hardly listening to the hard words as they ricocheted around the room without concern for any distress their assumptions might cause Mrs Jones. The names of murderers living in luxury at the tax-payers' expense were bandied around along with rapists and child molesters who were free to walk the streets. I nodded, when required, and made feeble attempts to point out that we didn't know what had happened to Colinette. I didn't want to reveal that at that very moment she was on the table in the PM room, spilling forth her secrets. My tea arrived and I sipped it gratefully. It was in a china cup and good and strong. A panacea for all ills.

There were three photographs on the sideboard. A handsome man in a Triumph Motorcycles T-shirt grinned from the large one in the middle; to the right he had a little girl on his shoulders and in the other he was snuggling up close to a young version of Mrs Jones in what could have been a Spanish bar. There'd have to be a new addition to the gallery, I thought, and wondered how she would arrange them. I finished my tea and as I looked for somewhere to put the cup and saucer a hand reached out and took it from me.

"Would you like a refill, Inspector?"

I shook my head. "No, but that was most welcome, thank you." I turned to Mrs Jones and told her that I'd be sending Maggie Madison to spend some time with her. "The newspapers will descend on you, I'm afraid, when they hear about this, but she'll deal with them." She nodded vacantly, as if I were explaining why the milkman was late. "I'd like to ask you a couple of questions," I continued, now that I had her attention. "About Colinette, if you don't mind."

The room fell silent. "He'd like to ask you a few questions, about Colinette," the big woman sitting next to her on the settee explained.

"Yes, I heard," Mrs Jones replied with a nod.

"Was your daughter carrying a handbag, do you know?" I asked.

She shook her head. "No, she hardly ever carried one."

"I don't know where they keep stuff, these days," the other woman stated.

"Right. Thank you. What about an umbrella?"

"I'm not sure. She had two or three, and I think she kept one at the shop."

"What sort were they?"

"Those roll-up ones that come down very small."

"I never know how to fold them," the woman complained.

"Joan, shut up," a man sitting near the window snapped. "Let the inspector ask his questions."

"That's all right," I said. "And what colour would they be?"

"Black. And I think she had a blue one."

"If I can speak," the woman said triumphantly, "if I can speak, the blue one's in the hall. I've seen it, just now."

"Thank you. So she probably had a black, telescopic umbrella with her?"

"Yes, I think so."

"Good. That's all for now, Mrs Jones. I'll get back to the station and Maggie Madison will be with you as soon as possible." I rose to my feet and felt for the plastic bag in my pocket. "There is just one other thing," I said as I unfolded it. "Have you ever seen this ring before?" I was fairly sure that it was irrelevant, but it added to the illusion that we were doing everything we could, following every avenue in our attempts to find her daughter's killer.

Mrs Jones took it from me and studied it for several seconds. Tears were welling up in her eyes when she looked at me again. "Yes," she whispered. "It was Colinette's."

"Oh," I said. That hadn't been the answer I'd expected. "Um, we found it in the recreation ground. Did she lose it?"

"I don't know. She had a boyfriend. Went out with him for years, ever since they were at school together. They were engaged when she was fifteen, but we didn't know. About, oh, two years ago she finished with him and stopped wearing the ring. I don't know why they finished, he was a lovely boy."

"I see," I said as I took the ring back from her, although I didn't see at all. "And would you happen to know this boy's name and address, Mrs Jones?"

Things are rarely straightforward. The ex-boyfriend was called Graham Allen, and the address was his parents' house, but nobody was home. It was a detached residence, definitely in a league above Colinette's modest semi, surrounded by well-tended gardens with rose beds and neat lawns. After gaining no answer to my knocks and pushes on the bell I wandered around and peered in through the windows. The rooms were large and elegantly furnished, and if the number of pot dogs were anything to go by they were canine freaks. Next door, over the wall, I could hear the noise of a motor mower, so I wandered in that direction.

When the gardener swung the mower round at the far end of the lawn he saw me standing at the end of his next stripe, ID already in my hand. He burbled towards me in a haze of blue smoke until he was almost on my toes, then stopped and turned off the engine.

"Can I help you?" he asked. It was a mild day but he was wearing leather shoes, grey flannels and a tank top over a shirt and tie, except he would have called it a sleeveless pullover.

"Is it dry enough for cutting?" I said.

"Hardly, but it needs doing."

I held my ID towards him, saying, "DI Priest, Heckley CID. Would you happen to know where your neighbours are?" He might have been the gardener, but I'd do him the courtesy of assuming he was the householder.

"CID, did you say?"

"Mmm."

"In that case there's probably no harm in telling you. Spain. Costa del Sol. They have business interests over there."

"And what about Graham?"

"Ah!" he snorted. "Thought it might be him you were after. What's he done now?"

"Nothing," I replied. "We just want a word with him. What makes you think he may have done something?"

"Oh, perhaps I'm being unfair," he replied, as cagey as I was. "He's young, enjoys life. That's all they think about, these days, isn't it?"

"So what time will he be home?"

"He lives in Heckley, with his girlfriend. Don't know the address."

"OK. Thanks for your help." I pointed at the mower. "You should buy a sit-on one," I suggested.

"Only exercise I get," he replied, pulling the starter cord and disappearing in a cloud of smoke.

We had a meeting in Gilbert Wood's office in the afternoon. Me and Gilbert, Maggie Madison and the pathologist from the General, Doctor Sulaiman. I helped Maggie make coffee with Gilbert's percolator and when we were all settled at one end of his conference table he said: "Right, Dr Sulaiman, what can you tell us?"

The doc is just as impatient and probably even busier

than we are. He might be thorough when he does the business, but when it comes to reports he's thankfully straight to the point. Colinette was a fit and healthy girl, athletic even, and had been strangled.

"She competed in triathlons," Maggie told us, "and would have started college in September to train as a sports therapist."

"Her musculature indicates that she had been training at an endurance event for some time," the doctor said.

"So you'd think she'd be able to put up some sort of a struggle," the super suggested.

"You'd think so, but there was no evidence of this. Let me tell you about the strangulation." The doctor looked in his pile of documents and withdrew a sheet of unlined paper from them. "Unfortunately the photographs are not ready yet, but my assistant made these drawings." He spun them round so I could see them. "These represent the marks on Colinette's neck. They are deep and quite savage. A great deal of force would be required to make them. The strange thing, however, is that they are only on the front of her throat, covering an arc of about one hundred and thirty degrees." He made a circle with his fingers and thumbs, saying: "In a normal strangulation, either with the hands or with a ligature, some bruising is found around the full circumference of the neck."

Maggie said: "So the marks go less than halfway round."

"That's right, Maggie."

"Any thoughts on that, Doc?" I asked.

"A few, Charlie, but I'd like to move on, if I may. Note that there are several marks, one above the other, and not just one. And you'll have to take my word for this, until we have the pictures, but the marks were remarkably smooth-edged."

"Smooth-edged?" Gilbert repeated.

"Yes. In a strangulation as violent as this the bruising and abrasions usually give an indication of the type of material the ligature was made from. In this case, it appears to be something lacking in any sort of surface texture whatsoever."

"Like what?" I asked.

"The material that comes to my mind is plastic-covered clothesline."

"Wouldn't that be too stretchy?" I wondered.

"No, it doesn't stretch."

"What about its size. Does the diameter indicated by the marks fit with clothes line?"

"Yes, precisely. In fact..." he reached down into his old-style briefcase and produced a short length of pink line, "...I have a typical sample here, courtesy of Mrs Sulaiman, but don't tell her."

"So it looks as if we have a murder weapon," Gilbert concluded as he ran it through his fingers.

"Yeah," I said reaching for my coffee and one of Gilbert's chocolate digestives, "available from every other shop in the country."

Gilbert offered the biscuits round but left the packet at his corner of the table. "Was there any sexual interference, Doc?" he asked.

The doc shook his head slowly as he swallowed biscuit, in a way that indicated he wasn't sure. "She was wearing those very brief knickers that are so popular these days," he told us.

"A thong," Maggie said. "She was wearing a thong. Lots of the younger girls wear them."

"The nurses at the hospital have started wearing them under their tunics," the doctor divulged. "I'm not sure if the effects on the patients are detrimental or restorative. However, back to poor Colinette. She was wearing a thong and it appeared to have been pulled down, but only a little way. As if our perpetrator had had a feel at her private parts, but that's all."

"Touched her up," I said.

"Yes indeed."

"Wonder if he'll be happy with that the next time?"

All eyes turned to me. I looked at Dr Sulaiman. "Back to the strangulation marks, Doc," I said. "Some of them were side by side and some were probably superimposed on each other. Would any one of them have killed her?"

"Yes," he replied. "Any one of them would have resulted in death had it been sustained for long enough."

I didn't voice my thoughts. He'd strangled her until she was unconscious, then let her revive for a while before doing it again and again. Six or ten murders for the price of one. And poor Colinette, waking each time from the worst nightmare anybody had ever had, only to find that it wasn't a nightmare, it was reality.

"You said, Doc," I began, "that you'd come back to the question of how she was strangled. I know you're not in the business of conjecture, but…"

"Ah yes," he replied. "Unfortunately once again I have to apologise for the lack of photographs, and I'm not even sure if the photos will capture what I saw, but I have put it in the record. When I studied the marks on her throat there was a slight suggestion that they were deeper at the right side than at the left. Now why could that be?"

I looked puzzled, Maggie said: "She struggled and twisted sideways?"

"Possibly," the doc agreed, "but when he did it again you'd think that she might twist the other way, wouldn't you?"

Maggie looked glum and nodded.

"The other explanation is that more force was applied at the right side than at the left."

"Spell it out, Doc," I invited.

"OK." He picked up the piece of clothesline and bent it into a horseshoe shape. "Colinette's neck is here," he said. "The perpetrator pulled back, like so." He pulled the loop towards himself. "As you see, it is necessary for him to have something to pull her back against."

"Like a car seat," I said. "She must have been in a car for him to dump her where he did, and he strangled her from behind while she was in the front passenger seat."

"With her head against the headrest," Maggie added.

"It's a possibility," the doctor agreed with a shrug of modesty.

"So why are the marks more pronounced at one side?" I asked.

"One reason," the doctor said, "could be that this end of the line was attached to the headrest support on the left hand side. He would then only have to pass the loop over her head and pull on one side."

"Brilliant, Doc," I said. "I think you've just given us his MO."

I walked downstairs with the doctor and thanked him again for his time. From the front desk I rang HQ and arranged for every policeman in the division to look out for a vehicle with a piece of rope, possibly clothes line, dangling from the passenger seat headrest. I wanted them to inspect every car or van they saw, and if they found it I wanted the driver arrested. It was a long shot, but murderers get sloppy, just like the rest of us.

"Has Maggie gone?" I asked when I was back upstairs in the super's office.

"Only to refill the perc," he replied.

"Good. Only place I know where you can get a decent cup of coffee. So what do you think?" It's a catchphrase. Say it first and you win yourself some time to consider your own thoughts.

Gilbert shook his head and looked grave. "Poor kid," was all he said.

"She was a thoroughly modern woman," I told him. "Fighting fit, training for the toughest sport there is but still feminine, liked her fashionable clothes. Not all the younger generation are couch potatoes and substance abusers, thank God."

Maggie came back and plugged in the percolator. "If you don't need me I'll get back to Mrs Jones," she said.

"Is anybody with her at the moment?" I asked.

"WPC Renfrew and several assorted neighbours. Claire Renfrew has the press statement if they start harassing her."

"Hang on a bit, then, Maggie," I said. "You can give us the female perspective, and three heads are better than two, as they say." I showed them the ring we'd found that had belonged to Colinette, and told them about the neighbour's indiscreet comment about ex-boyfriend Graham Allen.

"Sound like she hurled it there in a moment of reckless abandon," Maggie stated. "How far into the field was it?"

"About thirty-five yards."

"Phew! She must have been in a mood."

"If you're free this evening we'll go talk to young Mr Allen," I said.

"Right. I can't wait. Have you tracked him down?"

"Mmm. Got his address from the DVLC. He has form for speeding and careless driving, but that's all."

"Any word about the missing umbrella?" Gilbert asked.

"No, and she was only wearing one shoe when she was found, so finding the other is a priority."

"Are we assuming that she was picked up by someone in a car?"

"She must have been." I turned to Maggie. "OK, Maggie," I said. "Put yourself in her place. It's peeing down with rain, you're half a mile from home and wearing unsuitable shoes. Who would you accept a lift with?"

Maggie thought for a few seconds before answering and the percolator gurgled impatiently in the background. "I wouldn't attach too much importance to the rain," Maggie said, eventually. "It was quite bad but it wasn't a cold night and she'd be used to training in it. I don't think she'd accept a lift with anyone unsuitable just because it was raining."

"What if she'd lost a shoe or broken her heel?" I asked.

Maggie shook her head. "Nah. She'd either limp home or back to the shop."

"Might somebody stop in circumstances like that?" Gilbert asked.

"Yes," Maggie agreed. "Some white knight, or a chancer, might stop and proposition her. She was young and attractive. Who knows?"

"But you don't think she'd have got in the car if she didn't know him?"

"No. And we haven't found a broken heel, have we."

"No. So who *would* you get in with?"

Maggie raised a hand and touched the thumb with her other forefinger. "Someone I knew," she said.

"Yep. Go on."

"A policeman."

"Right."

"And…a woman. Perhaps I'd get in with a woman."

"Anyone else?"

"I don't think so."

"A taxi?"

"No, no way, not if I hadn't waved him down."

"Right."

"The coffee's ready." She walked over to the little table in the corner, near the plug, where Gilbert did his brewing.

"What about a man and a woman, Maggie," I called across to her. "Would you get in with a man and a woman?"

She came back with the percolator and poured Gilbert the first cup. "I don't think so," she replied, "but what if the man was hiding behind the seat? Then Colinette would have thought it was just a woman, on her own."

"Hiding behind the seat," I repeated as I offered her my mug for refilling, "with the loose end of the cord wrapped around his fist."

I picked up Maggie at seven o'clock, after she'd fed Tony, her husband. He's a schoolteacher, hanging on until early retire-

ment, and is used to me borrowing his wife at odd hours.
This is a job that tests relationships to breaking point. In the
car Maggie told me bits and pieces of information that she'd
gleaned from Mrs Jones about Colinette. Nothing heavy,
just snippets that helped fill in a few blanks in the picture I
had of a healthy, likeable girl.

Graham Allen lived in the downstairs flat in a converted
house on the edge of old Heckley, where once lived the management classes in the wool industry and all the related
occupations. The wool barons, who lived elsewhere, needed
managers to manage what needed doing, solicitors to tell
them what they were allowed to do, and accountants to
count the money. This was where *they* once lived, side by
side with each other in big stone houses, with room in the
attic for a servant or two and space in the cellar for the odd
bottle of port. Maggie pressed the bell and after a few seconds a woman's silhouette appeared behind the frosted
glass.

"DC Madison and DI Priest from Heckley CID," Maggie
said to her when the door opened. "I believe Graham Allen
lives here. Could we have a word with him, please."

The room was by Ikea, with a little help from Laura
Ashley and Modigliani. Graham and the woman were in the
middle of a take-away pizza, but we didn't offer to come
back later. First impressions of him were that he was a handsome so-and-so with enough charm to lure the linnets out of
the bushes, but they faded rapidly. He was tall, about six
feet, with a mop of fair hair that fell over one eye in a manner designed to melt the heart of every woman he met. The
black polo necked sweater emphasised his height and the
jeans were faded just the right amount. "Is it about
Colinette?" he asked, when I was alone with him.

His lady friend, whom he introduced as his partner, was
called Becky. She was nearly as tall as Graham, with platinum
hair that hung over her shoulders. Apart from that she had a
much more pleasing shape. Much more pleasing. Becky took

their food into the kitchen, to keep warm, and Maggie followed her.

"Yes," I replied. "When did you hear about her?"

"Tonight, driving home from work, on Pennine news. Do you know who did it?"

"Not yet. Where do you work, Mr Allen?"

"I manage a shop for my parents. Designer wear, in the mall."

"And how long did you know Colinette?"

"About, oh, five or six years. We were at the same school."

"I'd say you were a bit older than her. Is that so?"

"Um, yes. I was in the sixth form, she was in a lower one."

"How old are you now?"

"Twenty-six."

"So you'd be eighteen and she'd be...what...fourteen when you met?"

"Yes, I suppose so."

"Were you engaged?"

"No, nothing like that. We just palled about together, a whole crowd of us. Nothing serious."

"That's not what her mother said. She told me you were engaged when Colinette was fifteen."

His charm began to crumble at the edges, and so did his looks. First impressions had faded and now his mouth looked just a little too full, his teeth too big, like the wolf must have done to Little Red Riding Hood.

"Mrs Jones," he said, with a shrug of dismissal. "She was a bit...I don't know, possessive. It was Colinette this, Colinette that. Got on my nerves with it."

I fumbled in my pocket for the plastic bag containing the ring. "Ever seen this before?" I asked, handing it to him. The mop of hair fell across his face as he studied it, and I pictured Colinette or Becky reaching forward to brush it to one side for him.

"No," he answered, passing it back.

"Don't lie to me," I told him. "I'm told that you gave this ring to Colinette, and it was an engagement ring."

He brushed the hair away and stared at me defiantly. "What if I did? It was one like that, but it wasn't an engagement ring. Just a present, for her birthday, I think. Where did you find it?"

"Where did she throw it?"

"Into the rec – the recreation ground."

"That's where we found it. When was this?"

"Um, Christmas before last."

"And how long have you known Becky?"

"About three years, but I don't see what that's got to do with anything."

It hasn't, I thought, but it helps me determine just what sort of creep you are. "So where were you at seven o'clock last night?" I asked him.

"Here, where I am now, sitting in this chair. We watched a video after we'd eaten."

"What was it?"

"*Notting Hill*."

"Any good?"

"Yes, it was, as a matter of fact. Brilliant."

Julia Roberts, I thought. Not my type. Too wide-eyed and wide-mouthed for me. And old mop-head himself, of course. "Can anyone confirm that?"

"Only Becky. She was with me all night."

"Did you hire the video?"

"No, bought it. It's there, still on the player."

"Good," I said. "Good. Thanks for your help, Mr Allen. These are distressing times and I'm sure you'll understand that I have to ask these questions." I rose to my feet and opened the door to the kitchen. Maggie stood up and thanked Becky for her help. Graham led us to the door and I noticed that he'd carefully threaded his belt under the designer label on his jeans, so there was no mistaking their pedigree. Tosser, I thought.

"You first," I said, when we were in the car.

Maggie studied for a few seconds, probably trying to separate fact from impressions and finally abandoning the task. "She's an air-head," she stated. "Met Graham four years ago, when she was on a modelling assignment from some agency in Halifax."

"Halifax!" I echoed. "I bet Jerry Hall is quaking in her shoes."

"Jerry Hall? You're behind the times."

"Go on."

"Well, apparently he works for his parents, who have a chain of shops selling designer jeanswear and tops. Mister Blue, you've probably seen them."

"And heard them. They're the ones in the mall that deafen you as you go by."

"That's them. It was love at first sight, and they've been living together for nearly two years. She has a rock on her finger that would break your toe if it fell on it."

"So it looks as if the two relationships overlapped somewhat," I said.

"You can say that again."

"It must have taken some juggling to keep them separate."

"Not with Becky. She thinks the moon shines out of his rear orifice. If he told her that Bishop Auckland was the new Archbishop of Canterbury she'd believe him."

I fished in my pocket and pulled out the ring. "How did it compare with that?" I asked.

Maggie looked at it and sighed. "I never had an engagement ring," she replied. "I'd have been delighted with this. It's not the size of the stone that counts, but Becky's...it's in a different league."

"Put it in the connected property store, please," I said, then added: "On second thoughts, before you do, pop into a jewellers with it, see if it's genuine. Fancy a drink?"

Maggie fancied a gin and tonic, and once she'd put the

idea in my mind it sounded rather tempting to me too. However, husband Tony had been playing up lately, so she suggested we have a small one at her house.

Tony was engrossed in a programme about Nazi nurses on Channel 4 and declined joining us, so we sat in the kitchen with our drinks and I told her about my talk with the dashing Graham.

"He sounds a shit," Maggie concluded.

"A cad," I told her. "Years ago he'd have been called a cad and tolerated as being amusing and a bit of a lad."

Maggie changed the subject. "I see your name's down for the Three Peaks," she said.

"I know," I replied, downbeat, "but I just might strain a fetlock before then."

"It'll be tough."

"I know."

"Especially for someone your age, Charlie."

I grinned at her. "If that's meant to make me rise to the challenge, I'm impervious."

"Uh," was all she said.

"What does 'Uh' mean?"

"Oh, nothing." She filled the kettle and plugged it in. "Tea or coffee?"

"Tea please. Go on."

Maggie placed three mugs in a row and spooned loose tea into a brown teapot. The mugs had poppies and yellow flowers on them, and the spout of the teapot wasn't chipped. I'd never ever seen one before that wasn't chipped. "Do you know what they're raising money for?" she asked.

"The hospital, isn't it?"

"Mmm. They want to start a retina blastoma unit there. One of the firemen has a daughter who suffers from it."

"What's retina blastoma?" I asked. Soon I'd wish I hadn't.

"It's a cancer, in the eyes. They treat it with chemo and radiotherapy, but if they don't work…" She left it hanging in the air.

"What happens if they don't work?"

"If they don't work it spreads to the brain. So they remove the eyes."

I sipped my tea and had a Nice biscuit. As I left I popped my head round the front room door to say goodnight to Tony. He raised a hand and said: "G'night, Charlie," without taking his eyes off the screen. Rank after rank of nurses in white uniforms with cross-straps across their backs were marching away from the camera, black-stockinged legs all in time. Cut to Hitler pinning a medal on to the heaving bosom of one of them, her face glowing with devotion.

"Watch him," I whispered to Maggie as she showed me off the premises, "or he'll have you dressing up in jack-boots."

"Gymslips," she replied. "He prefers gymslips."

"So...who is the next Archbishop of Canterbury?" I asked.

"Go home, Charlie. I'll see you in the morning."

"No need for you to come in," I told her. "Go straight round to Mrs Jones's, if you want. I'll know where you are."

"Right. Thanks. I'll think about it."

I stepped down off the threshold on to the path and turned back to her again. "This girl," I began. "The fireman's daughter. How old is she?"

"Three," Maggie replied. "She's just three."

Chapter Three

Like I said, I rarely dream. I think a lot, though, and it keeps me awake. I had one murder a month old and a new shiny one. If this went to review they'd take me off the case. Graham Allen had been the rich kid at school, who always had a new cricket bat, went on all the trips and set standards of trendiness the others could only dream about. What was a new set of the latest trainers to a youth whose parents owned a shop that sold them?

Colinette wasn't quite from the other side of the tracks, but she lived within spitting distance of them. And she was the best looking girl in school. So the heap-big sixth-former started dating the impressionable younger girl and they became secretly engaged, which was probably about when he started having sex with her. He'd strung her along for six or seven years and then they'd fallen out. Either she'd found out about Becky and dumped him or he'd dumped her. Did that give him a motive for murdering her? Was she putting pressure on him?

No. According to her mother she was happy and looking forward to going to college. To Colinette, Graham Allen was history. My father was a copper, so I suppose I went into the family business, too, like he did. Mrs Jones was probably over-protective to her daughter, which was understandable after she'd lost her husband, but all Graham could say was that she'd "got on my nerves." And he hadn't once asked how she was taking this latest blow. Was that because he was totally uncaring or did he have something else on his mind?

Scafell Pike would be the difficult one, I thought, when we did the three peaks. It's the lowest of the three, but the route is ill defined, and we'd be up there late in the evening. The other two had decent paths all the way to the top, but not the Pike. We needed to do a couple of practice trips, so we could find the way in bad weather and not waste time looking at a map.

And I wasn't fit enough. All together we'd have to do about 10,000 feet of climbing, walk twenty miles and drive 500 miles in the day. Suddenly it didn't sound such a good idea. Perhaps it might be better if I volunteered to drive, and leave the difficult stuff to the Young Turks.

We'd have to have another look at Graham Allen and have a quiet word with his girlfriend. She'd expose any flaws in his story. I hadn't handled it very well, but we could always go back for another go. I'd let Maggie talk to him, next time.

Maggie hadn't asked about Annette, which was unusual. Perhaps she'd grown tired of me moping about her. Annette was a police lady, one of my DCs, and I'd broken the cardinal rule and started dating her. When push came to shove she left and moved to York, near her long-term boyfriend and his two young daughters. I stretched an arm across the empty half of the bed and wished she'd been there.

People die on Scafell. Those who were going up it would have to be fit and know the way. And it wouldn't be easy for the driver, either. He'd be behind the wheel for nearly a thousand miles, what with the trip down to Wales and then back from Scotland. I'd have to take lots of black coffee and get some fresh air while I waited for the walkers. I'd have time to make a brew, though, and maybe have something hot waiting for them when they came down.

Colinette competed in triathlons. Running, cycling and swimming. You have to be tough and dedicated to do something like that. The picture of her on the wall of the incident room showed a girl who was bubbling over with vitality, until someone snuffed it out. She was the type that might attract a stalker who'd fancied her for years. Had Graham been out there, or Mr Naseen, watching, following, drooling?

Someone was stooping over me and I couldn't move. His shadow grew larger, blotting out the ceiling. He smelled of curry and something gleamed in his fingers. They were inside latex gloves, like we wear, but he wasn't a cop. I could hear the roar of my pulse, like waves on a beach, rolling the pebbles back after each surge forward. I tried to lift a protective arm, but they were tied down. "This won't hurt," a voice said. "You won't feel a thing." "No," someone replied. "No, I don't want it. I don't want my eyes taking out."

I sat up and shivered. The window was a light patch against the shadows and my digital clock said five-seventeen. OK, maybe I do dream, now and again. I swung my legs out and sat on the edge of the bed. I imagined a man, in his forties perhaps, getting up on such a morning. He drove to work in his BMW and changed into a surgeon's gown, with mask and boots and everything else. When he was scrubbed up, or whatever the expression is, they wheeled the patient in. She was three years old and he was going to remove her eyes, all in his day's work. The image of Hitler's nurses flashed up before me and I shuddered. I couldn't have done it. Not even to save her life. I'd have said a little prayer, asking forgiveness, and placed my hands over her face.

I splashed cold water against my face in the bathroom and found an old pair of jogging bottoms and a sweatshirt. It's about a mile around the estate where I live, perhaps a little less. I did some stretching exercises in the hallway before plunging out into the grey morning. It felt good. Slightly foolish, but good.

I took it slowly, knowing how easy it is to damage your Achilles or strain a thigh when you haven't run for a while. If you look down you see your feet reaching forward, left-right-left-right, eating up the distance with the ground a blur beneath them, and you feel great, almost invincible. This would have to become a regular part of my regime, I decided, if I was hoping to climb those three damn mountains.

Mostly, we hold meetings. There is already a computer program with all the formal meetings on it, so that the ACC isn't at a divisional budget meeting when he should be handing out certificates at the training college or chairing a discussion with the Police Complaints Authority. Somebody must have worked it all out before it went on the computer. Interested parties, or their secretaries, must have sat down with the appropriate diaries and decided who should be where and at what time. They must have held a meeting about holding meetings.

The best ones aren't planned, they just happen. I was sitting in the big office, at Jeff Caton's desk, on Friday afternoon as the troops began to filter back, hoping to sew up the day's work and leave on time. We were talking about the foot-and-mouth epidemic, which had topped five hundred cases. A farmer near Howarth had died of heart failure after it was confirmed among his cattle. As each officer took off his jacket I gave an enquiring look but was only rewarded by shakes of the head. Nobody had struck gold. Jeff brought me a mug of tea and found himself another chair.

The early morning jog had given me a self-righteous feeling and an appetite, but I'd only grabbed a sausage roll and an Eccles cake for lunch. Dave came in and joined us, followed by Maggie.

"How is she?" I asked.

"Not too good," Maggie replied. "Worrying about the funeral. The money that was to put Colinette through college will now be used to bury her. Any ideas when the body will be released?"

"I'll have a word with the coroner. Any biscuits, Jeff?"

"Bottom drawer."

I reached down and pulled the drawer open. There was a book in there and a half-eaten packet of fig biscuits. "Custard creams," I said. "I don't like these, I prefer custard creams."

"That's why I bring figs," he replied.

"*The Beast Must Die*," I read from the cover of the book. "What's this? Looking for inspiration?"

"Catching up on the classics, Charlie. Have you read it?"

"Mmm, long time ago. By Nicholas Blake, aka CS Lewis."

"C Day Lewis."

"Near enough. I'll borrow it when you've finished."

He reached out and took it from me, saying: "Here, let me read you a piece." It was the first page and he soon found it. "Here we go: *Every criminal needs a confidante...Sooner or later he will blurt it all out...Or, if his will stands firm, his superego betrays him...forcing the criminal into slips of the tongue*, and so on."

"Those were the days," Dave said, "when you could nail someone on a slip of the tongue. Nowadays a signed confession isn't worth the paper it's written on."

"Ah!" I said. "But we have video evidence now. Show a young thug a blurred video of someone in a hooded top holding up a corner shop and he'll say: 'Yeah, it's me, bang to rights.' He's on TV, man, this is his moment of fame." I finished my tea and placed the mug on Jeff's blotter. "Right, what have we?" I asked, "and don't all speak at once."

We'd interviewed everyone who used the shop this week, everyone within quarter of a mile of it and everyone who used the road poor Colinette walked down and the lane where she was found. We'd had roadblocks out, knocked on doors and had a caravan near the shop. People came forward in their hundreds, mostly to say what a wonderful girl Colinette was, but nobody added to our sum of knowledge about her death. We'd even taken the names off the pile of wreaths and sprays of flowers that had accumulated outside the recreation ground, at the spot where we suspected she was accosted, and we'd relocated a CCTV camera to watch everybody who visited the place.

Late Thursday night, I was told, a brick was hurled through Mr Naseen's shop window and we were having to give him round-the-clock protection.

"We can't afford to let this become racial," I told them. "Anything like that needs squashing from the outset. Do we know who threw it?"

"The brick's gone to fingerprints."

"Fat lot of good that'll do." I looked at the DC who'd raised the subject. "Stay with it, please," I said. "Find out where the brick came from, who laid it, anything you can. Let it be known that we're not taking it lightly."

Peter Goodfellow, one of my more polite DSs, raised a finger as if to ask permission to speak. "Yes, Pete," I said.

"Um, I was just wondering, Charlie, have we considered that this murder might be linked to Mrs Heeley's?"

"Let's consider it now," I invited. "In what way are they similar?"

"Well, for a start, they are both murders," he began.

"There was the Robshaw case down in Doncaster about five years ago, when he murdered his ex-wife with rat poison and then killed her lover with a meat cleaver. It wasn't until a neighbour remembered that he used to chop logs with..."

"One of ours was a stabbing, one was strangled," someone interrupted. Pete might be polite and reticent, but once you launch him he's difficult to stop.

"Fair enough," Pete replied, "but they both ended up dead, for no apparent reason. Who's to say that our man didn't do the deeds in the way that was most expedient at the time, like Robshaw did. One night he just happened to have..."

"Let's not dwell on what might have happened, Pete," I suggested. "There could easily be a link. For a start both crimes are apparently without motive."

"As was young Robin Gillespie," Dave interrupted, "over in Lancashire, a fortnight before Mrs Heeley."

"OK," I said. "Let me tell you what we've done about it." I explained Dave's misgivings about Robin's murder and told them about my contact with NCIS. They were supposed to be looking into other apparently random murders for us. Initially, I said, we'd have to investigate Colinette's death as if it were a one-off, which it was. All murders which involve only one victim are one-offs. It's just that several of them may be committed by the same person. It didn't matter which you caught them for. As we were drawing a blank in our enquiries, now might be the time to consider possible links with other crimes, but whether that would open new avenues of enquiry was doubtful.

"It'll give us an insight into his mind," someone offered.

"True," I conceded, "but I'd prefer an insight into his address book."

"We need a reconstruction," one of the others suggested.

"You're right," I told him and turned to the sergeant who has the expertise to arrange one. "Any chance for next Wednesday?" I asked.

"No problem," he replied. "I'll start auditioning in the morning."

Tomorrow was Saturday, so I told them to be in the office at nine and sent them all home. In my own office I found an artist's A3 pad and a fibre-tipped pen and started drawing. From the window you can see the rooftops of Heckley, with the fells rising like a wall beyond them. I sketched it with hardly a look, from memory, with my chair twisted round and the pad on my knee. Somewhere up there, I thought, blowing about in the wind, are viruses that latch on to animals so that men with guns have to come and shoot them all. And was there someone out there with a virus of his own, that caused him to go out with murder in his heart? Or was he suffering from a mutant speck of DNA, one renegade base pair among three billions, that tipped him over the edge? I ripped the sketch off the pad and scrunched it up into a ball. It bounced off the wall and fell into my bin like they always do. Practise makes perfect. I pulled the chair up to the desk and started to write.

> *1.* I wrote, then drew a circle around it. *All deaths apparently motiveless.*
> *2. All outdoors.*
> *3. All in early evening.*

I looked out of the window. Lights were going out in offices all over town, but were coming on in homes at the foot of the fells. The outer office door opened and the two cleaning ladies came in.

> 4. *All three murders clinical and determined.*
> 5. *Car almost certainly used in M1 and M3.*
> 6. *Perpetrator "organised" in all three.*
> 7. *All victims creatures of habit. Movements predictable.*
> 8. *Murders committed Tuesday, Tuesday, Wednesday. i.e. working days early in the week.*
> 9. *Weapons: hammer, knife, ligature. Is this a progression?*
> 10. *Bodies M1 and M3 transported elsewhere but no attempt to hide them. Moving them apparently pointless.*

The cleaning lady popped her head round the door and asked if she could do my office. I said: "Sure," and moved out. I stood looking out of the window as she hoovered the floor and dusted the radiator. The road outside was jammed with traffic whilst an articulated delivery lorry attempted an impossible manoeuvre into Marks and Spencer's loading bay. One of my sergeants came in with a sandwich and said he wanted to do a report and some studying while things were quiet. Mr Wood looked in to say goodnight on his way downstairs, told us not to stay too long. *11,* I wrote, but I couldn't think of an eleventh.

I logged on, typed it out and ran-off ten copies. I wrote a brief note, put it in an envelope with one of the copies and addressed it to Dr Adrian Foulkes, Department of Psychology, Heckley General Hospital. The note ended with the words: *Are the murders linked and if so, will he kill again?* Even as I sealed the envelope I knew that the answer to both questions was "Yes".

On the way home I called in the supermarket to buy a curry from their oriental counter. They have them loose and you choose any combination you like, with different rices and naan bread. I'd decided to have chicken jalfrezi, but the container was nearly empty and definitely lacking in chicken. "Do you have any more jalfrezi?" I asked the big fair-haired girl whose nametag told me was called Julie.

"No problem," she said with a smile that was over and above that required by her employer. "I'll fetch some; won't be a sec."

She vanished backstage and returned almost immediately carrying a huge plastic box of the stuff. It had sticky address labels on the side with the name of the store and bar codes and the logo of one of those express delivery companies that you see hurtling up and down the motorway.

It was a revelation. I'd always thought that there was a little Indian or Bangladeshi chef in the back, a headband stopping the sweat running into his eyes, as he toiled away chopping meat and vegetables and carefully weighing out all the spices for the different flavours.

I hadn't appreciated the scale of the enterprise, but it suddenly hit me. This supermarket had about a thousand branches. Somewhere there must be a giant curry factory sending its wares to every city and town in the country. In Europe, possibly. Lorry loads of the stuff would be departing every minute of every day and night in the impossible task of alleviating our craving for spicy food. Huge tankers, labelled in some esoteric code only understood by supermarket managers and firemen, were at this very moment rumbling outwards to the distant corners of the land. That's what those orange stickers were on the backs of lorries. The Hazardous Chemicals code. When it said *Hazchem code 1234*, it probably meant that it was carrying vindaloo, so watch out.

And the opposite would be true. A similar number of articulated lorries, and probably trains, too, would be converging on the factory from all directions, bringing chickens and lambs on their final journey, together with onions, tomatoes, peppers and more exotic vegetables. Smaller, faster lorries, the equivalent of the old tea clippers, would race to bring spices and herbs from the far-flung outposts of the globe. They would carry cardamom from Cordoba, paprika from Papua, turmeric from Turkistan and basil from…Basildon.

Julie handed me the goods with another smile and I rewarded her with my best lopsided one. I collected a six-pack of Sam Smith's from the beer shelves and went home. That was Friday night catered for.

"Can I have a word, Charlie?" Pete Goodfellow asked as I poured hot water on to my Nescafé. "I've been thinking about the crimes again, if they are linked."

Pete never comes forward if he thinks somebody else has covered the ground, but he's knowledgeable and thorough, and has a near-photographic memory for trivia. We walked downstairs to the incident room, carrying our coffees, and he told me all about it. And I mean *all* about it.

Superintendent Gilbert Wood, my boss, was at the meeting, and so was Detective Superintendent Les Isles from HQ. He was the official senior investigating officer, keeping an overview in case I made a boo-boo. We talked about what we had done in the hunt for Colinette's killer and Les asked questions and made a few suggestions. We'd already covered most of them, but we agreed to have another look at one or two people. The only decision we made was to hold a press conference on Monday and a reconstruction on Wednesday. It's what we do when we're running out of ideas.

I then suggested that we look at the other two murders and consider if there were any similarities. I put my efforts of the night before on the overhead projector and invited comments.

"What sort of moon was there?" someone asked.

"Almost full for M1," I told them, "but no moon at all for M2 and M3. Sorry, but it was worth a try. Anybody else?"

Somebody asked about the first and third bodies being

moved. I explained that Robin had been killed in a fairly secluded part of his route, and the place where his body was dumped was, if anything, more public. It would have been more expedient to flee the scene, rather than bundle his corpse into a car. This was possibly true for Colinette, too.

"Do you think the killer wasn't alone?" somebody asked.

"It's a possibility," I replied. Peter Goodfellow was sitting to one side, leaning on the wall. I turned to him, saying: "Come on, Pete. You've a few thoughts on this, so let's hear them."

"Yeah," he said, uncurling from his chair and standing up. "I was thinking about it. Last night. The three victims were all people of habit. One was working, one had been to bingo, like she always did on a Tuesday, and M3 – Colinette – was on her way home from work. They were killed on Tuesday, Tuesday and Wednesday. If they were all killed by the same person there's a good chance that he had watched them, chosen them because he knew where they'd be at a certain time. But the two who worked were not attacked on Monday. I just thought, maybe…maybe he watched them on Monday, just to make sure they were working that week. We've spent a lot of time asking about cars and movements on the nights they were killed. Maybe we should ask about Mondays, too. There was a case in Belgium, back in 1975, when a series of women were murdered who all worked in launderettes, the Liege launderette murders. The perpetrator was caught because he had a part-time job at the weekend, and when he moved to Antwerp…"

"Cheers, Pete," I said, silencing him with a raised hand. "That's a good point. Anything else?" From the corner of my eye I saw Maggie fidgeting in her seat. "Yes Maggie," I said.

"What Pete just told us," she began. "As you know, I've spent a lot of time with Colinette's mum. Colinette didn't go straight home on Tuesday. She goes to the pool – Heckley baths – on a Tuesday. Well, she used to. Perhaps because of that she gained herself an extra day's life."

"OK," I said. "We start again with Colinette. Now we want to know where everybody was on Monday and Tuesday, as well as Wednesday, and more importantly, who they saw." It was something to do, but I couldn't help feeling that the trail was growing cold.

When the troops had dispersed Les and I went up to Gilbert's office and had another coffee, this time with a tot of the Famous Grouse in it. I prefer it without, but it's what cops do. Les produced a pipe and pouch of tobacco and asked if he could smoke. "No way," Gilbert told him, but Les opened a window and had a few puffs with his head hanging outside.

"When did you start that filthy habit again?" I asked, reaching for the pouch and sniffing the contents. "It smells quite nice until you light it."

"Only thing that keeps me sane," he replied.

"How long had you stopped for?"

"Ten years, eight months."

"So why did you start again?"

"This bloody stupid racial harassment case we've got. It'll be the death of me."

"Aagh!" Gilbert exclaimed.

"What does that mean?" I asked.

"It means that we've got one, too. Does the name Wilson McIntyre mean anything to you?"

"Light-fingered Willy," I said. "More convictions than you'll find in St Peter's Square on Easter Sunday."

"Well he's claiming racial harassment now. Says he's been stopped twelve times in the last four weeks."

"Because he's Scotch?" Les asked.

"He's not Scotch, he's black. The ACC rang me yesterday about it, but I'm trying to hold him off."

"Jeee-sus," I hissed. "What does Gareth have to say?" Gareth Adey is my uniformed opposite number, and it would have been his men who had stopped Willy.

"Haven't spoken to him yet. Since he was made OIC foot-and-mouth he's out all day nailing notices to trees and lampposts all over the division."

"And when you do," Les said, "you'll find that your friend Willy was stopped at three o'clock in the morning, wearing dark clothes and trainers, heading away from a reported break-in."

"I'll have a word with the men," I said. "Find out what it's all about. Now, this press conference. As you two far out-rank me, I suggest that you handle it between you. How does that sound?"

I had a banana sandwich for lunch and changed into jogging bottoms, lightweight boots and fleece jacket. In less than an hour I'd walked out of town and was nearly at the top of the fell, with sweat chilling my back every time a gust of wind came down from the North. I had to walk on the road, because every gateway was taped off, with a warning sign about the disease. We were living in a no-go area. I jogged the last quarter of a mile and nearly collapsed in the picnic lay-by at the top.

When I'd recovered I stood on the wall and surveyed my kingdom, spread out below me like a map. Along the valley buildings crowded next to each other in a hotchpotch of styles, like a collection made by someone who didn't know what to specialise in so he just kept everything. Churches – more churches than you'd believe – shoulder to shoulder with multi-storey car parks, department stores and office blocks. Gothic ornamentation jostled for position beside Sixties austere, Victorian art nouveau and pre-war utility. Steam rose from somewhere on the left of town and a Metro train left a smudge of black over the station as it pulled away. The train line cuts the town in half, while the canal borders it on the north side.

It was a dull day, and all the colours were muted.

Although we'd not had an outbreak of foot-and-mouth within twenty miles the fields and fells were uncannily quiet, devoid of livestock, as if they'd already surrendered to the inevitable. When the drizzle started it felt as if the sky was weeping. How soon, I thought, will the men with guns come and light the funeral pyres? It's a crazy world. A crazy world. I pulled my waterproof jacket out of my pack and headed downhill.

Willy McIntyre had gone to the press and the editor of the local evening paper tipped off the assistant chief constable that they were carrying an article about the case in Monday's edition. Forewarned is forearmed. The ACC sent for Gilbert to try to keep one step ahead of the game, which left me to handle the press conference on Monday morning. Les agreed to attend, to give the occasion a bit more clout, for which I was grateful.

While we were setting up the microphones and deciding who would sit where, Les pulled his pipe out and placed it on the desk. Our press officer latched on to it and insisted he take a few token puffs on camera. It would, he claimed, "create an aura of competence and authority." I pointed out that the room was fitted with a sprinkler system, and if he lit the thing it would create an aura of panic and ridicule, so we agreed that he would just hold it and point with it. Otherwise we might find ourselves on television a few more times than we'd bargained for.

Everybody came. They always do for the murder of a young woman. YTV and the BBC were recording us for a showing in the evening, the *Gazette* reporters came mob handed and a few tabloids sent their northern representatives, hoping to hear something to titillate their readers. You could recognise them by their fur hats and boots. They'd be disappointed, because we were presenting Colinette as a wholesome, home-loving girl and stressing that there was no sexual interference. All references to her underwear were lost in the pathologist's report.

Les outlined the facts of the case, saying what we'd done and talking about Colinette's movements on the night of her death and the two nights before. He said that we now needed to know from anybody who had been anywhere near the shop where she worked and her route home on Monday, Tuesday and Wednesday, and he explained the reasons why. He spoke in a low voice, his hands clasped together with the pipe stem pointing into space, like your headmaster explaining that your behaviour hadn't been quite what was expected of you.

Mrs Jones was too distressed to appear but she had provided an album of photographs and a few seconds of video taken at a barbecue in the garden of the ex-boyfriend's parents. It had been shot by his next-door neighbour and showed Colinette in happier times, wearing shorts and a skimpy top. Les told them that we'd had copies made and they would be distributed at the end of the conference. Meanwhile, if there were any questions, he and good ol' Inspector Priest would attempt to answer them.

A young woman with punk hair that I'd met before but forgotten the name of thrust her arm up with all the intent of a rearing cobra. Les invited her to speak with an expansive wave of the pipe.

"Superintendent Isles," she began. "Is it true that you are linking this murder with those of Laura Heeley a month ago and Robin Gillespie, over in Lancashire, a fortnight before that."

There'd been a leak. Someone had taken the pieces of silver and gone to the press. Les fidgetted with the pipe, hunched his shoulders and looked at me.

"No," I said. I don't know why, but a serial killer on the loose provokes hysteria in the media and that puts pressure on us. They give him a name and hurl it in our faces at every opportunity. It's as if committing one murder is almost acceptable – we all have one book and a murder in us – but more than that is aberrant. There was a rustle of unease in the room and more hands were thrust upwards. "If I can explain," I went on. "So far, we have found nothing to link any of these murders. We are in full consultation with West Pennine, who are in charge of poor Robin's murder, and Mrs Heeley's was on our territory, but there are very few similarities."

"What's your gut feeling, Charlie?" the editor of the *Gazette* shouted from the back of the room.

I sat up and stretched my neck so I could see him. "We don't have gut feelings," I replied. "We collect evidence and go along with that."

"So what does the evidence say?"

"Very little, I'm afraid, but that in itself is grounds for suspicion. It's the only factor that might link the cases."

"You mean that the very lack of evidence in each case suggests that they were committed by the same person?"

"No, but it's something we have considered."

"It sounds as if you're looking for someone who is extremely clever."

I shook my head. "Cunning and devious," I said. "There's nothing clever about hitting a young boy on the head with a hammer."

"So you do think the cases are linked."

"I didn't say that."

"You said you were considering it."

"It's a possibility," I admitted. I'd blown it, I'd really blown it.

"Have you called in a profiler?" someone asked.

"No."

"Why not?"

"It isn't the time."

"Can I ask a question please?" one of the hacks from the *Gazette* shouted. He was called Arnie Vernon and it was the first time I'd seen him outside a pub after ten o'clock in the morning. Les nodded at him and he said: "What about the ring? You haven't told us about the ring."

"What ring?" I asked.

"The one you found in the rec."

"Oh, that one." I turned to the rest of them and explained. "We did a fingertip search of the recreation ground adjacent to where we think Colinette was abducted. In the course of that search we found a lady's ring. In one of those incredible coincidences that sometimes occur in these situations it just happened to be one that Colinette had lost about eighteen months previously. So far we haven't attached any significance to it."

Our press officer, standing right at the back, made a cut-throat gesture to me. I said: "Can I thank you for attending, ladies and gentlemen. It's imperative that we keep this case in the public's eye in order to find Colinette's killer. We are grateful for your co-operation."

I took Les up to Gilbert's office and we attacked his coffee and biscuits with vigour. "Want anything in it?" I asked, but he shook his head.

"Go on then," I invited. "Tell me I cocked it up."

"You cocked it up."

"Thanks."

He pushed his tobacco pouch towards me, saying: "Want a fill?"

"No."

"Do you good." He sat back in Gilbert's big chair and sucked on the empty pipe.

"Make it something more exotic and I might be tempted."

"Somebody's squeaked," he stated. "They know that we're linking the cases, or that bird from *UK News* does. She's oiled someone's palm, or some other part of his anatomy. I bet they've already got a name for him."

"Yeah, I think you're right. And how did they know about the ring? That's never been mentioned."

"It had to come out sometime, Charlie, and the longer we'd concealed it the more they'd have been at our throats when it did come out. 'The public's right to know,' and all that."

"I was probably thinking that way myself, and when lives are at stake they've got a point."

"What about a profiler? It might be an idea."

"No," I replied. "I don't need anybody to draw circles on a map and tell me he lives within two miles of the town hall clock. And I don't need to know that his mother didn't love him. It's fingerprints and semen stains I want, not airy-fairy conjecture that might lead us up the wrong gum tree. I can do that for myself."

"They sometimes get good results."

"Yeah, in hindsight. When I've a specific question, Les, I'll ask. As a matter of fact, I've dropped a note to Adrian Foulkes at the General, asked him to contact me."

He grinned. "I should have known better than to push it. You're a good cop, Charlie. You might have fucked-up the press conference, but the enquiry is in safe hands."

"Thanks, Les. And patronising is the lowest form of bullshit. Do you really think a pipe would suit me?"

The considered opinion of the press was that if we spent less time harassing black people we might catch the murderers who were loose in society. Wilson McIntyre made the headlines, Colinette was pushed on to page five. It was probably a tough editorial decision, but in the absence of anything salacious, and considering the potential selling power of his story among the non-white population, light-fingered Willy just edged it.

Television was more objective, showing stills and the video of Colinette, and asking for anybody who was in the vicinity at the time of her death to come forward. They forgot to mention Monday and Tuesday, unfortunately, but my hair was tidy, Les looked avuncular and the pipe was a masterstroke.

Tuesday morning I spent some time with the people who were manning the telephones. We had a steady stream of callers, all concerned and trying to be helpful, all of doubtful value. We took the details, asked them their names and addresses and made it sound as if they'd solved the whole caboodle for us. Fortunately Pennine Radio had latched on to our request about Monday and Tuesday so several calls were new information about these evenings. I contacted the radio station and asked them to repeat the plea as often as possible. Community radio at its best.

One call was specifically for me. It was from Dr Foulkes at the General, saying that he'd be grabbing a sandwich in their canteen at lunchtime and I'd be welcome to join him. I dashed upstairs to knock some sort of a file together and made a list of questions.

Les Isles rang me just as I was about to leave. "I think I left my pipe and tobacco on your windowsill," he said.

I glanced across and saw them there, between the dead cactus and the framed department photograph. "I've thrown them away," I told him. "Thought you'd finished with them."

"No you haven't. Stick 'em in the internal, will you, please. I'll just have to chew my nails until they arrive."

"Will do. I'm on my way to see Adrian Foulkes."

"That should be interesting. Let me know what he says."

"OK. Ta-ra."

I collected the pipe from the window and looked in my bottom drawer for an envelope, but they were all too small. Never mind; they'd have something suitable at the front desk. I was halfway through the door when my phone started ringing again. I hesitated, decided that I couldn't afford to miss a call, and started back towards it, but it stopped just before I got there. Next time I made it out of the door.

Two people, male and female, were talking to the desk sergeant, who was laboriously taking notes. They were in cycling gear, with matching green helmets, black lycra leggings and Day-Glo pink waterproof tops. According to the legend across their backs they were part of the Mongoose team and were propelled along courtesy of Shimano. I nodded a hello and joined them at the desk. As my shadow fell across it the sergeant looked up and grinned with relief. "Ah! The man 'imself," he exclaimed. "Just tried ringing you. Inspector Priest, this is Mr and Mrs..." – quick glance down at his notes – "...Fletcher. Asked to see you about the appeal. I was explaining that you're a busy man, but as you're 'ere..."

I glanced at my watch. "I'm afraid I'm dashing off to an appointment," I told them. "What was it you want to see me about?"

"The appeal," the man replied. "On Pennine Radio. We were in the recreation ground near the shop on Monday night, about seven o'clock."

"Walking the dog," the girl explained, to dispel any thoughts I might be having that they were frolicking naked in the wet grass. "We can't take it in the fields, now, because of the foot-and-mouth."

"I see."

We were having a steady flow of citizens calling in with information about sightings, some useful, most not, some downright bizarre, but usually it went through a very fine filter before it reached me. Today I'd been unfortunate.

"This vehicle – a pickup – went by," he continued.

"She's called Trudy," the girl added.

"Right. Um, this pickup..."

"One of those big ones," he went on. "A Dodge or maybe a Toyota, with big wheels and a row of spotlights on the roof. I've always fancied one, think we ought to get one, so I noticed it, like."

"We don't want one of those big things," she told him.

"Why not? We could put the bikes in the back and go off for the day. Or the week. We could go all over. France even."

"It was too noisy," she stated.

I felt a cold draught and heard the rumble of traffic as the outer door opened and Peter Goodfellow walked in to join us.

"What else did you notice about it?" I asked, before they could have a full-scale major policy debate. "I don't suppose you got the number, but did you see what colour it was?"

"White," they replied in unison.

I looked at the desk sergeant and winked. "I think we can safely take that as white," I told him.

"And it was noisy," the man added. "We only saw it from the side, above the wall, but you could tell it was one of those big ones."

"This could be very important for our enquiry," I said, wanting to wind things up without antagonising them. "As you see, I'm on my way out, but Sergeant Goodfellow here is on the case and he'll take a statement from you, if you don't mind." Pete shrugged and looked mystified. "Mr and Mrs Fletcher have come in about the appeal," I told him. "They saw a white pickup. Could you take a statement from them, please, and tag it for the computer?" He nodded an OK and led them off to an interview room.

The sergeant and I watched them retreat. They were both a little below average height and slightly overweight and she really ought not to be in those leggings. "Make a nice pair of bookends," I said as they vanished into the interview room.

"Matching Lycra," the sergeant observed. "I wonder if I could get my missus interested in that?"

"Nah," I said. "She prefers rubber."

"Does she?"

"Mmm." I placed the pipe and tobacco pouch on the counter. "Have you an envelope for those, please, George?" I asked. "They want sending to Les Isles."

"Filthy 'abit," he said, gathering them up.

"I agree. Put a rude note in with them, if you want."

"Would you trust a man who wears a dickie-bow?" I said, sitting in the empty chair next to Dr Foulkes in the General Hospital's staff canteen. The room was buzzing, filled with white-coated doctors and nurses, a smattering of suits and a single sports coat and bow tie. I couldn't sit opposite him because that place was taken by a woman in a white coat, with dark-rimmed spectacles and a folded stethoscope poking out of her breast pocket. He twisted in his chair and shook my hand before introducing me to the woman.

"I'll be off then," she said. "Nice to meet you, Charlie. Don't let him baffle you with gobbledegook. See you tonight, Adrian."

I half rose and nodded a farewell to her, then moved round to the chair she'd vacated. It was warm, and I caught a whiff of her perfume.

"Mmm," I said, approvingly.

Dr Foulkes, Head of Psychology, fixed his gaze over my shoulder and watched her walk away. "That's the woman I intend to marry," he stated when I finally gained his attention.

"Congratulations!" I exclaimed with a big smile. "She's a very attractive lady. When's the happy event?"

"I don't know. I haven't told her, yet."

"Oh. But you're seeing her tonight."

"Giving her a lift home. And her husband. Their car is in for a repair and it's the highlight of my week. Can I get you something to eat?"

"You know, Adrian," I began, "I suspect that you have more hang-ups than any of your patients. It wasn't you who damaged the car, was it?"

"Got me in one, Charlie. Bang to rights. I believe that's the expression you use. We do a quite respectable tuna sandwich in a wholemeal baguette and the coffee's not bad. Can I tempt you?"

I shook my head. "No thanks. Let's talk, then I might grab something after you've had to dash off, as you no doubt will." I moved his prospective wife's coffee cup to one side and spread my papers on the table.

For ten minutes I outlined the three cases and he listened,

with just the occasional question. He was particularly interested in the positions of the bodies and the injuries. I
showed him the photographs.

"Have you drawn any conclusions from where the bodies
were found?" he asked.

"None," I told him. "M1 and M3 were dumped almost
arbitrarily."

"And M2 was left where she fell?"

"Mmm."

"The killer could have been disturbed."

"That's right, but nobody's come forward."

He speed-read the rest of the file, the nib of his fountain
pen tracing an invisible line down the pages. When he'd finished I said: "So, am I looking for three killers or just one?"

Adrian had taken a few notes and had my list of similarities in front of him. "I suspect you know the answer to
that," he replied.

"I'm a humble bobby," I told him. "What does the expert
say?"

"Look at all the murders you've ever heard about,
Charlie," he began. "List the variables and compare them
with your man. He's organised in all three cases and appears
to be forensically aware. They're all outdoors. The level of
violence is similar. No rapes. The locations are similar, neither rural or city."

"The MOs are different," I interjected.

"Yes, on one level, but the overall result is the same. The
victim is dead, with minimum of fuss. He's improving his
technique. All the victims were respectable and they were all
following a predictable routine. In fact, that's probably why
they were chosen. You said that a shoe and an umbrella are
missing from M3."

"Yes."

"But nothing from the others?"

"Not that we know of."

"I wonder if he's starting a collection of memorabilia.

The interference with M3's underwear is interesting."

"Tell me about him, Adrian. What are we up against?"

"It's as if he's suddenly discovered sex. You're looking for someone who is sexually inadequate, probably repressed for some reason, but who has suddenly found that violence gives him release. He's probably suffered from paraphilia all his life, but it's recently developed into an incipient psychosis followed by the real McCoy."

"What does that mean?"

"Mmm, sorry. Why he's killing in the first place, I don't know. Let's just say he's a nutter. He's always had a problem with sex – unable to get an erection when he needed one, unable to get rid of it at other times, and he's lived in a fantasy world. So he kills a couple of people and hey presto! he has an orgasm. Or, more probably, gets an erection and nearly has one. Violence, he's discovered, is the key to sexual release, so his fantasies – the paraphilia – are developing into reality."

I sat quietly, thinking about what he'd said. The doctor looked in his coffee cup, found it empty and replaced it on the saucer. "I'll have to go, Charlie," he said, "but we need to talk again. I'll give you my home number and you can ring me there, any time."

"Thanks, Adrian." I wrote his number at the foot of one of the pages and rotated my ballpen in my fingers, tapping each end in turn against the table: pointed end, other end, pointed end, other end. All around us people were rising to their feet, scraping chairs against the tiled floor, going back into the fray. "But we're only looking for one person?" I said.

"Well, unless he has an accomplice."

"Is that likely?"

"I don't know. What degree of effort was required to move the bodies?"

"A fair bit, but not enough to make a decision on."

"It's a possibility that he has a woman friend who shares

his inadequacies. It's surprising how these people seek each other out, and then one influences the other into their particular brand of perversion."

"But not two men?"

"I don't think so. If the victims had been raped, I'd have said yes, but not in these cases."

"So," I began, "if our friend has discovered that violence could give him the orgasm to end all orgasms, what will his next move be?"

The doctor grimaced before answering. "That's the frightening part, Charlie," he said. "I dread to think what he'll do next. I just dread to think."

Chapter Four

There was a note on my desk. It said: *You've been seen out jogging. Only a Yorkshireman would indulge in such ungentlemanly practices*, and was signed by Nigel.

"What did he want?" I asked David, handing him the note when he joined me in my little office.

"Dunno, wasn't in. Is it true?"

"What?"

"That you were out jogging."

"I might have been."

"Crikey, you are taking it seriously, aren't you."

"Yeah, well. I thought about that little girl, the fireman's daughter, and..." I pulled a face and shuddered. "...Whooa! It gave me a nightmare. I think we should make it special, go out for some corporate sponsorship, not just a few quid from family and friends."

"What about the foot-and-mouth. Everywhere's closed off."

"It'll all be open by June, won't it?"

"Might not be."

"OK," I said, "let's follow the fire brigade's example. They're doing it up ladders, aren't they?"

"So I believe."

"In that case, we'll do it here, up and down the back staircase. If we start at sea level, that's...oh, about eleven thousand feet of climbing – about two miles."

"Straight up."

"Yep. No problem."

"It'll be a killer."

I leaned forward on my elbows, saying: "*We choose to do these things not because they are easy, but because they are hard.* President Kennedy said that."

"They were going to the Moon."

"That's right."

"But they weren't *walking* it."

"It'll be fun. So how've you gone on?"

"Useless."

The troops had all been out doing follow-up interviews with the sightings resulting from the appeal. It's not a very efficient process. For every hundred contacts we only catch about twenty of them at the first call, and then about half of the remainder when we go back in the evening. We whittle it down until there is a residue of three or four that we never find. That's out of a hundred. Sometimes the figure we start with is in the thousands.

"Any mention of a white pickup?" I asked.

Dave shook his head. "No, why?"

"A young couple came in this morning, said they saw one on Monday night at about the right time. One of those great obstrockless things with the tyres and spotlights."

"Haven't heard anything about it. Want me to run it through the computer?"

"No, Pete was handling it. It's probably harmless."

"Did NCIS ever come back to you?"

"No," I replied, remembering that it was Dave who first suggested the link between the Gillespie and Heeley murders and reaching in my drawer for my diary, "let's give them a wake-up call."

Carl Warburton was at his desk, which was a surprise. Catching trout in the Calder is usually easier than finding the man you want in this organisation. I reminded him that our two murders were now three and pointedly asked him what he'd found out for us about possibly related cases.

"Hasn't anybody been back to you, Charlie?" he asked.

"Not a word," I told him.

"Oh. I started trawling through the database but when I mentioned to the boss what I was doing he told me to leave it with him. I got the impression he knew something and was going to ring you straight back."

"Well he hasn't."

"Let me have another word with him, then, and I'll

definitely get back to you. We have a few cases on the books, obviously, but let me see what he says."

"OK, as quick as possible, please."

"Will do."

Dave asked: "What's he say?" as I replaced the phone.

"He's done sod all about it," I told him.

"Typical. Fancy going for a jog after work?"

"Where?"

"Couple of times round the park."

"Good idea. Why don't you see if anybody else is interested."

To give my mind something different to think about I found a ruler and went to the foot of the back stairs. Each step was twenty centimetres high and there were thirty-two of them between the ground floor and the top, which gave a total rise of six and a half metres. The heights of the three mountains added up to 3,406 metres, so according to the calculator we'd have to run up and down the staircase 524 times to cover the equivalent height.

Sheest!

I was back in the office recovering from my efforts when Chief Superintendent Natrass of NCIS rang back. His message was short and simple: get my ass down to New Scotland Yard first thing in the morning, even if I had to hijack a plane. He wouldn't enlarge on the phone and I went home totally bemused, not knowing if he wanted to see me about the murders or something entirely different.

Four of us turned up for the jog in the park, including Big Geordie. We appointed him coach, because he turned out a few times for Halifax RL and plays union for the police, and he put us through some stretching exercises before we set off.

As they say: it's like banging your head against a wall – great when you stop. We did two turns around the park, partly on the path, partly over the newly-mown grass, and arrived back at the cars wheezing, coughing and sweating like there'd been a gas leak in an old-people's home. We'd a long way to go, but we'd get there.

I forsook the obligatory shandy and went home for an early night. The British Midland flight I'd managed to book a seat on left Leeds at 06:40, to give all the high-powered executives who used it a full day in town. To them this was routine, to a hick like me it was a novelty.

If they'd known a car was meeting me they'd have been impressed, even if it did turn out to be a Sierra with fake-fur seat covers, taken off observations in some South London borough. I tried small talk with the DC driving it, but his manner made it quite clear that he hadn't joined the Met to chauffeur people like me who couldn't read a tube map. I gave up trying and watched the traffic.

New Scotland Yard is on Victoria Street, handy for the Palace and the Department of Trade and Industry. My driver stopped under the familiar three-sided sign and I got out. The journey from the airport had taken five minutes less than the flight down, and the service was terrible.

It improved once I was inside. A stunning young lady in a uniform blouse with epaulettes took me upstairs to a meeting room and found me a coffee. I'd hardly taken in the view from the window when Chief Superintendent Natrass and a DI called Martin something joined me. Natrass had a grey crew-cut and bristly moustache, and favoured short-sleeved shirts. Handshakes all round and he asked if I'd had a good flight. I replied that it had been fine and that was the polite chat dealt with. We got straight down to business. At his invitation I spent the next fifteen minutes outlining the three murders and why we thought they might be linked. I told them about my conversations with the psychologist because I thought they'd be big on stuff like that and said that he'd confirmed our worst fear – that there was a steady escalation of violence.

The two of them shared uneasy glances and Natrass

cleared his throat. In front of him, on the table, was a pile of documents which he divided into three files, each about half an inch thick. He took a ten-by-eight black-and-white print from the first one and said: "You referred to your cases as M1, M2 and M3, Charlie. I know you don't mean to de-humanise the offences, but it does save confusion, so I'll do the same. This is case number one. Thirty-two-year-old female, found dead at the side of a road near Waltham Abbey." He turned to his colleague, saying: "Martin."

Martin slid a map across to me and pointed to the place. North London, just outside the M25. I wondered if there was still an abbey there. I looked from the map back to the photo of the victim. She was lying face down, with her arms and legs spread wide and a trickle of blood from her head making a dark patch against all the shades of grey.

"Killed instantly," the superintendent continued. "Injuries consistent with being struck by a motor vehicle."

I looked at him, wondering for a split second why he'd flown me to London to look at pictures of a hit-and-run, but I kept my counsel. He reached into the next file and slid another photograph my way. This time the victim was a teenage youth, lying on his back, arms flung upwards and ankles neatly crossed.

"Number two," Natrass said. "Nineteen-year-old male, killed by a single blow to the head with the proverbial, prob-ably a hammer. Weapon not found, body *apparently* not moved."

Martin pointed to the spot on the map again. North London, out towards Hatfield. I had dozens of questions to ask, including one about that stressed *apparently*, but I guessed he was skipping all the details to come to some big point, so I just said: "Go on."

"Victim number three," he continued, pushing the next picture my way. "Twenty-five-year-old female, again killed by a blow to the head, this time by something like a base-ball bat. Moved about five miles after she was killed and dumped in a field."

Martin showed me that she'd been killed near Harlow and her body left further towards the M25. I studied the photo. She was wearing a smart suit and had long fair hair. I turned the picture over and read her details: Samantha Jayne Wesley; date of birth 7th June 1974; lived in Harlow. It didn't say that she was a happy, outgoing girl, with lots of friends and a zest for life. It didn't say that she loved her mum and had a boyfriend and wanted to travel and get married and have at least four kids. It didn't say lots of things, like why some moron with the IQ of a fruit fly thought he had some God-given right to snuff her out. She was lying in what first-aiders call the recovery position, on her side with her knees drawn up and her arm reaching forward. I gently placed the photograph alongside the other two and looked at Superintendent Natrass.

"When?" I asked. "When did these happen?"

"October and November, 1999."

"Eighteen months ago. What time of day?"

"Evening. Seven, eight and ten o'clock, near enough."

"Similar to ours. I can understand the link between two and three, but why are you including the hit-and-run? There's obviously something you haven't told me."

He did what I think was the nearest thing to a grin he was capable of and said: "Roly Fearnside spoke very highly of you, Charlie. You know that, don't you?"

"Commander Fearnside," I said, smiling at the memory. "Yeah, we worked on a couple of good cases together and got lucky. How is he? Has he passed the stage where he's calling in every week to see how you all are?" The last time I'd spoken to him was when he phoned me to say that he was retiring.

Martin coughed and the superintendent stared at me for a few seconds. "You haven't heard, then," he said.

"Heard what?"

"That Roly died."

"Oh God, no. When was this?"

"'Bout a year ago, maybe less. He only had three weeks, poor sod, then a coronary got him."

"Oh heck," I said. I'd liked Roly. He was a brusque, military type, born to lead and doing it with style. The sort that died out along with trolley buses and unlocked churches.

"I believe he invited you down to work with him," Natrass was saying.

"Mmm," I agreed. "It was mentioned. He couldn't drag me away from God's own, though." Natrass had a North-Eastern accent, and I was aware of how parochial I sounded.

"You probably made the right decision, Charlie. It's all bloody paperwork here. But Roly was a good judge of a man, and if he wanted you, that's good enough for me." He rearranged his papers and went on: "You suggested that I was holding something back, and you were right. Four months after Samantha Wesley's murder, in March 2000, the SIO on the case received a note. Here's a copy."

I reached out and took the A4 sheet he held towards me. It was dark at the edges through being misaligned in the copier, but the three lines of typing were distinct enough. Bang in the middle of the page were the words:

*X Y Z*
*ha ha ha ha ha ha ha*
*This is the Eye Of The Storm*

"Anything else?" I asked, puzzled.

"Yes," the chief super said. "In with the note were press cuttings for the three killings, just so we knew what he was talking about."

"That's all?"

"Mmm."

"Any forensics from the envelope?"

"Not a thing."

"Posted locally?"

"Central London."

I was stalling for time and running out of ideas. Some nut was claiming to be a serial killer, but so what? It happened all the time. They knew that, so why were they bothering me. If this was some sort of test I was failing it, abysmally. I pushed the note forward until it was lined up neatly with the middle photograph, making a perfect capital T. It's something I've found myself doing a lot, lately. Maybe I should have a word with Adrian about it. He'd know a name for it, if not a cure.

*One, two, three*, I thought, looking at the pictures and remembering a snatch of song. *It's elementree. X,Y, Zee...*

"Oh my God!" I exclaimed. "Oh my giddy aunt! Now I see what it's all about." There it was in the photographs, spelled out by the bodies and arms and legs of the three victims. *X, Y and Z, I am the killer and I enjoy my work*, writ large, not in blood, this time, but in flesh.

"Let's stop for a coffee," Natrass suggested, and I agreed with him.

He gave me a lightning tour of the department, introducing me to more people than you could shake a truncheon at. Everybody was busy at a workstation, working on programs with acronyms that might someday pass into the language. We were using HOLMES, and I'd heard of HITS and CATCHEM, used in child murder cases, but what the devil was CORPSE? The sight of all those po-faced characters hunched over their keyboards made me think that I'd made a good decision when I rejected Roly Fearnside's offer, even if it had included promotion.

Martin had things to do, so Natrass and I had a serious head-to-head in his office. "You must've asked for psychiatric help on this one," I stated. "What did they say?"

"You're right," he told me. "We spoke to everyone we could. Considered opinion is that the first one, the hit and run, may have been an accident. He stopped initially, perhaps, but it gave him such a high that he fled the scene and resolved to repeat the experience."

"But with a bit more personal input next time," I suggested.

"Mmm, something like that."

"So why the XYZ business?"

"Because all the publicity reinforced his feelings. It was like a drug to him. Alternatively, he wanted to prove that he's so much cleverer than we are. He's laughing at us, as you saw. Who knows what goes through a mind like that?"

"But that's just what you're supposed to do," I said. "Get inside his mind, learn to think like him. Isn't that what it's all about?"

"Bullshit, Charlie. And meanwhile, while we're getting inside his mind, he's out killing. It's his guts I want to get inside, not his mind."

"I know the feeling. So you think he's re-surfaced and moved up North?"

"I'd say so, wouldn't you?"

"Where's he been for the last eighteen months?"

"Who knows? Maybe he had a scare, decided to lay low for a while. Got married, perhaps, but the gloss is wearing off. We thought that maybe he'd topped himself, but it looks as if we were wrong."

"You didn't go to the press."

"No. That was my decision. I thought it might rile him. We even leaned the other way a bit – denied they were linked. These pictures have never been made public, of course, so I hoped we might goad him into contacting us with more information to prove he was the killer, but we haven't. Now it's looking as if I've painted myself into a corner. Have you gone public with yours?"

"Yes. It wasn't an operational decision, we had a leak and made the best of it." No point in admitting that I'd goofed at the press conference. I clicked my ballpen and placed it in my pocket. He'd certainly given me something to think about. "Presumably you want me to keep mum about all this," I said.

He leaned forward on his hairy arms, saying: "What I want, Charlie, is for you to take the case on. We've had eighteen months of calm – the eye of the storm – and now we're through that and on your patch. Six murders so far, six separate investigations. We need someone with your experience and ability to think laterally to take an over-view. I can offer you Acting DCI and whatever resources you need. My advice would be to work on the quiet with a small, hand-picked team, at least to start with, but it's up to you. What do you say?"

It wasn't what I'd expected. Sometimes, with big cases, everybody with an eye on promotion wants to jump aboard. Other times they stay clear, especially when the press are on a witch-hunt and things aren't going too well. In those cases we find someone fresh-faced and ambitious and put them in charge, and it's muck or nettles for them. Alternatively, we bring out the old war-horse who thinks we're in business to catch criminals and doesn't know how to say no, and we let him get on with it. This looked like one of those.

So, I thought, I have a reputation for lateral thinking, whatever that meant. Somewhere on my file, next to the bits about being an ex-art student and failed goalkeeper, there must be something about my having a somewhat cavalier attitude towards proper police procedure. I didn't care, as long as they realised that it wasn't natural, and I had to work at it.

"I'm not keen," I told him. "I have a good relationship with Superintendent Isles and this would look as if I'm undermining him. Thanks for the offer, but he's the man you should be talking to."

"Les Isles is a plodder," he stated, "and this case needs something better than that. OK, so how does this sound: The Senior Command course is due to start at Bramshill next week and Les has had an application in for a couple of years. I could have a word with the director of studies about an extra place for him, which would leave the way clear for you to take over the investigation. You'd be doing him a favour."

I shook my head in disbelief and picked up a beer mat from his desk, turning it round and round in my fingers. The sunlight slanting in through the venetian blind made striped patterns across the desk and my outstretched arm. It would have looked good in a painting.

"No doubt you and the director of studies go back a long way," I said.

"Yes, we do. Shall I give him a ring?"

"If Les has applied," I said, my voice unreal, coming from someone else, "it would be churlish to disappoint him."

"Good man. Just what I thought."

"So who will I report to?"

"On a day-to-day basis, nobody, but I'm here if you need me and I'd expect to be kept informed of developments."

"Who'd know about me?"

"To begin with, your own super and the SIO for each case. And the chief constable, of course. That's all. After that, it's up to you how you handle it. If you decided that a higher, more open profile was appropriate, so be it."

"OK," I said. "You tell Admin that my new salary starts in the morning and I'll go back and kick up a storm of my own."

I spent a while looking at the files and then took the tube from St James's Park station to South Kensington, where I lost myself for a couple of hours in the V & A. I could have stayed there a fortnight, but I dragged myself away in time to catch the 17:35 plane back to Leeds. By eight o'clock I was sitting in front of my own flame-effect gas fire, pondering on the day's events. The fine words and the optimism had evaporated on the flight back, but they were paying me more for doing what I was already doing, so that couldn't be bad. A celebration was called for, and I was starving. I lingered only long enough to change my shoes and dump the junk mail, and went for steak and chips at a roadhouse on the bypass. It was my gesture of solidarity with the farmers.

Thursday morning I deployed the troops as usual, with the emphasis on the Colinette Jones enquiry. The reconstruction had gone well and jolted the memory of a few people who'd been on the streets that night, but there was nothing to send us dashing off with blue lights flashing. There never is. We'd had a stabbing the day before that sounded to have racial overtones, so I put Jeff Caton on to it, with instructions to placate everybody and keep it out of the papers. After that it was the morning prayer meeting, with Mr Wood and Gareth Adey, my uniformed counterpart. Gareth was up to his sweetbreads with the foot-and-mouth so we sent him on his way as soon as possible and I told Gilbert about my new job description.

He took it well, but wasn't too pleased when I said that I wanted Dave Sparkington and Maggie Madison working full time with me. I pointed out that nothing much would change. We'd concentrate on the deaths of the three in the North, but I would have an overview that would take in the other killings. I'd still be here to have a chocolate biscuit with him every morning.

Natrass didn't waste time and Les Isles rang me mid-morning to tell me his good news. He was apologetic about the case but said he'd recommend that I be left in charge and lifted to acting DCI. I expected to feel rotten about it, but he was obviously happy with the turn of events and made it sound like it was all his idea. I congratulated him on his selection and said he'd be sorely missed. My words sounded insincere even to me, and I knew I'd never make a politician.

Superintendent Natrass was oiling the wheels for me with the other forces, so all I had to do next was brief Dave and Maggie. I contacted them and said I'd see them in the canteen at lunchtime.

"Who wrote: *One two three, it's elementree*?" I asked, half singing the words between mouthfuls of bacon sandwich, when I met them there.

"Len Barry," Dave responded immediately. "Number three in 1963."

"Formerly of the Dovells," Maggie added. "Had another hit the following year with 'Like a Baby'."

"Blimey, I'm impressed," I said.

"Pub quizzes," she explained.

"I might have known. Anyway, you've passed the test, so here's the deal," and I told them all about it.

Friday morning they drove down to Hatfield and Waltham Abbey to familiarise themselves with those cases and the terrain, and to pick up the files that had been created for us. I had the usual meeting with Gilbert and when I went back to my office Peter Goodfellow was waiting for me in a state of high agitation.

"That pickup, Charlie," he said. "The white one. I just put it through the computer, and guess what? A white Toyota pickup with big wheels was reported near the scene of the Robin Gillespie killing, by three independent witnesses. One of them was a retired police officer, getting on a bit – seventy-four according to the report – but with all his faculties and he gave a good description..."

"Was it traced?" I asked.

"You bet. Owned by one Jason Towse. He works in Nelson and lives that way on. His wife gave him an alibi."

"Get the details. And a street map. I'll clear it with Nelson and we'll pay Mr Towse a surprise visit."

Pete drove, I navigated. I took us through Hebden Bridge and Heptonstall, where Sylvia Plath is buried, and then on a Z road over Heptonstall Moor. It's a wild landscape up there, and today it was at its best. The clear skies of the early morning had given way to steady drizzle drifting across from Lancashire, and the moors tapered away until land and sky merged in a grey smudge, barely an arm's length off. There were no sheep, no birds, and it wasn't hard to imagine that something was out there, something malevolent, drifting about in the miasma, waiting its opportunity to strike.

"Which way?" Pete asked as he slowed for a fork in the road.

"Um, right," I said. "Or left. Where are we going?"

"You're the flippin' navigator. It might have been better to take the A646 through Todmorden and Burnley, except we'd have hit all the traffic. Nelson's a nice town. If you want a new pair of shoes it's the place to go. There's this outlet, a factory shop, and all they sell is shoes, millions of them."

"I'm OK for shoes. They don't wear out like they used to."

"That's true. Did you ever stick rubber soles on them?"

"Mmm. Presumably Mr Towse will be at work. So let's see if his wife's at home, first. That might be interesting. Pull over and we'll look at the *A to Z.*"

Thirty minutes later we rolled into the cul-de-sac in Padiham where they lived and parked outside number twelve, a well-kept semi. There was no Toyota pickup on the drive, just an oilstain that indicated he did his own maintenance and a wishing well with a selection of gnomes patiently fishing and doing other things into it. The lawn had already had its first trim of the year and the daffodils were promising to look good in a day or two. Mrs Towse answered the door after our first push of the bell.

She was a pleasant looking woman, turning to blowziness, with bleached hair and high heels that gave a hint of glamour. We discreetly showed our IDs, conscious of the twitching curtains over the road, and she let us in.

"We didn't really expect to catch you, Mrs Towse," I said. "Do you work at all?" I make the small talk, butter them up, then Pete asks the meaty stuff.

"Oh yes," she replied. "I'm senior medical receptionist at

the practice and I was just getting ready to go. Will this take long?"

"I wouldn't think so," Pete answered. "I believe the local police have already interviewed you about your husband's movements on February 6$^{th}$."

"Yes. The night that poor boy was murdered. Someone saw a pickup like Jason's in the vicinity, but the time was wrong."

"Robin Gillespie was murdered a few minutes after five," Pete continued, "on his way home from his paper round. You said that Jason arrived home before then."

"That's right. He came in at about five o'clock."

"What does Jason do for a living, Mrs Towse?"

"He's a company director."

"But what does he do?"

"He manufactures high class kitchen units for several property developers and builders. Bespoke units, not mass produced ones that fall apart as soon as you fill them."

"I see. I've been led to believe, Mrs Towse, that people in small businesses have to work all the hours that God sends. Does your husband always finish at such a sensible time?"

"No, not always. It's just that he was between orders, just temporarily, of course, and had been to see a client. He rang me at about four thirty to say he was on his way. I had to go to evening surgery and it was a filthy night, but if I waited he'd be able to run me there. The police have been told all this several times."

"I know, Mrs Towse, and I appreciate your patience. Now, can we leap forward in time to just over a week ago. March the twenty-first, to be precise, which was a Wednesday. What time did your husband come home that evening, Mrs Towse?"

We were seated in the kitchen, surrounded by high-class bespoke units made in some fancy wood with a grain like a contour map of the Karakorams. There was a wine rack under the double sink and some of the cupboards had little pegs beneath them for hanging mugs on. Mrs Towse's hand made a small, involuntary movement towards her face and her cheeks flushed a shade under the makeup.

"The twenty-first, did you say?" she asked.

"Yes."

"That would be the third Wednesday of the month?"

"Yes, I suppose it would."

"He came home early, about four thirty."

"You seem very certain about that, Mrs Towse."

"Yes, well, I, er, I had the evening off. Wednesday evening is our quietest time, not that it's ever quiet for long, as you'll appreciate, and the doctors are very good about time off. Jason came home early and we had a quiet night in, just the two of us."

"You cooked something special," I suggested.

"Yes, as a matter of fact I did."

"What was it?"

"Pardon?"

"What did you cook?"

"Oh, er, Chicken Provençal, in a red wine sauce. It's his favourite."

"Sounds nice."

"Thank you."

Pete gave me a sideways look before saying: "Mrs Towse, this could be serious. Can anybody confirm that Jason was here with you on Wednesday the twenty-first?"

"Um, well, me," she said.

"Nobody else?"

"No, I don't think so."

"Nobody called, nobody phoned?"

"No, I'm afraid not."

Pete asked me if I'd anything else to ask, and I said: "No, I think that covers everything. What time will Jason be home this evening, Mrs Towse?"

"About five thirty, perhaps a little later," she replied.

"OK. Thanks for your time and we'll probably come back

then to have a word with him and verify what you said. Thank you."

"Oh no we won't," I said one minute later as I fastened my seat belt. "Let's have another look at the *A to Z*. With a bit of luck we'll catch him before she does, on his mobile. What did you reckon?"

"I reckon she was lying through her teeth."

"Mmm, me too. Take the motorway north and come off at J13, fast as you like."

He had a couple of units in an old cotton mill. Someone had gambled that there could still be a use for a solid stone building with acres of floor-space and lofty ceilings, and they'd been proved right. There was a canal running past the door, a motorway within three minutes and a market out there. A huge board listed the names of the resident companies, and only one unit was still available for rent. We parked in the visitors' section and saw the white Toyota pickup in the spot nearest the door. He was an early starter. As we walked past it I noticed the headrests and remembered the professor's theory about how Colinette had died. Was I looking at the place where she had gulped her last breath? Was I about to meet the man responsible? It's impossible to keep these questions from entering your head when you're on an enquiry.

JT Joinery was on the ground floor, and the communal receptionist rang him and said that a Mr Goodfellow and a Mr Priest had arrived. He came to a security door and let us in.

He was big and soft looking, with a chubby baby-face and the beginnings of a beer belly under his overalls that gave him a pear-shape. We followed him wordlessly down a short corridor, past doors marked with names like Pendle Dolls Houses and Lancashire Hot Pots. This was Craftsville UK, the new vision of working Britain. I suspected that JT Joinery was the only genuine industry in the place.

It certainly looked industrious. There were enough power tools to stock a small B & Q and the air was filled with a fine sawdust that stung your nostrils and made me want to sneeze, so I sneezed. Why deny yourself? He led us into a small partitioned-off office space, a bit like mine, cleared a pile of catalogues off two wooden chairs and invited us to sit down. There was a girlie calendar on the wall, plus dozens of notes, post-its and unpaid invoices. It was a typical small business, run by a craftsman who was slowly drowning under the paperwork.

"Sorry about the mess," he said.

"You were expecting us," I opened with, after the introductions.

"Er, yes. Janet rang me, said you'd called. I thought you might come straight round."

"How's business?"

"Not bad. Picking up after the winter."

Pete said: "This is serious, Mr Towse, so we'd like some straight answers. Where were you at seven o'clock on the evening of Wednesday the twenty-first of March? That's just over a week ago."

He blushed, pressed his hands together and did a funny little shake. "What's it about?" he asked.

Pete opened his mouth to speak but I beat him to it. "A pickup like yours was seen near the place where young Robin Gillespie was murdered, back in early February," I told him.

"That's right, and it was mine. I'd gone to measure up at a house in Trawden, but they weren't in, so I came home that way. Somebody saw the pickup and reported it. It's noticeable. I suppose that's why I drive it. The police have gone all over it and didn't find anything."

"So I understand. A week last Wednesday a young girl was murdered over in Yorkshire," I said, "and a similar pickup was reported near the scene. Now, Mr Towse, where were you on the evening of the twenty-first. It was the third

Wednesday in the month, if that helps."

Up to then he'd looked worried, but at that last state-ment you'd have thought I'd hit him in the teeth with an eight-by-four sheet of MDF. His mouth fell open and his arm shot out, knocking several letters on to the floor. I stu-diously bent down, tapped the sheets together and replaced them on his desk.

"Wednesday," I reminded him.

"Um, J-Janet told you I was with her," he began.

"That's right," I said. "She told us that you had a roman-tic evening in, all by yourselves. She cooked you coq-au-vin, which is your favourite, and you ate it off her stomach, while lying naked on the living-room rug. Now, we don't mean this as any reflection on yourself or your lovely wife, but we didn't believe her. So could we now have the truth, *please*!"

"She meant well," he said, brushing a hand through his hair.

"Commendable," I commented. "You're a lucky man."

"She thought it would just save trouble."

"Instead of causing it. Where were you, Mr Towse?"

"We went out to some friends. For a meal. Janet didn't want you calling round, embarrassing them. You know what women are like. The police call, asking questions...you might be completely innocent but mud sticks, doesn't it? And they're nice people. She didn't want to bother them."

"I'm sure she didn't. Do you have an address for them?"

"Yeah, somewhere." He produced a British Timber diary from a drawer and went to the page marked *Addresses*, near the back. I've never met anyone before who uses the Addresses page in a diary for addresses. Very suspicious. He read it out and Pete made a note.

"Name?" I asked.

"Um, Trevor and Michelle."

"Surname?"

"I don't know."

I said: "You went round to these people's house and had

a meal with them but you don't know their surname?"

"Mmm."

"Was anybody else there?"

"Yes, quite a few people."

"How many?"

"About forty, or so."

"Forty! Can you name any of them?"

"No, not surnames. They meet, now and again..."

"On the third Wednesday of the month."

"That's right. And talk and have a meal. That's all. It was the first time we'd been invited."

"I see. Sounds highly civilised. What time did you arrive?"

"Just after seven. We didn't want to be the first there."

"Do you have a phone number for Trevor and Michelle?"

"No."

I looked at Pete, who shook his head, and we left. "More lies," he said as he started the engine.

"He's certainly covering something up," I agreed. "Would you take him for a killer?"

"As much as anybody else. You get the impression there's something going off deep down inside him, and what sort of a grown man drives a vehicle like that?"

"Oh!" I exclaimed. "I was rather fancying one like it for myself."

Trevor and Michelle live in Skipton, which, to my eternal surprise, is not all that far away from these Lancastrian towns. Our *A to Z* didn't cover it, so we called in at the police station for directions and a quick consultation with the electoral roll told us that their surname was Young.

As soon as we turned into their cul-de-sac I knew where Janet Towse's aspirations lay. It was what the agents call an executive development, with four individual houses on large plots and not a wishing well in sight. Brookmere was second on the left, complete with integral sun lounge and double garage. There wasn't a car to be seen. Everyone must have either been elsewhere, in the reserved space outside the office, or safely tucked up in its heated garage. Pete tried to park his so that it didn't look abandoned, but found it impossible, and we walked up the block-paved drive to the front door. I searched for an oil stain from the pickup, but imagined that any such blemish would have been cleaned up within hours.

A white haired gentleman with a pink face and Shetland cardigan opened the door. "Sorry to trouble you, Sir," Pete said, "but are you Mr Young?"

Chapter Five

"Detectives, eh," he said, a few minutes later when we were seated in easy chairs which I would describe as chintz covered, although I don't know what chintz is. There were watercolours of Dales scenes on the walls, a rare burst of sun streaming in through the French windows, and if I'd had a pot of Earl Grey at my elbow I'd have been as content as a little green caterpillar in a peapod. "Always enjoy a good mystery myself," he went on. "Envy you chaps. Now, what's it all about?"

"I'm admiring the paintings, Mr Young," I said. "Do you have any problems with them fading in all this sun?"

"No," he replied. "Not so you'd notice, but Michelle does them, and what she doesn't sell ends up on the wall. She knocks them off like breeding rabbits."

"Don't belittle her talent," I chided. "They're very good." I meant it. Watercolours require something called painterliness, and these had it. Every stroke of the brush was done with confidence and there'd been no going back. And she'd caught the Dales in all their moods. "Where is Mrs Young?" I asked.

She was out walking the dogs. Funny, I thought, how "walking the dogs" carries connotations about class that "walking the dog" doesn't.

"We understand," Pete began, "that you held some sort of a dinner party here just over a week ago, on the evening of the twenty-first. Is that so, Mr Young?"

"Er, yes, as a matter of fact we did," he replied.

"Do you have a guest list, Sir?"

"No, I'm afraid not. We don't bother with anything like that; it's all rather informal. Not a dinner party, as such. We put on a buffet and just stand around and chat."

"How many attended?"

"Twenty-two couples. Forty-four including ourselves."

"So how do you draw up the invitations?"

"We don't. We're just a group of like-minded friends, and if you want to bring someone else along, that's fine. Could you tell me what this is all about, please? Is someone in trouble?"

I said: "And you hold one of these parties on the third Wednesday of the month?"

"Yes," he replied, "but not here. We don't hold them all here. We rotate, somewhere different each time."

"I see."

"Were a couple called Jason and Janet Towse at the party, do you remember, Sir?" Pete asked.

He looked thoughtful. "Jason and Janet?" he repeated. "No, I don't think I met them. You'll appreciate, of course, that one can't remember everybody's name, and there were one or two new faces present last Wednesday. Jason and Janet? No, I don't think so. We tend not to bother with surnames." A car door slammed and the sound of barking dogs interrupted our conversation until it receded to the back of the house. "That's Michelle," he said. "She might remember them."

"But you can't?"

"No, I don't think so."

A door closed and a voice shouted: "Hide behind the sofa, Trev, I think the bloody Mormons are in the street again," immediately followed by Michelle Young making her entrance.

I fell for her instantly. She was a big woman, wearing a long full coat and flowing silk scarf, with bleached hair and tinted spectacles. We stood up and I said: "Actually, we're the bloody CID."

She gave a hearty laugh and shook my hand, then Pete's, as we introduced ourselves. She'd have looked good in a trilby hat, tilted over one eye, drawing on a cheroot.

"So, what's the bloody CID want?" she asked, after telling us to sit down again.

"We came to ask a few questions about your Wednesday night party," I told her.

"Has Trevor offered you a coffee?"

"No, we're fine."

"Trevor! Where's your manners?" She turned back to me, saying: "Tch! I've tried to train him but most of it fell on deaf ears."

"No coffee," I protested. "We'd just like to clear up something about one of your guests, if you don't mind."

"Oh, if you insist. Which one?"

"Right, thank you. Now, can you tell us if a couple called Jason and Janet were at the party?"

"Yes," she stated, emphatically.

"You sound quite certain," I said.

"I am. They were here."

"Well I don't remember them," Mr Young admitted.

"Of course you do, darling. You spent most of the evening talking to him."

"I don't remember anyone called Jason. Damned stupid name. I'd have remembered that."

"Not Jason!" she declared. "Rowena! Surely you remember Rowena. Rowena and Janet."

"Ah, Rowena!" he exclaimed. "Now I remember. Does something in wood, I believe."

"Rowena?" I echoed.

"Rowena?" Pete added, determined not to be left out.

"That's right, Rowena," Mrs Young confirmed. "He was wearing a fetchingly simple fuschia button-through with white accessories. He couldn't get the handbag right, but it *was* the poor darling's first appearance in public, so to speak. He is all right, isn't he?"

I looked at Pete and he looked at her and I looked at Mr Young and she looked at me. "Um, yes, he's, er, all right," I mumbled. "He's, er, very...all right. But...I think I could manage that coffee, now, if that's, um, all right."

We didn't speak much on the drive back. Once a month forty-odd like-minded people of both genders met for canapés and dressed in their partners' clothes. They stood around and talked, mainly about fashions, had a few drinks and went home. It was a brief island of relief, a safety valve, before they immersed themselves once more in the daily grime of living a lie and being normal, whatever that meant.

"Reckon he's in the clear, Chas?" Pete asked as we swung into the station yard.

"Forty-three witnesses say he is," I replied.

"They weren't sure what time he arrived."

"True."

"And a pickup *was* seen."

"I know. Keep on it Pete – that only leaves four thousand nine hundred and ninety-nine others to check out."

"Thanks."

"Monday'll do."

Everybody had gone home, so we followed them. There was a note from Geordie on my desk telling me to bring my gear in the morning. He'd organised a jog round the park, followed by a swim at the sports centre, followed by a well-earned pint, so I abandoned my plan to go on a solo run and had a pizza from the freezer.

I was disappointed, no point in denying it. The pickup was the first red-hot lead we'd had, but now we were back to square one. Worse than that, square none. We had a database of possible offenders and could check the ones who owned motor vehicles, but Adrian Foulkes had told me that our man probably didn't have a criminal record.

I put a week's washing in the machine and gave it the *delicates* cycle. A lady a couple of doors away irons my shirts for me, and I'd take them round tomorrow. Ironing is one domestic task that I haven't mastered. I found a can of lager in the fridge and wandered into the front room to get a decent glass from the cabinet, but by the time I got there I'd forgotten what I wanted. Back in the kitchen I saw the can on the work surface and remembered that I needed a glass. I made it at the second attempt.

Dave rang to say that they were back from their trip south. Everybody had been helpful and they'd collected a load of paperwork. I told him to bring his kit in the morning and declined his offer of a swift half or two in a nearby hostelry. I emptied the swing bin and did all the washing-up and rounded off an evening at home with some laddish television. All in all, not a memorable Friday night, but better than someone's. Much better than someone's.

Gina Milner loved animals. She loved all animals, but not equally. At the first stutter of her alarm clock she was wide awake and swinging her legs out of bed, and a quick peek through the curtains confirmed that the sun was shining, for once. She loved animals with shells or scales or feathers or fur, it was all the same to her, but most of all she loved horses.

She'd never owned one but had taken riding lessons from an early age. Her dad had ferried her there and back, and even investigated the possibility of buying a horse and stabling it at the riding school, but the cost was prohibitive and there are too many horse traders in the horse trading business.

Mrs Milner was already downstairs, making toast, as Gina breezed into the sunlit kitchen. "Morning, love, want some toast?" Mum asked.

"Haven't time, thanks," Gina replied. "Is it all right if I take the car?"

"It's not good for you, you know, dashing about without any breakfast. Of course you can."

"I'll have some when I get back. Thanks, Mum."

She grabbed her anorak from behind the door, unhooked the car keys and was gone. Her mother shook her head and smiled, proud of the daughter she'd thought she would never have. She placed six rashers of bacon under the grill and shouted up to her husband that breakfast was ready.

Gina was in her A-levels year at Heckley High School, and was on course for a straight flush of grade A passes. Then it would be off to Glasgow, studying veterinary medicine. After that, who could tell? Set up in practise in Halifax, go into research or work for a while on some project in Africa? The world would be at her feet. Meanwhile, the horses had to be fed and then it was off to her Saturday job, earning money for a trip to see the famous Lipizzaner horses at the Spanish Riding School in Vienna.

None of her friends knew about her Saturday job, although they had all seen her at work. Her parents were in on the secret, but if one of them mentioned it she would collapse in a fit of giggling and change the subject.

Gina filled a plastic bag with carrots from the sack in the garage and transferred them to the boot of her mother's Fiesta. She drove to the greengrocer's shop at the end of the road and the proprietor gave her another bag filled with cabbage leaves and other waste items.

"There's some apples in there," he told her. "'Osses likes apples."

"Thanks Mr Moss," she replied. "You're a treasure. I'll tell them they're from you."

He smiled and shook his head as she drove off. "She'll go far, that lass," he said to his next customer. "She will, she'll go far."

Gina made an expert three-point turn and drove past her home, over the little bridge that crossed the canal and turned on to a minor road that led over the fells. The ponies were in a little triangular field just down from the tops, where a farmer had brought some of his sheep to have their lambs. They were all stranded there now, because of the foot-and-mouth restrictions, and the field was a quagmire. Gina had seen their plight a fortnight earlier, when out for a walk with her father, and had unofficially adopted them.

There was room to park but not enough to turn round. Usually she would feed the horses first, and after a long chat with them, and much rubbing of their ears, would drive another quarter of a mile to where an old drovers' road crossed the lane. She would turn round there and go home. This morning for some reason she decided to turn round first. The horses were waiting for her, their heads hanging over the wall like a pair of stuffed moose. Gina waved to them as she sped by, shouting: "Don't worry, I'm coming back."

A four-by-four came over a brow in the road, travelling in the opposite direction. Gina pulled into the side to give it room to pass and raised her hand to wave to the driver until she realised it wasn't the one she normally saw. She smiled at her mistake and saw the vehicle's brake lights come on through her rear-view mirror.

Gina stopped on the left-hand side of the lane, just beyond the drovers' road, and reversed into it. The ground was rough and stony, and the entrance narrow, so she concentrated hard on what she was doing. Mrs Milner would not be pleased if her car was returned minus its silencer. When she was far enough back she pulled the handbrake on and instinctively glanced in her right-hand wing mirror before moving forward.

Chapter Six

The same weak sun that had brightened Mrs Milner's kitchen was shining through the gap in the curtains of a Victorian terrace house on the outskirts of Heckley. The young woman lying in bed screwed up her eyes as the patch of light it cast on the duvet moved across her face. She turned away from it and put her arm around the man lying next to her.

"Are you awake?" he whispered.

"Mmm, are you?"

"Mmm."

"Did you sleep well?"

"Yes. I always do, after...you know."

"So do I." He moved her arm from across his chest and sat up, turning to plump up his pillows. "Put some music on," he said.

She reached out and pressed the Play button on the cassette player that sat on the bedside cabinet, then rearranged her pillows so she could sit up next to him.

*This is the eye of the storm*, came out of the speakers in a high-pitched voice, almost falsetto. *Watch out for that needle, Son, 'cos this is the eye of the storm.*

"Fast forward past this," he ordered her. "It's too slow."

She did as she was told and a few seconds later the tempo stepped up to a rap. "This is better." He put his arm across her shoulders and slapped out the rhythm with the palm of his hand against her skin as he sang along with the tape:

> *Teachers are liars, singing in choirs,*
> *Too much bread, I'd give 'em lead.*
> *Professors an' lawyers an' all their employers,*
> *Corruption is rife, I'd give 'em the knife.*
> *Man on the video, thinks he's a Romeo,*
> *He'll lose his aplomb if you send him a bomb.*

> *The congressman's niece is the chief of police,*
> *Don't choke on the smell, just send 'em to hell.*

"Ah, that's a good one," he declared. "Tim didn't fuck about when he wanted to say something. Now, listen to this next one and tell me all about it."

It was the song that Tim Roper wrote for his pal Zeke's new-born son, Theo. The collected voices of The LHO sang the lyric:

> *One two, buckle my shoe,*
> *Uncle Joe is stuck in the glue...*

"Now," the man began, "who are we talking about when we say Uncle Joe?"

"Joe Kennedy!" the girl answered, triumphantly.

"Very good!" he replied. "Dirty Joe Kennedy, who spawned the whole fuckin' Kennedy tribe. But who put an end to it?"

"Lee Harvey Oswald!" she replied.

"That's right. You're learning, my girl, you're learning. And who are The LHO named after and in tribute to?"

"Lee Harvey Oswald!"

"Off course they are. Probably the greatest American who ever lived. And who's Sister Mary?"

"Mary Warner!"

"That's right, marijuana. Now listen to this one. This one's poetry."

> *The property developer can see the possibilities,*
> *The hogan of the Navaho is now a tower of 'luminum,*
> *A pyramid of glass and steel*
> *Stands where the tents of Kedar leaned,*
> *And shareholders play endless golf,*
> *Where once the elk and pronghorn dreamed.*
> *Mojave and San Gabriel*

*Will soon be distant memories*
*The property developer has seen the possibilities.*

He reached across her and pressed the Stop button. "That's where Tim spent his last night," he told her, "in the San Gabriel mountains, composing himself, collecting his thoughts, before the CIA assassinated him. Maybe we should go there."

"What, to America?"

"That's right. I think they'd appreciate us there. Wouldn't you like to see the Mojave Desert just once, with the sun coming up behind the mountains, before they make it one big car park?"

Her face was alive at the thought of it. "Could we?" she asked.

"I don't see why not, when we've finished here. Did you enjoy last night?"

"Oh yes! It was the best so far." She snuggled against him, her face glowing at the memory of the previous night's activities. "When can we do it again?"

"Soon. I should be finished downstairs today or tomorrow. All it needs is some paint. And then we'll do something really special, I promise you."

"Have you found anyone?"

"I think so. And you'll like her. One I remember from the old days, back down home. It might be a good idea to go further afield, next time."

"Oh Timothy, you're so good to me."

"What!" he exclaimed. "What did you call me?"

"I'm...I'm sorry."

"Sorry's not good enough. What did you call me?" He pushed himself upright and placed his hand on her stomach.

"Timothy."

"And what happens to people who call me that?"

"They have to be punished."

"That's right. They have to be punished."

The sliver of sunlight slid off the bed and started its journey across the carpet and over the piles of clothes they'd left there the night before, and up on the roof a blackbird started singing.

People, some people, often drive out into the countryside to dump unwanted household effects. It's fairly commonplace to see some rural scene marred by the incongruous placement of a three-piece suite or a mattress that was surplus to the requirements of a townie who thinks of the countryside as one big dumping ground. Gina thought it was a mannequin, a store-window dummy, that some joker had abandoned there. It was sitting upright, legs spread wide, leaning on the wall as casually as if waiting for a bus. She opened her door to have a better view, and her smile slowly changed into a look of horror. Store-window dummies didn't have cellulite, she thought, or pubic hair.

The horses didn't get their carrots on Saturday morning. Gina drove downhill and stopped at the first house she reached, where she telephoned the police. The old lady who lived there made her sit by the fire and gave her a cup of tea, but she couldn't drink it because her hands were shaking too much. Much as she enjoyed it she didn't go to her weekend job that day, or the next.

We didn't have our jog in the park, or the swim, or the pint in the pub. We were congregating in the office, with Pete regaling everybody with the story of Rowena and his little fuchsia number in terms that were decidedly non-PC, when the call came through.

By the time I put the phone down the joking and laughter had stopped and all eyes were on me. "Looks like he's struck again," I said, very softly. "A woman's body's been found on Stone Rigg Lane, near the top of Whinmoor Hill." Here we go again, I thought. Here we go again. I mentally clicked up a gear. "Dave, you come with me. Maggie, I want you to talk to the person who found the body. I'll ring you with details. Peter, pick your team and follow us. Jeff and the rest of you, round up the specialists and stand by. Make some room downstairs for us and inform Mr Wood. You know the score. Christ, you ought to by now. C'mon, let's go."

We did what we do best: stood on the hillside in little groups, bare-headed with our jackets flapping in the wind. We looked suitably grave and I did a lot of pointing. I arranged for the lane to be blocked off and a tent to be erected over the scene before we let the specialists in. At lunchtime the pathologist did his stuff and I had my first close look at her.

The marks on her neck were similar to the ones we'd seen on Colinette Jones, but there were more of them. At first glance I'd have put her at about forty, but when I was closer I guessed she was younger than that. Late twenties, early thirties. Her tiny denim skirt was pulled up over her waist and she was wearing a skimpy top under a denim jacket. I could smell her perfume. It was one of those that sometimes knocks you over when a posse of sixth formers goes by. Cheap and strong and sold by the gallon.

There was no sign of her knickers, tights, handbag or shoes. In the pockets of her jacket we found a twenty pence piece, a used tissue and nine unused condoms in a packet that had once held twelve. We sealed these in evidence bags and I signed them. I suspected that our man had turned to a prostitute for his latest victim, and with any luck they'd done business before he'd killed her. Maybe this was his big mistake, I thought. Maybe this time we'd have him.

Finding out who she was and whom she'd been with were the top priorities, followed by the PM findings. Professor Sulaiman agreed to perform the autopsy on Sunday morning and I sent a team out trying to trace her. If she hadn't been reported missing an artist's drawing of her on TV or in the papers would probably do the trick.

The landlord of the pub in the village agreed to keep his kitchen open and at three o'clock fifteen of us descended on him for a belated lunch. I paid on my credit card and asked for a receipt.

There was nothing else we could do at the scene so I sent Dave and the others home and drove back to the office to start the paperwork. I left the space for the victim's name blank and wrote M4 after it. M4, I thought, plus XYZ makes seven. Not my lucky number. How long before we went public and announced that he'd done three others that we knew about?

Maggie rang to say that the body had been found by a seventeen-year-old schoolgirl called Gina Milner who had made a full statement but was taking it badly. She was an only child and Maggie suspected she'd led a sheltered life. I pictured the poor dead woman sitting back against the wall with her eyes bulging and her tongue hanging out and wondered how you could prepare a child for something like that. I called in at Sainsbury's on my way home and had my second cooked meal of the day in their restaurant, but this time I paid in cash. You can use the coffee machine as often as you like, so I sat there for an hour, watching people, wondering if he ever used places like this. Maybe yes, maybe no. Most of my officers wouldn't be seen dead in a supermarket, but I knew that a serial killer pushing a shopping trolley was not as incongruous as it sounded. He had to eat, and was probably a loner, so Sainsbury's was as good a place as anywhere to bump into him. I finished my coffee and went home.

Sunday morning I sent Dave to the General to witness the PM while I played at detectives. We'd been too late for Saturday night's papers and TV journalists like their week-ends off, too, so we were no nearer to identifying M4. Sixty or seventy people go missing every day, so we circulated her description and waited. I looked at my checklist of similarities between the cases and added another column for the latest victim. There were differences, but these were covered by the increased sexual activity theory, and the marks on her neck looked conclusive to me. I studied the pictures photographic had produced and put them in the file.

I knew Professor Sulaiman wouldn't hurry, and I needed some fresh air, so I drove through town and down the valley a short way until I reached the hamlet where Gina Milner lived. Her father let me in and led me to the front room where she was sitting.

Gina was a bonny girl, but her face was puffy, as if she'd been crying or not slept. She was fully clothed, in jeans and a sweater, with an unbuttoned dressing gown over the top of them. Her dad said: "This is Inspector Priest, come to see you. How're you feeling, love?"

She gave me a little smile and told her father that she was all right. Mrs Milner came in and asked me if I'd like a cup of tea, and I replied with a nod.

"DC Madison came to talk to you," I said. "Maggie. We call her Mad Maggie."

"Yes. She was nice."

"She said that you go up there every day, to feed some horses."

"Mmm."

Mrs Milner re-appeared with a mug of tea and placed it on a small table near the easy chair I was sitting in. Milky and sweet, just how I don't like it. I thanked her and turned back to Gina.

"Are they your horses?"

"No."

"You just feed them."

"Mmm."

"That's kind of you."

"They're gypsies' ponies," she said. "Well, I think they are. They put them in the field for the winter and left them.

There's no food because the sheep have eaten all the grass. The farmer feeds the sheep but the horses never get any. They're too shy and polite, and the sheep are greedy, so I take them some carrots and stuff from Mr Moss at the greengrocers. The farmer won't feed them because they're not his."

"She's been going up there every day before school," Mrs Milner added. "And at weekends too, before she goes to work."

"But you didn't feel like going to work today," I said, and she shook her head.

"I'm not surprised. It must have been quite a shock for you, yesterday morning. You did very well, ringing us as promptly as you did and I've come to say thank you."

"Have you identified the...the lady," her father asked.

"No, not yet," I replied.

"Was she murdered?"

"We believe so."

"Well I never," Mrs Milner added.

"Gina," I began. "When you go up there do you ever see anybody else?"

She shook her head.

"Never?" I asked.

"Just one person, sometimes," she replied.

"Who's that?"

"Don't know his name. Man in a Range Rover, comes over the hill. We sometimes meet on a narrow bit and he waves and smiles at me."

"What colour Range Rover?"

"Black, and it's always shiny, as if he washes it every day."

"When did you last see him?"

"Well, I thought I saw him this morning but it was a different colour car."

"What colour?"

"A reddish colour. Maroon."

"But a Range Rover?"

"I think so."

"What time would that be?"

"About half past seven."

I grinned and said: "You must love horses, to get up at that time."

"She does," her mother said, sitting on her chair arm and putting an arm around her. "Don't you, love."

"Have you seen anyone else, apart from these Range Rovers?"

"No, I don't think so."

"Well, if you remember anyone, let me know, please."

"OK."

"You haven't been up to see the horses today?"

"No."

"I don't think she wants to go up there again," her mother told me.

"So they'll be hungry."

"Yes."

"Get your coat, then," I said, "and we'll go feed them together."

She glanced up at her mother, her face filled with alarm. "Go on," her mother urged, giving her a gentle push. "You'll be all right with the inspector."

She wasn't sure, but the horses were starving and that was a bigger pull on her than the bogeyman she'd seen the day before. "We'll have to take some carrots," she said.

I rose to my feet. "OK, where are they?"

She had some stuff from the greengrocers in the garage, plus a sack of carrots. She removed yellowing cabbage leaves from a carrier bag and replenished it with carrots, telling me: "These were for yesterday's breakfast, but I didn't give them it."

"They *will* be starving," I said as I put them in my boot. "So let's go."

The horses were poor specimens. They had long broad noses that curled under like a walrus's, sprouting with coarse hair and twitching as we approached them. They stood there, heads over the wall, with sagging backs and clod-hopping feet, as patient and dignified as ancient Buddhists awaiting enlightenment. One was black and white and the other brown and white, with ribs like rubbing boards under their winter coats.

Gina was transformed, pulling their ears, talking to them and making a fuss. She shared out the food between them, telling them not to be greedy or they'd get colic, promising to come back tomorrow. I looked at the field, wondering if I ought to have a word with the RSPCA. It was just a churned up morass. A metal feeder was up at the top end, with about thirty sheep standing around it, waiting for the next meal to arrive. They were all looking towards us, wondering if it was worth the effort to investigate.

When the horses were fed we drove up the hill to where the tent was, where Gina had found the body. A patrol car was there and the driver got out and came to talk to us. I told him about Gina and he said it must have been quite a shock for her. We looked inside the tent and I showed her that there was nothing there now, all was back to normal, hoping she'd be reassured. Back in the car, heading down the hill, I said: "So what do you normally do on a weekend? Your mother said you had a job."

"O God, no," she said, smiling. "I'll...I'll..."

"You'll kill her," I finished for her. "It's all right to say it, you know."

"I suppose so."

"So what do you do?"

"Oh, it's embarrassing."

"Do they pay you?"

"Yes."

"Then there's nothing to be embarrassed about."

"Promise not to laugh?"

"On my goldfish's grave."

"Well, do you ever drive through town on a weekend?"

"Mmm, quite a bit."

"Right. So do you know where Henry's carpets is, in the old cinema at the corner of Church Lane?"

"I know it."

"Well, that's me."

"Who's you?"

"Me, on the corner, inside the lion suit, dancing about on the pavement. That's my weekend job."

I chuckled with laughter. I'd seen her dozens of times, waving to the cars, creating a traffic hazard with her antics. "Honest?" I said.

"'Fraid so."

"It's you, inside the suit?"

"That's right."

"Ha ha ha ha!"

"You promised not to laugh!"

"Last time I saw you, you were doing the can-can, twirling your tail around your head."

"One of my specialities."

"And I'd decided you were a quiet, shy girl."

"It's amazing what anonym...anomyn...ano..."

"Anno Domini?" I suggested.

"No!"

"Annapurna? Anaglypta?"

"No!"

"Anabolic steroids?"

"No!" She poked my arm with an elbow. "I can say it. Ano...nymity. It's amazing what anonymity can do for you."

"I'll have to try it, sometime, though I think I'm more a polar bear than a lion."

We were back at her house. "Thank your mother for the tea," I said as we came to a standstill.

"Right, and thanks for taking me up to feed the horses."

"Promise me you'll go up tomorrow?"

"It's a promise."

"Who pays for the carrots?"

"Dad does. They're called pony carrots, and they're dead cheap."

"Right."

As I drove away I saw her wave and I waved back. One reason for my visit was to see if she was all right, public relations, but I think she'd done far more for me than I'd done for her. It was impossible not to compare her with the schoolgirls I see in the mall at lunchtime, pulling on cigarettes, moping round the record stores and eyeing the boys in Burger King.

Dave arrived back at the station at the same time as I did. "No joy," he said.

"What, no sperm?"

"Nah. Not a trace."

"Damn! Did he have sex with her?"

"There were signs of penetration, but it could have been an object."

"Before or after death?"

"Um," he looked down at his notebook. "Perimortem, according to the prof. Didn't like asking what that was."

"*At about the time of*," I said. "Neither one nor the other."

"So it doesn't help."

"No. What about the marks?"

"Right. He was more forthcoming about them. He said the contusions were caused by a ligature across the front of the throat. I asked him how they compared with those on Colinette and he said that they were similar but there were more of them and they were not as pronounced."

"In other words, he's getting better at it."

"Yep. That's what the prof said."

She'd died sometime Friday evening. I walked across to the window and looked out. Down below, a patrol car left the station yard and a passing motorist let him out although there was no other traffic. The windows of the office block opposite were in darkness and the only sign of life was two pigeons in a courting ritual on a ledge with a third one looking on, awaiting an opportunity to oust his young rival. The sky had clouded over and somebody to the south was having a storm.

"It's been nine days between the last two," I said, still facing the window. "Last time I spoke with Adrian Foulkes he said it was like a drug. He said the highs level out, so he has to take a little bit more. And not only that, he has to take it more often." The female pigeon flew off with the young male in hot pursuit. The old one didn't bother. I turned around. "We've got to catch him, Dave. God help us, we've got to catch him."

Chapter Seven

Monday morning we still hadn't identified M4. There were old bruises on her arms and legs, and in the language of the PM she was a woman of some sexual experience, supporting my first impression that she was a prostitute. Fingerprints and dental impressions had been taken and the small amount of jewellery she was wearing – a wedding ring and a thin gold chain – was photographed. These would be circulated where appropriate in the hope of finding a match. After the usual round of meetings and deployment of the staff I collected Dave and Maggie and we locked ourselves in my office for a pow-wow.

"The Range Rover's in the clear," Dave told me. "Partner in a firm of estate agents in town. Likes to make an early start. The black one was in for a service and the garage loaned him the maroon one."

"Fair enough." I opened my notepad to a fresh page and laid a pen across it. "Outside there," I began, waving an arm towards the window, "a murder enquiry is under way. It's a routine investigation into the death of a young woman, coloured by the fact that the perpetrator has almost certainly killed three times before. We, however, are in a privileged position. We know that before this sequence of killings he – we'll call him *he* – has murdered another three people in the south. He arranged those bodies in an X, a Y and a Z, so that he could boast about them afterwards. In other words, there was a link between them all. Now, has he left a link between our killings? My guess is that he has, so have a think about it. It may not be much, and it may not help us, but we need to find it. Meanwhile, what else can we glean from the additional information we three have?"

Dave pursed his lips and Maggie looked puzzled. Dave said: "Up to now, we've been thinking that he probably lived in Yorkshire, Heckley, even. Meanwhile, the Hatfield police have been looking for someone who lives down there.

Knowing what we know, that the same person did all the murders, he probably lives in Birmingham."

"Which is a big help," I added, downbeat.

"Yep. A big help."

"Unless he's moved," Maggie suggested.

"That makes sense. There was an eighteen-month gap. Where was he then?"

"In jail?"

"Adrian thinks he's a first offender."

"Maybe he was in for something unrelated, like burglary."

"All the killings were out of doors. Burglars like to break and enter."

"In the army? Abroad? Had a job which didn't give him the opportunities? Maybe he'd fallen down a ladder and broken both legs and he spent all that time in traction. It's anybody's guess."

"You're right," I agreed, "so what we have to do is decide when to go public with all seven murders. What are the chances of the general public coming up with a list of suspects who fit in with laddo's movements: lived near Hatfield; somewhere else for over a year; then moved up here?"

"You'd get a list of suspects, all right," Maggie stated, "from all the grudge-bearers and crackpots. The Prime Minister top of the list, closely followed by Prince Charles."

"We've checked, but they were both out of the country. So if we don't publicise the fact that he's done seven, not four, we need another way to go pro-active on this one. He's gonna kill again in the next week or so. We can't just sit on our backsides while they look at ten thousand tyre prints and trace five thousand white Toyotas. He won't come to us, so we've got to take the hunt to him."

"When we identify the latest victim we might have something to go on," Dave said.

"Yes, but we might not," I argued. "It's looking as if she's a prostitute that he picked up on a street corner. I'm not an expert but I suspect that he didn't normally go with prossies. I'll ask Adrian about that."

"If he did he might not have turned to murder," Maggie interrupted.

"Perhaps not, but he did. We've asked everyone in Halifax, Huddersfield, Sheffield, Leeds, Bradford and Greater Manchester to hang on to their CCTV tapes for Friday night. When we learn where her patch was we can have a look at them, but it's a long shot, and we can't afford to wait."

"So what do you have in mind?" Dave asked.

"Going on TV again," I told him. "Another appeal. Ostensibly to try to trace the latest victim, but I leak out that we know he did the London murders. He wrote to one of the SIOs after them, so maybe we can get him writing to me. What do you think?"

"Worth a try, I suppose," Dave muttered. Displays of enthusiasm from him have all the substance of desert showers, but this was more like snowfall on Mercury.

"Well don't blow a gasket," I said.

"I think it's a great idea," Maggie said. "And it might check his momentum. He's due to kill again in a week or so, maybe if you give him something to think about he'll delay things."

"That's what I hoped," I agreed.

Dave looked thoughtful. After a few seconds he said: "When I suggested that he lived in Birmingham I wasn't exactly joking."

"I didn't think you were."

"It's possible that he drove a hundred miles south to do the first murders and now he's driving a hundred miles north."

"Yep, makes sense."

"OK. So how about this: you make the appeal, but to start with it only goes out on YTV and BBC Look North. Then, if he sees it we'll know he must live up here somewhere. If there's no response from him put it out nationwide in a day or two."

"Good idea. So you're agreed it makes sense?"

"Yep."

"Yes."

"Right. The papers will pick it up but we'll have at least twenty-four hours. You go see the press office, Maggie, and ask them to arrange it, if possible for tonight. Dave, you join the hunt to identify victim four, bearing in mind what I said about links. That's got to be top priority. Meanwhile, I'll notify the boss of what we're doing and compose my speech."

I spent a couple of hours reading reports then went for a walk through town to clear my head. I met Jeff Caton in the yard, on his way back from interviewing the man at the centre of Wednesday's racial attack. "Can we keep it out of the papers, Jeff?" I asked.

"Not sure," he replied. "He's playing the aggrieved hero. He has a defensive wound to his right hand which is genuine enough – he might lose the use of a couple of fingers – but the rest of it is decidedly fishy. There were four of them, he says, Pakistanis armed with knives, and he's given detailed descriptions of them all, right down to the makes of their trainers. He bravely fought them off but was injured in the process."

"Any witnesses?"

"His wife."

"Do we know him?"

"Yeah. Paul Usher, aged twenty-eight. He's been through the washing machine more times than a pub tea towel. All petty theft. He hangs around with younger kids, hasn't ever grown up."

"OK, keep on it."

"What about you? Anything new?"

"No, but I might be on TV tonight."

I walked into town, down the High Street and through the mall, stopping to look at trainers in a few shop windows. The weather had settled into a routine of cold, bright mornings and rainy afternoons, confusing the plants and the birds because they don't have calendars. Town was busy, as it always is, crowded with people, mainly couples, out shopping or meeting friends. Dress code for the day was shell suits for the men, fleece jackets for the women. I walked down the middle of the precinct, coat open, feeling the cool air on my stomach and hands. I like the cold. The buildings in that part of town are shops with living quarters and store rooms above them, built in Victorian times. I looked up, admiring the ornate stone and brickwork, wondering how they did it. Stone could be carved on the job, but bricks in special shapes, with curves and angles, would have to be purpose-designed and manufactured elsewhere. So was it all laid out on the floor first to make sure it fit together? I don't know, they were much cleverer than me. There were parapets around the roofs where a man could hide. A man with a gun. I scanned them as I walked, squinting into the bright sky. Last year somebody took a contract out on me. £50,000, for me dead. Is he still out there somewhere, watching and waiting? I doubt it, but I like to imagine he is. Anything is better than indifference.

I bought a mug of coffee and ham sandwich with plenty of French mustard and sat at a pavement table to eat it. A couple of retired officers saw me and we exchanged greetings. It's hard to go anywhere without meeting someone from the job, usually retired. I watched the people go by and thought about what I might say on the TV. Heckley is not a prosperous town, the good days went long ago, and they were only good for the fortunate few. But it's a friendly town. The people are ugly and overweight and speak in a vernacular as hard and abrasive as the millstone grit that tops the hills. But they hold doors open for you, and say "good morning" whether you know them or not, and if there is a mistake in your change it's just as likely to be in your favour as theirs.

And one of them kills people. Over the road from where I was sitting was a small patch of lawn with a couple of statues. A yellow council van drove over the block paving that designated the pedestrianised area and a workman extricated a lawnmower from the back of it. I watched him go through his routine: fit the grass box; remove fuel filler-cap and check the level. He gave the machine a shake to disturb the surface of the fuel and make it easier to see. Apparently there was enough in because he replaced the cap and produced the string that he used to start it. He wound it round and round a pulley and gave it a sharp pull. There was a handle, probably just a piece of wood, on the end of the string to make it easier to grip. The engine coughed but didn't start. He repeated the procedure and was lucky second time. Within seconds he was following the mower across the grass, barely able to keep up with it. The smell of newly-mown grass laced with two-stroke fumes and atomised dog turds is not my favourite perfume, so I finished my coffee and went back to the office.

We met on neutral ground, at Millgarth police station in Leeds, in a lecture theatre that they use for press conferences. YTV and the BBC co-operated fully with us and each other, agreeing to share the film, which meant that there were only two cameramen and one producer present. No press had been invited, so there'd be no questions. This was a straightforward statement and request for assistance. Our press officer was with me, and we'd prepared the statement together. I was told I could have three minutes.

I talked about the body that Gina had found on the edge of the moors, because this was the reason I'd put forward for the broadcast. We'd supplied an artist's impression of the woman and photos of her clothes and jewellery, which would be shown on the screen as I spoke. I told the viewers that she was the fourth murder that we believed had been committed by the same person and it was imperative that we find out who she was so we could bring her killer to justice.

"And now," I said, "I'd like to end on a more personal note. These deaths are a tragedy for the victims and their families, as we can all imagine, but the ripples spread much further than that. The latest body was found by a seventeen-year-old schoolgirl who had gone up on to the moor to feed some neglected ponies. She's that sort of kid. Someone any parent would be proud of, but now traumatised by what she saw up there. And it's not easy for my officers, either, and the back-up staff who are called to the scene of each crime. They have wives and families but they can't go home and talk about their day's work. So we have our own techniques for handling the pressure. For instance, the first three murders in this sequence were designated X, Y and Z, ostensibly to avoid confusion but also to remove the human aspect from the cases. We have to be dispassionate, but it isn't always easy. There is no escaping that X, Y and Z were real people who had died in horrible ways. So, if you can identify this woman, or have your suspicions about someone you know, please ring the number that will be shown at the end of this broadcast.

"And finally," I went on, "I'd like to appeal to the killer himself. So far we have received dozens of letters and calls purporting to be from you. If you do contact us, please give us some code word so we can more easily identify your approaches. It goes without saying that you need help and should give yourself up before you create more misery for yourself and others. Thank you."

Phone calls started coming in almost immediately and the letters began to arrive on Wednesday morning. Two names were suggested for the victim several times, and both were probably right. Ladies of the night often give themselves new, more erotic identities, so chances were that Naomi

Huntley and Norma Holborn were the same person. What you knew her as depended on the nature of your relationship with her, and the several men who identified her as Naomi had a marked reluctance to leave their own names.

All the mail was taken straight to the incident room. I'd supplied them with photocopies of the envelope received by the Hatfield SIO, in which the murderer had claimed the XYZ killings, and they had strict orders to look out for something similar. It arrived by the second post.

I dashed down when they rang me, closely followed by Dave. It was a long white self-sealing envelope, with the address typed slightly cock-eyed in Courier script, probably by a computer printer. "Just leave it there," I said, "until forensic have had a look at it."

Two hours later one of them, wearing latex gloves and a surgeon's mask, slit the envelope open with a scalpel and extracted the single sheet of A4 it contained. She unfolded it using a pair of tweezers and the blunt end of the scalpel and held it down on the desk. I peered over her shoulder, hold-ing my breath, but I couldn't make out the words and didn't want to go any closer.

"Could you read it, please," I asked, and she did. It said:

> *XYZ – very good! very good!*
> *You can call me The Property Developer*
> *as in the property developer has seen the possibilities*
> *ha ha ha ha ha ha ha ha ha ha*

I asked her to repeat it while I wrote it down. We'd have copies made but first the boffins would go over it with an electron microscope. If he'd as much as exhaled on the paper they'd find evidence of it.

"XYZ – so it's definitely from him," Dave said.

"You bet."

"Who's the Property Developer?"

"He is, he's the Property Developer."

"Which means what?"

"I don't know." I'd wanted more, not some enigmatic nonsense that probably had no intellectual foundation.

"So what's he saying?"

"I don't know!" I spun round, away from them, resisting the temptation to smash my fist down on a desk. "He's laughing at us," I shouted. "The bastard's laughing at us."

"Sorry," Dave said, "but you didn't expect his name and address, did you?"

"I don't know what I expected."

"Look at it this way, Charlie," Dave went on. "He's talking to you. That's got to be an improvement, hasn't it?"

We took mouth swabs from everybody we spoke to about the case. If you had a white pickup, or were in the vicinity of any of the murders, or came forward for any reason whatsoever, we asked you for either a mouth swab or six hair roots. "For elimination purposes only," of course. We had nothing to compare them with, so far, but when we had we'd be prepared.

Dave went to Leeds University with photographs and photocopies of both the envelopes and letters that the Property Developer had sent us. Graphology is the study of handwriting, but lexicography is slightly different and more scientific. It is the study of the content of a piece of writing, of the words and what they say, rather than the shape of the letters. We had no handwriting because the notes were typed on a word processor, but we did have a small amount of content. Small amounts of anything were gratefully received and analysed to destruction. He took them to the English department to let the experts have a look.

Letters and calls came flooding in after the appeal went out nationwide, but Dave's idea had paid off. Laddo's reply came after the local TV broadcast, so he must live in the North of England. This was another piece of near-worthless information that would confirm how clever we were, after some rookie PC had arrested him for peeing in the street and found his mask and club in his car boot. That's how he'd be caught, because that's where all the real policing is done: out on the streets, by the boys and girls in uniform. I had three days in the office, looking at reports, sifting information, typing names into HOLMES, checking for matches. A few came up. The trouble with requests for information is that they declare an open season for grudge-bearers. Noisy neighbours, the mentally impaired and the bloke at the office who was having it away with someone's wife all had the finger pointed at them by concerned members of the public, and we had to check every one.

A pair of Adidas Ballistics were what I finally decided on. Big Geordie took the team on training spins in the park but I elected not to join them. It would have looked bad if the press had seen us out *en bloc*, enjoying ourselves, so I trained alone. I was all in favour of the efforts we were making for several reasons. Ostensibly we were doing it for the retina blastoma unit, but, as with all these things, we'd be the ones who benefited most. It kept up the team's morale, and exercise, the harder the better, is the finest antidote to stress and depression yet discovered.

Saturday I finished at about four and went shopping. I bought the shoes and two chicken breasts. At home I seared the breasts in hot oil and put them in a casserole dish with sliced peppers, chilli beans, peas, string beans, sweetcorn, carrots, new potatoes and a tin of condensed mushroom soup. Five minutes in the microwave on *max* to heat it up, then ninety minutes on *de-frost* should do it, I thought. I changed into jogging bottoms and T-shirt and went out for a run while it cooked.

I walked to the edge of the estate, bouncing on my toes, stretching the tendons, feeling good. Once clear of the houses I did a few more stretches, rotating my shoulders and pushing against a telegraph post to stretch my hamstrings until I couldn't put it off any longer. It's about a mile and a half to the top of the hill, the road twisting and undulating all the way upward. Like they say, the first step is the hardest. I turned to face the slope and set off.

There are two schools of thought amongst distance runners. The first, favoured by the hard men, is that you listen to your body. Every stride, every breath, you feel the pain, watch out for trouble and meet it head on. If you find you are running easy, you step up the pace. Too hard, you slow down. In a race you put the pressure on when the other fellow is hurting. How do you know when he's hurting? Because that's when you're hurting. It's a savage sport, strictly for masochists.

School Two likes to think about something else. You chase dinosaurs, make love to Elizabeth Taylor, concentrate on anything but running, and hopefully next time you look up the miles have sped by under your feet and the finishing line beckons. Except it's not that easy.

I put my head down and saw the new shoes stabbing forward, the tarmac a grey blur unrolling beneath them. My breathing synchronised itself with the short strides at four strides breathing in, three out: in-two-three-four, out-two-three, in-two-three-four, out-two-three; and slowly the tiredness crept up my legs.

We'd catch him, that was for sure. But we wouldn't *detect* him. We never detect anybody. Jeff Caton had left the book on my desk, for me to read. *The Beast Must Die*, by Nicholas Blake. He said it was escapism, would take my mind off the case. I'd brought it home and left it handy. Our man wouldn't be caught by a slip of the tongue, like the narrator of the story said most villains were. We'd catch him by default, for something else, and realise who he was after the event.

My legs were wobbling and the length of my strides reduced to a shamble. I looked up and saw a short level stretch of road approaching. Thank God for that. Laddo –

ought I to be calling him the Property Developer? – had arranged the first three bodies in the XYZ formations, so that he could prove afterwards that they were his handiwork. No doubt he was making some link between the latest four murders, but what was it and would it help us if we knew? Probably not. The flat stretch soon passed under my feet and the next part was steep. I was almost running on the spot. Maybe mental arithmetic would help. There are sixty million people in the country, which we could reduce by a half by assuming he lived north of the Thames and south of the border. Thirty million. Assume he was male, fifteen million, and between twenty and forty. Five million. Chuck in all the assumptions made by Dr Foulkes and we were down to about three million. Nothing to it. All we needed was their names, a few thousand extra officers and some time.

The road levelled out and my strides lengthened. After the steep bits the long gradual slope near the top felt almost downhill. It's exposed up there, with nothing between you and the Urals. The wind was from the north-east and had an edge to it, chilling the sweat on my back. I kept going, right to the beacon at the very top, where they used to light a bonfire to warn of approaching armies, or the coronation of a new king, or, more recently, the turning of the millennium. Twenty miles to the north, on a similar hill, the peasants would see the blaze and say: "Hey, we're being invaded, or maybe we have a new king, or else it's a new millenium," and they'd hastily start to rub two sticks together to pass on the tidings, whatever they were.

Trouble was, someone was out there, someone with an aberrant brain, and fate had decreed that it was my job to find him. Millions of words have been expended on proving who Jack the Ripper was, but they were all wasted. Jack the Ripper wasn't somebody out of the history books, he was John Doe, Mr Nobody or Mr Everyman. Take your pick. Mark Twain said that Shakespeare's plays weren't written by William Shakespeare, they were written by somebody else with the same name. That's how this case felt. The Property Developer didn't do the murders, it was someone else with the same name.

It worked, I was at the top. I stopped and rested, bent over with my hands on my knees, the cold air searing my throat as my lungs dragged it in. I was knackered, but I'd done it. The track to the beacon was closed so I had to be satisfied with the lay-by and a brief rest in the shelter of the wall. There was nobody else up there, picnicking in the warmth of their Renault Megane, and for once I wished there had been. "Have you run all the way up?" they'd have asked, and I'd have smiled modestly and admitted that I had, but there was nobody at all to witness my righteousness, not even a sheep.

I spent a few moments taking in the view and letting my heart settle down to its normal rhythm. We were a five-minute drive out of Heckley, but it could have been the North Pole. The summit of the fell is a plateau, and all you can see in any direction is brown moorland for about half a mile, until it drops out of sight. It's the roof of the world, if you have a decent imagination and modest ambitions. "C'mon, legs," I said, "let's go," and started on the gentle jog back home.

The casserole was cold and uncooked when I checked it. Bugger! It looked as if I'd put it on for ninety seconds instead of ninety minutes. I gave it twenty minutes at *high* and went for a shower. This time it was done to perfection and there was enough left for Sunday lunch.

The nationals, even the Sundays, latched on to the killings with varying degrees of sensationalism but we were kept off the front pages of the tabloids by the foot-and-mouth, which topped a thousand cases that weekend. *Prostitute is victim number four* was the general tenor of the reports, and they called her Naomi Huntley because we hadn't made a positive identification of her as Norma Holborn. Nor had we released the information that three other murders were attributable to the killer, making his real tally seven. Monday morning, after troop deployment and morning prayers, I had a meeting with Dave and Maggie to discuss progress.

"No sussies over the weekend," Maggie stated.

"Thank God for that," I replied. Control had been instructed to let me know of any suspicious death anywhere in the region, but no call had disturbed my weekend.

"Either he couldn't find a suitable victim or he's gone into retirement for a while," Dave suggested.

"Dr Foulkes says he's out of control," I told them. "This time he won't stop until he's stopped, by us or someone else. We're just in a lull while he finds his next victim."

"The eye of the storm," Maggie said.

"Precisely." I turned to Dave, saying: "So what did you learn at Leeds University about the letters, if anything?"

He shook his head. "I spoke to a professor in the English department who's worked with the police before. Well, he said he has. He found the notes very interesting – fascinating, even – and said he'll let us have his conclusions as soon as possible."

"Jesus!" I cursed. "There's only about fifteen words for him to consider. Did you tell him that it was a murder hunt?"

"All the more reason for him to do it properly," Dave replied.

"And he wouldn't want somebody doing time because he'd condemned them for using the past pluperfect where it should have been the present bloody indicative, would he? What about the quotation, if it is one? Did he recognise that?"

"No."

"I thought not. Let's have a look at them ourselves." I pulled a photocopy of the two notes out of my drawer and Maggie unpinned one from the office wall. "Right, Mags," I said. "What do you see?"

She held the page between her fingertips as she studied it. "Done on a computer," she informed us, after a few seconds. "Set to centralise the printing."

"Good. What else?"

"The spelling is correct, which is probably unusual in notes from psychopaths, but his punctuation is erratic and he uses capital letters in some places and not in others." She paused for a while, and started seeing pieces of information in the note that had not been immediately visible to her. "He's computer literate," she continued, "and has that tendency to use small case letters that most nerds have, but he uses capitals when he calls himself the Property Developer. Maybe there's a deep psychological reason for that, or maybe it's just his inconsistency."

"OK," I said. "Well done, but let's leave the deep psychological stuff for Dr Foulkes. Does anything leap off the page?"

Dave said: "He uses capitals for Eye Of The Storm, as if it's the title of something. Maybe the line about property developers is a quote from something called 'Eye Of The Storm'."

"It does have a certain scansion about it."

"Yes."

"But your man at Leeds didn't recognise it?"

He shook his head. "No."

"Perhaps it was too lowbrow for him. You're the pub quiz whiz-kids, so this is your chance to put all that knowledge to use," but now they both shook their heads. "OK," I continued. "Let me tell you this. 'Eye Of The Storm' may be the title of a book or a poem or a song. We're agreed on that?" They nodded. "Right. In England we would normally write a title like that with small case letters for the little words, like *of* and *the*. However, in America they usually use upper case letters for all the words in a title. I just thought I'd share that with you."

"You mean, he's an American?"

"Not necessarily. If you get used to seeing titles printed like that there's a tendency to adopt the convention because there's a logic in it. It makes sense. I think the book or whatever is probably American."

Maggie looked puzzled, pursing her lips and pressing the end of a pencil into her chin. "How do you know something like that?" she asked.

"Um, it's a long story," I replied.

"We'd love to hear it."

"No you wouldn't."

"Oh yes we would, wouldn't we, Dave?"

"I'm falling off my chair with anticipation."

"Right. OK. Well, long time ago, when I was very young – at Art College, actually – somebody bought me a guitar and the Bert Weedon instruction book for a birthday present." I shrugged my shoulders, saying: "Everybody was doing it, those days."

"I wasn't," Dave said.

"Nor me," Maggie added.

"Well everybody with any talent. There were these books called *Sing Out!* which had all the words and music in them, and the titles were written like I said, with capital letters. They were considered terribly left wing and subversive, so when I joined the police my musical career went on hold. Otherwise, I might have been the next, um, Craig Douglas."

"Is this when you went through your Dylan phase?" Maggie asked.

"He's still in his Dylan phase," Dave growled.

Jeff Caton's face appeared at the window of my partitioned-off office and he made a knocking gesture, his knuckles not quite making contact with the glass. I waved for him to come in.

"Am I interrupting?" he asked, and I assured him that he was rescuing me from further embarrassing disclosures about my youth. Jeff was handling all the other crime while I was bogged down with the murders.

"We're neglecting you, Jeff," I told him. "I've wanted a word. What's happening on the streets of Heckley that I should know about?"

"All fully under control, Chas. Nothing at all for you to concern yourself with. I came in to ask about the Three Peaks. Are we doing it up and down the steps, or what?"

"Depends on the foot-and-mouth," Dave told him, "but it's looking like the stairs to me. This lot'll get worse before it gets better."

"Big Geordie's in charge," I said.

"I know," Jeff replied. "I've just been talking to him. Apparently he's organised some corporate sponsorship from the supermarkets and they've offered to supply drinks and stuff. It's looking good, if we can do it, but it'll be tough up and down the stairs – a lot tougher than the real thing."

"Which is why some of us are in strict training," I told him. I slid the photocopy of the first letter towards him, saying: "Have you ever heard of a song or book called that?"

"Eye of the Storm?"

"Mmm."

"No."

"Well thanks for trying."

"There's 'Riders on the Storm', by Jim Morrison."

"This is 'Eye of the Storm'."

"'Fraid not."

"Ne'er mind."

"Have you tried the Internet?"

I looked at Maggie and Dave. "Why didn't we think of that?" I asked.

Dave cleared his throat, saying: "I was just about to mention it."

"I bet you were. Thanks, Jeff, you've saved the day. Now, what's happening about the Pakistanis who attacked that youth? I see you've managed to keep it out of the papers."

"Ah!" he responded. "That is one small piece of grit in the Vaseline of Mr Wood's life. I went to the *Gazette* and asked them not to print it because it was definitely dodgy, and they agreed. However, his solicitor has just called the front desk wanting to know the crime number and the name of the investigating officer, because the little scrote is making a claim for criminal injuries. Gilbert will have apoplexy when he hears."

"Is this the youth who claims he was attacked by four Pakis?" Maggie asked.

"He's twenty-eight, but yes, that's him."

"And what's dodgy about it?"

"Just that the four Pakis don't exist and his chief witness is his wife. She has form stretching back to bullying at school, mugging and ABH on a neighbour. Word is that they are always arguing and had the mother and daddy of a row on the night in question, but nobody will make a statement on the record. We reckon she went for him with the carving knife and they're making the best of it."

"What's he called?" Dave asked.

"Paul Usher."

"And what's she called?"

"Maria-Helena."

He sat up at the mention of the name. "She wouldn't be Maria-Helena Smith, would she, of the Sylvan Fields Smiths?"

"That's her. Violence is a way of life with them and none of the neighbours dare say a dicky bird."

Dave poked his tongue into his cheek and stroked his chin, pondering on his next move. "Want me to sort it?" he said, eventually.

"How?" Jeff asked.

"Whoa!" I said, slamming my chair down on to all four legs and holding up a restraining hand. "Just what have you in mind?"

"Nothing too illegal, indecent or dishonest," Dave replied. "You bring Usher in for an interview and find out where his wife will be at the time. After I've had a quiet word with her I'd be very surprised if she didn't withdraw her statement."

Everybody was looking at me. Sometimes, an ounce of local knowledge is worth all the highfalutin' expertise you can throw at a case. Having all the acronyms in the alphabet backing you up is no substitute for a pair of eyes on the street and experience of the people you are dealing with. But there were risks, too. The Paul Ushers of the world had a good grasp of what we could do and what we couldn't, plus free legal advice on tap. They knew their rights, as they often reminded us, and had little to lose and much to gain by turning the tables on the police. And then there was his wife, Maria-Helena. We had her safety to think of, too.

"No," I said. "It's too risky."

We didn't have access to the Internet at the station because of fear of collecting a virus. For the same reason it is forbidden to bring diskettes from home or take any home. Command and control at HQ have access but they'd have wanted to know what it was all about and I was wary of leaks. Normally I'd have seen someone I knew in the pornography squad and done it on the QT, but Dave said that his son, Daniel, was at home on a revision day, so the three of us went to see him. He haggled like a Moroccan souk trader but I stuck out at minimum wage and he agreed to help us. Dave fetched three more chairs and arranged them behind Dan's.

"Which search engine do you want to use?" Dan asked.

"You tell us, we're paying you enough." He clicked a button and the screen was filled with advertising bumph.

"What are we looking for?"

"Try *Eye of the Storm*, please." He typed *eye* and *storm* into the box and clicked the search button. Within seconds we had a list of references. They included a couple to do with hurricane tracking, a company that made horse drawn carriages and book about a day in the life of Jesus. "That could be interesting," I said, pointing to the book – the Bible is the favoured reading of most serial killers. There was another site to do with the Florida presidential election and one that proclaimed: *Eye Of The Storm; the legend of Tim Roper*. "Print them out, please," I said, and Daniel leaned past me to switch on the printer.

"What next?" he asked when the printer had stopped.

"Try *Property Developer*," I said and within seconds we were staring at another list names and references. It started with a couple of books about how to make millions out of property developing, and was followed by dozens of companies who had probably done just that, with or without the book. They were mainly in the Far East, as far east as Australia and New Zealand, with a preponderance in Malaysia.

"They don't look very helpful," Dave said.

"There's hundreds of them," Daniel told us, and demonstrated by paging through a seemingly endless list. "Same with *Eye of the Storm* – there'd have been lots more."

"Try *XYZ*," I suggested. When it came up all we had was a predictable list of more companies, consultants and productions that had all chosen the name in an effort to stand out in their local telephone directory. The only intriguing item was details of a John Adams speech in 1797 about "the XYZ affair."

"Print us the first three or four pages of every reference we've looked at, please, Dan," I said, "and I think we'll have that one in full, plus the Jesus one." I pointed at the John Adams entry.

"Before that," Maggie interrupted, "can we have a quick look at this, please." She'd been studying the list that Dan had printed earlier, and now she was holding it in front of him, pointing at the name of Tim Roper. Dan back-paged several times until he was there, adjusted the mouse until a little fist appeared above the name and left-clicked it. The middle of screen went blank and I watched the blue bar

slowly extend in its little box, like the mercury in a ther-
mometer. It was probably coming all the way from America,
so I told myself to be patient.

*Eye Of The Storm*, it said. *Welcome to the official Tim
Roper and The LHO website*. There was a menu across the
bottom of the page and Dan clicked on *Tim*. A photo started to unfold, strip by strip, until we were looking at a clean-
shaven, handsome boy with long hair, wearing a T-shirt. He
was leaning forward, looking at the camera, with an electric
guitar across his body. *Tim Roper*, it said, *1944 to 1969 –
elegido por Dios*.

"He was quite a dish," Maggie observed.

"And died young," Dave added.

"What does that mean, Dan?" I asked, pointing at the
screen.

"*Chosen by God*."

"Thanks. It must be nice to be educated."

"It's OK."

"Let's see some more."

Tim Roper, we learned, was a singer-songwriter in Los
Angeles, forming his group, The LHO, in 1960 while at high
school. He earned fame of a sort for his anti-war lyrics and
his stance against commercialism, and died of gunshot
wounds in mysterious circumstances while being investigated by the CIA for un-American activities. His most famous
song was 'Eye Of The Storm' but he was believed to have
written one called 'Theo's Tune', which went to number one
in several charts in the winter of 1969, after his death.

I read it all twice, then said: "Click *The songs*, please."

The screen unfolded and there it was, near the bottom of
the list. "Oh my God," Dave whispered. "Oh my God. It's
there, look."

Chapter Eight

Tim Roper had written a song called 'The Property Developer'. We stared at the words, expecting them to blossom before our eyes into some multi-coloured fire-breathing shape with horns and a tail. Dan broke the silence. "Want to hear one?" he asked.

We did. It took nearly a minute to download, then the tapping of a cowbell slowly filled the room, followed by a twangy guitar and a keyboard. When he started singing he had a strained contralto voice like syrup being squeezed through a syringe. Neil Young on a bad day. He sang:

> *This is the eye of the storm*
> *Watch out for that needle, Son*
> *'Cos this is the eye of the storm...*

We'd been crowded around the computer in Dan's bedroom, and it suddenly felt oppressive in there. I stood up and went downstairs, the high voice following me until I closed the kitchen door and shut it off. I filled a cup with water from the tap and drank it. As the first words of the song came out of the little speakers the sweat on my spine had changed to ice. It was a voice from the grave, and thirty-two years later and six thousand miles away someone had been inspired by it. Inspired enough to kill seven strangers.

I went through into the front room and sat in an easy chair, waiting for the others to come downstairs.

By lunchtime next day we had our own Internet access in the incident room, plus transcriptions and photocopies of every lyric and poem Tim Roper had composed. We even had recordings of the songs themselves, kindly downloaded by Daniel and put on CD ROMs for us. He was probably breaking all sorts of copyright law but I granted him a dispensation. I shared out the song sheets and several of us spent the rest of the day poring over them. There was no contact address on the website and nobody in the office knew how to trace such things, so we handed that little problem to our technical department.

Most of the lyrics were fairly typical Sixties anti-establishment stuff that I'd happily have sung along with back in those days. Some of the later stuff was more poisonous, advocating bombing schools and shooting politicians. When I listened to them performed, however, the anger came over but the actual words were lost in the wall of sound. Most modern rap records were probably just as violent, had you been able to hear and consider the words. One or too had an uncanny topicality. What goes around comes around:

> You're dead, Mr Businessman
> Your shares won't repair
> The hole in your brain
> And the Oval Office
> Will make a place
> For dogs to sleep
> An' feel at home.

The phone rang, startling me. At the back of my mind was the fear that another body was lying somewhere, waiting for an unsuspecting jogger or dog-walker to find it. Every time the phone rang I hesitated, my hand hovering over it as I said a little prayer. This time it was the lab, and I heaved another sigh of relief. They told me that the letter from the killer had probably been printed on a Hewlett Packard 600 series printer. The paper transfer rollers leave evidence of their action behind and the paper rack leaves indents on the bottom edge of each sheet. The spacings were consistent with the HP, and that's all they could tell me. No DNA. No prints. When we caught him it would be another piece of circumstantial evidence, but it wouldn't help us catch him.

Five minutes later it was ringing again. This time I learned that Naomi had been positively identified as Norma Holborn, aged 33, a convicted prostitute who worked in Manningham Lane, Bradford. I gave our press office permission to release her name and sent someone to collect the CCTV tapes.

Tim Roper had written a series of short poems called *What Did You Do In The War, Dad?* My favourite was called *#23*, although there were only eight of them. It read:

> *You never saw a German or a Jap,*
> *but you had to zap someone*
> *You spread your seed from a lower altitude*
> *And ignored the moans of only one.*

Put Tim's mother in the family way, that's what Dad did in the war. Dr Foulkes might find something of interest in that fact and the effect it could have on an impressionable small boy, but it wasn't much help to me. I was working at a spare desk in the main office, because my little one gives me claustrophobia and it's noisy if I have the window open. I can't hear myself think for the pigeons cooing. Pete Goodfellow came over and asked me if I'd like a coffee.

"Please," I replied.

"Any joy?"

"Nah, not that I'm expecting any. His dad didn't go off to fight in World War Two, and he'd have liked him to have been a hero. Big deal. You?"

"Not much. Hogans are what Navajo Indians live in, and *Tents of Kedar* is a biblical reference, that's all. Haven't found any others."

"Don't tell me: Revelations. That's where all the nutters' Bibles fall open."

"Actually, it's the Song of Solomon."

"Well that's a change. Have you had a look?"

"Mmm. Doesn't mean a thing to me."

"Well it won't to me, that's for sure."

"Have you seen this morning's *UK News*?" Pete asked.

"About Madame LeStrang? Yeah, I saw it." Julia LeStrang was a self-styled psychic and a charlatan with a taste for publicity.

"She says she can help find the killer. Claims she told us where to find Georgina Dewhurst's body."

I felt my hands start to shake, like they had the day I'd slit open the bag that contained what had once been a delightful little girl. "The person who put it there told us where to find Georgina's body," I said, my voice almost a growl, "and if that old witch starts causing trouble by going round upsetting people, resurrecting ghosts, she'll be hearing from me."

"Right. I'll, er, make that coffee."

I moved back to my office and found an envelope in the bottom drawer. Inside it was a school photograph of Georgina wearing a blouse and striped tie, giving a gap-toothed smile at the camera. She'd been eight years old when her stepfather smothered her, and I'd found her body wrapped in a bin-liner in a rat-infested workshop at a disused coalmine. My wife was pregnant when she left me but I didn't know. I found out by accident, after her new boyfriend had signed the consent forms at the clinic. Eight would have been the same age as... Ah well, I thought, no point in going down that road again. I placed the picture back in its envelope and slid it under the files as Pete came in with my coffee.

Things were moving so I rang my opposite numbers at Hatfield and Hendon and arranged a meeting with them at the police training college. Chief Superintendent Natrass was on leave but Martin agreed to represent him. Not wanting to be too outnumbered, and preferring some company on a long drive, I took Maggie along.

We'd prepared files containing details of the Norma Holborn murder, the Property Developer note and transcripts of everything Tim Roper had ever written. Maggie handed them out as they fumbled in pockets for spectacles and cautiously opened the files.

"Does the Property Developer mean anything?" one of them asked as he reached that part.

"It's the name of a song," I replied.

"Property development – location, location, location," Martin said, presumably because it came into his head and he had nothing else to contribute. I looked at Maggie and she pulled a face.

It all fell a bit flat. They thanked me for keeping them informed and wished me the best of luck, but the hidden message was that it was on my patch, now. As I negotiated the junction of the M25 with the M1 and settled back for a three-hour blast northwards I said: "Well that was a waste of time, wasn't it?"

"I can say I've been to Hendon," Maggie replied, "and that's about it."

"I'll put you down for a course, any time you want," I told her.

"Yeah!" she exclaimed, "and put me down for a divorce at the same time, please."

"Is it that bad?"

"No, not really, but Tony gets a bit fed up when he has to cook his own meals. Schoolteachers have pressures on them, too, you know."

"So I believe."

We listened to the news and Maggie tried to find some decent music but couldn't, so we settled for talking.

"What about you?" Maggie asked. "Haven't noticed you coming in reeking of aftershave lately, or wearing your best shirts to work."

I shook my head and laughed. "It's not only the farmers who are having a lean time," I told her.

"Have you heard from Annette since she left?"

"No." Annette was one of my DCs, and I'd disregarded

the golden rule about becoming involved with a fellow officer. She had hair like a forest fire, and freckles and green
eyes, and I'd thought: stuff the rules.

"That's a shame. I thought you'd found it with Annette.
She's a nice girl."

"Yeah, well."

Maggie was quiet for a while, then she said, hesitantly: "I,
er, never really thought that, you know, Annabelle was for
you. She was an attractive woman, beautiful, but, I never
thought, you know... I'm sorry. Tell me to mind my own
business."

I smiled at the memories. Annabelle was the first long-
term relationship I'd had since my divorce. She was beautiful and sophisticated, the widow of a bishop, and far too
classy for me. We'd helped each other out of a difficult
patch, then gone our separate ways. I said: "Maggie, my love
life is your business. You've been sorting it out for me for
the last twelve years. I never thought Annabelle was for me,
either. It was an extremely pleasant interlude, but I always
knew it would end. It was just the manner of it that was
upsetting. I was very fond of Annette, still am, but it wasn't
to be. She had a boyfriend and he had two small daughters,
and she wanted to play happy families. I couldn't compete."

"I don't think I'd want to take on another woman's children," Maggie stated.

"It was her choice."

"It's a big gamble. Would you have her back?"

"Annette? Yes, I'd have Annette back. Not Annabelle,
though. Annette never cheated on me. I knew the score
right from the start."

We were streaking past Leicester Forest services when my
phone rang, jolting me out of my reverie and sending that
familiar trickle of iced water down my spine. I'd left word
that I didn't want any calls at all, unless it was urgent.

"Priest," I said, easing into the slow lane.

"That you, Charlie?" the voice asked. It took me a second

or two to realise it was Nigel Newley.

"Hello, Nigel. What can we do for you?"

"Hi, Boss. You're not in at home so I thought I'd chance your mobile. Where are you?"

I have a reputation for not switching my mobile on. I don't belong to the instant communications, anywhere, anytime, generation. There's a time and a place for everything, and telephones should be screwed to desks in offices. Mobiles are tolerable in an emergency. "Coming up the M1," I replied. "What's it about?"

"Just thought you'd like to know that a friend of yours was arrested a couple of hours ago."

"Who's that?"

"Graham Allen."

"Graham Allen? Remind me."

"Ex-boyfriend of Colinette Jones."

"I have him. What's he done?"

"Not sure of the details, but nobody from Heckley was available when the call came, so we have him downstairs on an assault with intent charge. He beat up his next-door neighbour. We'll be holding him until tomorrow so there's no hurry, but I thought you'd like to know."

"You bet I'd like to know," I said, but expecting me to wait until the next day was like asking an orphan to save his Easter egg until Whitsuntide. I told Nigel that I'd be there in an hour and I'd appreciate it if he'd clear the way for me to have a word with young Mr Allen. I offered to drop Maggie off but she insisted in coming along. Poor Tony would have to wait for his tea again.

When I joined the force Halifax nick was a Victorian building in the middle of town, built when labour was cheap and ornamentation was included in the price. Proportion erred towards solid rather than graceful, but in the event of an earthquake they would be the buildings left standing. Burgeoning business and increased technology revealed the old building's shortcomings, and the move was made to a modern police station on the edge of the town centre. Land prices may have been an influential factor too, but I'm not cynical enough to follow that argument. The rush hour had ended and the thought of another meeting with handsome Graham had injected a certain urgency into my driving, so we were there in quicksticks. I parked in the spot reserved for the chief constable's annual visit and took the steps two at a time.

The arresting detective had kindly waited for me and he told us what it was all about. Graham had been told not to say a word without his solicitor present, but when I heard his story it sounded reasonable. He'd gone round to his parents' house to collect any mail that might be for him and seen the next-door neighbour, called Neville Ferriby, locking the door behind him as he left. That was fair enough, because Mr Ferriby had been given a key by Graham's parents so he could water a rather large magnolia in the conservatory. But Graham claimed he had suspicions that the neighbour was overstepping his brief, so he'd laid a trap for him. He'd left a long blonde hair from his girlfriend across the door to his parent's bedroom, and when he checked he found it had been dislodged. Graham then went next door to challenge the neighbour, things got out of hand and Mr Ferriby found himself paying an unscheduled visit to Heckley General A & E department with a broken nose and facial bruising.

When the custody officer went to give Graham his routine check Maggie and I accompanied him. He unlocked the cell door and we stood there looking at a young man who was a shadow of the cocksure fellow we'd interviewed three weeks earlier. The hair was greasy and had lost its bounce, as had the rest of him. Prison changes a man, but he'd only been in for four hours. Maybe the problem was the pale blue one-piece disposable suit he was wearing. As far as I knew none of the major fashion houses were making them yet, but stick a decent label on, charge a hundred and fifty quid, and they'll soon be all over the place.

"Hello Graham," I said. "We've met before, I'm Inspector Priest from Heckley CID." I'd never get used to the Acting Chief Inspector bit. "Now I know you don't want to talk to us without legal representation, and I respect that, but as you know I'm investigating the death of Colinette. Do you mind if I ask a few questions regarding that enquiry?"

He was sitting on his bunk, elbows on knees, looking up at me. He shrugged his shoulders, which I took as assent. "What made you suspicious that Neville Ferriby was snooping round your parents' house?" I asked. He brushed a lank lock off his forehead while he wondered if this was a trick question. "This is off the record," I told him, "and nobody's writing anything down."

"I just thought he was," he replied, eventually.

"What put the idea in your mind?"

"I don't know."

"Something must have done." I started to ask if he'd seen him snooping around or spying on them, then realised I'd be putting my words into his mouth. "Think about it," I said.

"Once," he began. "Years ago. I was still at school. It was a hot day and I knew Mum would be sunbathing in the garden. I sneaked in the back way. There's a ginnel runs along the bottoms of the gardens. I was going to put the lawn sprinkler on to give her a surprise, or something, but I saw him, up in his bedroom window. He was spying on her, with his binoculars. That's all."

"And you've never liked him since."

"No."

"Did you tell anyone?"

"No."

"Did he ever make any approaches or advances to your mother or yourself?"

"No."

"In the summer before you finished with Colinette your parents held a barbecue, I believe."

"They were always holding them. That's how they live in

Spain. Dad's a barbecue freak."

"Mr Ferriby was at this one, with his video camera."

"They used to invite the neighbours in case the smoke or the music upset them. They weren't friends or anything. Ferriby was a camera bore. You know the type, thought he was Lord Lichfield. He keeps fish, as well."

"As well as what?" I asked, deadpan. "As well as Lord Lichfield keeps fish or as well as being a camera bore?"

"As well as being a camera bore," he replied without a flicker of a smile.

"Right. He took some film of Colinette," I told him. "Her mother has it. Did you know about it?"

"No. He must have given it to Colly sometime when she came round to see Mum. She often did."

"But you didn't know about it?"

"No."

"OK. Thanks for talking to us. I'm sure the magistrate will sort you out in the morning."

He called her Colly. It was the only display of any semblance of affection he'd shown towards poor Colinette, and it took sitting in a prison cell, feeling sorry for himself, to drag that out of him. We bought fish and chips and mushy peas and took them round to Maggie's house. Tony had laid the table for us, warmed the plates and had a pot of strong tea mashing as we arrived. Mobile phones do have their uses.

"London, was it, today?" he asked as he handed me the ketchup.

"Hendon," I replied. "We borrowed an office at the training college."

"About these murders?"

"That's right."

"So what do they know about them?"

"We took them copies of the files, to see if anyone had anything similar in their division."

"And had they?"

"They'll let us know."

I cleaned my plate but declined a slice of fruitcake and another cup of tea and left. My appetite was down and the atmosphere in the house was tense, like there were land-mines under the carpet and one wrong foot would cause an explosion. I have big feet. It was still daylight as I drove home through the empty town centre, and on an impulse I turned into the station yard and went up to the office. One day these impulses will get me into bother.

I found last year's diary, jotted down a number from the back and dialled it. After two rings a female voice that might have been at the next desk said: "Federal Bureau of Investigation, how can I help you?"

"This is Acting Chief Inspector Charlie Priest, speaking from England," I told her. "Could you possibly put me through to Agent Mike Kaprowski, please?"

She checked the name with me, consulted her lists and made the connection. Got him first time, surely a world record. "Charlie!" he boomed in my ear. "How're ya doin? Don't tell me – you're comin' over."

"I'm fine, Mike," I told him, "but far too busy for a holi-day." We joshed with each other like old pals, which felt com-pletely natural even though our friendship was based solely on a few telephone calls. It was impossible not to compare the ease with which I talked with him against the stiffness of my conversations with Natrass and Martin. After a couple of minutes on generalities I told him about the murders.

"Four, possibly seven, you reckon?" he said.

"That's right. He's written to us twice to confirm he's the killer, but nothing very enlightening. However, he quotes from old song lyrics, and we've traced them to someone called Tim Roper. Ever heard of him?"

"Tim Roper? New one on me, Charlie. What era are we talking about?"

"Ours, Mike. Roper was born in 1944 and died of gunshot wounds in 1969. In California. He was under investigation for un-American activities and rumour is that the CIA killed him, so there's a good chance you have a file on him."

"Charlie," he interjected, "we've got a file on the Partridge Family. Jee-sus, we've got a file on Billy Graham. They were heady times, back then."

"I'd appreciate anything you can find for me." We exchanged email addresses and then I spent five minutes assuring him that England wasn't sinking under a mountain of rotting animal carcasses and that the average citizen wouldn't know anything about foot-and-mouth and BSE if it wasn't for the sensationalist newspapers. It was a lie, but it helped redress the balance.

At home I poured a can of Sam Smith's into my best pint glass and put on the Tim Roper tape:

> *She's eighteen an' he's forty-four*
> *His gown is hangin' at the back o' the door*
> *He peels a bill from the wad on his hip*
> *Who is the judge an' who is the whore?*
>
> *You're at the bottom an' he's at the top*
> *He'll take his cut an' he'll never stop*
> *The only thing he won't take is lip*
> *Who is the thief an' who is the cop?*
>
> *Another deal is going down*
> *Just sign a cheque to buy renown*
> *To those who have it shall be given*
> *'Cos all is well in Tinsel Town.*

So much for the American Dream, I thought, but at least no one had ever called Tim Roper the New Dylan. I went to bed early and thought about Annette in the hope that I'd dream about her, but it didn't work. It never does.

"Suspects," the assistant chief constable said. "Do we have any suspects?"

Mr Wood's secretary came in carrying a tray with three coffees on it, giving me a few precious seconds to think of a number. I saw Gilbert glance towards his drawer where he keeps the chocolate digestives, but he decided that this was not the time.

As the door closed behind her I said: "We have a list of one hundred and four possibles, namely resulting from vehicle sightings and comparison with lists of known offenders. Unfortunately psychiatric evidence says that our man is a first timer, so he could be totally unknown to us. At the moment I have two officers studying video tapes of the last victim's usual territory, and hopefully they'll find something."

"Hopefully's not good enough, Charlie. We need something more positive than that."

"I'm open to suggestions," I said.

The ACC flung a copy of the *Gazette* on Gilbert's desk. The headline read: *Latest Victim Named*, and the page was divided into two linked stories. One was about Norma Holborn and her bleak life, the other was an assertion from Madame LeStrang that she could help find the killer. "What about *her*?" he demanded. "What have you done about *her*?"

"Madame LeStrang?" I asked, incredulous.

"Yes."

"Nothing."

"Why not?"

"Because it's complete bloody balderdash, that's why not."

Gilbert said: "Charlie…" and reached a restraining hand towards me. The ACC, his face white, tapped his fingertips together several times, composing his argument.

"My wife," he began, "once attended a seminar held by Madame LeStrang. She heard things there, things about herself, that were beyond belief. Personal things that Madame LeStrang could not possibly have known about. There are stranger things in heaven and earth, Charlie, than you or I ever dreamed of."

"She's a clever lady, Sir," I said. "That I've never doubted, but she does not have supernatural powers."

"Give her a try, eh. We've nothing to lose, have we?"

Only our marbles, I thought. "Right, Sir," I said, rising to my feet. "Is that everything?"

"No. Sit down, please."

I sat down.

"There's been a lot in the papers lately about institution-alised racism in the service," he said.

"Resulting from the Macpherson report," I replied.

"That's right. And the situation is tense in Heckley, I hear. This case involving the young man stabbed by the gang of Pakistanis hasn't helped. It isn't enough to be fair, Charlie, we've got to be seen to be fair, applying the law without fear or favour. Know what I mean?"

"No."

Gilbert rolled his eyes and looked away.

"What I mean, Charlie, is this: any form of racism will not be tolerated, and anyone who doesn't like it can get out."

I said: "That's exactly my attitude, Sir."

"I'm glad to hear it, but it works both ways, y'know. I want this stabbing case cleared up, no matter what the outcome. Black offences against white are just as intolerable as white on black."

"We tend to just regard them as offences, Sir," I replied.

"Good. Good. So let's have some results, eh?"

I unwound slowly from the chair, in case he told me to sit down again, but he didn't. I turned to go, then turned back to face him. "There's this group in Heckley," I began. "Fascists. Nazis. Call them what you will. Their sworn aim is to deport all the Blacks, all the Asians and, believe it or not, all the plumbers."

He looked at me, puzzled. "*Plumbers*, did you say?"

"That's right. Plumbers."

"Why on earth do they want to deport all the plumbers?"

"No idea," I replied, shaking my head and turning

towards the door again. Out of the corner of my eye I saw
Gilbert bury his face in his hands.

Nigel Newley was sitting in the main office, with one or two
of the others. He was wearing a pair of lightweight headphones
plugged into a Walkman and had a silly grin on his face.

Dave looked at me and said: "Blimey, you look grim. I
take it he wasn't handing out medals."

"No," I replied. "I think I've just had a bollocking. He
wants an arrest, soon, and he wants the Paul Usher stabbing
clearing up – *without fear or favour*."

"I've offered to sort it," Dave replied.

I thought about things for a few seconds, then asked: "If
his wife withdrew her statement how would she explain it to
him?"

"She's a resourceful girl," he told me. "She'd think of
something, and according to Jeff *he's* scared stiff of her family so he wouldn't dare lay a finger on her."

"It sounds as if you've already discussed it."

"Um, maybe."

"No comebacks?"

"None at all."

"OK, when you get the time, but don't do anything silly."
I turned to Nigel and shouted in his face: "What are you listening to!"

He pulled the headphones off with a grimace and poked
a finger in an ear. "This," he replied, shoving an empty cassette case towards me. It was from the Tim Roper tape.

"I thought you were more into string quartets," I told
him.

"Baroque. It's just this one track, it brings back memories."

"You mean – you've heard one? Nobody else has. Which
is it?"

He rewound the tape and transferred the cassette to the
portable stereo on Pete Goodfellow's desk. "This one," he
replied. "We had an American teacher for a year and she

taught us this. She was over on an exchange, or something. A Fulbright, perhaps. Platinum blonde, looked like something out of *Baywatch*. We had to stand up and do all the actions. I think that was the first time I fell in love."

"How old were you?" Pete asked.

"Thirty-three," Dave interjected.

"Six or seven," Nigel told him. He pressed the button and the combined voices of Tim's band, The LHO, filled the room:

> *One two, buckle my shoe*
> *Uncle Joe is stuck in the glue*
> *Two three, he'll never get free*
> *As long as he sits there in that tree*
> *Call the fireman, call the vet*
> *Call the doctor but not just yet.*

"C'mon then, Nigel," I urged, "let's see the actions." He blushed and shook his head.

> *Three four, lock the door*
> *Sister Mary just ate the floor*
> *Four five, saints alive!*
> *Sister Mary is learning to jive*

Dave jumped up and started twisting, standing on one leg, fists pumping to the beat. Pete clapped his hands in time with him.

> *Five six, take big licks*
> *Uncle Joe is practising tricks*
> *Seven eight, cats in a crate*
> *He'll make them vanish if you can wait*
> *Some are dancers and some play ball*
> *And all the others are much too tall.*
> *Eight nine, fish in a line*
> *Each one dressed in a coat so fine*

*Nine ten, I'll tell you when*
*You can bring your apricot hen*
*Come on an elephant, ride on a donkey*
*Come in a buggy with a wheel that's wonky.*

None of us was quite sure at which point the ACC came into the office. I saw Pete's eyes going round like a fruit machine and twisted in my seat to look behind me. Nigel clicked the off button and Dave sat down again, colour rising from under his collar. Maggie had been watching and listening with amused tolerance. "That's not listed as Tim and The LHO," she said, still unaware of the presence of God's first lieutenant, "but it sounds like them. It's called 'Theo's Tune' on the album and credited to Blue Coyote, whoever they are."

"Hello, Mr Pritchard," I said, too loudly, rising to my feet. "This is the music that we think inspires the killer. The letters he's written to us contain quotes from it. Maybe there's something in there that will lead us to him. We're just familiarising ourselves with the lyrics."

"Right," he said. "Right. I'm a James Last man, myself. You can't beat a good melody, I always say. I thought I'd pop in to say how much we appreciate all the hard work you're all putting in during these difficult times. I know it's not easy and family life suffers, but we wouldn't have joined the force if we thought it would be easy, would we? So good luck, and let's hope we soon have a change in fortune."

Everybody mumbled a thank you and I saw him out of the door. When I rejoined them Pete said: "Shit."

"Sorry, Chas," Dave added.

"He'll get over it," I said. "So where were we?"

Pete looked at Nigel, asking: "Did Miss Texas 1949 tell you who played it, Nigel? We had a teacher in junior school, Miss Kesteven, who used to bring records in, but nothing like that. It was stuff like *The Young Person's Guide to the Orchestra*, or *Peter and the Wolf*. She was nice, Miss Kesteven, used to come and sit next to me when we did..."

"Yes, Peter," Maggie interrupted. "We're talking about the case, not regressing into childhood, and we'd rather not know what you and Miss Kesteven got up to."

Nigel shook his head. "No, she never said who it was by."

"It's a bit different to all the others," I said. "Catchy. It's a children's tune. Maybe they released it under another name because they thought it would destroy their credibility."

"Like Paul McCartney and 'Mull of Kintyre'," Pete suggested.

"Something like that."

I saw the latest copy of the *Gazette* on a nearby desk so I retrieved it and spread it in front of Pete. "We've got to consult her," I said, tapping the photograph of Julia LeStrang, resplendent in a flowing cloak and enough gold ornamentation to plate an aircraft carrier. "It's a major new initiative inspired by the ACC's wife."

"You're joking!" was their collective response.

"'Fraid not. Drop her a line, please, Pete, from the ACC's office. Make a list of precise map references of the places where the bodies of our victims were found and say that you hope this will be useful. It might keep her quiet for a day or two. Apologise for being unable to supply any belongings of the deceased's because they are all held under our connected property rules, then slam it to HQ for him to sign."

"If you say so," Pete replied.

"I do." Turning to Dave and Maggie I said: "OK, now tell me all about the breakthroughs you've had from the videos. How many white pickups have you seen?"

Checking the tapes from the CCTV cameras was a tedious job. There were thirty hours of them, taken in the Manningham area on the night of Norma's death. Maggie and Dave had watched about a quarter, fast forwarding through the blank bits, stopping to make a note of every vehicle or person who wandered into focus. All the descriptions and any registration numbers would go into the computer and we'd finish with a list that included punters and local people, possible suspects and the totally innocent, with equal conviction. So far they hadn't seen any white pickups and there'd been no sign of Norma.

I drove over to the posh side of town, where Graham Allen's parents retreated when the tourists became intolerable on the Costa. They weren't home, as I expected, so I had a good look round the outside of the house.

The magnolia in the conservatory was wilting and the lawn needed cutting. A bricked-off area near the fence marked the place where the famous barbecues were held, although there wasn't a trace of ash or smoke staining. No doubt the contraption itself was one of those great hibatchi things with gas bottles and variable settings – an Aga on wheels – and would be parked securely in the garage. I was just nosey-parkering, not looking for anything in particular, wondering how the other half lived.

When I'd seen enough I moved next door. I gave a single push of the doorbell then wandered down the side of the house and round the back. There was a double garage and the stripes on the lawn were even more distinct than when I'd last seen them. I'd love a double garage. I peered through the window and saw his car standing there. It was a blue Rover 75. Between me and it, in the space designed for number two car, were all those things that accumulate in the best regulated households: step ladders, wheelbarrow, an old bookcase that was too good for the dump and several plastic boxes filled with magazines. Under the window was a chest freezer and by shielding my eyes with my hand I could just make out the lawnmower alongside it, the handles pointing towards me. One had a chrome lever that probably operated the throttle, and the pull-cord for starting the engine terminated on the other in a yellow grip, moulded to fit the fingers.

Behind the garage was a solid-looking shed that I hadn't noticed on my previous visit. It was about ten by eight, in the natural colour of the wood, and I suspected I'd seen similar ones advertised in the colour supplements. I was heading towards it when a voice said: "Where do you think you're going?" in an accusatory tone.

He had a black eye and a plaster across his nose, but I managed to keep a straight face. "Hello Mr Ferriby," I said. "I was looking for you. DI Priest, Heckley CID. We have met before. I tried the doorbell several times and wondered if you were out here." I nodded towards the shed, which I now recognised as being intended to contain a Swedish sauna. "Is that where you keep your fish?"

"Yeth," he replied. "DI Prietht, did you thay?"

"That's right."

"You came about that thad buthineth with Colinette, didn't you?"

"Yes, and I'd like to ask you one or two more questions, if you don't mind. I heard about the assault on you by Graham."

"Ith he thtill in jail?"

"No, the magistrate will have bailed him, this morning."

"Oh dear."

"Don't worry, he won't be back. What sort of fish do you keep?"

"Dithcuth."

"Discus?"

"Yeth. Do you want to thee them?"

"I'd love to."

He unhooked a bunch of keys from his belt and led the way to the shed. I stooped as he held the door open for me and stepped straight into a different world. The only light was from the tanks, and the room was filled with the sounds of air and water, as if we were on a scuba dive. The fish were deep-bodied, almost circular, coloured in muted shades of lilac, green and pink. They cruised with a lordly air, serene and sedate, turning at the end of their beat to do it all again, as if showing off at a stately ball for the benefit of prospective suitors.

There was one comfortable chair, facing the aquaria that covered one wall of the shed. I sat down and felt instantly at peace, more so than I've ever felt in a church. "This is wonderful," I said. "It should be available on the National Health. Do you ever take photographs of them?"

"Thometimeth," he replied.

"I'm told you're a keen photographer."

"I jutht dabble a bit."

"Mrs Jones gave us a video tape that you'd taken of Colinette at a barbecue. It was very useful but we were wondering if you had any more." I turned to look up at him, but in the light cast by the tanks it wasn't possible to judge his expression.

"No," he replied. "I juth took that bit."

"Did you take any still photos of her?"

"No."

"I'm surprised. She was a good-looking girl, didn't you ever offer to take her picture?"

"No."

"You took the video at a barbecue."

"Thath right."

"When?"

"One thummer, about two yearth ago."

"And you gave her a copy, next time you saw her."

"I thuppothe tho."

"Did you keep a copy for yourself?"

"I don't remember."

He was standing slightly behind me, and by tilting my head I could see his reflection in the glass of one of the higher tanks. His visage wasn't clear enough for me to read what he was thinking, but if he'd tried to bash me over the head with a jar of ants' eggs I'd have seen it coming. One of the discus, rooting about at the bottom of the aquarium, took in a mouthful of gravel and spit it out again.

"What about Graham's new girlfriend? Have you taken any pictures of her?"

"No."

"She's a professional model, I believe."

"Ith she?"

"Mmm. Have you seen her?"

"Onthe or twithe."

"A cracker, don't you think?"

"If you like that thort of thing."

I couldn't understand why he wasn't fighting back. He'd had ample opportunity to demand why I was asking all these questions but he was totally compliant, if somewhat unforthcoming. Unless he was cleverer than I thought. He might have had a room upstairs wallpapered with stills of Colinette from the video, and candid shots of Graham's mother and new girlfriend, blown up to life-size, but he knew there was no way I could get in there to find it.

"And don't you like that sort of thing?" I asked.

"She'th a tart," he replied.

"Well," I said, twisting round to face him. "What's wrong with being a tart? We all like to see a nice brassy tart with big bazookas, don't we?" He was wearing the same pullover as before, and now I could see that it was hand-made. The knitter had looked for a pattern that incorporated steam loco-motives, but all she'd been able to find was Thomas the Tank Engine. "Like Graham's mother," I went on. "She's like that, isn't she?"

"Thome might think she wath."

"Did you ever photograph her?"

"No. Except at the barbecue. She wath on the video."

"Are you married, Mr Ferriby?"

"Divorthed."

"How long were you married for?"

He hesitated before replying, and I saw that he was either blushing or feeling sick. The light from the tanks cast a pale green glow on to everything, including our faces, and as I watched him he turned from a delicate shade of sage to deep viridian.

"Not long," he whispered, looking away from me. That made two of us.

"Graham says he caught you snooping round the house," I said.

"He'th lying."

"Why would he do that?"

"I don't know. I watered the planth in the conthervatory, thath all. I never went anywhere elthe in the houthe."

"So why did he hit you?"

"I don't know."

"You must have some idea."

"Maybe he wanted to cover thomething up. He'th into all thorth of thingth. He'th a bad one, he ith. Why don't you athk him?"

"I will, Mr Ferriby," I said. "Rest assured, I will."

Back at the office I made some notes while eating the ham sandwich I'd bought. Neville Ferriby was definitely worth a closer look, I'd decided, and wrote out an interview request form. I'd let two of the others go see him, and tell them to be less circumspect than I had been. If they caught him indoors they could have a little snoop round while he made coffee, or one of them could use the loo, that sort of thing. I wanted to know about his marriage, his sex life, who knitted his jumpers and what he meant when he said that Graham Allen was a bad 'un.

After that I watched the video again. I counted about twenty different faces and decided that we needed to speak to every one of them. Maybe Graham could put names to them all. The longest sequence was of an overweight man in a striped apron, presumably Mr Allen senior, almost self-immolating as he doused the barbecue with lighter fluid, and the next longest was of a woman in a leopard print blouse making a production out of eating a sausage, her eyes never leaving the camera. His wife, I assumed. The sound was turned down low, but not so low that I couldn't hear *Una Paloma Blanca* in the background. No wonder they needed to placate the neighbours.

The two shots of Colinette were a few minutes apart. In the first she was facing the camera, as if asked to pose for a few seconds. She was wearing shorts and a skimpy top that showed her bare midriff and a healthy cleavage. Ferriby held the shot for too long and after a few seconds Colinette looked embarrassed and turned away. I rewound the tape a short way and froze the picture. By holding a plastic ruler diagonally across the screen I could draw an imaginary line from the top left to the bottom right corner. Then I repeated the exercise with the other diagonal. The two lines intersected at the exact spot Neville Ferriby had been focussing on, bang in the centre of Colinette's breasts. I fast-forwarded to the shot where she was walking away from the camera and repeated the exercise. This time the two imaginary lines crossed right in the middle of her bottom.

So what did that prove? That Neville Ferriby, wearer of Thomas the Tank Engine pullovers, was a healthy, heterosexual male after all? Probably, I said to myself as I ejected the cassette.

I was making coffee when Mike Kaprowski rang and we talked for nearly half an hour, mainly about Tim Roper and his band. During the Vietnam War he was accused of inciting anti-government feelings with his song lyrics, and there had been some rioting after three or four of his concerts. Policemen had been injured and two fans were stabbed to death, but all that was in the past. Tim and his band, along with Joan Baez, Tom Paxton, Neil Young and a whole galaxy of similar luminaries, were finally forgiven. They were now regarded as part of that marvellous hotch-potch of tastes, colours and opinions that made up the Land Of The Free, and indulged like talented but wayward children. Their files had been re-classified and in a hundred years or so would be destroyed, without prejudice. Tim would be an all-American boy again.

After a long silence I said: "But there's nothing in there to suggest he might incite an impressionable fan to murder?" What there could possibly be I couldn't imagine.

"'Fraid not, Charlie. There's not much at all. Let me see... Yeah, just as I thought. There's only one date on the file, and that's the one when it was opened. August third, sixty-nine."

"He died on Thanksgiving Day that year," I said.

"Fourth Thursday in November," Mike told me. "The file doesn't even have that little fact recorded."

"What? His death?"

"No."

"Anything suspicious in that?"

"Nah. He was low priority – this was a just-in-case file, is all. Covering our asses in case he made it big-time."

"The website says he was being investigated by the CIA and died under suspicious circumstances."

"Yep, I guess it would, just like for Elvis, Lenny Bruce, Grandma Moses and a whole mess of others."

"Mmm, sorry about that. OK, Mike, thanks for your efforts. I didn't know what to expect but we're clutching at any passing straw we can."

"Slow down, old son," he said. "This is not the end of the trail. I've done a little investigation of my own and have something for you. The drummer with the band was called David Zekolwski..."

"Zeke," I interrupted.

"You got him. OK, so according to the website his wife gave birth to a son, called Theo, in the summer of '69."

"Hence 'Theo's Tune'."

"The same. Having a DOB made it easier to trace him than any of the others. Young Theo Zekolwski is now the big shot vice-president of Glancing Spear Productions, over there in Hollywood, and will be happy to talk to you about his pa and The LHO. I just caught him at home and he says he'll be in the office for a couple of hours after lunch. Got a pen handy?"

I put a corned beef casserole in the microwave and jogged to the top of Beacon Hill again. It wasn't getting any easier. After a shower and the casserole I jotted a few notes and at ten o'clock I rang California. Mental arithmetic told me that he'd be thirty-one years old. Time flies. After a grilling by his secretary she put me through and I found myself listening to the *cafe au lait* voice of the inspiration behind Theo's Tune.

"Theodore Zekolwski here, Inspector," he said. "How can I help you?"

I didn't know if he had any musical talent but he could have done 'Coward Of The County' anytime. "Thanks for finding time to talk to me, Mr Zekowlski," I began. "I'd like to ask you a few questions about the group your father played the drums with back in the Sixties – The LHO – and about Tim Roper, their lead singer. Are you familiar with them?"

"Sure, I know all about them, but I'm intrigued by your interest, Inspector, and I haven't forgiven you yet for putting the FBI on to me."

"Sorry about that. I didn't mean to. I'm investigating a murder," I told him, "and the only decent information we have about the perpetrator is that he appears to be an LHO or Tim Roper fan. He's sent us a series of notes with quotations that we have identified as being from Tim's lyrics. Would you say that Tim had cult status over there?"

"In a very minor way, among just a few hard cases. My father had only told me the barest details about the band, but when I discovered that Tim had shot himself – did you know he shot himself...?"

"Yes, I did."

"OK, when I learned it I thought he might be a good subject for a piece of hagiography – we produce mainly TV documentaries here at Glancing Spear. You know the sort of thing – lots of Sixties music, leave it hanging in the air about his death, bring the surviving members back together to give their opinions. It's a pet project of mine so I've done the research, but it's only at the idea stage, so far."

"You said surviving members..."

"Yeah. Dad's still alive, that's for sure. He bought a Chirpy Chilli franchise with what he made out of The LHO and ended up with twenty. Peter Tontino – he was their sound engineer – died of an overdose back in the Seventies and Oscar Livingstone is an MIA. Carlo and Eddie are still in the business, up and down the West Coast."

"MIA?"

"Missing in action. He went to Vietnam and never came back."

"I see. Three dead out of, what, six? That's a dangerous place you live in."

"It was the lifestyle, I guess, and the war. I imagine life assurance wasn't easy to come by."

"No. Tim's *supposed* to have shot himself. Are you happy with that?"

"Completely. They'd had a big row on stage the night before and Tim had stormed off. The band finished the set without him. Next morning he sat in his father's Buick and blew his brains out with a revolver he found in the glove compartment. I've seen the photographs, Inspector, and they look just like that's what happened."

"No conspiracy theory, CIA involvement and all that?"

"Not at all. They probably had a file, like they had on everyone with left wing or anarchic leanings – this was not long after the McCarthy era, remember – but I don't think they went round shooting minor rock musicians."

"Some of Tim's lyrics were a bit strong, wouldn't you say? They were bound to attract attention. Did he have a weirdo following?"

"Possibly, but that's show business, Inspector. I asked Dad about them and he said they would rehearse with one set of words, which were not too controversial, but when it came to the concert Tim would sing something completely different. Claimed he just made them up as he went along. Dad said the rest of them didn't mind – the audiences liked it and they were only doing it for the money and laughs. I think he meant sex but he wouldn't admit it."

We chatted for a while about the song lyrics and he mentioned the names of several shows that Glancing Spear had produced, but I hadn't heard of any of them. I told him what sort of stuff I listened to and he recommended a couple of names. I'd long abandoned the idea that I might learn something useful, but I was fascinated listening to Theodore Zekolwski's velvet voice and these insights into the world of Sixties rock music. If only I'd stuck at the guitar lessons...

"So how come 'Theo's Tune' is credited to Blue Coyote?" I asked.

"Oh God! That song has dogged me all my life. If only you knew. It was a commercial thing, I imagine. Tim knocked it up especially for me but didn't want it including in The LHO repertoire. It wasn't their style, something like that."

"Did your father tell you what the row was about when Tim stormed off the stage?"

"No. I've mentioned it but he shakes his head, pretends he can't remember."

"Right. Well, thanks for your time, Mr Zekolwski. Do you mind if I call you again if I need anything else?"

"Not at all, Inspector, and drop by if you ever happen to be in this part of the world. Good luck with the investigation and let us know when you catch him – maybe there'll be a story in it for us."

"There'll be a story in it, that's for sure, but we've to catch him first."

"Well there you go – technical adviser. You've paid for your trip already."

"I like the sound of that. Thanks a lot."

"Just one small thing, Inspector. I take it that you've seen the website?"

"Yes, we have. That's where we found the lyrics and everything else we knew about The LHO. I've asked our technical people to try find who the author is but they haven't come back to me yet."

"I can help you there. She's a woman called Shiralee Weston, lives in a trailer in Desert Springs."

"Wow, thanks. That's a big help." I asked him for a spelling and wrote it down. "Who is she, do you know?"

"Yeah. Apparently she was a neighbour of Tim's parents and they were very close. I think there was possibly some involvement between her mother and Tim's father. They grew up together and Shiralee had a mighty crush on Tim. Now she keeps his memory alive with the website."

"It sounds as if we need to talk to her." If she ran a fan club we needed the names of any British members. Names, and addresses. I liked the sound of that. Perhaps we were getting somewhere at last.

"I'd hurry, if I were you," Theodore said. "She sits all day listening to LHO tapes and stuffing herself with ice cream and doughnuts, like the queen ant in a termite colony. Hasn't been out of the trailer for five years. When she dies they'll have to dismantle it from around her."

"Good grief. Have you met her?"

"Not personally. One of my research staff tracked her down, via the neighbours, and he had that pleasure. She claims to be Tim's ex-girlfriend, the love of his life wallowing in guilt for not saving him. She's intelligent, though – manages the website. I'd guess she's the source of all the CIA nonsense."

"Right, thanks. One last thing: what does LHO stand for?"

"LHO?" His voice lightened, went up an octave to put

him about level with Johnny Cash. "Don't you know?"

"No."

"OK. They all went to school together in La Habra. That's a district of LA. They played in the school band and kept the name when they left and turned professional. LHO was The La Habra Orchestra."

"It can't be done," Dave declared as he walked across the office, a plastic lunch box in one hand, his jacket dangling from the other.

I was seated next to Pete Goodchild with my feet on a spare chair. I swung them down to make room for him, saying: "What can't, Old Son?"

Pete said: *"He tried the thing that could not be done – and found he could not do it."*

"The walk," Dave replied. "I've just run up and down the back stairs four times and I'm knackered." He wiped the back of his hand across his brow and offered it as proof. "The steps are all wrong. If you take them one at a time they're too small and two at a time is too much. We've really taken something on with this, Charlie."

I patted him on the knee. "That's what makes it worth doing. Pacing yourself, David, that's the name of the game. Remember that we won't be carrying anything, we can wear shorts and T-shirts, and we'll arrange for certain off-duty PCs – those nice rounded ones with long hair – to ply us with refreshments throughout the twenty-four hours. It'll be fun. A party, you'll see."

"Were you out training over the weekend?"

"I might have been."

"No wonder you're so smug."

It was the Tuesday of Easter week and I'd stood the team down for Monday. Normally I would have done a walk somewhere, probably with Dave and Jeff, but the foot-and-mouth had closed all the footpaths and I'd settled for a couple of solo jogs to the top of Beacon Hill. We were still

tracking down and interviewing the owners of vehicles captured on various video cameras, but the main line of enquiry
was happening over in America. Her ISP had confirmed that
the Tim Roper website was owned by Shiralee Weston, but
our technical people hadn't been able to break into it or find
any membership lists. So I'd set the FBI on to her. If they
couldn't do it electronically they'd go round and scare her
skinny. All I could do was wait.

I picked up Dave's lunch box and opened it at one corner.
"Anything nice?" I asked, suddenly feeling hungry.

"Smoked salmon," he replied, taking it from me and
clicking the lid closed again.

"I don't like smoked salmon. I like my salmon cooked."

"It's not for you."

"Right. So where've you been until now, apart from running up and down the back stairs?"

"Ah!" he said.

"What does ah! mean?"

"It means ah! wouldn't you like to know."

I turned to Pete. "Peter," I began. "I have to put up with
him because we go back a long time, but if you ever become
as obstructive as he is, you're sacked. Understood?"

Pete grinned and nodded.

"It's a delicate matter," Dave said. "Let's just say that Paul
Usher will probably be withdrawing his complaint anytime
today."

"You've sorted it?"

"Consider it sorted."

"Good. Well done. I suppose I'd better do some work,
too. How's that letter to Madame LeStrang coming along?"

"Done it once," Pete replied, "but I've changed my mind
and decided to use the Outdoor Leisure maps. The
Landrangers are a bit too small and it looked as if we were
being deliberately obstructionist. I'm just working the references out more accurately so she won't be able to say we
were unhelpful."

Easter is a poor time for news, so there'd been a full-page spread about us in one of the Sunday tabloids. *Police Enlist Psychic*, it screamed out, and explained how we'd called upon the assistance, once again, of the extraordinary powers of Madame LeStrang.

"Try to get it off today, please."

"No problem."

A DCI had been bumped up to take over Superintendent Isles' workload, and he needed to know where the enquiry was heading. He knew the score, wasn't interfering, but he might have to field a few awkward questions. And he was hoping that the appointment might become permanent and didn't want to make a balls-up. I took Dave with me. On the way I asked what the hold was he had over Paul Usher.

"Not him, her," he replied. "Maria-Helena."

"Anything you can tell me?"

"Sure. I went round to the Smith's about three years ago, with a court warrant for Gary, the eldest of the sons. I'd hardly knocked on the door when it burst open and one of the younger ones stormed out, nearly knocking me over. I yelled: 'Is Gary in?' after him and he shouted back: 'Yeah, he's in bed.' Well, the door was open and the stairs were beckoning, so in I went. He was in bed all right, and his arse was going like a fiddler's elbow. Peeking out from under him was the lovely, if slightly embarrassed countenance of Maria-Helena. I said: 'Downstairs, both of you, in thirty seconds,' and they were."

"His *sister*?" I said.

"Half-sister, actually. Different mothers."

"It's still illegal."

"It's how they live, Charlie. Surprising thing is that they are all so well balanced when you talk to them. Totally immoral, but well balanced. Mrs Smith is an intelligent woman, lots of down-to-earth common sense. I brought him in on the warrant and forgot about the other."

"Until now."

"That's right. She's still playing home and away with her half-brother but Paul doesn't suspect a thing, so she's kindly offered to withdraw her witness statement about the Pakistanis who attacked her husband."

"Was it her who attacked him?"

"Mmm. They had a row and she thought he was going to hit her, so she grabbed the knife. Don't worry about her safety, Charlie, he's the one living dangerously."

"Right."

We brought the acting super up to speed, telling him about the assault on Neville Ferriby and our enquiries in America. He shook his head in disbelief when I laid it on about the ACC's intervention and the involvement of the mad Madame, and we parted the best of mates. Apart from that, it was another waste of time. As we drove into Heckley on the way back I stopped at a traffic light. It was showing red, so it was a wise action.

"There's a sandwich shop just round this corner," I said.

"Want me to leap out and get you one?"

"Please." The lights changed. I coasted round the corner and pulled into the kerb. The driver of the following car swung round me and glared as he passed.

"What do you want?" Dave asked, one leg out of the door.

"Um, something fast."

"Gazelle?"

"No, clot-head! Cheese, salad, whatever. Something that's ready made. Something where she doesn't have to defrost the prawns, or carve the ham, or cut the bread and slice her thumb and have to find a flippin' plaster, while I wait here and gridlock half of Heckley."

"OK, keep your 'air on."

It was cheese and pickle. Fine. I carried it into the nick and Dave drove off with Jeff Caton, who was just leaving to see if Paul Usher was having second thoughts about his complaint.

"Just the man!" the desk sergeant called as I walked through the doorway. He grabbed his phone and said: "I've found him, he's here, now," into it.

"Who is it?" I asked, taking the instrument from him.

"America," he replied in a confidential whisper, as if we were discussing his medical condition. "A woman."

I heard our operator say: "We've found Mr Priest, I'm putting you through," followed by the usual clicks and silences. After a couple of seconds I said: "Inspector Priest here."

"Inspector Priest?" The voice was straight out of Central Casting.

"That's right. Who am I speaking to, please?"

"This is Agent Gladys Jewel, Inspector. Good morning."

"Good morning to you, Gladys. Charlie Priest here, do you have some information for me?"

"*Gladys!*" I heard the desk sergeant hiss.

"Not what you were hoping for, I'm afraid, Charlie. Agent Kaprowski apprised me of the situation and we've approached the problem in a variety of ways. It's been the Easter weekend over here, so first of all I'd like to apologise for the delay in replying."

"Yes, we have the same festival this side of the Atlantic," I told her.

"Gee, I guess you do. OK. How to unlock the secrets of Shiralee Weston's computer, that was the problem. So first of all we hacked into it. No sweat, but we found nothing there and we couldn't discover any alternative sites operating from her address. That could mean that we were not clever enough or that there was nothing to find. We read all her emails and there was nothing to indicate she was running a Tim Roper fan club, no bulletin board, no *nuthin'*. So, plan two: I put on the funny voice and ring her. Say I've just discovered the works of Tim Roper and it was a revelation. This was what I'd been looking for all my life. Boy, did we have an animated conversation? That chick is one strange lady,

Charlie, believe me. She told me how to download all his stuff but guess what? There's no fan club. All the world are Tim's fans, she says, or they will be, once they've heard him. Which brings us to plan three: send a couple of agents round in the hope that she has a filing cabinet with it all in. Zilch. She doesn't have a filing cabinet with it all in. From what they said about her there's no room in the trailer for a filing cabinet. She's a mess, Charlie, a pitiful mess."

"I hope they weren't too hard on her."

"No. They told her what it was about and she co-operated. So the bottom line, Charlie, is that we haven't been much help to you."

A big stone was sitting somewhere at the bottom of my stomach. I'd been sure that the Tim Roper avenue would take us to the murderer, but it was a dead end, a false trail, a blind canyon. He could just as easily have used the lyrics of Abba or Brotherhood of Man to taunt us.

"Gladys..." I began, "you've obviously put a lot of effort into this, and I'm grateful."

"Yeah, well, I'm sorry to disappoint you but I think that's about all we can offer."

"I, well, I felt sure this was going to lead us to the killer."

"You sound desolate."

"I feel it."

"Don't take it to heart, Charlie. Do you know how many unexplained deaths we have in LA County?"

"No."

"About twenty-five a day."

"That doesn't make me feel any better."

"Who did he kill?"

"Seven. He's killed seven."

"Gee, I didn't know that. What are they, recreational killings?"

"It looks like it."

"They're the worst sort. Have you had a word with our people at Quantico?"

"I'm preparing a file for them."

"They're good, Charlie, believe me. Meanwhile, we'll have a think about things and keep looking for that fan club. How does that sound?"

"You're a treasure, Gladys. Many thanks for your help."

"You're welcome. Take care, Charlie, and good hunting."

Quantico is the FBI training college, and that's where they invented criminal profiling. Pete Goodfellow didn't know it yet but his next job would be to prepare that file and submit it to them. I wasn't expecting any results, but when lives are being lost and failure is staring you in the face, an important part of the job is covering your back. One day they'd be baying for a scapegoat, and I was the prime contender.

The offences were committed early in the evening. The implication from that was that the murderer lived miles away, outside the area. He'd be able to do the deed and then drive home while it was still early, without attracting attention. If he'd killed late at night he'd have to be on the roads when they were quiet and he'd be at risk of being picked up. That's what a profiler would tell us. Except that... Except that I didn't believe it. The killings were not opportunistic. He knew who his victims were in advance, of that I was sure. He'd known exactly where they'd be and at what time, and that took planning. Robin was doing his paper round. He wasn't going home after staying on late at school or after playing computer games at a friend's – he was following his routine. Similarly with Mrs Heeley and Colinette. They didn't just happen to be there, they were doing what they always did at that time on that day. Driving a hundred or even thirty miles trawling for likely victims would be a chore, and most criminals have a lazy streak in them. No, he lived and killed locally, first down south, and now here in West Yorkshire. As sure as my name was...Guiseppe Fatorini.

The team would be disappointed. We felt sure that our

luck was changing, that the website would put us on the trail, but now I'd have to tell them we were back where we started. We wouldn't catch our killer. He wouldn't be detected. Some fresh-faced PC would take a car number for driving without lights or parking carelessly, near where a future murder was committed, or a CCTV camera would pick him up at a couple of locations. He'd confess to everything, proud to have led us such a dance, enjoying the limelight. Then the celebrations would start. The chief constable would modestly tell the world that it was all down to good policing and he'd invite his favourite reporters and acolytes to drinky-poos in the office. Meanwhile, we'd quietly wipe the computer of the twenty thousand names and addresses we'd accrued and start thinking about burglaries again.

Pete was sitting at his desk when I entered the office, sleeves rolled up, an Ordnance Survey map spread out under his elbows. He looked up when he heard me, saying: "Hi Boss, the FBI's just been after you."

"I know, they caught me at the front desk."

"Any joy?"

"Sod all." I checked the weight of the kettle and switched it on, then shut myself in my little office. I'd completed my diary and was sitting with my knuckles pressed into my eyes when Pete opened the door and poked his head round it.

"So they couldn't find the fan club?" he asked.

My office has windows on three sides, and I can see my reflection in them. I raise my head without moving my hands, pulling my bottom eyelids down, followed by my cheeks and the corners of my mouth. It wasn't a pretty sight.

"There isn't one," I said as my face sprang back to its normal shape.

"Nothing at all?"

"Nothing at all."

"No names and addresses?"

"No names. No addresses."

"That's a blow."

"Putting it mildly."

"You sound pissed off."

I shook my head, lost for words. "I thought...I thought... Oh, what's the use. It looks as if Madame LeStrang is our best bet again."

"Uh!" Pete exclaimed. "I think you'd better come and see what I've discovered. I don't think you'll like this, either."

"What is it? What have you found?"

"The links, Charlie. I've found the links."

Chapter Nine

There were two Ordnance Survey maps on his desk, one on top of the other. He lifted a corner of the top one to show me the area around Nelson, where young Robin Gillespie's body had been found. Pete had marked the exact spot with a cross inside a circle. He folded the local map back, saying: "...and these are where Colinette, Mrs Heeley and Norma Holborn were found."

"Go on," I said. I'd seen the shape the pins made on the big map down in the incident room. Three of them in an irregular triangle, with Robin's pin way off to the west. We'd considered constellations, ley lines and mathematical ratios, all to no avail.

"The scale is one to 25,000," he told me, "and I've worked out six-figure references for all the places where the bodies were found. Three figures for the easting, three for the nor-thing, as you well know."

"I'm with you."

"OK. So the first figure of the three represents a ten kilometre square, the second brings it down to one kilometre, and the third figure is my estimate of the number of tenths of a kilometre to where each body was found."

"And what does it show?"

"Here's the list." He pulled a pad from under the maps, with columns of numbers written on it. "If you ignore the first figure, the ten kilometre square, we find that the reference for Robin is one two, two three. That for Mrs Heeley is three four, four five; Colinette is five six, seven eight and Norma is eight nine, nine zero. It's the words of the song, Charlie – *One two, buckle my shoe. Two three, he'll never get free.*"

I took the pad from him, studying the numbers, looking at the map, working out the references for myself.

"Norma was found smack on the line," Pete was saying. "Hence the zero. It explains why the bodies were found in what appeared to be arbitrary places, except that there was nothing arbitrary about it. He'd worked the spots out on a map, like I've just done."

The carpet tiles were coming up at me, pulsing and throbbing like something in a medical video. I stepped back, taking a deep breath, and stumbled against a waste paper basket. Something had to get in my way, and that was it. I spun round and toe-ended it across the office with all the venom that I once put into goal kicks. It clattered against a radiator and fell to the floor, rolling in a semi-circle before coming to rest.

"That's no good!" I yelled at Peter, slamming my fist down on his desk. "What frigging good is that? That doesn't help us at all!"

"He's not doing it to help us, Charlie!" he shouted back. "He's not doing it so we can catch him. He's doing it to prove he's the killer."

"He's mocking us," I said. "He's taunting us."

"Precisely! That's what he does."

I flopped into a chair and felt my chest heaving as I struggled to breathe. I said: "Location, location, location."

"What?"

"Somebody said that when I went down to N-CIS and told them he called himself the Property Developer. It's the three golden rules of property development – location, location, location."

"Which proves he's been working to a plan, a grand design, all along."

"Seven – nil to him." I said.

"Seven?"

"Yeah, seven." I ran my fingers through my hair. "You don't know the full story. I'll tell you all about it when Maggie and Dave are here. God knows, Peter, we need some fresh ideas with this one."

The evenings are the worst time. Eight through to midnight. Go to the pub and have a few beers is the usual solution, but it doesn't work with me. I read, listen to music, maybe watch some TV or catch up with housework, trying not to fall asleep. Lately, there'd been the jogging, but mostly, I use the time to think.

It had been seventeen days since Norma Holborn's murder but that one came only nine days after Colinette. He was overdue, unless a body was lying somewhere, undiscovered. I'd studied the maps, considering possible references where he could have left a body. There were a hundred of them in every ten kilometre square, but there was no need for him to stick to the rules anymore. He'd used up all the references in the song and proved his point. From now on he could leave the bodies anywhere.

Gladys Jewel had called it recreational killing, but there was more to it than that. Taunting us – the police – was a major part of how he got his kicks. We were a part of the equation, that was for sure. He was playing some deadly game with us, and so far he was winning hands down. I tried to remember words from the songs that might be relevant. *Who is the thief and who is the cop? Who is the judge and who is the whore?* There was something in his past that had turned him against us, and the words of Tim Roper had found the sweet spot, reinforced his feelings. But with the last two killings a new dimension had entered the equation. He'd discovered sex and the joy of inflicting pain, and he'd had the magnificent realisation that, for him, one was a function of the other. The game had entered a new phase.

Find the last victim, if there was one, and find the next victim before she became one. Those were the priorities. We were running out of white pickups and tyres to check, so I had a few more troops to play with. At the Wednesday morning briefing I set a team up to find all the locations on the map where there might be a body and then we had a brainstorming session. If we were the killer, where would we look for our next victim?

She had to be a person of habit, available in the evening.

Hospitals came top of the list. I gave someone the job of finding the shift times, not just for nurses but for the ancillary workers and anyone else who might work the twilight shift.

"And visitors," someone suggested.

"Good one," I agreed. "Regular visitors who come and go between times."

After that it was filling station attendants, fast food workers, librarians, office cleaners, barmaids and waitresses. Laura Heeley had been to the bingo, so we added bingo halls to the list but rejected the cinema and theatre. Many shops in the town centre had late night opening, as did the supermarkets, so we included their staff. We'd talk to the management, see who arranged transport and who didn't, warn vulnerable people to be aware of the situation and not to accept lifts.

Then we'd go looking ourselves.

I wasn't happy with the subterfuge – some of the team knowing the full extent of the case, most of them not – so I told Jeff Caton and Pete Goodfellow to meet me and Dave and Maggie in my office, after I'd had my morning meeting with Mr Wood.

When I returned Dave was in full flow, relating a story about the time he went to Boots to buy a deodorant. "...so the girl behind the counter said: 'Do you want the ball type, Sir?' and I said: 'No, it's for under my arms.'"

Thanks, Dave, it was the first smile I'd had all week. I told Maggie why I'd invited Jeff and Pete, and asked her to fill them in with details of the other murders. They sat in silence until she'd finished, ten minutes later.

"So it's seven?" Jeff said. "Not four, seven."

"Christ!" Pete added.

"No wonder you're so crotchety."

"It doesn't seem right, lumbering us with it."

"Well, they've hardly lumbered us with it. He's still murdered three on our patch."

"All the same..."

That's when the phone rang. Dave picked it up, listened

for a few seconds then handed it to me.

"It's Arthur, Charlie," the desk sergeant informed me. "There's another letter. It's addressed to you and it looks just like the first one."

"Right," I said. "Don't touch it again, I'm on my way down."

I drove straight to the Home Office lab at Wetherton with the unopened letter sealed in an evidence bag. What it said in words was irrelevant compared with what it might tell us in other ways. I had a coffee with my old buddy Professor van Rees who is senior scientist there, and told him all about it while his staff worked their alchemy on the envelope and its contents. If the sender had a recent criminal conviction they'd be able to convert a speck of spittle or a drop of sweat into a name and address. If he didn't have a conviction they'd still be able to label him in such a way that if he ever came to our notice we'd have him.

The prof is a busy man but courteous to a fault. I finished my coffee and told him that I'd wait in the canteen rather than take up more of his time. I was sitting in there, reading a magazine article about exons, introns and codons that went completely over my head, when the same scientist who'd opened the first letter came through the door. She gave me a smile of recognition and came over, carrying a single sheet of A4 paper.

"This is a hand-written copy I made," she said, placing it in front of me. "We didn't want to put the original through the copier. Does it make any sense to you?"

"Presumably the original was typed," I said.

"Yes, same as the other."

She'd written:

> *Old Holborn! Put that in your pipe and smoke it.*
> *Ha ha ha ha ha ha ha ha ha ha ha ha ha ha ha*
> *The Property Developer. Ha ha ha ha ha ha ha ha*

"Does it make sense?"

I shook my head.

"It's tobacco, isn't it, Old Holborn?"

"Yes, and the last victim was called Norma Holborn. He seems to find that amusing." I stared blankly at the paper for a few moments, then said: "I don't think it's pipe tobacco, though. I think it's roll-your-own stuff. There was an advert for it on TV, long before your time. 'Why do I smoke Old Holborn?' or something. Can't remember what the answer was. 'Because I want to catch cancer,' probably." My father was a heavy smoker, and for a few days after every budget he would experiment with rolling his own, to try save a few pence.

"I smoke Old Holborn because...it keeps hands that do dishes as soft as your face?" She was blushing slightly from the compliment I'd paid her.

I gave her the weary smile. "Yes, that's it. Well done."

"I'd better do some work," she said. "Sorry I can't help you with the jingle. It will be a couple of days before we know if there's anything on the letter, I'm afraid."

"I know you'll do your best, and thanks for this." I tapped the note with my knuckle and watched her walk towards the exit, white-coated, her sensible shoes not making a sound on the tiled floor.

The M62 snakes across England like a blood vessel. If the M1 is the country's aorta, then the M62 is the jugular vein. It stretches from Hull to Liverpool, dividing the country in half. Five miles south of Leeds it crosses the M1 at what must be a contender for the title Crossroads of England. In America it would have a name. In America two imaginary lines, state borders, cross at right angles at a spot they call Four Corners. It's in the middle of a God-forsaken desert, miles from anywhere, but a whole industry has sprung up around a map-making curiosity. The place where the M62 crosses the M1 is known as just that – the place where the M62 crosses the M1, but the distribution companies, hard nosed and unromantic, have not been slow to recognise the importance of the location. They've built their warehouses there, windowless, functional shelters that shadow the road like hyenas following a herd of wildebeest. I was driving fast but I could read their names out of the corner of my eye: Pioneer, Argos, Asda, Wicks, Royal Mail. Brand names, the new currency.

Fifteen minutes and twenty miles later I'd reached my exit, but I kept going. Off J22 there's an old-fashioned transport cafe that all the truckers use. The portions are generous, the quality high and the prices reasonable. If I had a decent lunch I wouldn't have to cook in the evening, and the menu was more comprehensive than at home. The route took me over the Scammonden Dam. After the dam two great bulwarks of rock rear up at either side of the road, with the bridge a delicate arch linking them, a hundred and fifty feet high. All the foot-and-mouth outbreaks in Yorkshire had been to the north of the motorway. It occurred to me that it was a *cordon sanitaire*, splitting the county in half, with the bridges the only weak spot, like aneurysms. I have these fanciful thoughts when I'm driving, but I usually keep them to myself.

It was going to be the steak and kidney pie, with garden peas and new potatoes, but when it was my turn to be served I didn't have the appetite. I settled for apple pie and custard, with a mug of strong tea, and that was enough for me. A quick look at the girlies in the paper, a visit to the loo – spotless – and then it was back to the station, although a nap in the car would have been nice.

"He's taking the piss," Dave declared when he read the note. "I'd like to stuff an ounce of Old Holborn up his nose and light it with a blow torch."

"Why did we smoke Old Holborn?" I asked.

"Because it would make us sick if we ate it," Pete Goodfellow suggested.

"Does it help you work, rest and play?" Maggie asked.

"That's a Mars bar, Dumbo."

"Only trying to be helpful."

"OK," I went on. "Which of you knew it was roll-up tobacco and not pipe tobacco?"

Maggie didn't know the difference but both Pete and Dave knew you had to wrap it in a piece of paper before you put it in your mouth and ignited it.

"He obviously thinks it's pipe tobacco," Pete said.

"So according to our highly scientific straw poll, *he* is a woman," Dave told us.

"Or maybe he's too young to remember the adverts."

"Or he never watches TV."

I stood up and walked across to the window. A light drizzle was falling and the evening rush, such as we have in Heckley, was tapering off. Shop girls and office managers, the last to leave, were making their way to the bus stops, the station and the multi-storey.

Dave came and joined me, leaning against the cold radiator, reading my thoughts. After about a minute he said: "He's out there, somewhere, Charlie. Watching us, watching them." We scanned the rooftops, acres of ornate brickwork and glistening slate, as if we might see the flash of light on binoculars marking his presence.

"Yeah," I said, "and all we can come up with is that he might be under thirty and he might not watch TV."

"Maybe forensic will find something."

"That's right." I repeated his words like a zombie. "Maybe forensic will find something."

I dressed accordingly and went into town. Black jeans, black polo-necked, leather jacket and trainers. I thought about boot-polish stripes across my face, diagonally to break up the shape, but decided it was unnecessary. I'd rearranged the shifts, brought some of them on late, split others in two, so we could cover the evenings. He was out there, all right, looking for his next victim, and I had to do everything in my power to stop him.

The women's groups had organised transport for late night revellers and most of the town's employers had identified vulnerable workers and arranged transport for them. But there were plenty who disregarded our advice. Heckley has more than its share of sweatshops, employing young Asian girls, whose owners didn't give a toss about them. They worked long hours, often late into the night, so we were giving them special attention. And there were others, the stupid ones who did nothing, who believed that when your number was up, your number was up. As if God had decreed that a certain number of young women were destined to die of lung cancer or be strangled by a maniac and there was nothing anyone could do about it, so they smoked like kipper factories and wandered alone down dark streets. I parked on the edge of town and walked over the bridge, into the centre.

Heckley in the evening does not have the air of menace that the big cities have. We have our muggers and nutters, spoiling for a fight, just like they do, but the overall level of aggression is much lower. The gang of youths spilling out of the pub are more likely to apologise for knocking you over than steal your wallet. I walked towards the precinct, noting the places that were still open, looking at closing times, assessing the gender of the staff.

The rain had stopped but the pavement was still wet, reflecting the lights, reducing the noise of passing cars to a soft swish. A knot of people, all young, stood at the cash machine outside Barclays. Burger King was full, a kids' party taking up one end of the place. They wore funny hats and painted faces, and were having a whale of a time. Kids and junk food. Brand loyalty. Get them young. I looked at my watch, then remembered it was the school holidays. A little girl with a tiger face waved at me through the window and I wiggled my fingers back at her.

All the aluminium chairs had been removed from outside the coffee shops in the precinct. What might appear cool on the Left Bank was downright frigid in Yorkshire. I looked up into the night, into the blackness above the lighted windows, trying to see into the shadows. If I were in his shoes where would I go, where would I look? That's what we're supposed to do, isn't it? Put ourselves in his shoes.

It was late night opening at the library. Late night is a relative expression, and in library usage it meant nine thirty. I like libraries. And librarians. There's something otherworldly about them, a throwback to an age when people spoke softly and cared about the way we interact with each other. I've never been called to a punch-up in a library. I walked round the block on the other side of the road and when I was back where I started the big lights went out in the library, leaving only a few fluorescent tubes casting a suspicious glow on the shelves, to deter any local thieves with literary tastes. I slipped into the doorway of a solicitors' office and stood in the shadow, watching.

The library door opened and two women came outside and waited. In a few seconds they were joined by a third who presumably had just set the burglar alarm. She pulled the door shut and locked it. Two of them unfurled umbrellas before realising it had stopped raining and collapsing them again. They set off walking and I followed.

At the entrance to the multi-storey car park they stopped for a few moments, saying their goodnights, and two of them went inside. I followed the third, all the way to the station, and watched her board a train that would stop at Huddersfield, Oldfield and Manchester. Eight other passengers boarded it at Heckley: two couples, two other women and two men. The two men carried briefcases, and somehow I thought that our man wouldn't. I terminated the chase at Heckley, on the grounds that I'm not good at trains and I couldn't be sure of catching one back at that time of night. Tomorrow I'd put someone on to it.

Leads are like decent TV programmes. You wait weeks for one and then two or three come along at the same time. I was under my desk, looking for something that I saw scurry across it, when the phone rang. I'd been sitting there, reading a report from one of the DCs, when I glimpsed it out of the corner of my eye. Nothing distinct but more than a shadow. It ran, or possibly flew, towards the far right-hand corner of my desk top. I stood up and grabbed the pile of papers that live there. Nothing. I looked on the floor, moved the waste paper bin, lifted a box filled with files that needed to go back to the registry. Nothing.

"Priest," I said into the phone. At least I could still remember my name.

"It's Rod, Boss," a familiar voice informed me. It was the DC whose report I'd just been reading.

"Hi, Rod," I said. "Just been reading your reports. Your spelling doesn't improve."

"Ah, but the content's first class."

"Presentation, Rod. Presentation is all. What can I do for you?"

"Neville Ferriby. He's up to something. I don't know what but it looks like no-good."

When we run out of lines to follow we don't admit that we've nothing to do and sit back, waiting for someone high up to disband the team. We run round like scalded cats, finding jobs, however improbable, to keep the team together and focused for when the break comes. I'd decided to have all the leading players followed, low key, low grade, learning how they lived. If we had any of them in again we'd put the frighteners on, know more about their movements than they did themselves. Get them talking about everyday stuff, then prove they're lying – that's how to do it. Rod and his partner had been given the task of building a dossier on the fishy Mr Ferriby, neighbour of Colinette's boyfriend.

"Tell me about it," I said, pulling my chair back up to the desk, the real or imaginary furry intruder forgotten.

"He's been on the move all morning. First he visited the Halifax in the precinct, followed by Jessops, and then he drove out to Sheepstone. We're there now. He parked the car and walked into the cemetery, carrying this holdall. He's ensconced in some bushes at the old end of the graveyard with a packet of sandwiches and a flask and he's spying on the houses at the other side of the valley. He has a camera with a lens on it like a bloody bazooka."

"Interesting," I agreed. "What's in his sandwiches."

"Tuna."

"Very nice. He probably bought a film in Jessops. Something high speed. Did you know he was a camera buff?"

"Yeah, I read it in the file."

"OK. Stay with him until he moves, then find the addresses of the houses he's watching and check the electoral roll for who lives there. You know the form."

"Right, Boss."

"Oh, and one other thing."

"What's that?"

"Remember that you're on hallowed ground, so don't go peeing behind the gravestones."

At that very moment the second lead was click-clacking on high heels up the steps and through the front door of the nick. I put the phone down and wondered about Neville Ferriby. He wasn't what I'd call a suspect, not for the murders, but he knew something about Graham Allen, of that I was sure.

We get circulars, dozens of them. The registry pins a distribution list to each and every one and sends them upstairs. Some are about possible terrorist attacks, some are to say that the laws relating to lights on bicycles have been relaxed. Every summer we receive one to say that uniform branch can now wear their short-sleeved shirts and occasionally we are told that standards of tidiness are falling, particularly with regard to the length of certain officers' hair. Gilbert always draws a triple circle round *DI* on the distribution list for that one and sends it straight to me.

The collection had built up over the last few weeks and there was quite a bunch of them, so some creativity was called for. I ticked all the boxes and wrote suitable dates alongside them, so it looked as if Gareth Adey, my uniformed counterpart, had hung on to the documents and only passed them on in the last week or so. I was checking in my diary that he hadn't been on leave when the phone rang. It was the front desk.

"Inspector Priest, there's nobody in the incident room and I've a lady here saying she thinks she's being followed. Is there anybody can see her?"

"*Compos mentis?*" I asked in a soft voice. We were having a steady procession of potential witnesses through the nick, a large percentage of who were one or two cogs short in the gearbox department.

"Yes, Sir, I'd say so."

"I'll come down."

Bugger. I'd just been thinking that I'd hotfoot round to Neville Ferriby's place to meet him when he came home. I'd quiz him about his whereabouts and maybe bring him in. And I'd confiscate the film from his camera. Contrary to popular belief we don't have an anti-stalking law, but we do have the Harassment Act, and *conduct likely to cause a breach of the peace* is a good catch-all.

She was about forty, slim, with straight hair and stiletto heels. I don't pay too much attention to my own personal appearance, and consequently, I am not all that bothered about that of any woman I happen to be friendly with. I like to think that they have other values that transcend good dress sense. But Caitlin Jordan-Keedy was a mess. Nature had been kind to her, her clothes looked expensive, but she was still a mess. Her hair was lank because, I suspected, she'd had a shower and not bothered to dry it. It was held off her face by an old-fashioned hair slide. Her long black skirt was crumpled, the grey jacket didn't go with it and her blouse hadn't seen an iron this side of wash day. Arthur, behind the desk, introduced us and I pointed her in the direction of one of the interview rooms.

She placed a tiny mobile phone on the desk and a bunch of keys with a Porsche fob alongside it. I checked the spelling of her name and wrote it down.

"Tell me all about it, Mrs Jordan-Keedy," I invited.

The words came out in staccato bursts, falling over each other in a way that is peculiar to certain very intelligent women. It's as if normal speech is not able to keep up with their thought processes. My brain took a second or two to adjust and I gathered that she lived in Salford, in the regenerated area near the Lowry, and commuted to Heckley by train every day. Except that today she'd come in the Porsche. Not the car, the Porsche. Tuesday evening she'd got off the train at Salford and seen a youth who appeared to be watching her. He had a notebook and she'd assumed he was a trainspotter. Wednesday she'd seen him again, on Heckley station but he didn't board the train.

Her mobile phone rang. "Mrs Jordan-Keedy," she said into it, then, after a pause: "I'm with a client at the moment, call me later."

Yesterday, Thursday, the youth had boarded the train, seating himself about four rows behind her. He followed her out of the station but she lost him by calling in a restaurant and pretending to ask for a table. When she arrived home she jumped in the car – make unspecified – and drove to the station again. He was waiting on the platform at the other side, for a train back the way he'd come.

The muscles at the back of my jaw were tightening and I wondered if it showed. "You called him a youth, Mrs Jordan-Keedy," I said. "How old would you say he was?"

Her phone rang again. "Mrs Jordan-Keedy." Longer pause this time, then: "I said I needed it today. Tuesday just isn't good enough, you'll have to come in tomorrow and have it ready for Monday. Yes, I know you're time-starved but aren't we all. The meeting's at ten thirty."

She put the phone back on the desk but didn't apologise for the interruption.

"Would you mind switching it off, please," I said.

For a second or two she looked as if she might protest, but she reached forward and pressed a button. There, I thought, it's easy once you decide to do it. "I asked you how old he was."

"Early twenties at a guess, but he could be older. You know the type: an anorak, anally retentive."

"Could you describe him?"

She could. He was nearly six feet tall, skinny build, wearing a khaki jacket, probably from the Army Stores, and he had bushy, unkempt hair.

"Clean shaven?"

"Absolutely."

"Spectacles?"

"Obligatory."

"Would you recognise him again?"

"Undoubtedly."

I wrote her answers down, drew a line across the page and tapped my pen against it. Her fingers were long and white, with neatly trimmed nails, and she wore no rings or any other jewellery. I wished Dave or Maggie was there with me, for a second opinion.

"You say you came to work in the car, today," I began.

"That's right. I was concerned so I decided to change my routine."

"That's what I'm coming round to. You have a daily routine?"

"Yes. I come in on the 07:19 and try to go home on the 18:28 or the 19:58." The times came at me like a burst of machine gunfire, far too fast to register in my feeble brain.

"Well you did right to change it, but how do you feel about going back to your usual routine next week? You'll probably notice that the train will be more crowded than usual."

"With police officers?"

"Mmm."

"No problem. That's how I'd have handled it."

"Good. Meanwhile, could you tell me a few things about yourself, please?"

"What do you need to know?"

"For a start, whereabouts in Heckley do you work?"

"Aire and Calder Water."

"Ah, the Cattery," I responded, giving the tower block its local name, bestowed on the building because of the number of fat-cat scandals that had been attached to it. Our water might taste like Domestos but the board had just shared ten million in windfall profits amongst themselves.

"That's right," she said. "I'm the senior accountant."

I felt my eyebrows shoot up like a couple of crows taking flight. When I'm in trouble I grin, but I struggled to hold it back. "Does that give you a seat on the board?" I asked, matter-of-fact. See if I care. I talk to captains of industry every day.

"Yes, but is that relevant?"

"It could be." I was extemporising like a non-swimmer who's just fallen in the cut. "He could be following you for any number of reasons. For a start, you're a young woman." I gestured with a hand, leaving the rest of it unspoken. "Now it transpires that you have a position of responsibility in a controversial industry. That could be of interest to certain pressure groups. And, of course, you're fairly well-off. There's no point in going too far with the speculations. If he follows you again we'll nab him and ask. How does that sound?" I hadn't voiced the possibility that was uppermost in my mind. That her movements were predictable and he didn't need any other motive for killing her.

"It sounds fine. What do I do?"

"Go back to your routine, that's all. It might be helpful if you kept us informed of your movements. I'll give you a number to ring."

I walked to the door with her and watched her drive away. I'd had a little bet with myself that the Porsche's registration would be H2O, but it wasn't. It began with CJK, though.

I was on dangerous territory, telling her to resume her normal routine, but I couldn't see any alternative. I rang Salford and they agreed to keep a weather eye on her over the weekend. Come Monday I'd have her followed in both directions. I wanted to talk to someone about it. This could be the break we'd been waiting for but there was nobody to discuss it with. I put the kettle on, then decided I'd been in the office long enough, I needed some fresh air.

I drove to Neville Ferriby's house in its neat little development of up-market dwellings. I should have talked to Rod, asked if he was moving yet, but I didn't. I'd park on Ferriby's drive and wait for him, listening to the radio. I could afford the time.

The sun was shining when I arrived so I strolled round the back to where I knew there was a garden seat. An hour or so there, away from the phone, gathering my thoughts, sounded inviting. Then I'd have the pleasure of putting the shifty Mr Ferriby on the spot.

His car wasn't on the drive or in the garage, but the door to the shed where the fish were kept was wide open. I walked towards it and peered inside.

The tanks were dark and silent, the fish congregating listlessly up near the top, seeking the warmer water, their once-vibrant hues reduced to shades of dirty brown. There was nothing exotic about them now, and if somebody didn't do something they'd soon be carrion. First thoughts were that a fuse had blown, but then I remembered the open door.

I looked on the wall just inside the door and found an electric cable. I traced it downwards and where it emerged from the floor there was a white plastic box with a switch on it. If it was wired up like all the switches at my house it was in the off position. I pulled a pen from my pocket and used it to operate the switch, just in case we needed to find whose finger had done the dirty deed. Dave would have been proud of me.

Things happened. A loud buzzing came from everywhere, soon settling to a steady hum, lights in the tanks flickered then sprang into life and after a few seconds bubbles burst forth from the gravel and produced the familiar, reassuring sound of lapping water. The fish panicked for a few seconds, dashing about, then realised that they were saved and settled down. Heat, light and oxygen, they thought, there is a God. I decided to do the job properly and feed them, so I hunted around and found a box labelled Freeze Dried Tubifex Worms. When I took the lid off and saw the gruesome contents I remembered that you should never over-feed fish, so I put it back on and went outside.

That's when I noticed that the back door to the house was open, too. The lawn was spongy under my feet as I walked across it, looking up at the windows, all tightly closed. I placed my fingertips against the door, pushed it wide and listened.

Somebody or something was in there. I stepped inside and moved across the kitchen to the door that gave way to the hall. The noise was louder now, more distinct.

"Uh, uh, uh, uh," it grunted, guttural, almost obscene. "Uh, uh, uh, uh."

It was coming from upstairs. I stood with one foot on the bottom step and listened again. "Uh, uh, uh, uh," then: "Ah, uh, yes, uh, uh."

Whatever they were doing they were doing it with energy, gusto and enthusiasm. I climbed the steps, well over to the left in the hope that they wouldn't creak, trying to peer round the landing as I climbed.

There were four bedroom doors off the landing and one of the middle ones was ajar. There had been a slight pause in the noises, but now they were coming again. "Uh, uh, uh."

I gently pushed the door all the way open and beheld the scene inside. A figure was standing in front of the built-in wardrobes and every door was flung open. She was surrounded by piles of clothes – suits and sweaters – and her right arm was jerking up and down in time with all the grunts as she slashed more of them with the Stanley knife she was holding. "Uh, uh, ah, uh."

"Mrs Ferriby, I presume," I said.

She spun round, her mouth and eyes wider than nature ever intended, and stood there, paralysed by more emotions than there are names for.

"Detective Inspector Priest, Heckley CID," I said. "Could you put the knife down, please?"

It took a while for the words to register, then she dropped the knife and flung herself sobbing on to the bed.

I picked it up by the blade. "I'll be downstairs," I told her. "Sort yourself out and be down there in two minutes."

I found a plastic bag in the kitchen and put the knife in it. Habit, I suppose. Makes me feel as if I'm doing the right thing. I sat on the windowsill surveying Neville Ferriby's little kingdom and waited for Madame F to present herself. The room was overstuffed and overbearing, a swirling mass of conflicting patterns. No marriage could have survived that room. I heard bathroom noises and eventually she appeared, sniffing into a tissue. I told her to sit down.

"It is Mrs Ferriby?" I asked, and she nodded.

"First name?"

"Monica."

"And where do you live now, Monica?"

"Sheepstone."

"Anywhere near the cemetery?" I was surprised how attractive she was. Petite, with a tendency towards plumpness, but well-groomed with a face that would be pleasant under different circumstances.

"Just over the road from it."

"And what exactly were you doing upstairs just now?"

She sniffed into the tissue, then gave me a little smile. "Exacting revenge, I think you'd call it."

"I'd call it criminal damage. Was it you who turned the fish off?"

She blushed and nodded.

"That wasn't very nice."

"No, I don't suppose it was." She half rose to her feet, saying: "I'll switch them back on, it may not be too late..."

"That's OK, I did it."

"Oh, thank you."

"So what were you exacting revenge for?"

She sank back in the chair and sighed. "Money problems."

"Go on."

"Well, when we divorced we came to an arrangement about the house. An *amicable* arrangement, we called it. Uh! He kept this place but is supposed to help me with the mortgage for mine. Now he's saying that my boyfriend lives with me and that excuses him from payment. He's been spying on me, gathering evidence against me. He's doing it right now, so I sneaked out the back way."

"Does your boyfriend live with you?"

"He stays overnight once or twice a week. He lives at Stockton-on-Tees, ninety miles away. What else could he do?"

Shag her earlier and go home? "It doesn't sound unreasonable to me, Monica, but I don't know the rules."

"How much trouble am I in?"

"That depends on whether your ex prefers charges."

"It's up to him?"

"Yes."

"Then he will."

"Tell me," I began, "what does Mr Ferriby do for a living?"

"He's retired."

"But he's not that old."

"No. He retired on ill health and a full pension."

"What's wrong with him?"

"It's a long story."

"I've got all the time in the world."

She looked around the room and her eyes settled on the cocktail cabinet, as if she needed a drink, but then she remembered this was not her home anymore.

"I'm listening," I said.

"Neville worked for the Inland Revenue," she stated, looking back at me. "As a statistician. I believe the expression is they 'let him go', on full pension and with a nice little compensation payment."

"Why?"

"Because his work wasn't up to scratch."

"I thought you said ill health."

"His work wasn't up to scratch because of ill health."

"So what's wrong with him?"

"Neville has a problem."

"Which is…?" I went through the possibilities in my mind. Little girls, little boys, bigger girls, bigger boys, photography and all the ramifications of that.

"He takes drugs, Inspector. Neville is a heroin addict."

I let it sink in, trying to figure out if it changed anything. I wasn't even sure what I was doing there. Mrs Ferriby came to my rescue, volunteering information for once, without my having to crowbar it out of her.

"I suspect he's having trouble with his supplier, and that's why he's unable to pay me."

"The price of heroin is at an all-time low," I told her. We measure our success by what effect we have on the street price. *Failure is no success at all*, as the troubadour sang, and prices were rock bottom.

"Not to Neville, Inspector. Neville is not what you might call street-wise. If he had to go out and find some heroin he'd probably wander into a city centre pub with his money in his sticky little hand and ask the first person he met."

"So how does he get it?"

"He's had the same supplier since he started taking it, about eight or nine years ago."

"And who's that?"

She sat back, looked up at the ceiling, turned her head towards the wall.

"A name, Monica."

"Graham Allen. Graham Allen, the boy next door, is his supplier."

I could see how it might have happened. Graham would have been fourteen, maybe sixteen, tall and handsome. Neville would have invited him to come and look at the fish, showed him some photographs, explained how a camera worked, insinuating his way into the boy's affections. But Graham had seen Neville watching Mrs Allen, and had a different agenda. He'd told Neville about the drugs that were on sale at school, brought some home, and they'd experimented together. And Neville had become hooked, completely under Graham's control. A nice little earner for him, you might say.

"I think we'd better go to the station, Monica," I said. "I need a statement from you."

Forensic didn't find anything on the latest letter, apart from traces of talcum powder as used to lubricate some types of latex gloves. Our man, scientific branch suggested, was "forensically aware". This meant that he was either a police officer or he watched true crime programmes on Channel 5.

I'd sent Mrs Ferriby on her way and was up in my office, catching up on the day's mail, when Pete and Dave came in.

"Bugger all!" I said, handing them the report.

They read it together and one of them said: "That's a disappointment."

"A disappointment! A disappointment! It's a sodding tragedy."

"There's still Mrs Whatsername's stalker," Dave said. "That might turn to gold."

"Yeah, I suppose so. So what else is new?"

"Young Graham Allen is up to something," Peter replied. "He's mixed up with a character called Bernie Cole who has lots of form for receiving and fraud. Cole leases the unit next door to Mister Blue in the precinct but he doesn't trade from it. This morning he took delivery of two huge boxes and Graham supervised the unloading. Then he met Cole for lunch and they had a cosy *tête-à-tête* over beef Wellington at Fidelio's."

"I hope your man wasn't watching from the next table."

"No. He had his nose pressed against the window."

"Good, but it's not much, is it?"

"That's not all. Cole then went off and visited a little factory off Bean Street, where they produce children's clothes for the cheaper end of the market. It's a sweatshop. After he'd left we had a word with the foreman there and leaned on him a little. He no doubt has things he'd prefer the authorities not to know about so he was eager to co-operate. Cole spoke to a couple of the girls, offered them some extra work for Saturday afternoon at his shop in the precinct."

"Maybe he wants some sewing done."

Pete shrugged his shoulders. "Maybe."

"So what do you think they're up to?"

"Something."

"That's not enough to get a warrant to raid the premises."

"I know."

"OK. Let me tell you what I know. Graham Allen is a dealer. Well, a pusher. He's been supplying Ferriby, the man next door, with heroin for the last eight years."

"You're kidding!"

"Scout's honour."

"Who told you this?"

"Monica Ferriby, his wife."

"Well that should be enough for a warrant."

"Can I leave it with you?"

"You bet! Tomorrow afternoon?"

"Is there a match on?"

"Only Chesterfield."

"Tomorrow it is, then."

I told the super what was happening and finished doing paperwork. One of the by-products of a murder hunt is that all sorts of other crimes are cleared up. We'd catch a small-time dealer but were no nearer the murderer. At about half past six I was tidying my desk when the phone rang again. It was Rod. I'd forgotten about Rod.

"Hi, Boss. It's Rod at the cemetery. Ferriby's just packed all his stuff in his car, looks as if he's going home. What do you want us to do?"

"You'd better do the same, then, Rod," I told him.

"Do you want us to pick him up again in the morning?"

"Um, no, come in here. Oh, and keep the afternoon free."

I told the front desk that very shortly they'd be receiving a call from an irate citizen who'd found all his clothes slashed and I had a word with drug squad. They had no intelligence whatsoever about Cole, Graham Allen or Mister Blue, but wanted part of the action. I gave them a formal invitation to the party, put my jacket on and placed my mug on the tray with the other dirty ones. If we don't take her for granted the cleaning lady washes up for us.

There was a reception committee waiting on the front steps for me, comprised of a young woman in an ambitious suit and an I-mean-business hairdo, a cameraman and a spotty youth with a sound boom.

"Inspector Priest," she gabbled, "Belinda Mayhew, Triple K News, is it true that you have consulted a medium in your attempts to find the murderer who is terrorising the district."

"No," I replied, ducking under the boom which the youth was waving around as if he'd just caught a squirrel on the end of a pole.

"That's not the information that's coming out of head-quarters."

"Well have a word with headquarters, then."

"We have done. They say that Julia LeStrang, the well-known psychic healer and medium, is assisting you with your enquiries."

I'd reached my car. I opened the door and stood with one foot inside. "Perhaps," I began, "perhaps she's assisting us on the psychic level, and the news hasn't filtered down to me yet. Meanwhile, I deal with facts, not hocus-pocus."

"Are you any nearer finding the killer."

That was the sucker punch. I dropped my head for a second, then shook it. "No," I admitted. "I'm afraid we're not."

"Do you expect him to kill again?"

"It's a possibility."

"Then why not allow her to help you?"

I was on TV. People were being murdered and this woman with the *fuck-you* haircut was making me look like a monster. I said: "We need all the help we can get. If any of your viewers have any suspicions about somebody they know, then I beg of them to inform us. Somebody somewhere must know who this person is. He has brothers and sisters, parents, a wife or a girlfriend. Please voice your suspicions before he kills again."

I slipped into the driving seat and slammed the door. She turned to the camera looking pleased with herself as she recited her by-line, and I drove off.

Saturday morning Mrs Jordan-Keedy came in to work on the train but the only person following her was one of the team. She had a busy morning in the office and caught the 13:17 back to Salford.

The drugs squad brought their latest secret weapon with them. She's called Delilah and she stared at me with eyes like chocolate marshmallows all through the briefing. I desperately wanted to tickle her behind the ears, but wasn't sure if that was permissible. At five to two we received a message saying that two Asian girls had arrived at Mister Blue and Graham Allen had taken them next door, to the unit leased by Bernie Cole. Everybody except me decanted down to the mall.

I picked up all their coffee cups and took them along the corridor to the kitchen. This time I rinsed them under the tap myself and left them to dry, upside down. Back in the office I found my drawing pad again and spread it out on a spare desk, but I wasn't in the mood for sketching.

The psychologists call it his signature. The MO is how he does the deed – in this case bludgeoning, stabbing and strangling – but everything else he does, all the unnecessary stuff, is his signature. Except, with this one, it was more what he didn't do.

One thing was certain – he wasn't mentally ill. At least not by the normal parameters. He was cold, calculating and intelligent, and that meant sane. A classic sociopath if ever I knew one. The phone rang.

"Charlie," I said into it.

"It's Dave. T1 is back in Mister Blue. He's left the girls in the shop next door."

"Can you see them in there?"

"No, they're in the back room. There's some right talent going in and out of Mister Blue, though. You ought to be here."

"No sign of Cole?"

"Afraid not."

"OK, keep me informed."

"Will do."

Chances were that our strangler had lived down south, in North London, and had moved up here. Not necessarily, but it looked that way. I had somebody checking the feasibility of comparing electoral rolls, but they are not updated very often and he could have changed his name. And if he was drawing benefits the DSS in both places would know about him, so we were checking with them, too, but they were longshots.

Was he married? That was a dodgy one. Inadequate singletons often try to strike up a relationship with their victims, but this one just killed them. If he'd come into the killing business by accident, after a road traffic accident as Chief Superintendent Natrass had suggested, it was probably arbitrary whether he was married or not. Then there was that eighteen-month gap. Had he married in that time, or divorced? Had he found a soul-mate and resumed his evil ways with her? A female friend would certainly help with the abductions. I left that one open.

"These seats in the mall aren't half uncomfortable," Dave complained, next time he rang. "My arse is as numb as a penguin's fanny, and they don't have a backrest."

"That's so you don't linger too long on them," I told him. "They want you on your feet, doing the shops, not lounging around all afternoon."

"The crafty so-and-sos."

"There's no clock anywhere for the same reason. You're supposed to lose all track of time as you enjoy the unique shopping experience. The architects who design these malls are cynical bastards. So what's happening?"

"I'm having a doughnut."

"Good, keep your strength up."

How old was he? Twenty to thirty? No, probably older than that. Rapists were usually younger, serial killers a bit older. Call it twenty-five to thirty-five, but what difference did it make?

Lifestyle and class. Did he work for a living and if so, at what? Did his job not bring him into contact with the opposite sex? Was he a loner, introverted?

How was I supposed to know? How the *fuck* did they expect me to know? I ripped the sheet off the pad, which was a waste of paper because I'd hardly written anything on it, and ripped it into shreds.

The phone rang again before I could snap all the pencils and trash the office.

"Charlie!"

"T2 has arrived but unfortunately T1 is back in Mister Blue."

"Damn. We need both of them in there, if possible."

"I know. I'm in the Happy Burger now, having one, just across the way. It's much more comfortable in here."

"As long as you're happy."

One of the problems was that the game was changing all the time. Sex was starting to rear its ugly head. The reasons for the latest killings were probably different to those for the early ones. I tipped my chair against the wall, put my feet on the desk and closed my eyes.

The phone woke me. "Don't tell me – you're having a milk shake."

"No."

"You've been sick."

"No."

"Go on, then."

"We're working, you know. We're not just having a good time. I could be at the match this afternoon, even if it is only Chesterfield."

"I'm suitably chastised. So what's happening?"

"T2 joined T1 in Mister Blue, then they went for a bite at the Italian place upstairs. Now T1 is in Mister Blue and T2 is next door, or maybe it's the other way round."

"Allen's in his shop and Cole's in his."

"That's it."

"Well why not say so."

"Because that's not the proper way."

"OK, keep watching. What's Delilah up to?"

"Don't know. They don't allow dogs in the mall."

"Eh! Since when?"

"It's a by-law."

"So the whole operation is in jeopardy because of some poxy little by-law?"

"They'll bring her in when necessary."

"They'd better."

At four o'clock I made a coffee and took it into my little office. The phone was ringing again before I'd taken the first sip.

"Charlie," I said.

"Sorry to disturb you, Sir," I heard Sparky intone. "This is DC Sparkington. Just thought you'd like to know that we have apprehended two gentlemen in a shop in the mall under suspicious circumstances."

"I'm on my way!" I told him as I grabbed my jacket from behind the door.

Quite a crowd had gathered around the entrance to the shop. I muscled my way through and winked at the two bobbies standing implacably in either side of the doorway. Their big hats made them look about seven feet tall and their uniforms bristled with all the paraphernalia that a modern policeman carries: extending side-handle baton, radio, pepper spray, handcuffs and a pouch of documents, ready to start the paperwork. Mustn't forget the paperwork. The front of the shop was empty, all the activity taking place in the back rooms.

The two Asian girls were sitting at one side, looking like a pair of frightened mice. Serena, our only Asian WPC, was kneeling before them, pouring on the reassurance. Graham Allen and Bernie Cole were seated in another corner, dejection oozing from every fibre of their bodies as Sparky went through the routine of asking them the preliminary questions.

"I'm not saying nowt without my solicitor," Cole asserted.

"Take him in," I said to Dave with a shrug. He was already handcuffed. They'd march him through the mall to the police van with his jacket over his head, and that would probably be the hardest part of whatever happened to him.

Indignity and embarrassment are powerful forces. Once he was in the dock, with his senses and sensibilities gathered and reinforced by a solicitor, he'd be as cocky as a bantam. But right now he was smarting, and if I could have rubbed salt in I would have.

This was the stockroom, I thought, looking around. The walls were lined with shelves and about a quarter of them were piled up with denim clothing, probably all jeans. Two heavy-duty sewing machines were against one wall, illuminated by Anglepoise lamps, and two of my detectives and two from drugs were rummaging about in a pair of large cardboard boxes that stood next to the sewing machines.

One of the detectives came over with a large manila envelope and handed it to me. It was bulging with designer labels as sewn on the backs of jeans. He gestured for me to follow him and indicated piles of the labels on the sewing machines, then pointed to the floor which was scattered with other labels. These had strands of cotton blurring the edges and had been removed by the girls from all the garments that were heaped near their machines. A movement caught my eye and I realised it was Delilah's tail, poking out from a pile of cardboard boxes, vibrating like a fiddler's elbow.

So Graham Allen was in the counterfeit jeans racket. Big deal. A fine, maybe community service, and a short jail sentence for Cole, who had previous. There's no such thing as victimless crime, they say, but counterfeit clothing must come close. The jeans are made in sweatshops in the Far East, paying pennies to kids who are little more than slaves. The big names pass them on at several thousand percent mark-up and the people who buy them can't tell the difference between the eighty quid ones and the fifteen quid ones, apart from the label. I wouldn't be shedding tears for them.

"Nice business associate you have," I said to Graham.

He looked up at me but didn't answer.

"Did he set this up?" I hoped he would agree with me,

accept the lifeline and tell me all about it, but he still didn't answer.

"I was talking to Monica Ferriby yesterday," I told him, "and I know all about her husband's little problem. You could help yourself by telling us where to find whatever it is we're looking for."

He said: "I am not saying anything until I have spoken to a solicitor." The words came out all wrong, as if it were the first rehearsal of a Shakespearean play. He wasn't as well versed as his partner in crime, but he'd learn. I was about to tell him to have it his way when Delilah started barking.

OK, I admit it. I have a thing about designer labels. I also have a thing about the type of training shoe that is categorised as *air*. Put them together – designer air shoes – and I go into a tizzy.

When you pay a lot of money for a pair of trainers, what you are buying is lightness. That's fair enough. Exotic materials used in the construction of shoes are light but they are also expensive. Hence the price hike. But air is free. And it's light, too. "Why not," Mr Heap Big Trainer Manufacturer said, "simply hollow out the soles and heels and let air do the work? We could even put the price up a bit for the innovation." So that's what they did.

"She's found something," the dog handler said, diving into the pile of boxes after her. "Find it, girl! Find it!"

We gathered round and after a few seconds he emerged holding a shoe box. It said: 'Top Speed Air training shoes' on the side, with a logo of a sprinter in full flight. Delilah was jumping around, yelping with excitement. He patted her head and gave her a biscuit from his pocket. The shoes inside the box were wrapped in tissue paper. Delilah's handler lifted one out and turned it over in his hands, carefully sniffing it. He held it down for the dog and she looked up at him and barked again, as if to say: "I've told you once."

I wanted to say something, but decided that they were the experts and besides, it was probably obvious. The hero-

in was in the air space. This time the trainers really did warrant their price. I looked across to see Graham's reaction but
his head was in his hands.

It was a result, of sorts, and would let the ACC know that
we weren't sleeping on the job. Sunday I was invited round
to Dave's for lunch. We went for a brisk walk along the road
to the top of the fell and back via the Ancient Shepherd,
where we stayed a little too long, but not long enough to
spoil the Yorkshire puddings.

The ACC wasn't impressed, and invited me to HQ for a
review meeting, ten fifteen Friday morning. He might not
have been impressed but Dave, Maggie and Pete were,
Monday morning, when I put the phone down and told
them.

"Ten *fifteen*," Pete said. "That sounds serious."

"They'll take it off us," Maggie added.

"They'll bring in some mutton-head from another division, who'll rake over everything we've done and come up
with nowt," Dave asserted.

"OK," I said. "Let's go over it again. What have we forgotten?"

That evening I had another long telephone conversation
with Dr Foulkes, but nothing new came out of it. Sex
offenders were not his main speciality but he agreed to talk
to someone in that field. It might be possible to type-cast
our man, find someone who'd done something similar and
use him as a template. Meanwhile, we'd continue monitoring
everybody who'd ever wiggled their winky in the park who
happened to live within twenty miles of Heckley. None of
them had ever lived in North London – we'd already
checked that.

Afterwards I did the town again. It was raining, so I put
on my Gore-Tex coat and hung around the hospital watching the visitors. People came and went, carrying their bur-
dens: nervous husbands, chain smoking, sprays of carnations

held at an awkward angle; women with umbrellas and carrier bags of goodies; Asian taxi drivers who deposited whole families right in the doorway. It's not easy to be invisible, to hang around for half an hour or more without being noticed, but that's what Laddo must have done as he selected his victims. Mrs Jordan-Keedy and a few others had claimed that they were being stalked, but apart from Mrs J-K these had been investigated and dismissed. One woman who contacted us in a state of high agitation had been followed on three successive nights from her place of employment at the DSS offices in Huddersfield all the way to her home in Church Grove, Heckley. On the fourth night we nabbed him and discovered that he was an auditor with the DSS, currently working in Huddersfield and living in Church Grove, Heckley.

A thin woman in a plastic mac walked straight past the bus stops and headed towards town. There's a dark stretch of road where it passes the cemetery, so I followed her. At the edge of town she went into a pub called the Marquis which is frequented by city workers during the day and gays late at night. In between times, you might be standing next to a barrister having a swift one before retreating to his New York-style loft apartment or an out-of-work choreographer soaking up local colour. I went in and saw her approach a man in a Greenwoods jacket and a cap with fur earflaps, turned up. He was sipping a pint and a glass of dark liquid stood on the table, waiting for her. I decided I didn't need a drink but as I turned to leave I saw a figure I recognised hunched at a table, deep in conversation with somebody else I knew. They didn't see me so I sneaked out and fetched the car.

I parked about fifty yards down the road and waited. Their glasses had been nearly empty and I didn't think they'd be staying for a session. After a few minutes I saw Tony Madison, Maggie's husband, appear in the doorway. He paused to look at the weather, turned up the collar of his coat and stepped into the road. I drove past him and stopped, reaching across to open the passenger side door. He looked inside, saying: "Hello, Charlie," as he recognised me.

"Get in," I said. "I want to talk."

Halfway back to his house I pulled into a lay-by. "What was it tonight?" I asked. "Night class?"

"Yeah. Spanish for beginners. How to say five pints please, with egg and chips, in twelve easy lessons."

"I'd have thought you'd've had enough of it through the day."

"I know, but I'm being unkind. The night classes are a joy, Charlie, believe me, a joy. And the money's welcome. It's the days that are the problem. We start again on Wednesday and I've already got the twitch back. What do you want to talk about?"

"I'm displeased, Tony, to put it mildly."

"What about?"

"About the company you keep."

"What company?"

"Arnie Vernon. He's a hack of the worst kind. To call Vernon a journalist would be an insult to the profession. Apart from being a sot he is an unscrupulous liar who would sell his sister to the Mujahedeen if there was a by-line in it. Somebody's been running to the press agencies with tit-bits of information, for money of course, because somebody else has leaked it to them. First of all they knew we were linking the murders, then they knew that the assistant chief constable wanted to call in the LeStrang woman. Nothing important, as it happens, but it could have jeopardised the enquiry."

His shoulders slumped and his head fell forward. I went on: "This is a murder hunt, Tony. A big one. People have died in extremely unpleasant ways and it's not over yet. I can't afford to have anybody on the team who isn't with us one hundred and twenty per cent. If you'd seen them, poor Colinette Jones and the others, you wouldn't be as eager to talk to Vernon and his likes."

Tony reached out and placed one hand on the dash, then twisted in his seat to face me. "It's not Maggie," he said. "She doesn't come home and blabber on about everything that has happened. She just sometimes lets a little bit slip, when she's frustrated. She knows I'm having a rough time – we have the OFSTED inspectors in next week – so she might tell me about her day, to make me feel involved. That's all, and I don't ask about it. She's never in when I come home, you see more of her than I do, so I started to call in the Marquis of an evening. That's how I met Vernon."

"What did he do – knock your drink over?"

"No, not quite, but I see what you mean."

We sat in silence for a few seconds. The rain had built up on the windscreen so I pressed the wiper lever down and they swept it clear. A vehicle going in the opposite direction kept his headlights on main beam as he passed us, flooding the car interior with light. Probably thought we were a couple of faggots having a tiff.

"She'll leave me," Tony said.

I didn't comment.

"She loves working for you, Charlie," he continued. "She'd walk to the ends of the Earth on broken glass for you. It's my fault, not hers. I know you've got pressure on you, but you're not the only ones, you know. And I'm sure you have your good times, your successes. They're few and far between in the classroom these days, believe me. Sometimes ...sometimes..." He gave a big sigh and left it at that.

I kept quiet, aware of the awkwardness, waiting for it to wear him down. After about an age he said: "My dad was a miner. Did you know?"

I didn't.

"Well he was. The pits this way on weren't much good. Thin and wet, with lots of faults. He was crippled with rheumatism. They were always on the point of closing, losing money, limping from one crisis to the next. And, of course, the miners took the blame. Dad used to say that it wasn't their fault: good coal made good colliers and bad coal made bad colliers. It's the same with schools, Charlie. These days it's all league tables, performance assessment, but it's good kids who make good schools and bad kids who make bad schools. Teachers can only do so much."

"Maggie's a good officer," I said. "And a good friend. You both are, and I don't want to lose either. This job puts a strain on marriages, God knows I learnt that the hard way, but that's the price we pay. We've just got to pull together and try to understand."

"We've been having it rough lately, Charlie," he admitted. "I think you sensed that when you came last week. This could finish us. Maggie tries, but I've been depressed, lately. I've just lost it, somehow. Lost my grip on things."

"Talking to Vernon's not the answer," I said. "If you need to talk to someone talk to me or Maggie."

"What will you say to her?"

"Maggie? I don't know. Nothing, probably. I don't think it'll be necessary, do you? Anyway, we have a review meeting on Friday. They'll probably appoint someone over my head and disband my team, so we should all have a bit more time after that."

He gave a little snuffle of a laugh but didn't speak.

"What?" I asked.

"Oh, nothing."

"Go on."

"Bad taste joke of the week. I was going to say can I quote you on that?"

I gave him a half smile and put the car in gear. As we moved off he mumbled something about appreciating it, said it wouldn't happen again. I wondered if I was growing soft.

They found half a pound of heroin concealed in the soles of the trainers, with a street value of about a quarter of a million pounds after it had been diluted with powdered milk and divided into individual hits. It would have cost about ten grand to buy, which made it, as Dave said, a nice little earner. Becky, Graham's model-girl partner, was inconsolable when the news was broken to her, but there'd be no shortage of volunteers wanting to try. His parents doused the barbecue over on the Costa and caught the next flight home. We'd wondered if they'd dabbled themselves, but they appeared genuinely shocked when we eventually met them. Another supply line had been closed off which would be reflected in a small blip in the street price, and the hapless Neville Ferriby would have to either go cold turkey or wander round the pubs of Heckley clutching his money, looking for another source.

Monday and Tuesday Caitlin Jordan-Keedy made it to work and back home again without let or hindrance. The only figure she might have seen furtively dodging between shop doorways, the collar of his dirty mac turned up against the rain, was Peter Goodfellow. I talked to her on the phone, reassured her that we were watching, trying to convince her that we were taking her story seriously. She'd never know how badly I wanted it to be true, how much danger I wanted her to be in.

"Just the man," someone said as I walked into the office and checked the kettle.

"Empty again," I snapped, half-heartedly. "What's the golden rule? If you empty it, you fill it."

There were about ten of them sitting round in the office, with Sparky the centre of attraction, as usual. The only uniform was Geordie Farrell, a white mug looking like an egg cup in his fist. Someone jumped up and took the kettle from me.

Dave said: "Jeff's been telling us about the latest drugs craze that's sweeping the county."

"What's that?" I asked, turning to Jeff.

"Oh, the kids have started injecting themselves in the

mouth with ecstasy," he replied.

I grimaced. "In the mouth?"

"Yeah, it's called E by gum."

I stroked my chin. "Right. Right. So what else is new?"

"Not much, apart from a couple of schoolkids downstairs, Charlie, in for a caution. I assume you'll want to handle it yourself."

I found a chair and pulled it towards the others. "Under normal circumstances, Jeff, you know I'd leap at the opportunity, but just this once I'm happy to delegate that responsibility to you. Regard it as something you can put on your CV."

"Cheers. I appreciate the sacrifice you're making and I'm grateful for the opportunity."

"No problem. Ask them if they know any good jokes. What've they done?"

"They were caught fighting liars in the school dumpsters."

I blinked as someone jumped in with: "*Fighting liars?*"

"*Lighting fires*, deaf lugs. I said lighting fires."

"No you didn't, you said fighting liars."

"You need your ears testing."

"He said fighting liars, didn't he, Charlie?"

I shook my head and raised both hands in a gesture of peace. "I don't know, I wasn't listening. I never listen to anything Jeff says."

Somebody else said: "This foot-in-mouth disease is getting worse, isn't it?"

"Get lost!"

"Oh what a shining wit."

"And you can piss off, too. It was a slip of the tongue. Anyone can make a slip of the tongue."

The phone in my office started ringing. Phones are inanimate objects. They transmit and receive electrical impulses and convert them to sounds. In theory they should transmit one sound as implacably as any other, but sometimes there's something about the ring, the tone, that makes you hesitate before you lift it. We all turned towards the offending sound as it cut across the office like an assegai, and the silence between rings was as evocative as the noise.

"I'll get it," Dave said, picking up the phone at his elbow. He tapped in the appropriate code and the phone in my office fell silent.

"No, he's not here," he told someone, presumably referring to me. I relaxed, encouraged by the tone of his voice, and reached towards him for the handset, but he ignored me. "No, I don't know where he is." He listened for a few seconds then concluded the conversation with the words: "OK. I'd give it another hour, if I were you, and then call it a day. S'long."

"Who was that?" I asked.

"Rod. He says not much is happening."

"You should have told him to go home."

"No, he likes watching people."

Someone placed a mug of coffee in front of me and I thanked him. Big Geordie coughed to attract attention, as if we could ignore him, and asked: "Who's coming training tonight? Five laps roond the park."

Two or three said they'd be there but I declined.

"Is it true that the firemen are doing the three peaks thing by climbing up ladders and sliding down a brass pole?" Jeff asked.

This caused a flurry of disapproval and widespread agreement that it would be cheating. Walking down the mountains was almost as hard as walking up them.

"Somebody's talking rubbish," Geordie informed us. "'Hoo are they going to put a pole up in the middle o' the park? Anyhoo, we'll do it the hard way, up and doon the back stairs."

"So the real thing is definitely off?" Another fifteen cases of foot-and-mouth had been confirmed, mainly in the Lake District, and there was no sign of it easing.

"It looks like it."

Dave broke a brief silence, saying: "Just think, Jeff. If you did the scoring as the rest of us went up and down, you could tell us when we'd mounted three counts."

"*Fuck off*!"

That broke up the meeting. Big Geordie stood up and I did the same. My coffee had cooled down so I was heading for the kettle to revitalise it when the phone in my office rang again. Sparky did his trick but this time it wasn't Rod. He raised an arm to silence us and the smiles slipped from our faces as he listened.

"Yeah. He's here. I'll put him on."

I reached for the phone as he told me the news: "They've found a woman's body, just outside Leeds."

Chapter Ten

I sat in the back as we drove there, not speaking, watching the fields and telegraph poles going by, remembering when I used to go off with my parents. Scarborough, Whitby or the Dales. I'd stuff myself with ice cream and Dad would slip into a pub to buy cigarettes and have a quick pint. He'd cough and smoke all the way home, and we'd stop at the Four Alls for a shandy and some more cigarettes. *It's not the cough that carries you off...*

Dave was driving, with Peter in the front passenger seat. We'd not been able to raise the chief inspector doing the initial investigation, so we had to be content with second-hand messages from their HQ. They gave us the location of the body and we headed there. A council worker giving the grass its annual trim had found her in the middle of a roundabout, but she was newly dead. Dave was inches behind a woman in a Nissan Trooper doing the school run, nosing out every few seconds as he looked for an opportunity to pass.

"Take it easy, Dave," I said. "She won't be going anywhere."

They'd closed off one segment of the roundabout and diverted the traffic through a garage forecourt. We showed our IDs and were allowed through the cordon to join the crush of vehicles parked haphazardly at the crime scene, some on the grass, some on the road. The sun was low and bright, casting long shadows, and a tent indicated the location of the body.

Faces turned to us as we slammed the car doors and walked over to the knot of suits who might have been insurance salesmen or Jehovah's Witnesses deciding who was going to knock on which side of the street. They were all strangers to me.

"Acting DCI Charlie Priest, Heckley CID," I said to the swarthy man with a pencil moustache who projected himself to the front of the group. "And this is DC Sparkington and DS Goodfellow. I don't think we've met..."

He introduced himself and we shook hands, but without much cordiality, and he asked why we were there.

"We've had three," I told him. "Possibly more. We're looking at all suspicious deaths to see if they might be linked with ours."

"This one isn't like yours," he replied.

"Perhaps not, but I need convincing."

"We'd have sent for you if it was."

"I'm sure you would."

"OK. Come and see for yourself."

He strode off towards the tent and we followed him. It was a green tent and everything inside was bathed in green light. Only the blanket over her body provided a contrast. The DCI stooped and peeled the top three feet of blanket back, revealing its ghostly cargo.

She was huddled in the foetal position and looked about eighty years old. Grey-green hair, green face, blue-green nightdress. He covered her again and lifted the blanket off her feet. Legs like cocktail sticks ending in fluffy slippers.

"Poor old lass," Pete said, very quietly.

"Come outside," the DCI ordered. When we were back in the fresh air he said: "Hypostasis indicates that she died where she is lying. Time of death in the early hours of today, cause of death probably hypothermia but the PM scheduled for in the morning." He turned and pointed. "See that building?"

"Er, which one?"

"Other side of the trees, with the tower."

It was a castellated tower, poking above the trees, with a clock face and a flag pole, about half a mile away.

"With the clock?"

"That's it. St Joseph's, known locally as Holy Joe's. One-time septicaemia hospital, one-time isolation hospital, now an old people's home. We asked them to do a stock-take and would you believe it, one of their clients is missing. Miss Jane Middleton, aged 77, hasn't been seen since supper last night, and her bed hasn't been slept in. We're just waiting for permission to move the body. Anything else you need to know?"

Dave said: "They probably have supper at about seven."

"So they haven't missed her for nearly twenty-four hours."

"Poor old lass."

"That'll do for me," I said. "Thanks for your help."

"Glad to be of assistance." He warmed slightly once he realised I wasn't there to steal his case. "So how's it looking with your jobs?" he asked as we walked back towards the cars.

"Grim. No progress at all."

"Rather you than me."

I didn't even look out of the window on the way back. I sat gazing at the back of the driver's headrest, letting thoughts tumble through my head like newspapers blown about by a gale. I wasn't getting any younger. What a stupid expression. Nobody was getting any younger. I was getting older, rapidly, that was it. No known relatives. Outlook, bleak. Pension prospects were good, so that was a relief. Friday we'd be on the carpet and they'd probably take the case off me. Perhaps that would be the time to leave. I had an option that wasn't available to most officers. Somewhere in my abdomen were three shotgun pellets. Two were deep in my liver, too difficult to recover but not doing any harm, the surgeon assured me, and the third was pressed against my spinal column. Too dangerous to retrieve. Anytime I wanted I could keel over with a stabbing pain in my back and I'd be out of the force on full pension before the ink dried. That was my insurance plan.

As we approached Heckley I said: "Is your phone on, Pete?"

"No, it hasn't been. I'll ring in."

He told the front desk that we'd been on a wild goose chase and I heard him ask for a number. He twisted in his seat, saying: "Rod's been after you."

He dialled the number and spoke to Rod. "Yeah, he's here. We've been out. Charlie's asleep in the back. Oh God! his mouth's open and he dribbles. It's disgusting. OK."

Pete terminated the conversation abruptly and turned back to me. "Said he'll ring back. Sounds as if he's on to something but didn't want to speak."

"Good old Rod," I commented.

"Where is he?" Dave asked.

I thought about it. "Do you know," I said, "I believe it was his turn to tail Mrs Jordan-Keedy tonight."

"Lucky for him," Dave mumbled.

Five minutes later Rod rang back. He was in the toilet of the trans-Pennine flyer and a youth of the appropriate description had followed Mrs Jordan-Keedy on to the train at Heckley. He was now sitting about four rows behind her and the train was full. Rod had phoned her on his mobile and she'd answered in the pre-arranged way. We'd made contact.

I pulled my mobile from my inside pocket and unfolded it. Mrs Jordan-Keedy's number was in my diary. I dialled it and she answered with a brisk hello.

"It's DI Charlie Priest," I said. "Just answer yes or no. Can you speak?"

"Some."

"Is it the same youth?"

"Yes. Absolutely."

"Last time, I believe you said you went into a restaurant and he gave up the chase. Is that right?"

"Yes."

"OK, so do the same tonight, except that one of our men – he's called Rod – will walk to the restaurant with you. Just say hello to him as you get off the train. Pretend he's an old friend and you're pleased to meet him. Then we'll follow laddo back and nab him at this end. Are you happy with that?"

She was, so I rang Rod and told him to stick to her like the proverbial. It takes one second to stab someone, and she mustn't be left alone for that time.

Almost everyone had gone home when we arrived at the office. Maggie was typing a report and another DC was swatting for his sergeant's ticket. Two more were busy at computer terminals, but whether they were consulting HOLMES or *lovelyladies.com* I didn't enquire. I told the uniformed sergeant what was happening and asked for some weight to be handy near the station in case we needed it.

"Guns?" he asked.

I shook my head. "No. We have no reason to believe he has a gun."

"ARV standing by?"

"That might be a good idea."

After that it was have a coffee and wait. All the sandwich shops would be closed but one of the DCs suggested a pizza and we sent him out for a supply.

I was in my office, reading Pete's *Telegraph*, when Maggie came in and shut the door behind her.

"Hi, Mags," I said, folding the paper. "You look busy, anything interesting to report?"

She pulled the spare chair out and sat down.

"No, I've been waiting for you."

"Right."

"Tony and I had a long talk last night..."

"Something all married couples should do," I said.

"You know what I'm on about. I feel I've let you down, Charlie."

I tossed the *Telegraph* into the bin. "It's over, Maggie," I told her. "Forget about it. Are things OK between you and Tony? That's all that matters."

"We've agreed to work at it. I'll resign from the CID if you want me to."

"What? Back to shifts? That's a marriage killer if ever

there was one. No, Maggie, forget all about it. Tony was a bit silly, that's all. I'm not always as discreet as I could be myself. Just don't talk to newspapermen, that's the thing. Meanwhile, I need you on the team." Over her shoulder I saw the DC enter the outer office, laden down with flat boxes. "The pizzas have arrived," I said. "So be a good girl and fetch me a spicy beef, with extra olives, oh, and a fresh coffee."

She rose to her feet and gave me a half smile, opened her mouth to speak and hesitated.

"No sugar," I told her. "I've stopped taking sugar."

"Right," she replied and went to fetch the pizza.

Rod timed it perfectly, ringing just as I was nibbling over-cooked cheesy bits off left-over crust. As the train approached Salford station he'd walked down the carriage towards the doors and accidentally-on-purpose met Mrs Jordan-Keedy. She'd given him a broad smile and they'd walked to the Italian restaurant about a quarter of a mile away. Pleasantries were exchanged on the doorstep before she went inside and Rod crossed the road and made himself invisible. The youth had waited outside the restaurant for about twenty minutes and then gone back to the station. "Long enough to establish that she was staying for a meal and not just buying a take-away," Rod had suggested, although the image of the senior accountant with Aire and Calder Water tottering home with a ten inch Hawaiian clutched in her Virginia Woolf fingers didn't ring true with me.

And now he was on the train. "What time do you arrive?" I asked.

"Not sure, but in about half an hour."

"OK. We'll be waiting. I want him followed home and arrested as soon as he puts his key in the door. You drop back as soon as you see the others, and well done, Rod. The boy done good."

I gave the team a lightning briefing, alerted uniformed and went upstairs to tell Mr Wood what was happening. And to wait. That's the hardest part. Once upon a time I was the youngest inspector the force ever had, and now I'm the longest serving. Because I couldn't wait. Sitting at a desk, waiting for news, is not my style. I like to be out there on the streets, the adrenaline flowing, where the real policing is done. That's how I got the pellets in the liver.

It wasn't a long wait. Twenty minutes and I received the message that the train was pulling in. Fifteen minutes later they had him and ten minutes after that I was in the custody suite, looking at the real thing.

Six feet tall, built like a wind-blown reed. Wire specs, bushy hair, ex-German army anorak. Mrs Jordan-Keedy was right: his natural habitat was the end of a station platform, writing train numbers in a notebook. I watched and listened as they informed him that he'd been arrested under the Protection from Harassment Act, 1997, and told him his rights. He declined the offer of a phone call and didn't want to inform either a solicitor of his own choice or the duty solicitor.

His name was William Desmond Thornton.

Age twenty-eight, unmarried, lived alone. Didn't want his parents notifying.

Everybody came to have a look. We had uniformed officers guarding every doorway and corridor and two ARVs in the yard in case he made a break for it, but I knew he wouldn't. From now on he'd rely on his mental agility to foil us. He answered the questions as briefly as possible, volunteering nothing extra, in an educated voice. He wasn't scared, accepting everything he was told, almost as if he was expecting this and was prepared for it. I'd given instructions for the minimum of questioning, just the essentials, until we had him in the interview room, but I stepped in as his pockets were being emptied.

The custody sergeant produced a plastic evidence bag and

explained that this would contain connected property and would be under the control of an exhibits officer. His keys, wallet, some loose change, two pens and half a tube of mints were all placed on the counter. The money was counted and the amount noted. He had a Lloyds TSB cheque guarantee card but no credit cards. The PC frisking him found a note-book and, after a more thorough feel-around, produced a small penknife from a sleeve pocket of the anorak. On to the pile it went.

As the sergeant was placing the bounty into the evidence bag I picked up Thornton's doorkeys. "Is there anything spoiling, back home?" I asked.

He shook his head. "No."

"Not left the electric fire on?"

"No."

"No pets that want feeding?"

"No."

"No rabbits, gerbils, hamsters?"

"I don't have any pets."

"No tarantulas, boa constrictors, Tasmanian devils, Abyssinian garter snakes?"

"No."

"Tortoises?"

He didn't have any tortoises.

"Right," I said, dropping the keys into the bag. "That saves us a journey."

The sergeant sealed the bag and we both signed it. I asked him for a big envelope and placed the evidence bag inside it. I licked the flap, stuck it down and asked for the stapler. Three staples completed the job.

When the processing was complete they took him down to the cells. As he vanished from sight I held my hand out towards the sergeant. "Keys, please," I said.

He unsealed the bag, made me sign for them and the notebook and resealed the bag, forgetting the brown enve-lope and the staples this time.

I threw the keys towards Sparky and he caught them.

"First thing in the morning," I said. "Take it apart."

Upstairs I rang Dr Foulkes at home. This time he answered the phone himself.

"It's Charlie Priest," I told him. "I was, um, half expecting your friend to answer."

"Hi, Charlie. No, it's over, I'm afraid."

I didn't want the details, so I said: "Oh, I am sorry, but listen, we have someone in the cells and I need some help."

"For the killings?"

"That's right."

"Is he admitting it?"

"No, he doesn't know he's a suspect, yet, and I'm not expecting him to. I want to do a substantive interview in the morning and I could use some guidance. Any chance of you cancelling a few appointments?"

"What time?"

"Er, well the clock started at eight forty-five. We're just tucking him up and hopefully he'll get his full eight hours, but we've things we need to do. Providing he doesn't start demanding a solicitor in the middle of the night we should have him available about ten in the morning."

"Ten it is. I'll see you then."

"Cheers, Adrian. I appreciate it." I put the phone down, swung my feet up on to the desk and opened William Desmond Thornton's notebook.

"William Thornton," he replied to my question, voice confident with no trace of an accent.

"And your address?"

"Flat one, number eight, Herdwick Street, Heckley."

"And your date of birth?"

"Three, two, seventy-three."

"And how long have you lived in Heckley?"

"No comment."

"William, as I've just told you, you are still under caution.

You do understand that, don't you?"

"Yes."

"And I strongly advise you to engage the assistance of a solicitor. Do you want me to send for the duty solicitor?" Actually, I didn't give a toss whether he had one or not, but it sounded good on the tape.

We were in interview room number one, ten minutes to eleven on Thursday morning. Thornton was sitting with his back to the door, where the light from the high window fell on him, with me to the left, facing him, and Sparky to the right. The table was pushed against the wall, behind Sparky, so we all had a clear view of each other. It's how they do things in social services, with no artificial barriers between participants. They reckon it's based on Native American pow-wows, but we wouldn't be handing round a pipe of peace. It meant I had no table to thump or leap over, and I felt naked, but it also meant that the camera was recording every twitch Thornton made, from his nose to his toes. A PC sat at the table, away from the door so as not to intimidate him, ready to change the video or sound cassettes, as necessary.

"No."

"You don't want a solicitor?"

"No."

"OK, so how long have you lived in Heckley?"

"No comment."

I leaned forward. "What's so secret about that, William. Why won't you tell me?"

"Because under the Geneva Convention I'm not obliged to. Name, number, unit and date of birth, that's all."

"So what's your number and unit?"

"I don't have one."

"This isn't the Second World War, William. You're not some German paratrooper we found hiding in a haystack. You could be in very serious trouble and I strongly advise you to co-operate, because this isn't a game." I wanted to add: "*So answer the fucking questions and don't be such a smartarse*," but the camera works both ways.

"Do you work for a living?"

"No."

"You're unemployed?"

"I'm a student."

"Where?"

"Nowhere. I'm between courses."

"What were you studying?"

"IT."

"Where?"

"Huddersfield."

"When was this?" Keep it going, I thought. Keep it simple and keep it going.

"Two years ago."

"So what have you been doing since then?"

"I worked at Computers R Us."

"But you don't now?"

"No."

"Why not?"

"We fell out."

"What over?"

"Nothing. I didn't get on with them."

"How long did you work there?"

"Not long."

If he was twenty-eight there were big gaps, the numbers didn't add up, but now wasn't the time to worry about it. When he came in he'd been wearing brown brogues and khaki corduroys, all highly polished but seriously deformed through constant wear. Now he was dressed in a blue tracksuit and lace-less trainers, out of our community chest, while his own clothes were examined by the lab. He sat with one foot behind the other, heel to toe, and occasionally swapped them over. His right hand rested on his right thigh, with the other hand grasping its wrist, and his fingers drummed his knee periodically.

"Where were you born, William? You don't sound like a Yorkshireman."

"No comment."

"It's not an offence."

"No comment."

"Are you worried we'll tell your parents?"

"No comment."

After each answer I paused for a beat, allowing his movements to settle down while I formed the next question, giving him time to expand his answer, which he never did. One of the tapes made a squeak-squeak-squeak as it turned and behind me I could hear a bluebottle flying against the window. Sparky cleared his throat and shuffled in his chair. Next door Dr Foulkes would be watching the monitor, analysing every blink, twitch and tick.

"I get the impression from your earlier answer," I said, "that you are interested in warfare. Do you ever play war games?"

"Sometimes."

"Any particular theatre?"

"The European conflict."

We're not supposed to lie to suspects, or mislead them in any way, but it's hard to avoid the temptation. He was sitting there believing his door keys had spent the night sealed in two envelopes, whilst my *impression* was really based on the eight-by-four table that had greeted Sparky, Maggie and Pete when they visited his bed-sit, laid out in a diorama of the D-Day landings. Maggie estimated that there were about a thousand tiny figures on it, plus all the other paraphernalia of war, suitably scaled-down.

"Any particular battle?"

"No."

"Do you have a...whatever...a set-up?"

"Just a few bits."

"So which side are you on?"

He shrugged his shoulders.

"I read General Patton's biography a few months ago. Brilliant. Have you read it?"

"No."

"You should. You'd like it."

A long silence, then I said: "There are clubs for war games, I understand. Are you a member of one?"

"No."

"But presumably you play against someone?"

"No."

"Against yourself?"

"Yes."

"There must be someone you play against."

"No."

"Doesn't that get boring?"

"It's not a game. We go for historical accuracy, so the outcome's already decided."

"We?"

"I. Me."

I looked at the clock, making sure that the tape wasn't going to click to a standstill in the next few seconds, then looked across at Sparky. He pulled himself upright, saying: "Why were you following a certain woman last night, William?"

William twisted in his chair to look at his new adversary. His shoulders curled forwards and he placed his feet side by side. The left hand let go of the right and took up position on the other knee, but he didn't answer the question.

"Why did you follow her. All the way to Salford, on the train?"

"I didn't. I don't know who you're talking about. I went for a ride, that's all. No law against that, is there?"

"Do you often go for a train ride to nowhere and back?"

"No, not often. Just sometimes."

"On that same train?"

"Not always."

"When did you last go on it?"

"I can't remember."

"Try."

"I can't."

"Did you go on it last week?"

"No comment."

"What about Tuesday the seventeenth?"

"No comment."

"Did you or didn't you?"

"I don't remember."

"But you might have done?"

"No. You're putting words in my mouth."

"And on Thursday the nineteenth?"

"No."

"You were seen, William. And you were at the station on Wednesday the eighteenth, too, but you didn't board the train. So why were you following her?"

"I wasn't. No comment. I'm not answering any more questions."

"In that case," I said, "we might as well suspend proceedings and have lunch. Interview terminated at...eleven forty-two."

They took William back to his cell and I pulled my chair over to the table. I crossed my arms on it and leaned my head against them, faking sleep. I'd had none at all for two nights, and hardly any for a fortnight. I could have dropped off, there and then, but two hands gripped my shoulders and started massaging my neck muscles.

"Lower, Bridgette, lower," I moaned, then lifted myself up to confront a grinning Dr Foulkes.

"This isn't easy, you know," I told him. "All this softly-softly stuff. I want to ring the lanky creep's neck for him."

"You're doing great, both of you."

"We'll have to hit him with something more substantial before too long, Adrian. We haven't got forever."

"I understand that. So far we've built up a comprehensive database of his behaviour under different stress levels, in other words, when he's lying and when he's telling the truth. If you can quickly go through some of it again, particularly when we know he's lying, to reinforce what we have, and then you can move on to the heavy stuff, start asking him about the murders. Keep him talking and then start to point out where he's being economical with the actualities. Now, what are we doing for lunch? How about that Italian place round the corner?"

We had bacon sandwiches up in the office, with mugs of coffee and chocolate eclairs. Maggie was waiting for me, with one of the boffins from technical branch who'd spent the morning unlocking the secrets of William Thornton's computer. I studied the summary sheet which Maggie had prepared and compared it with what I'd gleaned from the notebook. William was in cahoots with someone called Martin Daley, who lived in Loughborough, Nottinghamshire, and there were vague references to something called the Company. The notebook was filled with initials and times and numbers which were meaningless so far, but the computer was more explicit. It held the names and addresses of people that an unemployed ex-student wouldn't normally have on his Christmas card list.

Mrs Jordan-Keedy wasn't the only captain of industry he was interested in. We found the chiefs of all the other major utilities in there with the chairmen of several local companies, plus the head of the council, local millionaire with strong political views, manager of the football club, owner of the shopping mall, right down to the chief constable. I couldn't wait to tell *him*. I compared their names with the initials in the notebook and found a few matches, including those of Mrs Jordan-Keedy, but there was nothing anything like the names of our murder victims. I heaved a great sigh and scratched my head.

"What are you thinking?" Adrian asked, peering over my shoulder.

"You tell me. You're the shrink."

"I think he's one weird young man, that's what I think."

"Is that your considered clinical assessment?"

"It'll do for now."

Peter Goodfellow came in and gave me another sheet of paper. "He has form," he told us. "Arrested at the Manchester airport demos and at the Newbury bypass demos. Released without charge."

"That's hardly form," I said.

"No," Dr Foulkes agreed, "but it explains why he's not fazed by his predicament. He has experience at being interviewed by the police and knows how to give unco-operative answers."

Dave said: "For what it's worth, I'd say that Loughborough is about halfway between here and where the first three murders were done."

I turned to Maggie. "Have this Martin Daley picked up, Mags. Let's see what he has to say." Then, to the doctor: "Any last minute instructions?"

"No, you're doing OK."

"Want me to wear the earpiece?"

"I don't think so. He'd notice it, know someone was prompting you."

"Right. Let's go, then."

"What did they give you for lunch, then, William?" I asked, after I'd reminded him about the caution.

"Baked potato, with coleslaw."

Presumably he wasn't lying about that. I thought about poking my head in front of the camera and asking if that would do, but resisted the temptation.

Instead I talked to him about war games, concentrating on who he played with, knowing he wasn't telling the truth when he said he played alone. According to Outlook Express he exchanged several emails every day with his pal Martin Daley, describing lines of supply, launching counter attacks and falling back into defensive positions.

Dave said: "What was the name of the lady you were following last night?"

"I wasn't following her." He wriggled in his seat, caught on camera.

"So you know who I mean."

"I didn't say that."

"Have you ever followed Joe Albright, chairman of Albright Construction?"

"No."

"Cyril Wheeler, chairman of the..."

"I'm not answering any more questions."

"...chairman of the borough council?"

"No comment."

I leaned forward with my elbows on my knees. "What about Laura Heeley, William. Did you ever follow her?"

"No comment."

"Photo, Dave."

Dave picked up his folder from the floor and produced a photo of Mrs Heeley, taken in happier times. He passed it to me and I held it in front of William. "Have you ever seen this woman before?"

He shook his head, then remembered he wasn't co-operating and said: "No, no comment."

"What about Norma Holborn? Did you ever follow her?" Dave passed me another picture and I held it towards William. He looked at it then turned away.

"And then there was Colinette Jones. Did you ever follow Colinette Jones, William?" I'd saved the best until last. Dave handed me the picture of Colinette that had been emblazoned on the front of all the tabloids, a beautiful girl radiating happiness and vitality. The stuff of dreams for any man who was ever swayed by a shapely calf, a bountiful blouse or a sideways glance. I held it towards him. "Take a good look, William. Did you ever follow this girl?"

He looked, briefly, as if against his better judgement,

looked away, and then was drawn back to the photograph.

"How many times did you follow Colinette, William?"

He stared at her. I pushed the picture at him and he took it from me.

"How many times, William?"

He looked at me, back at the picture, then at me again. His mouth was open and his cheeks were pink.

"How many times?"

"She was murdered," he whispered.

"How many times?"

"She was murdered. And you think I murdered her. You think I'm a murderer, don't you?"

"We know you've told us a pack of lies, William. Now I suggest you start telling the truth. You were arrested for offences under the Protection from Harassment Act, 1997, for what is commonly referred to as stalking. But now we want to question you about a series of murders that occurred over the last four months. The caution still applies but we strongly recommend that you have a solicitor present. We'll have a short break while you consider your position." I gave out the time and terminated the session.

Twenty minutes later we tried again.

"You don't want a solicitor?"

"No."

"Why not?"

"Because they're the enemy."

"But you've used solicitors in the past, surely, when you went on demos."

"No. We used people who'd studied law and used that knowledge for the greater good. There's a difference."

Whose greater good, I thought? Yours or mine? But I didn't pursue it. "Can you drive?" I asked.

"Drive?"

"A car. Do you hold a licence?"

"Erm, yes, but I don't have a car now."

"Have you ever been to Nelson, in Lancashire."

"No." He shuffled his feet, drummed his fingers on his knees and ran his tongue over his teeth. I hadn't noticed that before.

"You sure about that?"

"Positive."

"What about Hatfield?"

"I've never been to Hatfield."

"And Waltham Abbey?"

"Never been there, either."

"Do you know where it is?"

"Where what is?"

"Waltham Abbey."

"Yes, I do, as a matter of fact. It's on the zero meridian, just outside London."

The taste of bacon sandwich and something more bitter came flooding up into my mouth and images of maps and grid lines flashed in front of me. "That's a strange piece of information to carry about with you," I said, swallowing the taste.

"I've studied the tactics and strategies of the Battle of Hastings, and Harold is believed to be buried at Waltham Abbey. One of the books I've read just happened to mention that it was on the zero meridian."

Well I did ask. Next door Dr Foulkes would be grinning like a five-barred gate at my discomfort. "But you've never been there."

"No."

"Where were you on the night of Tuesday, February 6th?"

He looked uncomfortable, massaged his neck with his left hand, but it didn't help him remember where he'd been, and he was equally blank about February 20th , March 21st and March 30th.

"Do you have a diary that might tell you?"

This solicited an unconvincing shake of the head.

"Nothing stored on your computer that might help you remember?"

But there wasn't. I grilled him about the car he'd owned and tried jogging his memory with the headline stories from the papers on the days when Robin Gillespie, Laura Heeley, Colinette Jones and Norma Holborn were murdered, but it didn't work.

Then I asked him about music. He listened to Indie, whatever that is, and when pressed confessed to liking Phut Phut Jag and the Pink Town Boys. I don't think he was taking the piss but he might have been.

"What about Tim Roper?"

"Who?"

"The LHO. 'Eye of the Storm'."

"Never heard of them."

There was a knock at the door and a DC came in with a sheet of paper for me. It had a few background details on it about William's friend, Martin Daley. I read it slowly, folded it and passed it to Dave.

"Do you smoke?"

"No."

"Have you ever?"

"No."

"Do you know what Old Holborn is?"

"Tobacco."

"What sort?"

"Roll-up tobacco."

"How do you know that if you never smoked?"

"Lots of the students use it."

"Why are you lying to me, William?"

"I'm not lying to you."

"OK, then tell me about Martin Daley."

Everything moved at once: his feet, hands, fingers, nose and tongue, but he didn't reply in words. I stayed silent too, so that Dr Foulkes next door could get it all down on the diagrams he worked with. I let the silence hang in the room like a poison gas cloud for what must have been a whole minute, with the tape going squeak-squeak-squeak in the background.

"Martin Daley," I reminded him.

"I, er, don't know him."

"That's not our information," I declared, surprising myself with the hardness that had crept into my voice. "Our information is that he emails you several times a day about the wargames you insist that you play by yourself. Our information is that you and Martin Daley were buddies at university and have stayed close ever since you both fluffed your second-year exams. And my information, William, is that you are in serious trouble and have told me a pack of lies so far today." I pulled myself back into my chair and sat upright. In a softer voice I said: "The time has come to start telling the truth. As things are, you are just digging a deeper hole for yourself. Get it all off your chest, William, right from the beginning. You'll feel a lot better for it. You can start by telling me all you know about the Company."

More reaction from William. All good stuff for the doctor to analyse and show his second-year students, none of it any use in a court of law.

"The C-Company?" he stuttered. "W-what do you know about the C-Company?"

"You don't understand," I told him. "I'm investigating a series of murders. I ask the questions and you provide the answers. Start by telling me about the Company."

He slumped forward, placing his elbows on his knees and staring at the floor. He had long legs and big feet that jutted out awkwardly and there was a wide gap between the bottom of the tracksuit we'd supplied and the cheap trainers. I made a mental note to suggest that when we did video-taped interviews in future we make an effort to dress the accused in a way that didn't immediately gain him the viewers' sympathy. We were due a pee break but I wanted to keep him talking.

"Sit up, please," I said.

He did as he was told and started massaging his neck again.

"I strongly advise you to have a solicitor present."

"I don't want one."

"OK. Tell me about the Company."

"It's just what we do. A silly thing."

"Who's *we*?"

"Me and Marty."

"Martin Daley?"

"Mmm."

"And what do you do?"

"We follow people."

"So you *do* follow people. Tell me why."

"Just for fun."

"Where's the fun in that?"

"We just pretend. Like, we were police, or spies or something. There's no harm in it. We never hurt anybody."

"So you admit that you have been following a certain woman on the train to Salford?"

"Yeah, I suppose so."

"Do you know who she was?"

"Caitlin Jordan-Keedy, a director of Aire and Calder Water."

"Where did you learn that?"

"Her picture's in their annual report."

"She was scared stiff."

"Good. Last year EPW sacked nearly two thousand employees and all the directors rewarded themselves with a nice fat bonus. Mrs Jordan-Keedy swapped her year-old Porsche for the latest model out of hers."

"What did you do with the information?"

"What information?"

"Train times, when she finished work, whatever."

"Just wrote it in my book, that's all."

"Was she meant to see you?"

"No."

"Tell me about Joe Albright."

"What about him?"

"You followed him. Why?"

"Because he's a crook. His daughter works in the council planning office and he has total disregard for the Health and Safety laws."

"That's a bit vague."

"OK. In 1998 two men were killed on one of his sites when scaffolding gave way. He claims they were both experienced men and had convinced his site manager of this. The site manager was fined a trivial amount for not keeping proper records. In 1997 a sixteen-year-old boy was badly hurt by a truck on which the audible warning was not working. Several of his men said it had been working the day before. Since then others have sworn that it hadn't worked for over a year, and every other piece of equipment was in the same state."

He was leaning forward now as if lecturing me, glad to have an audience. I'd stumbled into something he held passionate views about but I wasn't sure how relevant it was. "He's got the contract for the by-pass extension, hasn't he?" I asked, eager to keep him talking.

"If it goes ahead."

"Don't you think it should?"

"It goes through the only place in Yorkshire where fritillaries grow."

"So why did you follow him?"

"I told you – for fun."

"What did you do with the information?"

"Nothing."

"The people you followed were people you don't like. Why not follow someone you admire? Celebrities."

"That would be stalking, and we're not stalkers. We're more like, you know, spies, doing it for society. That's how we see ourselves."

"Spies? MI6 and all that."

"Mmm."

"Licensed to kill?"

"No, we never hurt anybody."

"So what did you do with all this information about where these people lived and what their movements were?"

"Nothing. We just saved it."

"As if it were just train numbers."

"That's right. Like train numbers."

"Which of you followed Colinette Jones?"

Neither of them was the answer. I kept at him for another hour until my bladder could take no more. We had a coffee break and then I let Sparky loose on him for another hour. All they did was follow people, for fun. He was twenty-eight years old, had never had a proper girlfriend, didn't think he was gay and followed people for fun.

Strange thing was, I knew what he meant. We follow people, and sometimes the buzz is electric, like standing under the power lines on a foggy morning. Maybe one day it would be a national sport, if it wasn't already.

Mr Wood granted us an extension and we sent him back to his cell. Up in the boss's office we all gathered round his conference table and compared notes. Dr Foulkes started it off, saying that the interview technique we had adopted had worked well and although it had little forensic value he was confident he could tell when William was lying and when he wasn't.

"So when is he telling the truth?" Maggie asked.

The doctor hedged. "Um, well, I'd prefer to formalise my observations before being specific."

"I'll tell you when he's lying," Pete Goodfellow declared. "He's lying when he says they do it for fun. Fun my backside. He's feeding the information to his pals who do all the protesting. Swampy and co. That's why he's following all these people. One of the names we found is for a farmer up near Stonedale who breeds beagles for laboratories. Last year all the dogs were released and his barns were torched, on the very night he and his family were at the village pantomime. I bet I know who supplied the information."

"That's a distasteful business," Gilbert said. "Breeding

dogs for experiments. Can't say I have much sympathy there."

"We've taken our eye off the ball," I told them. "OK, so we can do him for stalking, which he claims he does for fun."

"Rapists do it for fun," Maggie interrupted.

I held up a hand to silence her. "I know, I know, but he hasn't raped anybody. Apart from the stalking there's a good chance that he's into something more sinister: supplying intelligence to direct action groups, as Pete suggested."

"I've wondered how these groups are so well-informed," Dave said. "They're always one step ahead of the authorities."

"Can I finish a sentence!" I protested.

"Sorry Chas."

"As I was saying: we can do him for stalking." I turned to the super: "I suggest we charge him under the Prevention of Harassment Act, then we can keep hold of him."

Gilbert nodded his approval.

"Also," I continued, "we need to investigate the theory that he's supplying information to other parties, in some sort of conspiracy. I'd like to hand that side of the case over to Jeff Caton." Again Gilbert nodded. "Which leads us to the reason we are all here. This is a murder enquiry and William Thornton is our twenty-four carat gold plated suspect. How does he measure up to that job description, Adrian?"

The doctor was sitting back from the table, one hand extended to rest on it. I could see his cufflinks reflected in the polished wood. He pursed his lips, gazing at his hand and turning it to inspect his fingernails, then raised his eyes and focused on me. He coughed and shuddered, as if shaking himself out of some reverie.

"Um, like I said, Charlie, I'd like to study the data more thoroughly before I commit my findings to paper. He's a mass of contradictions, young Mr Thornton. An interesting case study. He'll probably be the subject of text books, one day."

"What's your gut feeling?"

"About the murders?"

"About the murders."

He held my gaze for several seconds, then slowly shook his head. "Sorry, Charlie," he said, "but I think you've got the wrong man."

I had beans on Ryvita for supper because the bread had green spots on it, followed by a chunky KitKat that I'd put in my pocket during one of the coffee breaks. Long time ago I heard this nature programme on radio about a beetle – a giant water bug – that eats frogs. It sneaks up on the frog and injects it with a poison and a dose of digestive juices. The frog dies as its innards are turned into some nutritious brew and when they are nice and runny the beetle draws them up, as if drinking some obnoxious milk-shake. To the observer, the frog sits there with its head out of the water, watching the world go by. I think its eyes glaze over, but I may have invented that bit. Then, quite unexpectedly, it sags and wrinkles like a deflating balloon as its insides are sucked from it.

That's the best way I can describe how I felt: as if my insides had been sucked out. It was raining and I wasn't in the mood for a walk or jog. The house was a tip so I decided to do something about it. Two days' washing-up would be a big help. Washing-up can be quite therapeutic, I'm told, and I was ready for some therapeuting. The Fairy Liquid was empty, but by squeezing the container under the hot tap I made a decent lather with the dregs.

One of the mugs I washed had poppies on it. A girlfriend bought it for me for the office, but it was real china, much too good for there. *Papaver somniferum*, it said. One day, when I retire, I'll learn the names of all the flowers. I'll point out bedstraw and bugloss with the same authority that the average person has for daisy and dandelion. And the birds, too. Not obsessively, not enough to tell a willow warbler from a chiffchaff, but when I was out walking and I saw a silhouette against the clouds I wouldn't be calling the humble buzzard a golden eagle.

When I retire I'll read all those books I've heard clever people discussing. The ones they thrust at us in school when all we wanted was *Biggles* and *Roy of the Rovers*. I'll read poetry, learn whole chunks of it. Not Omar Khayyam or Roger McGough, but proper poetry. I'll quote from Yeats and Keats whenever the opportunity arises, and I'll remember which was which. I'll mark the constellations as they cartwheel overhead, and have time to watch the spider weave its web. When I retire I'll paint my masterpiece.

And will I look back on the one big case where I failed? Yeah, almost certainly. It would dominate my thoughts until the end of my days.

I didn't have a clean shirt for my meeting with the assistant chief constable. All the decent ones were in the linen basket and I was down to the Ben Shermans with the floppy collars. I'd look like George Harrison in his heyday. Not the impression I wanted to create.

I found the least-creased blue one in the linen basket and sniffed it. It was OK. I hung it on a hanger and wondered if the creases would fall out overnight. No chance, it'd have to be ironed. I looked at the clock but it was too late to take it to the neighbour who does these things for me. I put the other dirty ones in the washing machine, on the delicates cycle, and looked for the ironing board.

Perhaps if I just did the collar and the front it would pass muster. He wouldn't invite me to take my jacket off. I was spitting on the iron, wondering if it was hot enough, when the doorbell rang. I carefully stood the iron on end and went to answer.

Chapter Eleven

She was wearing jeans and a jacket over a striped rugby jersey, and in the gleam of the outside light her hair glowed like a maple tree in autumn.

"Hello Charlie."

"Annette. I...wasn't expecting you."

"I was passing. Thought I'd call."

"Good. Good. I'm glad you did. Come in." I stood aside and let her pass me. "I'll put the kettle on. You'll stay for a coffee?"

"Yes please."

"Come through into the kitchen."

I dried two mugs and spooned Nescafé into them. "Well, this *is* a surprise."

"I was in town. I've been to see the flat."

"I thought it was sold. The notice vanished."

"We took it down. It hadn't sold and I heard about a relief teacher who was looking for somewhere for three months – covering for maternity leave – so I leased it to them."

"I wish I'd known. I thought you'd severed all your connections with Heckley. It made me sad."

"I'm sorry."

"Nothing for you to be sorry about. Just me being silly. I have a look whenever I pass that way, that's all. I could have kept an eye on it for you if I'd known it wasn't sold." I was chattering, lost for words and finding all the wrong ones. "Have they left it OK?"

"Not really. 'Professional couple', they said. I specified non-smokers and they didn't mention the two toddlers and the dog. Nothing that you'd call damage, but more wear and tear than I'd make in a lifetime."

"It's a dodgy business, letting property."

"So I've found out."

"Will you put it back on the market?"

She heaved a sigh and shook her head. "I don't know."

"So how's the grand affair going? Are you a married woman now?"

Another shake of the head. "No."

That was the lead question. "How are the children?" I asked, trying to look concerned, or disinterested, anything but what I was really feeling. What was it Maggie said? That she wouldn't want to take on another woman's children.

"They're fine. The kids are fine."

I fixed the coffees, hers with milk, mine black, and we sat at the table. "I haven't any biscuits," I said.

"Coffee's fine."

"And how are you enjoying teaching?"

"That's good, too. I'm enjoying it. I miss some things, the joshing, but it's OK."

"I'm glad. I thought you wouldn't like it."

"No, it's fine. Better than I expected. What about you?"

But it wasn't fine. There was a sadness about her, a lack of spirit, that I'd never seen in her before. I gazed at her, studying her mouth and eyes. She caught me looking at her and held my gaze for a long moment, her cheeks pink. I'd forgotten how easily she blushed, and how my insides lurched whenever I saw it.

"They made me acting chief inspector," I told her, breaking the silence.

"I know, I saw you on television. You didn't look well. That's why I came."

"I'm OK."

"No you're not. You're probably living on takeaways and working too hard." She jumped to her feet. "And what's this? Doing your own ironing? The great Inspector Priest actually ironing a shirt. I thought a neighbour did them for you."

"She does but I forgot to take...forgot to collect them. I'm seeing the assistant chief constable in the morning. It's a review meeting. I think he'll take the case off me."

"Let's have a look." She spread the shirt on the board, buttons down, and picked up the iron. Thirty seconds later she was holding up a perfectly pressed shirt for my inspection.

"That's smashing. Thanks."

"Any more?"

"No."

"Where are they all?"

"In the washing machine." I pointed and we both looked at the porthole, filled with suds.

"This has a mark on it," she declared, pointing to the front of the shirt.

"Where?" I stood up to join her.

"There."

"I can't see it."

Annette picked up a J-cloth and carefully rubbed the front of the shirt. "It's come off," she said. "Looked like ketchup. This wasn't a clean shirt, was it?"

"I'd only worn it for a couple of hours."

"Oh, Charlie."

I gave her my hangdog, sorry-I-ate-your-slippers look and she gave me her best school ma'am one.

"Come here," I said, holding my arms out, and she walked into them.

I squeezed her until she couldn't breathe and buried my face in her hair. She smelt of Camay, and something else. A perfume that was strange to me. I'd once asked her what it was but she wouldn't say. Just laughed. They say it's a sad woman who has to buy her own perfume. I'd never given her any but I doubted if she'd ever bought her own. It was her secret, her precious memory, and she didn't want anybody else encroaching on it. I felt her relax and took it as a signal that my time was up.

"That's what I'm missing," I said, dropping my hands to her waist. "A hug. It works wonders."

She nodded and turned away, reaching for her coffee.

I said: "Let's go in the other room, where it's more comfortable."

The two girls had been brought up on the fairy stories, knew all about wicked stepmothers. They were all right, little angels, Annette told me, when Harvey was there, but when she had them to herself they made it quite clear that she wasn't their mum, could never be their mum.

Harvey, I thought, suppressing a smile. I'd never heard his name before. Wonder if he had big ears?

I turned the fire on, made some more coffee, told her all about the case. Everything, even about the first three killings, and the interview we'd just given the strange Mr William Thornton. It was an excuse, as if I needed one, to go over it all again. Maybe I'd become a bore on the subject. One day, perhaps, when I went to the pub, the locals would shrink away from me lest I corner them and insist on relating my last big case: the one that got away.

About ten past eleven, just as I was considering the sexual politics of the situation, Annette jumped to her feet and announced that it was work in the morning, she'd better be off. I helped her on with her jacket and walked out into the garden with her. In the shadow of the house I caught hold of her hand and pulled her closer. "Thanks for calling, Annette," I said. "You've been a tonic."

We kissed each other, quite gently, on the lips.

"Look after yourself, Charlie," she said.

We walked down the short drive, out into the street where her car was parked. "You've still got the yellow flyer," I remarked, running a finger over the wheel arch of her Fiat.

"Yep. Can't afford another on teacher's pay."

The indicators flashed as she unlocked the doors and I pulled the driver's open. "So what will you do with the flat?"

"I'm not sure. I ought to sell it, but a little bit of me thinks of it as an insurance policy. My safety net. I don't know."

"Well, you know where I live."

"Yeah. Goodnight. Thanks for the coffee."

"Take care."

I watched her drive down the cul-de-sac and turn out into the main road, indicator signalling although there was no other car in the street. Her lights vanished behind the houses and I knew how Captain Bligh must have felt, abandoned in his dinghy, as the *Bounty* faded over the horizon.

I rinsed our mugs, put a CD on and tidied away the rest of the crockery. Mary Black, *The Moon and St Christopher*. I turned the volume high and went upstairs to the bathroom. After I'd cleaned my teeth I found some clean clothes for the morning, checked the alarm and climbed into bed.

It's a sort of sleep, I suppose. You feel wide-awake, but the images flooding your brain are out of control, beyond your knowledge, out of context. I was facing a big rabbit behind a desk, buck teeth and whiskers stained with blood. His secretary was a little girl, a bandage round her eyes as she took notes.

"Why did you do this?"

"Because it seemed a good idea."

"Take that down."

"Yes, Sir."

I opened a filing cabinet. It was filled with dead fish. I closed it again. Someone was watching me, pointing a camera. A body leaned against a wall, legs wide apart, grinning at me. "Hello Charlie. Looking for business?" I had to climb these stairs to escape, but each bend I went round brought me to the bottom of the stairs again, like in some M C Escher drawing. If I went faster I could make it round the bend before they changed ... not quite ... faster this time ... faster still.

I kicked the duvet off, woke up shivering, went to the bathroom for a pee. I dried my back on the towel and had a drink of water from the tap.

When I was in bed again I pulled a corner of the duvet over me and lay on my back with my hands clasped behind my head. What was it Annette had said about the apartment? That it was her safety net, her insurance policy. Is that what

I was, too? An insurance policy? Was tonight's visit just her way of keeping up with the premium?

Ah well, I thought, if that's a price I have to pay, so be it. I was in a corner, with nowhere to run to, and my tanks were dry.

I transported myself to a lake, in a canoe, with the sun rising from behind the Rockies and the mist lying across the water. *New World Symphony* from the orchestra hidden in the pine trees. I caught a small trout, brought it on board and unhooked it, but when I looked at my hands they were covered in blood. I leaned over the side to wash them and the lake turned crimson.

Carcasses of cattle were burning. A great pile of them, falling out of the back of a white pickup. "Why did you do this?" the rabbit asked.

"It wasn't me."

"Take that down."

"Yes, Sir."

"Someone must have ordered it."

"Not me."

"It was a slip of the tongue."

"Why do you smoke Old Holborn?"

"Because it makes me sick if I eat it."

"Well put that in your pipe and smoke it."

"A slip of the tongue?"

"A slip of the tongue."

"Is that why you're burning them?"

"That's right. They always give themselves away."

They always give themselves away.

I sat up, leaned forward with my elbows on my knees, giving my brain time to clear. The digital clock said 01:13, its red glow spilling on to the pillow at that side of the bed. I pinched my ear, decided I was awake. I sat like that for nine minutes, going over it in my mind. *They always give themselves away.* Over it and over it. Over and over and over again. As the clock slipped to 01:22 I reached for the phone.

It only rang twice. "Yes Charlie?"

"It's me, Dave," I said.

"I gathered that. Can't you sleep, Old Son?"

"No."

"It's Charlie," I heard him say, aside, then: "Neither can I."

"Sorry."

"Never mind. Look, why don't we both go downstairs, make a cup of tea and continue this conversation from there? How about that?"

"No. It won't wait."

After a pause he said: "What won't?"

"I've been thinking about the case."

"Haven't we all?"

"How does this sound?" I replied, still wondering if I was missing something, if I'd overlooked a glaringly obvious piece of information that would immediately rubbish what I was thinking. "About a month ago a young couple called in the nick, just as I was on my way out. I spoke to them. They said they'd been walking the dog in the recreation ground on the Monday night, two days before Colinette was murdered. A white pickup went by. A big, noisy, white pickup."

"Mmm," Dave mumbled. "We checked all the white pickups, Charlie. You went to interview the owner of the one seen in Nelson yourself. He was the gay guy, wasn't he, with an alibi like the Rock of Gibraltar?"

"Cross-dresser, that's right, but hear me out."

"Sorry."

"OK. In Nelson three independent witnesses reported seeing a white pickup, and we eventually traced it and eliminated the driver from enquiries. But when Colinette was murdered nobody else saw a noisy white pickup, not on the Monday, Tuesday, or Wednesday."

"So..."

"So what if there wasn't one? What if our visitors saw one in Nelson when little Robin was murdered because they were there? They killed him. They needed an excuse to come into the police station, for bravado, to show how clever they are, so they reported seeing the pickup in Heckley, following our appeal, in the hope that the one in Nelson had been reported. Spreading misinformation. Maybe the one in Nelson drove by as they did the deed, scared them."

"You're saying that the murderers came into the nick, large as life, to show off. Would they do that?"

"I don't know. Sounds likely, to me. We're talking about nutters, remember. Goading us has been part of the deal right from the beginning. Maybe I should ring Adrian..."

"Whoa, Charlie," Dave interrupted. "Before you wake half the county. Can you remember what they were called?"

"No."

"Any idea who talked to them?"

"Peter did in the nick, and he probably did the follow-up. Somebody else will have done a second follow-up. It'll all be in the book, on the computer."

"It sounds good, Chas. It sounds bloody good, but it might look different in the cold light of day. Nothing's spoiling, so grab a couple of hours and I'll see you in the office at seven. How's that?"

"That's fine...except..."

"Except what?"

"Except...that's just supporting evidence. It's not the real reason why I rang you."

A long pause, followed by: "So why did you ring?"

"I think I'm going mad, Dave."

"No you're not. Not any more than anyone else is. You've just got things on your mind, that's all. It'll pass, believe me."

"This couple."

"Mmm."

"I met them at the desk."

"So you said."

"When we did the first television appeal Les Isles did

most of the talking. He was holding his pipe in his hand."

"That's right. Made him look avuncular, or something."

"The last letter, the one after Norma Holborn, it said: 'Put that in your pipe and smoke it.'"

"I remember."

"But it was addressed to me, not to Les."

"I know. We assumed whoever sent it confused you."

"That's what we assumed, but we were wrong. Les left his pipe and tobacco on the windowsill in my office. I dropped them off at the front desk, asked for them to be posted them to him. That's when I met this couple. They're not confused, Dave – I was holding Les's pipe in my hand as I spoke to them. That's why they think I'm the pipe smoker."

I could hear him breathing down his nose, considering what I'd told him: heeeee haaaaa, heeeee haaaaa, heeeee haaaaa. I was beginning to think he'd fallen asleep, sitting up with the phone pressed against his ear, until he said: "What's the fastest you've ever made it to the office, Charlie?"

"Thirteen minutes."

"I'll beat you there."

I slammed the phone down and rolled off the bed. My suit was on the chair but I didn't want that. Jeans, T-shirt, trainers. No time for socks. Leather jacket off the peg downstairs. The tyres protested as I reversed out of the drive, and screamed like a banshee as I accelerated up the street. The big security light on the end house flicked on as I streaked through its detection zone, but it missed me, I'd already gone.

Dave's car was parked in the super's place, next to the entrance. I swerved to a standstill next to it and yanked the brake on. As I slammed the door I could hear his engine ticking and hissing as it cooled.

"Where's Dave?" I shouted to the desk sergeant as I sprinted through the foyer to the foot of the stairs.

"There's a message for you, Charlie," he called after me.

"Tomorrow. Where's Dave?"

"In the incident room, what's happening?"

But I was out of earshot, taking the steps three at a time. The CID office was in darkness but there was sufficient light coming in from outside for me to see by. I went straight into my own office, pulled the drawer open and found my diary.

"This message, Charlie..." the sergeant began as I passed him again, on my way to the incident room.

"It'll have to wait. Who've we got that's handy?"

"Geordie Farrell. It's important."

"So is this. Call him in, we need him."

"I was going to ring you at shift change..."

"Later, Arthur, later. Get Geordie, fast as you can." I transferred the diary to my left hand and reached for the handle of the incident room door.

"A woman's missing..."

His words hit me like a missile, right between the shoulder blades. I leaned on the doorjamb, not breathing, wishing I'd heard him wrongly.

"What did you say?" I hissed, slowly turning round.

"A woman's missing. Hatfield rang, about fifteen minutes ago, said to tell you. I was going to ring you at shift change."

Hatfield. Not one of ours. A little comfort there, but not much. "Get them on, Arthur," I told him. "Find out what you can. Say I might have a name for them in a few minutes."

Dave was hunched over a computer, looking at one of the interminable lists. If there's one thing computers are good at doing it's making lists. As I pulled a chair alongside his he said: "Anything to narrow it down?"

"In a sec," I replied, opening my diary. "After I'd seen them I went straight to see Dr Foulkes." And for that I'd claim mileage, so it would be in my diary.

"Here we are. Tuesday, March 27th."

Dave went back to the Home page, typed the date and *white pickup* into the little box and hit the Enter key.

The search, we were told, took all of a billionth of a second and produced only one entry. Typed across the screen, with a blue band above and below, it said:

*Timothy Fletcher  14, Ladysmith Grove, Heckley.*

I don't think either of us believed it. Two months' work, living, breathing, eating and sleeping the case, and suddenly we had a name and address. No evidence, yet, but we were getting there.

"Let's give him his wake-up call," I said.

But first we had other things to do. I spoke to Hatfield, gave them the name and address and the number of Fletcher's car. He drove a blue Peugeot 306. The missing woman was a twenty-year-old nurse at a local hospital. She should have finished work at ten but when she didn't arrive home her boyfriend started making enquiries. They found her car still in its usual place, but with two tyres slashed. It looked as if some not-so-good Samaritan had come to her assistance, given her a lift.

I rang Dr Foulkes and asked him if it was likely that our man would have called in the station. He was in bed, alone. Must be going through a lean spell, I thought. "God, it would be audacious, Charlie," he replied, "but yes, it's just the thing that would appeal to him."

Dave rang Peter Goodfellow. He'd done the first follow-up but not the second. He remembered them, thought they were an odd couple, but not unduly so.

"Did they have a dog?" Dave asked. "They were supposed to be walking the dog in the recreation ground. Did you see it?"

Pete hadn't seen a dog, asked if we wanted him to come in. Dave said he'd better.

But the real reason we delayed was because we wanted more manpower. Geordie works alone, because he's big enough for two. He came back to the nick as did another car with two officers in it. We alerted traffic and an ARV. Asked them to look out for the Peugeot, to stand by. Then we drove in my car to 14, Ladysmith Grove.

It was on the outskirts of Heckley, in the buffer-zone where the back-to-back terraced cottages of the once-upon-a-time mill workers give way to the more substantial dwellings of the middle classes. There were three or four streets of through-terraces built into the hillside, probably where the overseers or the lower echelons of the professionals lived in Victorian times. Schoolteachers and policemen, perhaps. Number 14 was the top house, and beyond it a wall extended across the road in a recent initiative to stop cars using it as a rat-run. There were no windows in the end gable, making the cross street that ran past it surprisingly private. Cars were parked everywhere, mainly bangers but I saw a Mitsubishi Shogun and a decent BMW.

We'd driven past the Grove and turned up the next street, Ladysmith Avenue, and parked as silently as we could right alongside the end of number 14. The two officers from the panda went to the back door and Dave, Geordie and I padded round to the front. Every house in the street was in darkness apart from one upstairs window a few doors down, on the other side of the street. It was a bedroom window with red curtains. An invalid, I wondered, or someone working late, or left on by accident? There was a gate and a tiny walled garden, just a yard, with four steps leading up to the door.

The bell worked. We could hear it inside, chiming like the Bells of St Mary's each time we pressed the push, but nobody answered it.

"There's nobody in," Dave declared after five minutes. People give off waves, emanations, which are absent when a house is empty. Science has never proved their existence, but we all recognise the feeling.

"Do your stuff, George," I said.

Geordie tested the door with his shoulder, feeling if there

were any bolts. The steps made it awkward for him to take a kick at the lock, so Dave and I supported him while he stood on the top step, leaning backwards, and raised his size fourteen boot.

The first kick sounded like a mortar shell exploding. I looked down the street but no more lights came on. A taxi went past on the road at the bottom of the hill, followed by a motorbike. Geordie leaned back and took another kick. The third one burst the door open. I took a final quick look around and followed them inside.

I let the other two in through the back door while Dave and Geordie ran upstairs shouting "Police! Police!" but nobody was home.

There was an upstairs and a downstairs, plus a cellar, a hallway and two attics. We switched on all the downstairs lights and looked around. "Keep your hands in your pockets," I told them. The kitchen was big, taking up half of the ground floor, with a deep, old-fashioned porcelain sink and modern units. Highly desirable to some tastes. The floor was polished floorboards with a big Chinese rug covering half of it. The iron range had an electric fire where the real thing had once blazed, and a dining table with two chairs stood against one wall.

"Not bad," one of the PCs remarked.

"Very homely," I agreed.

We filtered through into the other room, probably called the lounge. The one that the original tenants only used on high days and holidays, or when the vicar called. There was a log-effect gas fire with a bulbous settee in a ghastly material in front of it and a matching easy chair to one side. A coffee table supported two wineglasses, used, and the only picture on the walls was that one of a clown with a painted smile and a big tear rolling down his cheek. The striped curtains clashed alarmingly with the wallpaper and three teddy bears sat next to a mini hi-fi centre and a Playstation on top of the cheap sideboard, dispassionately watching us.

I was getting some good ideas about interior design, mainly how not to do it, but nothing that helped with the case. I posted one of the PCs at the front door, in case the householders made a sudden appearance, and went back to the lounge.

As I entered the room Dave was standing near the side-board with one hand raised. He looked round, wondering where I was, and beckoned me over.

"What is it?" I asked.

"Look." He was pointing at the window of the cassette deck in the Sony player. "See what it's called."

I stooped until my face was level with it. There was a cassette in the machine with a hand-written label. I couldn't read it all, but the middle bit said:

*Of The Storm. Tim Rop*

It was like toothache in all my teeth at once. But not painful toothache. Pleasant, spine-tinglingly, bladder-releasingly glorious toothache. More pleasant than you can bear, like it must be when your numbers come up or a loved one arrives back from war. The muscles for my jaw were contracting, clenching my teeth together and sending pins and needles up the sides of my head. I straightened up, looked at Dave, unable to speak.

He felt the same. I could see it in his face.

"Bingo!" he said.

"It's him! We got him!"

He threw his arms round me in a bear hug and lifted me off my feet. "You did it, Kid! You did it!"

"Waaa! That's enough," I grunted as he put me down. "We've work to do."

The remaining PC and Geordie were grinning like schoolboys at an Anne Summers party. "Worrizit?" one of them asked.

"It's a tape by Tim Roper," Dave explained. "He was an

American rock musician in the Sixties, and we know the killer was a fan of his."

Geordie's smile widened and he thumped me on the arm. I staggered sideways, my shoulder nearly dislocated.

We sent for the SOCOs, collected some latex gloves from the cars and started to give the house a search. "What are we looking for?" the PC asked.

"Anything that might link the killer with the victims. Photos, newspaper cuttings, the weapons, anything like that. He may have collected a few items: shoes, an umbrella, handbag, knickers. Anything."

The cellar was directly beneath the lounge and echoed its dimensions. I searched it with Geordie, his hands in his pockets because they don't make gloves to fit him. Two mountain bikes leaned against the end wall, incongruously modern in these surroundings. Once it had been the laundry and an old zinc set-pot still stood in one corner, with a mangle like my grandma used, but now all that was done up in the kitchen. Now it was a storeroom and workshop. One wall was lined with rickety shelves that held paint cans going back to the days when lead poisoning was endemic amongst painters and decorators, and a Black & Decker Workmate held centre stage, looking as if it was still in use. It was surrounded by sawdust and off-cuts, and several assorted lengths of three-by-two timber lay nearby.

"He's been busy," I said.

"Yeah, but doing what?"

We climbed the stone steps out of the cellar and gave the kitchen the treatment. Apart from the knives it was a waste of time. Dave and the PC came downstairs and reported finding nothing of interest except for another Tim Roper tape. He'd been careful, very careful. We double-checked, Geordie and me going upstairs and the other two plunging into the cellar. The attics were huge – just *asking* for a big train set or a four-lane Scalextric to be spread across them – but held nothing for us: rolled up carpets, surplus wallpaper,

*Sunday Times* supplements going back to the Ice Age. I thumbed through a few but the dust found its way into my nose and I had a sneezing spell.

The tape was in the bedroom, in a Panasonic rasta-blaster on the bedside table. He wore expensive jeans and Debenhams underpants, she wore M & S big knickers and small bras. The bed was unmade and two people had slept in it. I collected some hairs, put them in evidence bags and sealed them, but I wasn't sure why. While we were in there my phone rang. It was the front desk.

"Hatfield have sent us some information on Timothy Fletcher, Charlie."

"I'm listening."

"Right. He doesn't have a record but he's known to them. Apparently his foster parents were burned to death in a house fire, four years ago, and he inherited £350,000. Fletcher was in the house at the time but escaped from an upstairs window on to the roof of an outhouse. No cause for the fire was ever found but it was suspicious. He was given a hard time but there wasn't enough to charge him."

"Mmm, it all fits. Anything on the missing girl?"

"No, nothing. Have you found anything?"

"No, not much."

The euphoria was fading. Losing your parents, even your foster parents, in a house fire was unfortunate. A jury might find it suspicious, but on the other hand it might win him the sympathy vote. Having a liking for an obscure, dead, American rock musician wasn't a good enough link to win a conviction. We went downstairs, joined up with the others again and I told them the news.

"No dog," Dave said. "They don't have a dog."

"That's not illegal," I told him.

"Isn't it? Bugger."

"Any luck?" the other PC asked when we joined him on the doorstep.

"No," I told him. "Not a thing." I turned to the others.

"Did we double check everywhere? Let's go through it. Did we all do the front and back attics?"

"*We* did," Dave replied.

"An' so did we," Geordie added.

"Good. Front bedroom?"

"Yep."

"Aye."

"Back bedroom."

"Yes."

"We did."

"Bathroom?"

"Yes."

"Yes."

"Kitchen?"

We'd all done the kitchen.

"Front room."

Again, we'd all searched it.

"What about the hallway?"

"We checked it out."

"So did we."

"And that only leaves the cellar."

"We did it."

"And us."

"That's it, then. Let's hope forensic can find something."

"Two cellars," the PC who'd been waiting outside stated. "There are two cellars. Did you do them both?"

"There's only one," I told him.

"No there isn't. I was brought up in a house like this. There's a front and back cellar, same as the rooms on every floor."

We all looked at each other, shaking our heads, certain we hadn't missed a whole cellar.

"Show us," I said, stepping back inside.

He led us down the stone steps into the room we were now so familiar with. The Workmate and bits of timber were still there.

"Oh!" he exclaimed, looking at the blank wall. "It should be there. That's where the door normally is. These houses must be different."

His colleague rapped his knuckles against the wall, but they hardly made a noise against the solid brickwork. It was covered in woodchip wallpaper, painted white.

"Did you paper the walls in yours?" I asked.

"No. We kept coal in it. Never seen one papered before."

"Keep tapping," I told his pal.

He worked his way from left to right, towards where the door was supposed to be. When he was there his knuckles made a hollow booming sound.

Geordie pointed to the wood on the floor. "That's what he's been doing: blocking off the other cellar. This paper and paint's brand new."

We all started tapping the wall and in a few seconds had the outline of the doorway delineated. "Let's go through," I said, and turned to look for a suitable implement.

"Don't bother, Boss," Geordie said. "Leave it to me."

He lowered his head, pointed his shoulder at the wall, adopted a grimace that had terrified many an opposing prop-forward and charged.

There was a splintering and snapping of woodwork and the big fellow vanished from sight. We all peered through the hole in the wall and saw him picking himself up, wood and plasterboard hanging round his neck, bits in his hair and a cloud of dust slowly settling around him.

"Well that's one way," Dave said.

I pulled the loose bits down, widening the hole, and stepped through it. "You OK?" I asked.

"Great!"

It was dark in there, but we fumbled around until some-one found a light switch. It controlled a single, naked, 150 watt bulb that hung in the middle of the room. Against the central wall was an aluminium loft ladder leading to a trap door in the ceiling, just about under the Chinese rug and the table. We'd come in the hard way.

But it was the chair that held our attention.

It was directly under the light and reminded me of a picture I'd seen of the electric chair in which the Rosenbergs were executed for selling nuclear secrets to the Russians. It was primitive, made of pieces of wood crudely nailed together, without a dovetail or tenon to grace its construction. Four blunt legs, a back, armrests, all at right-angles to each other, and two pieces sticking forward, for the legs. And nailed to all of these was a succession of leather straps.

"What in Christ's name is that?" I hissed.

We slowly circled it, hypnotised by the horrors it suggested, as if in some nightmare-induced pavan. I counted the straps. There were eleven of them, some plain black leather, some coloured red or green. They were dog collars, put to use for something else.

Dave crouched down inspecting it closely, sniffing the woodwork and the leather.

"Don't touch it," I said.

"It's brand new," he replied. "It's never been used."

"You know what this is, don't you, Boss," I heard Geordie say, his voice strangely hushed.

I turned to look at him and thought he was about to faint. His face was ashen and beads of sweat were forming on his brow. "What, George?"

"It's a torture chamber. That's what it is. A torture chamber."

I stared at him, then at the chair and back at him. "She's alive!" I exclaimed. "She's still alive and they're bringing her back here!"

Fresh air has rarely smelt sweeter. I took great gulps of it as we emerged into the little garden. "We'd better be ready for them," I said. "Fix the door, George, if you can." He broke a few splintered pieces free and pulled the door shut, jamming it with a wedge of wood.

"Well done, so here's what we do. Get rid of the pandas

round the corner, one in each street. Warn the others off but tell them to stand by. Dave and I will wait in the street in my car and we'll try to rustle up some more unmarked cars. If she went missing at ten they've had nearly five hours to come back home. Taking it steady they should..."

They should have been here by now. That's what I was going to say, but before I could my prediction was confirmed by a dark car that cruised silently into the top of the street. Its lights were out, but the familiar Peugeot badge glinted under the street lamps as it turned the corner. I stopped in mid-sentence, transfixed by it, and the others turned to follow my gaze.

"It's them," I shouted. "They're back! It's them!"

Geordie was nearest. He jumped into the middle of the road and held up his arm. The car's engine revved and it headed straight at him.

"After them!" I cried as I he dived clear.

Dave ran round to the driver's door of my car and started the engine. I climbed in beside him and we were accelerating down the road as I pulled my door closed. The Peugeot turned left at the bottom of the hill and was about two hundred yards clear of us as we straightened out after the corner.

"Seat belt," I said, after I'd pulled mine on. The Peugeot is a fast car, and this wasn't going to be a cakewalk. Dave pulled a length of belt and I held the wheel as he fastened it. We were doing eighty, still accelerating, still losing ground. I looked back and saw the blue light of one of the pandas, way back in the distance.

The road was well-lit and deserted, millions of watts of off-peak electricity being used to illuminate the way home for the odd late-night reveller and the man who changes all the prices outside the filling stations when nobody's about. A young couple emerged on to the pavement, holding hands, pulling against each other. There was a zebra crossing and he took hold of the pole, swinging her around it. Dave hit the horn button and we shot past them, horn blaring, as they suddenly sobered and watched us disappear into the distance.

"Heading west on Milltown Road," I told control, on my mobile. "In pursuit of suspect. He's in a blue Peugeot 306." I told them the number. The road curved to the left and we lost sight of our quarry. When we came out of the curve its rear lights were two specks nearly a quarter of a mile away.

"We're losing them," I reported. "Just passing the Yorkshire Outlets place – Texas, Curry's – nearly at the bypass. At a guess they're heading for the motorway."

Dave said: "If they've been to London and back they could be low on fuel."

"Good point." I relayed the information to control. If they turned on to the motorway we, or someone else, would just have to follow them until they ran out. A bread delivery van came out of a side turning without looking, like he'd done at the same time every morning for the last twenty years. Dave gave him the horn treatment and a minor cardiac arrest. I nearly wet myself.

The bypass, built only a few years ago, runs across Milltown Road, and the junction is controlled by traffic lights. They were at red. We saw the Peugeot's brake lights come on as he slowed and moved from side to side, deciding which way to go. He didn't stop for them, no chance of that, and went straight on, through the reds.

"Perfect," I heard Dave whisper to himself as we hurtled towards the junction and the red lights.

"He won't get on the motorway that way," I said.

At a hundred and ten miles per hour it takes less than two seconds to cover a hundred yards. I worked it out, later. At that moment I didn't think I'd ever have a later. I saw the traffic lights, bright red, racing closer and closer, growing redder and redder as Dave kept his foot firmly down against the floor. A Post Office van moved across the junction. I saw my left hand reach out towards the dash board, felt my right foot press down on the carpet, wishing there was a brake pedal under it. With a hundred yards to go, at the point of no return, the lights flipped to amber and I breathed again. The suspension bounced and bumped as we hit the change in camber, then the crossroads were behind us. The streetlights were less bright now, and the Peugeot was only fifty yards ahead.

"He hasn't taken the bypass," I reported to control. "Heading south. Get the chopper airborne. We need the chopper."

There's an in-between land where the urban development runs out but the moors haven't started. A thousand years of agriculture have wrested a patchwork of handkerchief-sized fields, hundreds of them, from the encroaching heather and cottongrass. They hug the low ground in a jigsaw puzzle of irregular geometric shapes, bounded by stone walls and straggling hedges. The road, laid out when the only traffic was horse-drawn, zigs and zags between them. I braced myself against the door as the tyres scrabbled for grip. The G-forces tried to propel me from the vehicle and the headlights illuminated a moss-encrusted wall as it raced across the windscreen in a green blur. We'd left the street lamps behind but the sky was lightening in the east.

Dave let the gap stretch to a hundred yards or more, throwing my car into the bends with an enthusiasm that can only be experienced when driving somebody else's car with the law on your side. I gritted my teeth as he explored the limits of adhesion.

"It's a maze," I said. "Where's that chopper?"

Fletcher didn't know where he was going, either. He took corners and side turns haphazardly, left and right, without apparent reason. His only aim was to lose us. Around one corner we found dirt and a big stone lying in the road where he must have clipped the wall.

We came out on a wider road and as we turned to the left I saw the pale surface of a lake swing into view, the sky reflected in its flawless surface.

"We're on a middling road," I told control, "heading south again, and there's a reservoir to our right." There are dozens of them up here.

"It's Ringstone," Dave told me. "Ringstone Edge."

I passed the information back to Heckley nick. "Looks like you're on Saddleworth Road," I was told, "heading towards the Scammonden Bridge."

"We're heading towards Scammonden Bridge," I told Dave. It was one of those roads that looks straight on the map, but maps are flat. We were up to the ton again, with the car leaping from bump to bump, brow to brow, as we kept up the pressure.

"Look!" he replied.

"Where?"

"Straight ahead"

All I could see was Tarmac rolling under us, then we cleared another brow and the sky came back into view. Blue lights were flickering against the clouds like a summer lightning storm.

"Traffic!" I said.

"Got the bastards," Dave added, taking his foot off the accelerator.

There was nowhere else for them to go. Brake lights came on as the Peugeot reached the bridge and slowed. The two big traffic division Volvos stopped at the far end of the bridge, their sirens and light bars rending the dawn and washing the surroundings with blue as they formed into a roadblock. We were way back, creeping forward now, watching in case Fletcher turned round and came at us. He didn't.

We dropped on to the bridge and stopped. Down below us the traffic on the M62 looked like a procession of Dinky toys, streaming endlessly in both directions. Fletcher was out of his car, dragging a woman by the hand. We got out and slammed the doors. Another blue light was behind us. I turned and saw Geordie arrive. Fletcher had his back against the rail, still holding the woman, as we converged on him.

"I'll kill her," he shouted at us. "Get back or I'll kill her."
We all stopped. He was grasping her hair, pulling her head
back and holding a knife at her throat. I was fairly certain she
was the woman who'd been with him when he came to the
police station to report the white pickup. The noise of the
traffic down below was a monotonous roar and the air was
cold. It's the coldest part of the night, just before daylight.

So where was the other woman? The nurse from
Hatfield? Fletcher wasn't going anywhere so I walked over
to the Peugeot and pressed the button on the boot lid. She
was lying inside, huddled in the foetal position in the tiny
space. Her hands and feet were tied with plastic-covered line
and her mouth covered in gaffer tape. Only her nose was
free for her to breathe through and her face was resting in a
pool of mucus. Her eyes were wide with terror like a trapped
animal's, and she was convulsing, fighting to pull some air
into her lungs. I don't think she could have lasted much
longer.

"One of you over here," I shouted, and they turned to
me.

"I'm a police officer," I told her, clearing the mucus from
her nose. "It's over, love. You're safe now." I tried to find the
end of the tape covering her mouth, but couldn't, and my
fingers wouldn't go under it. She had a choking fit and I
tried to steady her.

"Knife?" I demanded of the traffic officer who had joined
me, and he produced a small penknife. Within a few seconds
I had sawed through the tape and she was breathing through
her mouth.

I cut the rope around her hands and feet and we massaged
some circulation back into them. When she was looking better, breathing as normally as we could expect, I lifted her
out. She wrapped her arms around my neck and clung to me
like a koala bear clinging to a tree. I carried her to one of the
Volvos and the driver helped me load her into the back seat.
I told him to take her to Heckley General and let Heckley

nick know that she was safe. They'd pass the news on to her boyfriend.

"It's over, love," I told her again. "It's all been a bad dream, but it's over now." I squeezed her hand and she nodded.

Fletcher had upped the stakes. He'd climbed over the railing and was poised a hundred and fifty feet above the westbound middle lane, still holding the knife to her throat although she was on this side. His leg was hooked through the railings to stop him falling backwards. Dave, Geordie and the two remaining traffic officers stood in a semi-circle around them.

"Joomp then, yer bastard," Geordie was urging him. "Gan on then, joomp. Do the decent thing for once an' joomp."

I put my hand on his arm and pushed between him and Sparky. The two from traffic dropped back. This wasn't their field. It occurred to me that I was the only one of us who knew who the woman was. That she was a full partner, and not an unwilling victim. I decided to withhold that piece of information from Geordie.

"We've met before," I told him. I should have had a set-piece speech prepared, but I didn't. I'd have to make it up as I went along. "It's cold, and I haven't had my breakfast. Drop the knife and climb back and I promise not to let this big lout loose on you. Otherwise..."

Otherwise, I don't mind one way or the other if you do jump. That's what I started to say, but I didn't get the chance. The woman turned on him and clawed at his face, her fingernails digging into his cheeks, pulling his bottom eyelids down and leaving livid stripes behind.

He yelled with pain and fell backwards as we all leaped forward. Dave bundled her to one side, I grabbed the front of Fletcher's anorak and Geordie grabbed me.

He was leaning out over the drop, supported only by me grasping two handfuls of anorak and his hands trying to find a grip on the leather sleeves of my jacket. Geordie had one arm round my neck and one round my waist, so Fletcher couldn't take me with him, but the rail was chest high and it would have taken a superhuman effort to hoist me over it. Still, madmen have the strength of ten, or so we're told. Somewhere behind me I could hear his partner shouting that it wasn't her, he'd made her do it.

"Keep still," I told him. "Keep still and relax." I was looking straight into the face of the man who had killed seven people and terrorised the North of England. The claw marks down his face were symmetrical, like animal markings. The lesser-striped psychopath. He had blue eyes, like me. All I had to do was open my fingers...

"Now," I said. "Gently does it. Come this way."

It wasn't until afterwards that I remembered. Or thought I remembered. I was heaving him upwards, gradually pulling him towards me, when his toes slipped off the ledge. For a second or two I had all his weight and he stared at me with terror in his eyes. His blue eyes. Then the anorak slowly swallowed him. His face sank into it as his fingers slid down my arms in a hopeless quest for grip and his hands were consumed as the sleeves of the anorak turned inside out.

He screamed. I was glad about that. I was left hanging over the rail, flapping a blue and lilac Regatta anorak at the traffic, as his scream was lost in the screech of tyres and brakes as thirty-two tons of Yorkie bars heading for Liverpool went into a terminal jack-knife.

Geordie heaved me back and I fell over on to my arse.

"This'll get us on Radio Four if nothing else will," Sparky said. The jack-knifed lorry had completely blocked the road and we were watching the traffic come to a standstill, a wave of hazard flashers slowly spreading back down the motorway like a nasty rash. I told Dave to look after the cars and deployed Geordie and one of the traffic officers to take Mrs Fletcher, if that was her name, to the nick. As they loaded her into the car, still protesting that he'd made her do it, I saw Geordie reach down and rub his ankle. Then he eased himself into the driving seat and pulled the door shut.

I climbed the sheep fence and set off at a jog to find a place where I could scramble down the banking and identify Timothy Fletcher's mortal remains. A crowd had gathered around his body. He was lying on his back, half on the embankment with his head dangling in the drainage channel. One arm was doubled under him at an impossible angle and blood had dribbled upwards from the corners of his mouth, giving him a clown's painted grin. I remembered the picture on his wall that I'd seen barely an hour earlier.

I told everyone that I was a police officer, asked them to sit in their cars and be prepared to supply names and addresses when asked. The inevitable businessman with an urgent appointment came forward but I brushed him aside. Others had planes to catch, so I told them ten to fifteen minutes, that's all. The lorry driver was taking it badly. His windscreen had a big crack running diagonally across it where he'd hit the falling body and he was gabbling about not having a chance.

The ambulances and police cars came the easy way, on the empty road from the wrong direction, and within minutes the air was filled with flashing lights and the buzz of radios. I led the driver to the ambulance and sat him inside it.

One of the paramedics produced a blanket. "Shall I chuck this over Laughing Boy?" he asked, nodding towards Fletcher.

I looked from him to the body, still grinning at the sky, and back at him. "No," I replied. "Leave him be."

Motorists were leaving their cars to come and look at him. They'd peer at the broken body, grimace and turn away. Let them look, I thought. Let them have something to tell their families when they go home. This is what happens to people who think they can kill for their own gratification, or cause, or gain. People who believe that they have some God-given right to deprive others of life for their own pathetic reasons. Once upon a time he would have been suspended in a cage until his bleached bones disintegrated and fell through the bars. Well, we don't do that now, we're more civilised, but let him lie there for a few more minutes and let the people come and look at him.

"You OK, Mr Priest?"

It was a traffic sergeant from Halifax. "Yeah, fine," I said. "Never felt finer."

"Do you know who he is?"

I nodded. "Yeah, don't shed any tears. Can I leave you to it?"

"Of course. Any requests?"

"A couple of photos, that's all. It's straightforward. And about twenty names and addresses. Get the traffic going. My car's up there." I pointed. "Thanks for your assistance."

"Do you want a lift round?"

"No, it's OK. The exercise will do me good."

Because I had some mountains to climb, and I'd fallen behind with the training. I set off down the empty road, walking in the middle of the slow lane just for the hell of it, already thinking about the questions I needed to ask Fletcher's woman. When and where did she meet him? That was the burning one. The answer to that would determine her involvement with the early murders. I'd leave the fancy stuff, like why did the killings start and how come Fletcher was so influenced by Tim Roper, to Dr Foulkes. *Because he was stark staring mad* was probably as near as we'd ever get to an answer. I'd done about fifty yards when I realised that my left ankle was hurting and stooped to rub it. I wasn't wearing socks and there was a graze and a lump just above the bone, where it must have taken a knock during the struggle.

That's when I remembered Geordie grabbing me as I held Fletcher, his leg banging against mine just before Fletcher's toes slipped off the ledge. And later, I saw him rubbing his own ankle. But maybe it was only my imagination.

Yes, that's what it was: my imagination. It had been playing tricks on me, lately. The lorry's big engine juddered into life and I turned to see a cloud of smoke come from its exhausts. Beyond it a streak of silver marked the sunrise, like a trap door opening. A panda did a U-turn in the road and came towards me. I moved to one side but it stopped and the passenger door opened.

"Hop in, Mr Priest," the driver said. "I'll run you round."

It was churlish to refuse so I climbed in beside him. I'd accept that ride, after all.

What the heck, I deserved it.